The Beast Within

The Beast Within

Émile Zola

MINT EDITIONS

The Beast Within was first published in 1890.

This edition published by Mint Editions 2021.

ISBN 9781513282138 | E-ISBN 9781513287157

Published by Mint Editions®

 MINT
EDITIONS

minteditionbooks.com

Publishing Director: Jennifer Newens
Design & Production: Rachel Lopez Metzger
Project Manager: Micaela Clark
Translated by: Edward Vizetelly
Typesetting: Westchester Publishing Services

Contents

Preface

This striking work, now published for the first time in England, but a hundred thousand copies whereof have been sold in France, is one of the most powerful novels that M. Émile Zola has written. It will be doubly interesting to English readers, because for them it forms a missing link in the famous Rougon-Macquart series.

The student of Zola literature will remember in the *Assommoir* that "handsome Lantier whose heartlessness was to cost Gervaise so many tears." Jacques Lantier, the chief character in this *Bête Humaine*, this *Human Animal* which I have ventured to call the *Monomaniac*, is one of their children. It is he who is the monomaniac. His monomania consists in an irresistible prurience for murder, and his victims must be women, just like that baneful criminal who was performing his hideous exploits in the streets of the city of London in utter defiance of the police, about the time M. Zola sat down to pen this remarkable novel, and from whom, maybe, he partly took the idea.

Every woman this Jacques Lantier falls in love with, nay, every girl from whom he culls a kiss, or whose bare shoulders or throat he happens to catch a glimpse of, he feels an indomitable craving to slaughter! And this abominable thirst is, it appears, nothing less than an irresistible desire to avenge certain wrongs of which he has lost the exact account, that have been handed down to him, through the males of his line, since that distant age when prehistoric man found shelter in the depths of caverns.

Around this peculiar being, who in other respects is like any ordinary mortal, M. Émile Zola has grouped some very carefully studied characters. All are drawn with a firm, masterly hand; all live and breathe. Madame Lebleu, caught with her ear to the keyhole, is worthy of Dickens. So is Aunt Phasie, who has engaged in a desperate underhand struggle with her wretch of a husband about a miserable hoard of £40 which he wants to lay hands on. The idea of the jeering smile on her lips, which seem to be repeating to him, "Search! search!" as she lies a corpse on her bed in the dim light of a tallow candle, is inimitable.

The unconscious Séverine is but one of thousands of pretty Frenchwomen tripping along the asphalt at this hour, utterly unable to distinguish between right and wrong, who are ready to do anything, to sell themselves body and soul for a little ease, a few smart frocks, and some dainty linen. The warrior girl Flore, who thrashes the males, is a grand conception.

But the gem of the whole bunch is that obstinate, narrow-minded, self-sufficient examining-magistrate, M. Denizet; and in dealing with this character, the author lays bare all the abominable system of French criminal procedure. Recently this was modified to the extent of allowing the accused party to have the assistance of counsel while undergoing the torture of repeated searching cross-examinations at the hands of his tormentor. But in the days of which M. Émile Zola is writing, the prisoner enjoyed no such protection. He stood alone in the room with the examining-magistrate and his registrar, and while the former craftily laid traps for him to fall into, the latter carefully took down his replies to the incriminating questions addressed to him. It positively makes one shudder to think how many innocent men must have been sent to the guillotine, or to penal servitude for life, like poor Cabuche, during the length of years this atrocious practice remained in full vigour!

The English reader, accustomed to open, even-handed justice for one and all alike, and unfamiliar with the ways that prevail in France, will start with amazement and incredulity at the idea of shelving criminal cases to avoid scandal involving persons in high position. But such is by no means an uncommon proceeding on the other side of the straits. Georges Ohnet introduces a similar incident into his novel *Le Droit de l'Enfant*.

M. Émile Zola has made most of his books a study of some particular sphere of life in France. In this instance he introduces his readers to the railway and railway servants. They are all there, from the station-master to the porter, and all are depicted with so skilful a hand that anyone who has travelled among our neighbours must recognise them.

By frequent runs on an express engine between Paris and Havre, and vice versâ, the author has mastered all the complicated mechanism of the locomotive; and we see his trains vividly as in reality, starting from the termini, gliding along the lofty embankments, through the deep cuttings, plunging into and bursting from the tunnels amidst the deafening riot of their hundred wheels, while the dumpy habitation of the gatekeeper, Misard, totters on its frail foundations as they fly by in a hurricane blast.

The story teems with incident from start to finish. Each chapter is a drama in itself. To name but a few of the exciting events that are dealt with: there is a murder in a railway carriage; an appalling railway accident; a desperate fight between driver and fireman on the footplate of a locomotive, which ends in both going over the side to be cut to pieces, while the long train of cattle-trucks, under no control, crammed full of inebriated soldiers on their way to the war, who are yelling patriotic songs, dashes along, full steam, straight ahead, with a big fire just made up, onward; to stop, no one knows where.

This is certainly one of the best and most dramatic novels that M. Émile Zola has ever penned; and I feel lively pleasure at having the good fortune to be able, with the assistance of my enterprising publishers, to present it to the English reading public.

EDWARD VIZETELLY

SURBITON,
August 20, 1901.

I

Roubaud, on entering the room, placed the loaf, the pâté, and the bottle of white wine on the table. But Mother Victoire, before going down to her post in the morning, had crammed the stove with such a quantity of cinders that the heat was stifling, and the assistant station-master, having opened a window, leant out on the rail in front of it.

This occurred in the Impasse d'Amsterdam, in the last house on the right, a lofty dwelling, where the Western Railway Company lodged some of their staff. The window on the fifth floor, at the angle of the mansarded roof, looked on to the station, that broad trench cutting into the Quartier de l'Europe, to abruptly open up the view, and which the grey mid-February sky, of a grey that was damp and warm, penetrated by the sun, seemed to make still wider on that particular afternoon.

Opposite, in the sunny haze, the houses in the Rue de Rome became confused, fading lightly into distance. On the left gaped the gigantic porches of the iron marquees, with their smoky glass. That of the main lines on which the eye looked down, appeared immense. It was separated from those of Argenteuil, Versailles, and the Ceinture railway, which were smaller, by the buildings set apart for the post-office, and for heating water to fill the foot-warmers. To the right the trench was severed by the diamond pattern ironwork of the Pont de l'Europe, but it came into sight again, and could be followed as far as the Batignolles tunnel.

And below the window itself, occupying all the vast space, the three double lines that issued from the bridge deviated, spreading out like a fan, whose innumerable metal branches ran on to disappear beneath the span roofs of the marquees. In front of the arches stood the three boxes of the pointsmen, with their small, bare gardens. Amidst the confused background of carriages and engines encumbering the rails, a great red signal formed a spot in the pale daylight.

Roubaud was interested for a few minutes, comparing what he saw with his own station at Havre. Each time he came like this, to pass a day at Paris, and found accommodation in the room of Mother Victoire, love of his trade got the better of him. The arrival of the train from Mantes had animated the platforms under the marquee of the main lines; and his eyes followed the shunting engine, a small tender-engine with three low wheels coupled together, which began briskly bustling to and fro, branching off the train, dragging away the carriages to drive them on to the shunting lines. Another engine, a powerful one this, an express engine, with two great devouring wheels, stood still alone, sending from its chimney a quantity of black smoke, which ascended straight, and very slowly, through the calm air.

But all the attention of Roubaud was centred on the 3.25 train for Caen, already full of passengers and awaiting its locomotive, which he could not see, for it had stopped on the other side of the Pont de l'Europe. He could only hear it asking for permission to advance, with slight, hurried whistles, like a person becoming impatient. An order resounded. The locomotive responded by one short whistle to indicate that it had understood. Then, before moving, came a brief silence. The exhaust pipes were opened, and the steam went hissing on a level with the ground in a deafening jet.

He then noticed this white cloud bursting from the bridge in volume, whirling about like snowy fleece flying through the ironwork. A whole corner of the expanse became whitened, while the smoke from the other engine expanded its black veil. From behind the bridge could be heard the prolonged, muffled sounds of the horn, mingled with the shouting of orders and the shocks of turning-tables. All at once the air was rent, and he distinguished in the background a train from Versailles, and a train from Auteuil, one up and one down, crossing each other.

As Roubaud was about to quit the window, a voice calling him by name made him lean out. Below, on the fourth floor balcony, he recognised a young man about thirty years of age, named Henri Dauvergne, a headguard, who resided there with his father, deputy station-master for the main lines, and his two sisters, Claire and Sophie, a couple of charming blondes, one eighteen and the other twenty, who looked after the housekeeping with the 6,000 frcs. of the two men, amidst a constant stream of gaiety. The elder one would be heard laughing, while the younger sang, and a cage full of exotic birds rivalled one another in roulades.

"By Jove, Monsieur Roubaud! so you are in Paris, then? Ah! yes, about your affair with the sub-prefect!"

The assistant station-master, leaning on the rail again, explained that he had to leave Havre that morning by the 6.40 express. He had been summoned to Paris by the traffic-manager, who had been giving him a serious lecture. He considered himself lucky in not having lost his post.

"And madam?" Henri inquired.

Madame had wished to come also, to make some purchases. Her husband was waiting for her there, in that room which Mother Victoire placed at their service whenever they came to Paris. It was there that they loved to lunch, tranquil and alone, while the worthy woman was detained downstairs at her post. On that particular day they had eaten a roll at Mantes, wishing to get their errands over first of all. But three o'clock had struck, and he was dying with hunger.

Henri, to be amiable, put one more question:

"And are you going to pass the night in Paris?"

No, no! Both were returning to Havre in the evening by the 6.30 express. Ah! holidays, indeed! They brought you up to give you your dose, and off, back again at once!

The two looked at one another for a moment, tossing their heads, but they could no longer hear themselves speak; a devil-possessed piano had just broken into sonorous notes. The two sisters must have been thumping on it together, laughing louder than ever, and exciting the exotic birds. Then the young man gained by the merriment, said good-bye to withdraw into the apartment; and the assistant station-master, left alone, remained a moment with his eyes on the balcony whence ascended all this youthful gaiety. Then, looking up, he perceived the locomotive, whose driver had shut off the exhaust pipes and which the pointsman switched on to the train for Caen. The last flakes of white steam were lost amid the heavy whirling cloud of smoke soiling the sky. And Roubaud also returned into his room.

Standing before the cuckoo clock pointing to 3.20, he gave a gesture of despair. What on earth was keeping Séverine so long? When she once entered a shop, she could never leave it. To stay his famishing hunger he thought of laying the table. He was familiar with this large apartment lighted by two windows, which served as bedroom, dining-room, and kitchen; and with its walnut furniture, its bed draped in Turkey-red material, its sideboard, its round table, and Norman wardrobe.

From the sideboard he took napkins, plates, knives and forks, and two glasses. Everything was extremely clean, and he felt as much pleased to perform this little household duty, as if he had been a child playing at dining. The whiteness of the linen delighted him, and, being very much in love with his wife, he smiled to himself at the idea of the peal of laughter she would give on opening the door. But when he had placed the pâté on a plate, and set the bottle of white wine beside it, he became uneasy and looked about him. Then he quickly drew a couple of small parcels from his pockets which he had forgotten—a little box of sardines and some Gruyère cheese.

The half hour struck. Roubaud strode up and down with an ear attentive to the staircase, turning round at the least sound. Passing before the looking-glass as he waited with nothing to do, he stopped and gazed at himself. He did not appear to be growing old. Although getting on for forty, the bright reddishness of his curly hair had not diminished. His fair beard, also verging on red, which he wore full, had remained thick. Of medium height, but extremely vigorous, he felt pleased with his appearance, satisfied with his rather flat head, and low forehead, his thick neck, his round, ruddy face lit up by a pair of large, sparkling eyes. His eyebrows joined, clouding his forehead with the bar of jealousy.

There was a sound of footsteps. Roubaud ran and set the door ajar; but it was a woman who sold newspapers in the station, returning to her lodging hard by. He came back and examined a box made of shells standing on the sideboard. He knew that box very well, a present from Séverine to Mother Victoire, her wet-nurse. And this trifling object sufficed to recall all the story of his marriage, which had taken place almost three years previously.

Born in the south of France at Plassans, he had a carter for father. He had quitted the army with the stripes of a sergeant-major, and for a long time had been general porter at the station at Mantes. He had then been promoted head-porter at Barentin, and it was there that he had first seen his dear wife, when she came from Doinville in company with Mademoiselle Berthe, the daughter of President Grandmorin.

Séverine Aubry was nothing more than the younger daughter of a gardener, who had died in the service of the Grandmorins; but the President, her godfather and guardian, had taken such a fancy to her, making her the playmate of his own daughter, sending them both to the same school at Rouen, and, moreover, she possessed such an innate air of superiority herself, that Roubaud for a long time, had been content to admire her at a distance, with the passion of a workman freed from some of his rough edge, for a dainty jewel that he considered precious.

This was the sole romance of his existence. He would have wedded the girl without a sou, for the joy of calling her his own; and when he had been so bold as to ask her hand, the realisation of his hopes had surpassed his dream. Apart from Séverine and a marriage portion of

10,000 frcs., the President, now pensioned off, a member of the Board of Directors of the Western Railway Company, had extended to him his protection. Almost immediately after the wedding he had become assistant station-master at Havre. No doubt he had good notes to his credit—firm at his post, punctual, honest, of limited intelligence, but very straightforward,—all excellent qualities that might explain the prompt attention given to his request and his rapid promotion. But he preferred to believe that he owed everything to his wife whom he adored.

When Roubaud had opened the box of sardines he positively lost patience. It had been agreed that they should meet there at three o'clock. Where could she be? She would not have the audacity to tell him that it required a whole day to purchase a pair of boots, and a few articles of linen. And as he again passed before the looking-glass, he perceived his eyebrows on end, and his forehead furrowed with a harsh line. Never had he suspected her at Havre. In Paris he pictured to himself all sorts of danger, deceit, and levity. The blood rushed to his head, his fists of a former porter were clenched, as in the days when he shunted the carriages. He became the brute again, unconscious of his strength. He would have crushed her in an outburst of blind fury.

Séverine pushed open the door, and presented herself quite fresh and joyful.

"Here I am! Eh! you must have fancied me lost," she exclaimed.

In the lustre of her five-and-twenty years she looked tall, slim, and very supple, but she was plump, notwithstanding her small bones. At first sight she did not appear pretty, with her long face, and large mouth set with beautiful teeth. But on observing her more closely, she fascinated one by her charm, by the peculiarity of her blue eyes, crowned with an abundance of raven hair.

And as her husband, without answering, continued to examine her with the troubled, vacillating look she knew so well, she added:

"Oh! I walked very fast. Just imagine, it was impossible to get an omnibus. Then, as I did not want to spend money on a cab, I walked as fast as I could. See how hot I am!"

"Look here," said he violently, "you will not make me believe you come from the Bon Marché."

But immediately, in the delightful manner of a child, she threw herself on his neck, closing his mouth with her pretty little plump hand.

"Oh! you wicked creature! you wicked creature!" she exclaimed; "hold your tongue; you know I love you."

She was so full of sincerity, he felt her still so candid, so straightforward, that he pressed her passionately in his arms. His suspicions always ended thus. She abandoned herself to him, loving to be petted. He covered her with kisses, which she did not return; and it was this that caused him a sort of vague uneasiness. This great, passive child, full of filial affection, had not yet awakened to love.

"So you ransacked the Bon Marché?" said he.

"Oh! yes. I'll tell you all about it," she replied. "But, first of all, let us eat. You cannot imagine how hungry I am! Ah! listen! I've a little present. Repeat, 'Where is my little present?'"

And she laughed quite close to his face. She had thrust her right hand in her pocket, where she held an object she did not take out of it.

"Say quick, 'Where is my little present?'" she continued.

He also was laughing, like a good-natured man, and did as she asked him.

"Where is my little present?" he inquired. She had bought him a knife to replace one he had lost, and which he had been regretting for the past fortnight. He uttered an exclamation of delight, pronouncing this beautiful new knife superb, with its ivory handle and shining blade. He wanted to use it at once. She was charmed at his joy, and, in fun, made him give her a sou, so that their friendship might not be severed.

"To lunch, to lunch!" she repeated. "No, no!" she exclaimed, as he was about to shut the window; "don't close it yet, I beg of you! I am too warm!"

She joined him at the window, and remained there a few seconds, leaning on his shoulder, gazing at the vast expanse of the station. For the moment the smoke had disappeared. The copper-coloured disc of the sun descended in the haze behind the houses in the Rue de Rome. At their feet a shunting engine was bringing along the Mantes train, all made up, which was to leave at 4.25. The engine drove it back beside the platform under the marquee, and was unhooked. In the background, beneath the span-roof of the Ceinture line, the shocks of buffers announced the unforeseen coupling-on of extra carriages. And alone, in the middle of the network of rails, with driver and fireman blackened with the dust of the journey, the heavy engine of some slow train stood motionless, as if weary and breathless, with merely a thin thread of steam issuing from a valve. It was waiting for the line to be opened to return to the depôt at Batignolles. A red signal clacked, disappeared, and the locomotive went off.

"How gay those little Dauvergnes are!" remarked Roubaud. "Do you hear them thumping on their piano? I saw Henri just now, and he asked me to give you his compliments."

"To table, to table!" exclaimed Séverine.

And she fell upon the sardines with a hearty appetite, having eaten nothing since she bought the roll at Mantes. Her visits to Paris always made her excited. She was quivering with pleasure at her run through the streets, and still enraptured with her purchases at the Bon Marché. Each spring she spent all her winter savings at one stroke, preferring to purchase everything at the capital, and thus economise the cost of the journey, as she said. Without losing a mouthful, she never paused in her chatter. A trifle confused, and blushing, she ended by letting out the total of the sum she had spent, more than 300 frcs.

"The deuce!" remarked Roubaud, startled; "you get yourself up well for the wife of an assistant station-master! But I thought you were only going to buy a little linen and a pair of boots."

"Oh! my dear! but I have got such bargains. A piece of silk with such lovely stripes! A hat, in exquisite taste, something to dream of! Ready-made petticoats with embroidered flounces! And all this for next to nothing. I should have paid double at Havre. They are going to send the parcel, and you'll see!"

She looked so pretty in her delight, with her confused air of supplication, that he resolved to laugh. And besides, this little scratch dinner was so charming in this room where they were all alone, and much more comfortable than at a restaurant. She, who usually drank water, threw off restraint, and swallowed her glass of white wine without knowing what she was about. The box of sardines being empty, they attacked the pâté with the beautiful new knife. It cut so admirably that it was a perfect triumph.

"And you—what about your affair?" she inquired. "You make me chatter, and you don't tell me how your matter with the sub-prefect ended."

Thereupon he related in detail how he had been treated by the traffic-manager. Oh! he had received a thorough good wigging! He had defended himself, he had told the truth. He had related how this little whipper-snapper of a sub-prefect had insisted on getting into a first-class carriage with his dog, when there was a second-class carriage reserved for sportsmen and their animals, and had given an account of the quarrel that had resulted, and the words that had been exchanged. In short, the manager had said he was right to have insisted on the regulations being complied with; but the bad part of the business was that sentence which he confessed having uttered: "You others will not always be the masters!" He was suspected of being a republican. The discussions that had just marked the opening of the session of 1869, and the secret alarm about the forthcoming elections, had made the government distrustful. And had not President Grandmorin spoken warmly in his favour, he would certainly have been removed from his post. As it was, he had been compelled to sign the letter of apology which the latter had advised should be sent, and had drawn up himself.

"Ah! you see!" broke in Séverine. "Wasn't I right to drop him a line, and pay him a visit along with you, this morning, before you went to receive your wigging? I knew he would get us out of the trouble."

"Yes, he is very fond of you," resumed Roubaud, "and is all powerful in the company. What is the use of being a good servant? Ah! the manager did not stint me of praise: slow to take the initiative, but of good conduct, obedient, courageous, briefly, all sorts of qualities! Well, my dear, if you had not been my wife, and if Grandmorin had not pleaded my cause out of friendship for you, it would have been all up with me. I should have been sent to do penance at some small station."

She was staring fixedly into space, and murmured, as if speaking to herself:

"Oh! certainly, he is a man with great influence."

There was a silence, and she sat with her eyes wide open and lost in thought. She had ceased eating. No doubt she was thinking of the days of her childhood, far away, at the Château of Doinville, four leagues from Rouen. She had never known her mother. When her father, the gardener Aubry died, she was commencing her thirteenth year; and it was at this period that the President, already a widower, had placed her with his daughter Berthe in charge of his sister, Madame Bonnehon, herself the widow of a manufacturer, from whom she had inherited the château.

Berthe, who was two years older than Séverine, had been wedded six months after the marriage of the latter with Roubaud, to M. de Lachesnaye, a little, shrivelled-up, sallow-complexioned man, judge at the Rouen Court of Appeal. In the preceding year President Grandmorin was still at the head of this court at Rouen, which was his own part of the country, when he retired on a pension, after a brilliant career.

Born in 1804, substitute at Digne on the morrow of the events in 1830, then at Fontainebleau, then at Paris, he had afterwards filled the posts of procurator at Troyes; advocate-general at Rennes; and finally, first president at Rouen. A multi-millionaire, he had been member of the County Council since 1855, and on the same day as he retired, he had been made Commander of the Legion of Honour. As far back as she could recollect, she remembered him just as he was now—thick-set and strong, prematurely grey, but the golden grey of one formerly fair; his hair cut Brutus fashion, his beard clipped short, no moustache, a square face, which eyes of a hard blue and a big nose rendered severe. He was harsh on being approached, and made everyone about him tremble.

Séverine was so absorbed that Roubaud had to raise his voice, repeating twice over:

"Well, what are you thinking about?"

She started, gave a little shudder, as if surprised, and trembled with alarm.

"Oh! of nothing!" she answered.

"But you are not eating. Have you lost your appetite?" he inquired.

"Oh! no; you'll see," she replied.

Séverine, having emptied her glass of white wine, finished the slice of pâté on her plate. But there was a cry of alarm. They had eaten the small loaf; not a mouthful remained for the cheese. They clamoured, then laughed, and finally, after disturbing everything, found a piece of stale bread at the back of the sideboard cupboard of Mother Victoire.

Although the window was open, it continued very warm, and the young woman, seated with her back to the stove, could not get refreshed; and she had become more rosy and excited, by the unforeseen talkative lunch in this room.

Speaking of Mother Victoire, Roubaud had returned to Grandmorin; there was another who owed him a famous debt of gratitude. The mother of a child who had died, she became wet-nurse to Séverine, whose birth had sent her mamma into the grave. Later on, as wife of a fireman of the company, who spent all he earned in drink, she was leading a wretched existence in Paris by the aid of a little sewing, when, happening to meet her foster-daughter, the former intimacy had been renewed, while the President, at the same time, took her under his protection. He had now obtained for her the post of attendant at the lavatory for ladies. The company gave her no more than 100 frcs., but she made nearly 1,400 frcs. out of the gratuities, without counting the lodging, this room where they were lunching, and her coals. Indeed, she had a most comfortable post. And Roubaud calculated that if Pecqueux, the husband, had brought home the 2,800 frcs. which he earned as fireman, wages and gratuities together, instead of running riot at both ends of the line, they would have had between them more than 4,000 frcs. a year, double what he received as assistant station-master at Havre.

In the meanwhile, their sharp hunger had become appeased, and they dawdled over the rest of the meal, cutting the cheese into small pieces to make the feast last longer. Conversation also flagged.

"By the way," said he, "why did you decline the invitation of the President to go to Doinville for two or three days?"

In the comfort of a good digestion, he had just been running over in his mind, the incidents of their visit in the morning to the mansion in the Rue du Rocher, quite close to the station; he had seen himself again in the large, stern study, and he again heard the President telling them that he was leaving on the morrow for Doinville. Then, as if acting on a sudden impulse, the latter had suggested taking the 6.30 express with them that evening, and conducting his god-daughter on a visit to his sister, who had been wanting to see her for a long time. But the young woman had given all kinds of reasons which prevented her, she said, from accepting the invitation.

"For my part," he remarked, "I saw no inconvenience in this little trip. You might have remained there till Thursday. I should have been able to manage without you; don't you think so? We have need of them in our position. It is rather silly to show indifference to their politeness, and the more so as your refusal seemed to cause him real pain. And that was why I never ceased pressing you to accept, until you tugged at my coat; and then I spoke as you did, but without understanding what it meant. Eh! Why wouldn't you go?"

Séverine, with restless eyes, gave a gesture of impatience.

"How could I leave you all alone?" she exclaimed.

"That isn't a reason," he replied. "During the three years we have been married, you have paid two visits of a week to Doinville. There was nothing to prevent you going there a third time."

The young woman, more and more uneasy, turned away her head.

"Well, I didn't care about it," said she. "You don't want to force me to do things that displease me."

Roubaud opened his arms, as if to say that he had no intention of forcing her to do anything. Nevertheless, he resumed:

"Look here, you are hiding something. Did Madame Bonnehon receive you badly the last time you went there?"

Oh! no; Madame Bonnehon had always welcomed her with great kindness, she was so amiable. Tall, and well developed, with magnificent light hair, she still remained beautiful, notwithstanding her fifty-five years. Gossip had it that since her widowhood, and even during the lifetime of her husband, her heart had frequently been occupied. They adored her at Doinville, where she made the château a perfect paradise. All Rouen society visited there, particularly the magistracy; and it was among this body that Madame Bonnehon had met with a great many friends.

"Then own that it was the Lachesnayes who gave you the cold shoulder," continued Roubaud.

It was true that since Berthe had married M. de Lachesnaye, she had not been on the same terms with Séverine as before. This poor Berthe, who looked so insignificant with her red nose, was certainly not improving in character. The ladies at Rouen extolled her noble bearing in no mean measure. But a husband such as she had, ugly, harsh, and miserly, seemed likely to communicate his bad qualities to his wife, and make her ill-natured. Still, Séverine had nothing in particular to reproach her with. Berthe had been agreeable to her former companion.

"Then it's the President who displeases you down there," remarked Roubaud.

Séverine, who had been answering slowly and in an even tone, became impatient again.

"He! What an idea!" she exclaimed.

And she continued in short, nervous phrases. They barely caught sight of him. He had reserved to himself a pavilion in the park, having a door opening on a deserted lane. He went out and came in without anybody knowing anything about his movements. His sister never even knew positively on what day he arrived. He took a vehicle at Barentin, and drove over by night to Doinville, where he remained for days together in his pavilion, ignored by everyone. Ah! it was not he who troubled them down there.

"I only mention it," said Roubaud, "because you have told me, over and over again, that in your childhood, he frightened you out of your senses."

"Oh! frightened me out of my senses!" she replied. "You exaggerate, as usual. It is a fact that he rarely laughed. He stared at you so with his great eyes, that he made you hang your head at once. I have seen persons confused, to the point of being unable to say a word to him, so deeply were they impressed by his great reputation for severity and wisdom. But as for me, I was never scolded by him. I always felt he had a weakness for me."

Once more her speech became slow, and her eyes were lost in space.

"I remember," she resumed, "when I was a little girl, and happened to be having a game with playmates on the paths, that if he chanced to appear, everyone ran into hiding, even his daughter Berthe, who was always trembling with fear lest she should be caught doing something wrong. For my part, I calmly awaited him. He came along, and seeing me there, smiling and looking up, gave me a pat on the cheek. Later on, at sixteen, whenever Berthe wished to obtain some favour from him, she always entrusted me with the mission of asking it. I spoke. I never looked down, and I felt his eyes penetrating me. But I did not care a fig, I was so sure he would grant whatever I wanted. Ah! yes; I remember it all. There is not a piece of brushwood in the park, not a corridor, nor a room in the château that I cannot see, when I close my eyes."

She ceased speaking, and lowered her lids. The thrill of incidents of former days seemed to pass over her warm, puffy face. She remained thus for a few moments, with a slight beating of the lips, something like a nervous twitch, that drew down the corner of her mouth as if she were in pain.

"He has certainly been very good to you," said Roubaud, who had just lit his pipe. "Not only did he bring you up like a young lady, but he very shrewdly invested the little money you had, and increased it when we were married, without counting what he is going to leave you. He said in my presence that he had mentioned you in his will."

"Ah! yes!" murmured Séverine, "that house at La Croix-de-Maufras, the property the railway cut in two. We used to go there, occasionally, for a week. Oh! I don't much count on that. The Lachesnayes must be at work to prevent him leaving me anything. And, besides, I would rather have nothing—nothing at all!"

She had uttered these last words in such a sharp tone, that he was astonished, and, taking his pipe from his mouth, he stared at her with rounded eyes.

"How funny you are!" said he. "Everyone knows that the President is worth millions. What harm would there be in him putting his god-daughter in his will? No one would be surprised, and it would be all right for us."

"Well, I've had enough of the subject," answered Séverine; "let us talk about something else. I will not go to Doinville because I will not, because I prefer to return with you to Havre."

He tossed his head, and appeased her with a motion of the hand. Very good, very good! As the subject annoyed her, he would say no more about it. He smiled. Never had he seen her so nervous. No doubt it was the white wine. Anxious to be forgiven, he took up the knife, went into another fit of ecstasy about it, and carefully wiped the blade. To show that it cut like a razor, he began to trim his nails with it.

"Already a quarter past four," murmured Séverine, standing before the cuckoo clock. "I have a few more errands to do. We must think about our train."

But, as if to get quite calm before making the room tidy, she went to the window and leant out of it. Then he, leaving his knife, leaving his pipe, also rose from the table, and, approaching her, took her gently from behind in his arms; and holding her enlaced, placed his chin on her shoulder, pressing his head against her own. Neither moved, but remained gazing at the scene below them.

The small shunting engines went and came without intermission. Similar to sharp and prudent housewives, the activity of their movements could barely be heard as they glided along with muffled wheels and a discreet whistle. One of them ran past, and disappeared under the Pont de l'Europe, dragging the carriages of a Trouville train to the coach-house. Over there, beyond the bridge, it brushed by a locomotive that had come alone from the depôt, like a solitary pedestrian, with its shimmering brass and steel, fresh and smart for the journey. This engine was standing still, and with a couple of short whistles appealed to the pointsman to open the line. Almost immediately he switched it on to its train, which stood ready made up, beside the platform, under the marquee of the main lines.

This was the 4.25 train for Dieppe. A stream of passengers hurried forward. One heard the roll of the trucks loaded with luggage, and the porters pushing the foot-warmers, one by one, into the compartments. The engine and tender had reached the first luggage van with a hollow clash, and the head-porter could then be seen tightening the screw of the spreader. The sky had become cloudy in the direction of Batignolles. An ashen crepuscule, effacing the façades, seemed to be already falling on the outspread fan of railway lines; and, in this dim light, one saw in the distance, the constant departure and arrival of trains on the Banlieue and Ceinture lines. Beyond the great sheet of span-roofing of the station, shreds of reddish smoke flew over darkened Paris.

Séverine and Roubaud had remained some minutes at the open window without speaking. He had taken her left hand, and was playing with an old gold ring, a golden serpent with a small ruby head, which she wore on the same finger as her wedding-ring. He had always seen it there.

"My little serpent," she murmured, in an involuntary dreamy voice, thinking he was looking at the ring, and feeling an imperative necessity to speak. "He made me a present of it at La Croix-de-Maufras when I was sixteen."

Roubaud raised his head in surprise.

"Who was that?" he inquired. "The President?"

As the eyes of her husband rested on her own, she awoke, with an abrupt shock, to a sense of reality. She felt a little chill turn her cheeks icy cold. She wished to answer, when, choked by a sort of paralysis, she could say nothing.

"But," he continued, "you always told me it was your mother who left you that ring."

Even at this second, she could have annulled the sentence she had thoughtlessly let slip. She had only to laugh, to play the madcap. But, losing her self-command, unconscious of the gravity of what she was doing, she obstinately maintained her statement.

"I never told you, my dear," she replied, "that my mother left me that ring."

Thereupon, Roubaud, also turning pale, stared at her threateningly.

"What do you mean," he retorted, "by saying you never told me so? Why, you've told it me twenty times over! There's no harm in the President giving you a ring. He has made you other presents of much greater value. But what need was there to hide it from me? Why lie, in speaking of your mother?"

ÉMILE ZOLA

"I never mentioned my mother, my darling," she persisted. "You are mistaken."

This obstinacy was idiotic. She was aware that she was ruining herself, that he could clearly see through her. And she then wanted to retrieve her position, to swallow her words. But it was too late. She felt her features becoming discomposed. Do what she would, the truth burst from all her being. The chill on her cheeks had spread all over her face, and a nervous twitch dragged down her lip.

Roubaud looked frightful. He had suddenly become red again, so red that it seemed as if his veins were about to burst. He had grasped her by the wrists, looking close into her face so as to be better able to follow, in the terror-stricken distraction of her eyes, what she dared not utter aloud. He stammered a great oath, which threw her into a fright, and, foreseeing a blow, she bowed her head, covering her face with her arm.

A trifling, wretched, insignificant incident—the failure to recollect the falsehood she had told about this ring—had just now, in the few words they had exchanged together, supplied evidence of a matter she had every desire to conceal. And a minute had sufficed to bring this about.

With a jerk, he threw her across the bed, and struck her haphazard with his two fists. In three years he had not given her so much as a flip, and now he was beating her black and blue, in the brutish fit of passion of a man with coarse hands, who had formerly shunted railway carriages.

Uttering another frightful oath, he exclaimed:

"You did something wrong! Something wrong! Something wrong!"

As he repeated the words, his rage increased, and he belaboured her with his fists, each time he pronounced them, as if to drive them into her flesh. His voice at last became so thick with anger, that it hissed, and ceased to be intelligible. It was only then that he heard her, quite weak from his blows, saying "No." She could imagine no other defence. She denied the accusation, so that he might not kill her. And this utterance, this obstinate clinging to the lie, made him completely furious.

"Confess that you did something wrong," said he.

"No, no!" she answered.

He had caught hold of her again, supporting her in his arms, preventing her from resuming her position with her face against the bed-covering, like some poor creature hiding herself. He forced her to look him in the face.

"Confess that you did something wrong," he repeated.

But, slipping down, she escaped, and tried to gain the door. In a bound he was upon her again, his fist raised; and furiously, at one blow, near the table, he felled her. He threw himself beside her, he seized her by the hair to nail her to the boards. For an instant they remained thus, on the ground, face to face, without moving. And in the frightful silence, could be heard, ascending from the floor below, the singing and laughter of the young Dauvergnes, whose piano, fortunately, frantically poured forth its notes, stifling the sound of the struggle. It was Claire singing nursery-rhymes, while Sophie accompanied her with all her might.

"Confess that you did something wrong," said he.

No longer daring to say no, she remained silent.

"Confess that you did something wrong," he exclaimed with an oath, "or I'll rip you open!"

He would have killed her; she could see it distinctly in his eyes. In falling, she had perceived the knife, open on the table, and now she fancied she saw the flash of the blade again. She thought he was extending his arm. She was overcome by cowardice, by an abandonment of herself and everything, a necessity to have done with the matter.

"Well, yes," said she, "it's true. Let me go."

What followed was abominable. This avowal, which he had so violently exacted, had just come upon him, point blank, like something impossible and monstrous. It seemed that he could never have imagined such an infamy. He caught hold of her head, and knocked it against a leg of the table. She struggled, and he dragged her across the room by the hair, scattering the chairs.

Each time she made an effort to rise he knocked her back on the floor by a blow from his fist. And he did this panting, with clenched teeth, in savage and senseless fury. The table, thrust away, almost upset the stove. Blood and hair were sticking to a corner of the sideboard. When they recovered breath, stupefied and reeking with this horror, weary of striking and of being struck, they had got close to the bed again; she, still stretched on the floor, he squatting down, holding her by the shoulders. And they had breathing time. Below, the music continued. The laughter rippled away, sonorous, and very youthful.

Roubaud, with a jerk, raised Séverine into a sitting posture, setting her back against the bedstead. Then, still on his knees, weighing down on her shoulders, he could at last speak. He had ceased beating her;

he tortured her with questions. She wept. She was so upset that she could not utter a word; and, raising his hand, he half stunned her with a blow from his palm. Three times, at intervals, receiving no answer, he slapped her face. Why should she struggle any longer? She was already half dead. He would have torn out her heart with those horny fingers of a former workman. And so, the cross-examination proceeded, with the threatening fist uplifted, ready to strike if she hesitated in her replies.

All at once he shook her, and inquired with an oath:

"Why did you marry me? Don't you know it was infamous to deceive me in this manner? There are thieves in prison, who have not half what you have on their conscience. So you despised me? You were not in love with me? Eh! why did you marry me?"

She gave a vague gesture. She did not exactly know, now. She was happy to marry him, hoping to get rid of the other. There are so many things one would rather not do, and which one does, because they are after all the wisest. No, she did not love him; and she carefully avoided telling him that had it not been for this business, never would she have consented to become his wife.

Séverine, by an effort, had risen to her feet. With a vigour that was extraordinary in such a weak, vanquished creature, she had thrust Roubaud from her. And as she freed her hand he felt the ring, the little golden serpent with the ruby head, forgotten on her finger. He tore it off, crushed it beneath his heel in another fit of rage. Then he began striding up and down, from one end of the room to the other, mute and distracted. She sank down, seated at the edge of the bed, staring at him with her great fixed eyes. And a terrible silence ensued.

The fury of Roubaud was not calmed. No sooner did it seem to moderate a little, than it returned at once in great waves of increased volume, which bore him along in their vertiginous flood. No longer under self-control, he struck about in space, a victim to all the gusts of the violent tempest lacerating him, only to awaken to the imperative necessity of appeasing the howling brute within him. It was a physical, an immediate necessity, a thirst for vengeance that wrung his body, and which would leave him no repose until it had been satisfied.

Without stopping in his walk, he struck his temples with his two fists, and he stammered out in a voice of anguish:

"What shall I do?"

As he had not killed this woman at once, he would not kill her now.

His cowardice in allowing her to live exasperated his anger, for it was cowardly. It was because he still cared for her that he had not strangled her. Nevertheless, he could not keep her with him, after what he had discovered. Then he would have to drive her out, put her into the street, never to see her again? And at this thought, a fresh flood of suffering overwhelmed him. He experienced an execrable feeling of disgust when he recognised that he would not even do this. What then? It only remained for him to accept the abomination, and to take this woman back to Havre, there to continue to live quietly together, as if nothing had occurred. No, no! Death rather. Death for both of them that very instant! He was stirred with such intense distress that his head seemed to have gone astray, and he cried out louder than before:

"What shall I do?"

Séverine, from the bed, where she remained seated, continued following him with her great eyes. She had always felt the calm affection of a comrade for him, and the excessive grief in which she now saw him plunged, aroused her pity. The ugly words and blows she would have excused, if this wild fit of passion had caused her less surprise—a surprise that she had not yet got over. Passive and docile, she had consented to her marriage simply from a desire to settle down, and she was at a loss to understand such an outburst of jealousy about a former error which she repented.

She watched her husband, going and coming, turning furiously round, as she would have watched a wolf, or an animal of some other species. What was the matter with him? There were so many husbands without anger. The thing that terrified her was to perceive the brute, whose presence she had suspected for three years, from certain sullen growls, at this moment unchained, mad and ready to bite. What could she say to him to avert a misfortune?

At each turn he came near the bed before her. She awaited him there, and had sufficient courage to address him.

"My dear, listen," said she.

But he heard not. He went back to the other end of the room, like a bit of straw beaten about in a storm.

"What shall I do? What shall I do?" he continued asking.

At last she seized him by the wrist, and retained him a minute.

"My dear, listen," she said. "You know it was I who refused to go to Doinville. I should never have gone there again. Never! Never! It is you I love."

"Look here," he answered, "if I am to live, I must kill the other! I must kill him!—kill him!"

His voice rose louder. He repeated the word, erect, grown taller, as if this utterance, in bringing him to a resolution, also brought him calm. He ceased speaking. He walked slowly to the table, and there, with a gesture of indifference looked at the knife, whose shimmering blade was wide open. He closed, and put it in his pocket. Then, with his arms swinging at his sides, his eyes lost in space, he remained at the same place thinking. Obstacles that presented themselves to some plan he was elaborating in his brain, caused two great wrinkles to appear on his forehead. To get the better of his difficulty, he went and opened the window, standing before it with his face in the chilly air of twilight. His wife in another fright stood up behind him; and, not daring to question him, waited with her face to the expansive sky, endeavouring to guess what was passing in that hard skull.

In the falling shades of night, the distant houses stood out black, and a violescent mist clouded the vast site of the station. The deep cutting seemed as if smothered in dust, particularly in the direction of Batignolles, and the ironwork of the Pont de l'Europe began to fade away. Towards Paris a final gleam of daylight whitened the windows of the great iron marquees, but within they became densely obscure. Suddenly one saw a glitter of sparks. The men were lighting the gas-lamps along the platforms. Here a great white spot was formed by the lantern on the engine of the Dieppe train, crowded with passengers. The doors of the compartments were already closed, and the driver only awaited the order of the assistant station-master on duty, to start. But some hindrance had occurred. The red signal of the pointsman closed the line, while a small locomotive came and picked up a few carriages, which a defective manœuvre had left behind.

Trains flew along without intermission, in the increasing darkness, over the complicated network of rails, threading their way through lines of carriages standing motionless on sidings. One started for Argenteuil, another for Saint Germain. A very long train arrived from Cherbourg. Signals succeeded one another, accompanied by whistles and blasts of the horn. Lights appeared on every side, one by one: red, green, yellow, white. There seemed to be a regular confusion at this troubled hour when day glides into night, and it looked as if a tremendous smash would ensue. But everything passed on. The trains brushed by each other, detaching themselves from the entanglement, in a smooth, creeping motion that could only be perceived indistinctly in the deep crepuscule. But the red light of the pointsman was effaced, the Dieppe train blew its whistle, and rolled off. A few drops of rain began to fall from the wan sky. It was going to be a wet night.

When Roubaud turned round, it was with a face cloudy and obstinate, as if overcast by the shadow of this night that was drawing in. He had made up his mind. His plan was formed. In the vanishing darkness, he looked at the cuckoo clock, and exclaimed aloud:

"Twenty minutes past five!"

He was astounded; one hour, barely one hour, and so much to do! It seemed to him that they had been devouring one another there for weeks.

"Twenty minutes past five!" he muttered. "We shall have enough time."

Séverine, without daring to ask a question, continued following him with her anxious eyes. She saw him rummage in the cupboard, and bring out some notepaper, a small bottle of ink, and a pen.

"What!" she exclaimed. "Are you going to write a letter? To whom?"

"To him. Sit down."

And, as she instinctively drew away from the chair, ignoring as yet what he was about to exact from her, he brought her back, and weighed her down so heavily as he seated her at the table, that she remained there.

"Write this: 'Leave tonight by the 6.30 express, and do not show yourself before you arrive at Rouen.'"

She held the pen, but her hand trembled. Her fright increased at the thought of all the unknown gaping before her in those two simple lines. And she had the courage to raise her head, and say in a pleading tone:

"What are you going to do, my dear? I beg you to tell me."

He only repeated, in his loud, inexorable voice:

"Write, write!"

Then, with his eyes on her eyes, without anger, without ugly words, but with such obstinacy that she felt the weight crushing and annihilating her, he answered:

"What I am going to do, you will see, well enough. And listen, what I am going to do, I mean you to do with me. In that way we shall remain together. There will be something binding between us."

He terrified her. She drew back again.

"No, no; I want to know!" she exclaimed. "I will not write without knowing."

Then, ceasing to speak, he took her hand—the small, delicate hand of a child, and pressed it in his iron fist, with the continuous pressure of a vice, until he almost crushed it. He was driving his will into her flesh with the pain. She uttered a cry. All her spirit was broken, all her will surrendered. Ignorant creature as she had remained, in her passive gentleness, she could but obey. Instrument of love, instrument of death.

"Write, write!" he repeated again.

And she wrote painfully, with her poor, sore hand.

"That's all right; you are very good," said he, when he had the letter. "Now tidy the place up a bit, and get everything ready. I'll come back and fetch you."

He was quite calm. He arranged the bow of his tie before the looking-glass, put on his hat, and took himself off. She heard him double-lock the door, and remove the key. Night was drawing in more and more. For an instant she remained seated, her ear catching every sound outside. A continual, low whine came from the adjoining room in occupation of the newspaper woman: no doubt a little dog forgotten by its mistress. Below, in the apartment of the Dauvergnes, the piano had become silent. There was now a merry clatter of stewpans and crockery. The two little housekeepers were busy in their kitchen, Claire looking after a mutton stew, Sophie picking a salad. And Séverine, prostrated, listened to their laughter in the frightful distress of this falling night.

At a quarter past six, the locomotive of the Havre express, issuing from the Pont de l'Europe, was switched on to its train and there secured. Owing to the metals being occupied, they had been unable to lodge this train under the marquee of the main lines. It waited in the open air beside a prolongation of the platform forming a sort of narrow jetty, in the gloom of an inky sky, where the poorly furnished row of gas lamps displayed but a line of smoky stars.

A shower had just ceased, leaving behind a trace of icy dampness spread over this vast uncovered space, which the mist threw back as far as the pale glimmers on the façades in the Rue de Rome. This immense, dreary expanse, bathed in water, here and there studded with a gory light, was broken up by opaque lumps, engines, and solitary carriages, parts of trains in repose on the shunting lines. And from the depths of this sheet of darkness came sounds,—giant-like respirations, breathless with fever, whistles resembling the piercing shrieks of women, distant, lamentable blasts of horns mingled with a rumble in the adjoining streets. Orders were shouted out to add on a carriage. The engine of the express stood motionless, losing by a valve a great jet of steam, which ascended into all this obscurity to spread into small clouds and sprinkle the boundless veil of mourning drawn across the sky with white tears.

At twenty minutes past six, Roubaud and Séverine appeared. She had just returned the key to Mother Victoire, as she passed by the lavatory, near the waiting-rooms. And Roubaud, impatient and blunt, his hat on the back of his head, urged her on, after the fashion of a husband with no time to lose, who is being delayed by his wife; while she, with her veil drawn tight over her face, advanced slowly as if broken down with fatigue.

Joining the flood of passengers streaming along the platform, they followed the line of carriages, on the look-out for an empty first-class compartment. The footway became alive with porters rolling trucks of luggage to the van at the head of the train. An inspector was busy finding seats for a numerous family, the assistant station-master on duty, with his signal lantern in his hand, glanced at the couplings, to see that the spreaders had been properly screwed up. And Roubaud, having at length found an empty compartment, was about to assist Séverine to get in, when he perceived M. Vandorpe, the head-station-master, strolling along in company with M. Dauvergne, his deputy-chief of the main lines, both watching the manœuvre connected with the carriage that was being added to the train. Roubaud, exchanging greetings with them, found it necessary to stop and have a chat.

First of all they spoke of the business with the sub-prefect, which had terminated to the satisfaction of everyone. Then the conversation turned to an accident that had happened in the morning at Havre, the news having come by telegraph. A locomotive, called La Lison, which on Thursday and Saturday took the 6.30 express, had broken its connecting-rod, just as the train entered the station; and the repairs would give two days' holiday to Jacques Lantier, the driver, who came from the same part of the country as Roubaud, and to his fireman, Pecqueux, the husband of Mother Victoire.

Séverine remained standing before the door of the compartment, while her husband affected great freedom of mind in conversation with these gentlemen, raising his voice and laughing. But there came a shock, and the train recoiled a few yards. It was the locomotive, driving back the first carriages to the one that had just been added on, the No. 293, so as to have a reserved coupé. And Henri Dauvergne, the son, who accompanied the train as headguard, having recognised Séverine through her veil, had prevented her from receiving a knock from the wide-open door, by pulling her away without ceremony. Then, excusing himself, smiling, very amiable, he explained that the coupé was for one of the directors of the company, who had sent to ask for it half an hour before the time for the train to start. She gave a little, senseless laugh, and he ran off to attend to his work.

The clock marked 6.27. Three minutes more. Roubaud, who was watching the doors of the waiting-rooms in the distance, while chatting with the station-master, suddenly left the latter to return to Séverine. But the carriage having moved back, they had to make their way to the empty compartment a few paces off. Roubaud pushed his wife along, and with an effort of the wrist, made her get into the carriage; while she, in her anxious docility, looked instinctively behind her, to see what was going on.

A passenger behind time had just arrived, carrying only a rug in his hand. He had the broad collar of his blue top-coat turned up, and the rim of his bowler hat brought down so low over his eyebrows that nothing could be seen of his face, in the vacillating gaslight, but a bit of white beard. M. Vandorpe and M. Dauvergne advanced and followed the passenger, notwithstanding his evident desire to avoid being seen. He only greeted them three carriages further on, when in front of the reserved coupé, in which he hurriedly took a seat. It was the President. Séverine, in a tremble, sank down on a seat, her husband bruised her arm in his grasp, as if in a final act of taking possession of her, exulting, now that he was certain of doing the thing he had thought out in his mind.

A minute later the half hour would strike. A newspaper seller stubbornly offered the evening editions, a few passengers still strolled along the platform finishing cigarettes. But all took their seats. The inspectors could be heard coming from both ends of the train, closing the doors. And Roubaud, who had met with the disagreeable surprise of perceiving a sombre form occupying a corner in the compartment which he had thought empty, no doubt a woman in mourning, who remained mute and motionless, could not restrain an exclamation of real anger, when the door opened again, and an inspector pushed in a stout man and a stout woman, who flopped down on a seat, gasping.

They were about to start. The very fine rain had recommenced, drowning the vast, dark expanse, which was crossed incessantly by trains that presented nothing distinguishable but a moving line of small, bright windows. Green lights had been lit, a few lanterns danced on a level with the ground; and there was nothing else, nothing but black immensity, where alone appeared the marquees of the main lines, pale with a dim reflex of gas. All had disappeared, even the sounds had become muffled. The roar of the engine, opening its exhaust pipes, to let out a whirling wave of white steam, alone could be heard. A cloud ascended, unrolling like the winding-sheet of an apparition, and divided by dense black smoke springing from some invisible source. The sky was once more obscured, a volume of soot flew over nocturnal Paris, ablaze with luminosity.

Then the assistant station-master on duty, raised his lantern for the engine-driver to inquire if the line was free. Two whistles were heard; and away, near the box of the pointsman, the red light vanished, to be succeeded by a white one. The headguard, standing at the door of his van, awaited the order to start, which he transmitted. The driver gave a long whistle, and opening the regulator, set the locomotive moving. They were off. At first the motion was imperceptible, then the train rolled along. Darting under the Pont de l'Europe, it plunged towards the Batignolles tunnel. All that could be seen of it were the three lights behind, the red triangle looking like gaping wounds. For a few seconds longer, it could be followed in the chilling darkness of night. Now it flew on its way, and nothing now could stop this train, launched at full speed. It disappeared.

II

The house at La Croix-de-Maufras stands aslant, in a garden which the railway has cut in two, and is so near the metals that it feels the shock of every train passing by. A single journey suffices to bear it away in memory. The entire multitude, who have flown along the line, are aware of its existence at this spot, without knowing aught about it. Always closed, it looks as if deserted in distress, with its grey shutters turning green through the effects of the rain beating against them from the west. Standing in a wilderness, it seems to increase the solitude of this out-of-the-way corner, where scarcely a soul breathes for three or four miles around.

The only other house there, is that of the gatekeeper, at the angle where the road crosses the rails on its way to Doinville, four miles off. Low in build, the walls seamed with cracks, the tiles of the root devoured by moss, it lies crushed, with a neglectful aspect of poverty, in the middle of the garden surrounding it—a garden planted with vegetables, enclosed by a quickset hedge, and where a great well rises almost as high as the habitation itself.

The level crossing is just half-way between the two stations of Malaunay and Barentin, being three miles from each. It is but little used. The old decaying gate rarely rolls back, save for the stone-drays from the quarries at Bécourt, half a league distant in the forest. It would be difficult to imagine a more out-of-the-way place, or one more completely separated from humanity, for the long tunnel in the direction of Malaunay, cuts off every road, and the only way to communicate with Barentin is by a neglected pathway beside the line. Visitors therefore are scarce.

On this particular evening, as night was drawing in, a traveller who had just left a train from Havre, at Barentin, followed with long strides the pathway of La Croix-de-Maufras. The country thereabouts is but one uninterrupted set of hills and dales, a sort of waving of the soil, which the railway crosses on embankments and in cuttings, alternately. The continual unevenness of the ground, the ascents and descents on either side of the line, make walking difficult and add to the feeling of deep solitude. The impoverished, whitish land lies fallow, the hillocks are crowned with small woods, while brooks, shaded with willows, run at the bottom of the narrow ravines. Certain chalky elevations are absolutely bare, and sterile hills succeed one another in the silence and abandonment of death. The young, lusty traveller hastened his steps, as if to escape from the sadness of the twilight, falling so gently over this desolate country.

In the garden of the gatekeeper, a girl was drawing water at the well: a tall lass of eighteen; fair, robust, with thick lips, greenish eyes, a low forehead, and a heavy head of hair. She was not pretty, and had the heavy hips and muscular arms of a young man. As soon as she perceived the traveller coming down the path, she let go the pail and ran to the garden gate, exclaiming:

"Hullo! Jacques!"

He raised his head. He had just completed his twenty-seventh year. He also was tall, and very dark. A handsome fellow, with his round face and regular features, which nevertheless were marred by too heavy a jaw. His thick hair curled, as did his moustache, which was so full, so black, that it seemed to add to the pallidness of his complexion. From his delicate skin, carefully shaved on the cheeks, anyone would have taken him for a gentleman, had it not been for the indelible imprint of the workman that he bore on his engine-driver hands, which were already turning yellow with grease, although remaining small and flexible.

"Good evening, Flore," he simply said.

But his large dark eyes, studded with golden sparks, had become troubled with a reddish cloud, which made them dim. The lids were blinking, the eyes turned away in sudden constraint, and he experienced a feeling of uneasiness that went so far as to cause him suffering. His whole frame instinctively made a movement as if to draw back.

She, standing motionless, her eyes looking straight at him, had perceived this involuntary shudder, that came on him, and which he endeavoured to master, each time that he approached a woman. It seemed to make her quite serious and sad. Then, when he asked her, in view of concealing his embarrassment, if her mother was at home, although knowing she was unwell and unable to leave the house, the girl only answered with a nod, standing aside so that he might come in without touching her; and, erect and proud, she returned without a word to the well.

Jacques crossed the small garden at his rapid stride, and entered the dwelling. There, in the centre of the first room, a sort of large kitchen where the family took their meals and lived, Aunt Phasie, as he had called her from infancy, was alone, seated near the table on a rush-bottomed

ÉMILE ZOLA

chair, with her legs wrapped in an old shawl. She was a cousin of his father, a Lantier, who had stood godmother to him; and who, when he was no more than six, had taken care of him, at the time when his father and mother had flown off to Paris, and there disappeared. He had then remained at Plassans, where, later on, he had followed the classes at the École des Arts et Métiers. He bore Aunt Phasie great gratitude, and was in the habit of saying that if he had made his way, it was entirely due to her.

When he became a driver of the first class in the Western Railway Company, after passing a couple of years on the Orleans Railway, he had found his godmother married again to a level crossing gatekeeper named Misard, and exiled with the two daughters of her first marriage to this out-of-the-way place, called La Croix-de-Maufras. At the present time Aunt Phasie, although barely forty-five, and who formerly had been so tall and strong, looked sixty. Moreover, she had grown thin and yellow, and was a prey to constant shivers.

She welcomed Jacques with joy.

"What! is it you, Jacques?" she exclaimed. "Ah! my bonny lad, what a surprise!"

He kissed her cheeks, explaining that he had suddenly come into a couple of days' enforced holiday. La Lison, his engine, on reaching Havre in the morning, had broken its connecting-rod; and as the repairs would take four-and-twenty hours, he would not resume duty until the following evening for the 6.40 express. So he had come over to see her. He would sleep there, and catch the 7.26 train from Barentin in the morning. And he kept her poor, withered hands in his own, telling her how anxious her last letter had made him.

"Ah! yes, my lad, I am not well, I am not at all well. How nice of you to have guessed my desire to see you! But I know what little time you have of your own, and did not dare ask you to run over. Anyhow, here you are, and I have so much, so much on my mind!"

She broke off to cast a timid glance out of the window. On the other side of the metals, in the twilight, her husband could be perceived in his box, one of those wooden huts erected every four or five miles along the line, and connected by telegraph to ensure the satisfactory running of the trains. While his wife, and, later on, Flore, had been placed in charge of the gate at the level crossing, Misard had been made a watchman of the line.

In fear of him hearing her, she lowered her voice, and said with a shudder:

"I verily believe he is poisoning me!"

Jacques started in surprise at this disclosure, and his eyes, also turning towards the window, were again deadened by the peculiar trouble to which he was accustomed, that little reddish haze which dimmed their brilliant black full of golden sparks.

"Oh! Aunt Phasie, what an idea!" he murmured. "He looks such a gentle, weak creature."

A train had just passed, going in the direction of Havre, and Misard had left his box to block the line behind it. Jacques looked at him as he pulled up the lever to show the red signal. He was a little puny man, with thin, discoloured hair and beard, and a lean, hollow-cheeked face. Moreover, he was silent, retiring, never angry, and obsequiously polite in presence of his chiefs. But he had returned to his box to note down in his register the hour at which the train had passed, and press the two electric buttons, one opening the line at the preceding post, the other announcing the coming of the train at the box after his.

"Ah! you don't know him," resumed Aunt Phasie; "I tell you that he must be giving me some filth. I, who was so strong, who would have eaten him up; and it is he, this bit of a man, this insignificant creature, who is devouring me!"

She was burning with concealed timorous spite, and unbosomed herself, delighted to have at last found someone who would listen to her. What could she have been thinking of to have married such a cunning fellow, without a sou and miserly, she who was more than five years his senior, with two daughters, one already eight, and the other six? It was now close on ten years since she had done this famous business, and not an hour had passed without her repenting it—a poverty-stricken existence, exiled to this icy quarter in the north, where she was shivering with cold, wearied to death at not having a soul to speak to, not a single neighbour. He, formerly a plate-layer, now earned 1,200 frcs. a year as watchman; she, from the commencement, had received 50 frcs. for the gate, which was now in charge of Flore. Such was the present and future, no other hope; the certainty of living and dying in this hole, far away from their fellow creatures.

"I tell you," she repeated to conclude, "that it is he who is tampering with me, and that he'll do for me, little as he is."

The sudden tinkling of an alarum made her cast the same anxious glance outside as before. This was the preceding post informing Misard that a train was coming in the direction of Paris, and the needle of the apparatus, standing in front of the window, pointed that way. Stopping the ringing, he went out to signal the train by two blasts of the horn, while Flore, at the same moment, came and closed the gate. Then, planting herself before it, she held the flag up straight in its leather case. The train, an express, hidden by a curve, could be heard advancing with a roar that grew louder as it approached. It passed like a thunderbolt, shaking, threatening to carry away the low habitation in a tempestuous gust of wind.

Flore returned to her vegetables; while Misard, after blocking the up-line behind the train, went to open the down-line, by lowering the lever to efface the red signal, for another tinkling, accompanied by the rise of the other needle, had just warned him that the train which had gone by five minutes previously was clear of the next post. He returned to his box, communicated with the two watchmen, jotted down the passing of the train, and waited. It was always the same kind of work that he did, for twelve consecutive hours, living there, eating there, without reading half a dozen lines of a newspaper, without appearing even to have a single thought in his slanting skull.

"Perhaps he is jealous," suggested Jacques.

But Aunt Phasie shrugged her shoulders in pity.

"Ah! my lad, what is that you say? He jealous!"

Then, with the old shiver upon her, she added:

"No, no, he never cared for me. All he cares for is money. Why we quarrelled, you see, was because I would not give him the 1,000 frcs. I inherited from father last year. Then, just as he threatened me that it would bring me bad luck, I fell ill. And the complaint has not left me since. Yes, it is exactly from that time that I have been unwell."

The young man understood her idea; and, attributing it to the gloomy thoughts of a sick woman, he still endeavoured to dissuade her. But she obstinately shook her head, like a person who has made up her mind. So that he ended by saying:

"Very well then, the remedy is as simple as can be. If you want to put an end to the thing, give him your 1,000 frcs."

By an extraordinary effort she rose to her feet; and, resuscitated, as it were, she violently answered:

"My 1,000 frcs.? Never! I would sooner burst. Ah! they are hidden, and well hidden, take my word! The house may be turned upside down, but I defy anyone to find them. And he has had a good try, the demon! I have heard him at night time, sounding all the walls. Search,

search! The mere pleasure of watching his nose grow longer, would suffice to give me patience. We shall see who will give up first, him or me. I am on my guard, and swallow nothing that he touches. And if I kick the bucket, well, he will not even then get my 1,000 frcs. I prefer leaving them to the earth."

She sank back into the chair exhausted, shaking at another sound of the horn. It came from Misard, who, standing at the door of his box, this time signalled a train on its way to Havre. In spite of her obstinate determination to withhold the legacy, she had a secret and increasing fear of him, the same kind of fear as that of a giant, for the insect he feels devouring him.

The train signalled, the slow train which had left Paris at 12.45, was coming along in the distance with a dull rumble. It could be heard issuing from the tunnel and puffing louder in the open country. Then it passed amidst the thunder of its wheels, and its mass of carriages, with the invincible might of a hurricane.

Jacques, with his eyes raised towards the window, had watched the small squares of glass file past. Wishing to turn aside the gloomy ideas of Aunt Phasie, he resumed in a joking vein:

"Godmother, you complain that you never see a soul in this hole; but there are people for you!"

Failing, at first, to catch his meaning, she looked astounded, and inquired:

"Where are there any people?" Then, understanding, she added: "Ah! yes, those folk who go by. What good are they? One does not know them, one cannot chat with them."

He continued in a merry tone:

"But me, you know me well enough; you often see me pass."

"You, that's true. I know you, and I know the time of your train," she answered. "Only, you fly, fly along! Yesterday you did so with your hand. I can't even answer. No, no, that's no way of seeing people."

Nevertheless, this idea of the multitude the up and down trains carried along daily before her, amidst the deep silence of her solitude, made her pensive, and she turned her eyes to the line where night was drawing in. When in good health, and she went and came, planting herself before the gate, her flag in her hand, she never thought of such things. But since she had been remaining for days on this chair, with naught to think of but her underhand struggle with this man, confused reveries, barely formulated, had set her head topsy-turvy.

It seemed to her so strange that she should be living here, lost in the depths of this desert, without a soul in whom she could confide, when so many men and women filed past in the tempestuous blast of the trains, shaking the house, tearing along full steam, day and night continually. Certainly all the inhabitants of the earth went by there, not only Frenchmen, foreigners also; persons come from the most distant lands, as no one could now remain at home, and as all people, according to what had been written, would soon be but one. This was progress: brothers all, rolling along together, yonder towards a land of plenty.

She endeavoured to count them, to arrive at an average, so many for each carriage; but there were too many, she could not manage it. Frequently she fancied she recognised faces: that of a gentleman with a light beard, doubtless an Englishman who travelled to Paris every week; that of a little dark lady, who went by regularly on Wednesday and Saturday. But the flash bore them off, and she was not quite sure she had seen them. All the faces became confused, blended together, as if alike, disappearing one in the other. The torrent ran on, leaving nothing of itself behind. And what made her sad at the sight of this constant movement, amid so much well-being and so much money, was to feel that this panting multitude was ignorant of her being there, in danger of death, so that if her husband some night polished her off, the trains would continue passing one another, close to her corpse, without anyone even suspecting the crime within the solitary habitation.

Aunt Phasie had remained with her eyes on the window, and she summed up what she felt; but her feelings were too vague to be explained at length.

"Ah! it's a fine invention, there's no doubt of it. People go along quick, and become more learned. But wild beasts remain wild beasts, and people may invent even finer machines still; but, nevertheless, there will be wild beasts in spite of all."

Jacques tossed his head to say that he thought as she did. For a few moments he had been watching Flore, who had opened the gate for a quarry dray loaded with two enormous blocks of stone. The road only served for the Bécourt quarries, so that the gate was padlocked at night, and Flore rarely had to get up to unlock it. Observing her chatting familiarly with the quarryman, a dark young fellow, Jacques exclaimed:

"Hullo! Cabuche must be ill, as his cousin Louis is in charge of the horses. Poor Cabuche! Do you often see him, godmother?"

She raised her hands without answering, heaving a great sigh. The previous autumn there had been a regular drama which had not contributed to improve her health. Her younger daughter, Louisette, in service as housemaid with Madame Bonnehon at Doinville, had ran away at night, half crazy and black and blue, to go and die at the hut which her sweetheart, Cabuche, occupied in the middle of the forest. All manner of tales had got about reflecting on President Grandmorin; but no one dared repeat them aloud. Even her mother, who knew what had happened, did not like returning to the subject. Nevertheless, she ended by saying:

"No. He never looks in. He is becoming as shy as a wolf. Poor Louisette, who was such a pet, so white, so sweet! She really loved me, and would have nursed me, she would! Whereas Flore, well, I don't complain of her, but she has certainly something wrong with her head, always doing just as she likes, disappearing for hours together. And then proud and violent! It is all very sad, very sad."

Jacques, while listening, continued following the stone-dray with his eyes. It was now crossing the line, but the wheels had got clogged by the metals, and the driver had to clack his whip, while Flore shouted to excite the horses.

"The deuce!" exclaimed the young man, "it wouldn't do for a train to come along now. There would be a smash!"

"Oh! there is no fear of that," replied Aunt Phasie. "Flore is sometimes funny, but she knows her business. She keeps her eyes open. It is now five years since we had an accident, thank God. A long time back a man was cut to pieces. We have only had a cow, which almost upset a train. Ah! the poor creature! We found its body here, and its head over there, near the tunnel. With Flore one can sleep soundly."

The stone-dray had passed on. The loud shocks of the wheels in the ruts could be heard growing less distinct in the distance. Then Aunt Phasie returned to the subject that constantly occupied her thoughts— the question of health, in regard to others as much as herself.

"And you," she inquired, "are you quite well now? You remember, when you were with us, that complaint you suffered from, and of which the doctor could make neither head nor tail?"

His eyes became restless.

"I am very well, godmother," said he.

"Truly? It has all disappeared?" she inquired again. "That pain boring into your skull behind the ears, and the abrupt strokes of fever, and those periods of sadness, which made you hide yourself like an animal at the bottom of a hole?"

As she proceeded, he became more and more troubled, and got so dreadfully uneasy that, at last, he interrupted her, saying in a brief tone:

"I assure you I am very well. I feel nothing of all that. Nothing at all."

"Well, so much the better, my lad," said she. "The fact of you being ill would not cure me. And then, you're of an age to enjoy good health. Ah! health! there is nothing like it. It is all the same very kind of you to have come to see me, when you could have been enjoying yourself somewhere else. You'll have dinner with us, won't you? And you'll sleep up there in the loft, next to the room Flore occupies?"

But another blare of the horn interrupted her. Night had closed in, and, turning towards the window, they could only confusedly distinguish Misard talking with another man. Six o'clock had just struck, and he was giving over his service to the night watchman. At length he was about to be free after twelve hours passed in this hut, furnished only with a small table under the shelf supporting the apparatus, a stool, and a stove which threw out so much heat, that he was obliged to almost constantly keep the door open.

"Ah! here he is, he is returning home," murmured Aunt Phasie, in a fright again.

The train signalled was coming, very heavy, very long, roaring louder and louder as it approached, and the young man had to bend forward to hear what the invalid said, feeling pained at the wretched state she was putting herself in, and anxious to relieve her.

"Listen, godmother, if he really has bad intentions, perhaps it would stop him if he was to know that I have taken up the matter. You would do well to entrust your 1,000 frcs. to me."

She gave a final outburst.

"My 1,000 frcs.!" she exclaimed. "Not to you any more than to him! I tell you I'd sooner die!"

At this moment the train passed in its storm-like violence, as if it would sweep everything before it. The house shook, enveloped in a gust of wind. This particular train, on its way to Havre, was very crowded, for there was to be a fête on the following day, a Sunday, in connection with a launch. Notwithstanding the speed, by the lit-up glass of the doors one caught sight of the full compartments, of the lines of heads side by side, close together, each with its particular profile. They followed one another and disappeared.

What a multitude! The crowd again, the crowd without end, amidst the rolling of the carriages, the whistling of the locomotives, the tinkling of the telegraph, the ringing of bells! It was like a huge body, a gigantic being stretched across the earth, the head at Paris, the vertebræ all along the line, the limbs expanding with the embranchments, the feet and hands at Havre and at the other termini. And it passed, passed, mechanically, triumphant, advancing to the future with mathematical precision, careless as to what remained of man on either side of it, who, although concealed, was still replete with life, the embodiment of eternal passion and eternal love.

Flore came in first, and lit the lamp, a small petroleum lamp without a shade, and laid the table. Not a word did they exchange. She barely threw a glance at Jacques, who stood before the window with his back turned. A *soupe-aux-choux* was being kept warm on the stove. When Misard made his appearance she was serving it. He showed no surprise to find the young man there. Perhaps he had seen him arrive. He displayed no curiosity to know what had brought him there, and asked no questions. A pressure of the hand, three brief words, and nothing more. Jacques had to take the initiative of repeating the tale about the broken connecting-rod, and how he had then thought of running over to kiss his aunt. Misard was content to gently toss his head, as if to say he considered this quite proper, and they sat down, eating slowly, and, at first, in silence.

Aunt Phasie, who since the morning had not taken her eyes from the pot where the *soupe-aux-choux* was simmering, accepted a plateful. But her husband having risen to give her the iron-water forgotten by Flore, a decanter in which a few nails were rusting, she did not touch it. He, humble, puny, coughing with a nasty little cough, did not seem to remark the anxious look with which she followed his slightest movement. When she asked for salt, there being none on the table, he told her she would repent of eating so much, that it was this that made her ill; and he rose to take some, bringing her a pinch in a spoon, which she accepted without distrust, salt purifying everything, as she said. Then they spoke of the really mild weather that had prevailed for some days, and of a train that had run off the rails at Maromme. Jacques began to think that his godmother must suffer from nightmare while wide awake, for he could see nothing suspicious about this bit of a man, who was so civil, and had such expressionless eyes. They remained more than an hour at table. Twice Flore disappeared, for a few moments, at

ÉMILE ZOLA

the signal of the horn. The trains went by, making the glasses ring on the table; but no one paid the least attention.

Another blare of the horn, and Flore, who had just cleared the cloth, withdrew and did not return. She left her mother and the two men seated at table before a bottle of cider brandy. All three remained thus another half hour. Then Misard, whose ferreting eyes had been resting for a minute or two on a corner of the room, took his cap and went out, with a simple good-night. He was in the habit of poaching in the little neighbouring brooks, which harboured superb eels, and never went to bed without examining his lines.

As soon as he had gone, Aunt Phasie looked fixedly at her godson, and exclaimed:

"Eh! What do you think of that? Did you see him searching over there with his eyes in that corner? He has got an idea that I have hidden my hoard behind the butter-jar. Ah! I know him, I am certain he will move the jar tonight to have a look."

But she began perspiring, and trembling from head to foot.

"You see, there it is again! He must have drugged me. My mouth is as bitter as if I had been swallowing old sous, though God knows I have taken nothing from his hand! It's enough to make one drown oneself. I can't sit up any longer tonight. It's better for me to go to bed. So good-bye, my lad, because if you leave at 7.26 it will be too early for me. And come again, won't you? And let's hope I shall still be here."

He had to assist her to her room, where she got into bed, and went off to sleep, exhausted. Left by himself, he hesitated, thinking whether it would not be as well if he were to retire for the night also, and stretch himself out on the hay awaiting him upstairs in the loft. But it was only ten minutes to eight; he had plenty of time for sleep. And so, he too went out, leaving the little petroleum lamp alight in the empty, slumbering house, shaken ever and anon by the abrupt thunder of a train.

Jacques was surprised at the mildness of the air outside. No doubt it would rain again. A uniform milky cloud had spread over the sky, and the full moon, concealed behind it, lit up the whole vault of heaven with a reddish reflex. He could clearly distinguish the country. The land around him, the hills, the trees stood out in black against this equal, deadened light, soft as that of a night lamp. He walked round the little kitchen garden. Then he thought of going towards Doinville, as the road in that direction was not so steep as the other way. But the sight of the solitary house planted aslant on the opposite side of the line having caught his attention, he crossed the metals, passing by the side gate, the big one being already closed for the night.

He knew this house very well. He gazed at it on each of his journeys, amid the roar and jolting of his engine. It haunted him, without him being able to understand why, save for a confused sensation that it had something to do with his existence. Each time he went up and down the line, he first of all experienced a sort of dread lest he should find it no longer there, then he felt a kind of uneasiness when he perceived it still in the same place. He had never seen either the doors or windows open. All he had learnt about it was that it belonged to President Grandmorin, and on this particular night he was beset by an irresistible desire to wander round about it, so as to ascertain something more.

Jacques remained a long time on the road, facing the iron railings. He stepped back, raised himself on his toes, endeavouring to form some idea of the place. The railway, in cutting through the garden, had only left a small plot enclosed by walls in front of the house; while behind was a rather large piece of ground, simply surrounded by a quickset hedge. The dwelling, with its distressful-looking appearance, had an air of lugubrious sadness in the red reflex of this fumy night; and Jacques was about to leave it, with a shiver running over his skin, when he noticed a hole in the hedge. The idea that it would be cowardly not to go in, made him push through. His heart was beating; but, immediately, as he passed beside a greenhouse in ruins, he stopped at the sight of something dark, in a heap at the door.

"What! Is that you?" he exclaimed, astonished, recognising Flore. "What are you doing here?"

She also started with surprise. Then she answered tranquilly:

"You can see; I'm taking cords. They have left a heap there, that are rotting, without being used by anybody, and as I am always in need of them, I run over and take them."

And, indeed, seated on the ground, with a stout pair of scissors in her hand, she was undoing the bits of cord, cutting the knots, when she failed to get them apart.

"Doesn't the owner come here any more, then?" inquired the young man.

She began laughing.

"Oh! since that affair of Louisette," she replied, "there's no fear of the President risking the tip of his nose at La Croix-de-Maufras. I can pick up his cords without fear."

He remained silent for a moment, and seemed troubled by the thought of the tragic adventure she alluded to.

"And do you believe what Louisette said?" he asked.

Ceasing to laugh, she suddenly became violent, and exclaimed:

"Louisette never lied, nor did Cabuche. He is my friend."

"Perhaps your sweetheart?" suggested Jacques.

"He, indeed!" she replied. "No, no; he is my friend. I have no sweetheart, and I don't want one."

She raised her powerful head, with its thick yellow mane curling very low on the forehead, and from all her massive, supple body, burst a savage energy of will. Already a legend was growing up about her in the neighbourhood. Stories were related of heroic deeds of salvage: a cart torn with a mighty jerk from before a train; a railway carriage stopped while descending the declivity at Barentin alone, like some furious beast bounding along to encounter an express. Then there was the tale of her adventure with a pointsman at the Dieppe embranchment, at the other end of the tunnel, a certain Ozil, a man about thirty, whom she seemed to have encouraged for a short time, but who having been so ill-advised as to attempt to take a liberty, had almost met his death from a blow she dealt him with a club. Virgin and warlike, she disdained the male, which finally convinced people that she certainly had something wrong with her head.

Jacques, hearing her declare that she did not want a sweetheart, continued his fun:

"Then your marriage with Ozil can't be in a good way? Yet I've heard it said that you run to meet him every day through the tunnel."

She shrugged her shoulders.

"Ah! To Jericho, my marriage!" she retorted. "What you say about the tunnel makes me laugh. Two miles to gallop over in the darkness, with the thought that you may get cut in two by a train if you don't keep your eyes open. You should hear them snorting in there! But Ozil worried me. He's not the one I want."

"Then you want someone else?"

"Ah! I don't know. Ah! faith, no!"

She had burst into a laugh again, while a slight embarrassment made her give her attention to a knot in the cords which she could not manage to undo. Then, without raising her head, as if very much absorbed by her occupation, she said:

"And you, have you no sweetheart?"

Jacques, in his turn, became serious. He avoided looking at her, his eyes moved restlessly from side to side, and were at last fixed on space in the night. Abruptly he answered:

"No."

"Just so," she continued; "they told me you held women in abomination. And, besides, I've known you for a very long time, and you have never said anything nice. Why? Tell me."

As he gave no answer, she made up her mind to leave the knot, and look at him.

"Do you only love your engine?" she inquired. "People joke about it, you know. They pretend you are always polishing, and making it shine, as though you had caresses for nothing else. If I tell you this, it is because I am your friend."

He looked at her, now, in the pale light of the fumy sky. And he remembered her when she was a child. Even then, she was violent and self-willed, but she sprang to his neck, as soon as he entered the house, with all the passionate impulse of a madcap. Later on, having frequently lost sight of her, he had found her grown taller each time he saw her. She continued to put her arms round his neck, troubling him, more and more, by the flame of her great light eyes.

She was now a superb woman, and no doubt she had loved him a long time—from childhood. His heart began to beat. A sudden sensation told him that he was the one she awaited. He felt a swimming in the head, his first impulse, in the anguish he experienced, was to flee. Love had always made him mad, and he felt bent on murder.

"What are you doing there, on your feet?" she resumed. "Why don't you sit down?"

Again he hesitated. Then, his legs suddenly becoming very tired, and himself vanquished by the desire to try love once more, he sank down beside her on the heap of cords. But he said nothing; his throat was quite dry. It was she, now, the proud, the silent one, who chattered merrily until she lost breath, deafening herself with her own verbosity.

"You see, the mistake mamma made was to marry Misard," she began. "He'll play her a nasty trick. I don't care a fig, because one has quite enough to do with one's own business. Don't you think so? And, besides, mamma sends me off to bed as soon as I want to cut in. So she must do the best she can by herself! I pass my time outside the house, I do. I am thinking of things for later on. Ah! you know, I saw you go by this morning, on your engine. Look! over there, from those bushes, where I was seated. But you, you never look—I'll tell you the things I'm thinking of, but not now, later, when we have quite become good friends."

She had let the scissors slip away from her, and he, still silent, had caught hold of her two hands. Delighted, she abandoned them to him. But when he carried them to his burning lips, she gave an affrighted start. The warrior woman awoke, prepared, and warlike.

"No, no! Leave me alone!" she exclaimed. "I won't have it. Keep quiet. Let's talk."

Without heeding her, without hearing what she said, he grasped her brutally in his arms, crushing her lips beneath his own. She uttered a feeble cry, which was more like a moan, so deep, so sweet, that it revealed the tenderness she had so long concealed. Then, as he, breathless, ceased his kisses and looked at her, he was all at once seized with frenzy, with such frightful ferocity, that he glanced round about him in search of a weapon, a stone, something, in fact, to kill her with. His eyes fell upon the scissors, shining among the bits of cord. At a bound, he secured them, and he would have buried them in her bosom had not an icy chill brought him suddenly to his senses. Casting the scissors from him, he fled, distracted, while she imagined he had left her because she had resisted his caress.

Jacques fled in the melancholy night. He ascended at full speed a path on the hillside, which brought him down to a little dale. The stones he scattered beneath his feet, alarmed him, and he tore off to the left among the bushes, there he bent round to the right, and came to a bare plateau. Abruptly descending from the high ground, he fell into the hedge bordering the line; a train flew along, roaring and flaming. At first he failed to understand what it could be, and felt terrified. Ah! yes, all this multitude that was passing, the continual flood, while he stood there in anguish!

He started off once more, climbing the hill and descending again. He now constantly encountered the railway line, either at the bottom of deep cuttings, resembling unfathomable depths, or else on embankments that shut out the horizon with gigantic barricades. This desert country, broken up into hillocks, was like a labyrinth without issue, where he, in his folly, wheeled round and round in the mournful desolation of the fallow land. And he had been beating up and down the inclines a long time, when before him he perceived the round opening, the black jaw of the tunnel. An up-train plunged into it, howling and whistling, leaving behind, when it had disappeared, absorbed by the earth, a prolonged concussion that made the ground quake.

Then, Jacques, with weary feet fell down beside the line; and, grovelling on the ground, his face buried in the long grass, he burst into convulsive sobs. Great God! So this abominable complaint of which he fancied himself cured, had returned! He had wanted to murder that girl. Kill a woman, kill a woman! This had been ringing in his ears from his earliest youth. He could not deny that he had taken the scissors to stab her. And it was not because she had resisted his embrace. No; it was for the pleasure of the thing, because he had a desire to do so, such a strong desire, that if he had not clutched the grass, he would have returned there, as fast as he could, to butcher her. Her, great God! That Flore whom he had seen grow up, that wild child by whom he had just felt himself so fondly loved! His twisted fingers tore the ground, his sobs rent his throat in a horrifying rattle of despair.

Nevertheless, he did his utmost to become calm. He wanted to understand it all. When he compared himself with others, how did he differ from them? Down there at Plassans, in his youth, he had frequently asked himself the same question. It is true that his mother Gervaise was very young at the time of his birth, barely fifteen and a half; but he was the second. She had only just entered her fourteenth year when his elder brother Claude made his appearance; and neither Claude nor Etienne, who came later, seemed to suffer from having such a child for a mother, or a father as young as herself—that handsome Lantier, whose heartlessness was to cost Gervaise so many tears. Perhaps his two brothers also had his complaint, and said nothing about it. Particularly the elder one, who was dying with such incensement to become painter, that people said he had gone half crazy over his genius.

The family was not at all right, several of its members were wrong in the head. Himself, at certain hours, felt this hereditary flaw. Not that he had bad health, for it was only the apprehension and shame of his attacks that formerly had made him thin. But he was apt to suddenly lose his equilibrium, as if there existed broken places, holes in his being, by which his own self escaped from him amidst a sort of great cloud of smoke that disfigured everything. Then, losing his self-control, he obeyed his muscles, listening to the mad animal within him. Nevertheless, he did not drink, he even deprived himself of an occasional dram of brandy, having remarked that the least drop of alcohol drove him mad. And he began to think that he must be paying for others, the fathers, the grandfathers who had drunk, the generations of drunkards, whose vitiated blood he had inherited. It seemed like slow poison, which reduced him to savagery, taking him back to the depths of the woods, among the wolves, devourers of women.

Jacques had raised himself on an elbow, reflecting, watching the dark entrance to the tunnel. Heaving another great sob, he sank down again, rolling his head on the ground, crying out with grief. That girl, that girl he had wanted to kill! The incident returned to him, acute and frightful, as if the scissors had penetrated his own flesh.

No reasoning appeased him. He had wanted to kill her, he would kill her now, if she happened to be there. He remembered the first time the complaint had shown itself. He was barely sixteen, and one evening, while playing with a young girl, a relative, his junior by a couple of years, she happened to fall, and he at once sprang at her. In the following year he recollected sharpening a knife to bury it in the neck of another girl, a little blonde, whom he noticed pass before his door every morning. This one had a very fat, rosy neck, and he had already selected the place, a beauty spot under one of the ears. Then, there were others, and others still, quite a procession of nightmares, all those whom he had glanced at, with an abrupt desire to murder them. Women he had brushed against in the street, women whom accident made his neighbours, one particularly, a newly married bride seated beside him at the theatre, who laughed very loud, and from whom he had to run away in the middle of an act, so as not to rip her open.

As he did not know them, why was he so furious against them? For, each occasion, it seemed like a sudden outburst of blind rage, an ever-recurring thirst to avenge some very ancient offences, the exact recollection of which escaped him. Did it date from so far back, from the harm women had done to his race, from the rancour laid up from male to male since the first deceptions at the bottom of the caverns? And, in his access, he also felt the necessity to fight, in order to conquer and subjugate the female, the perverted necessity to throw her dead on his back, like a prey torn from others for ever. His head was bursting in the effort to understand. He could find no answer to his inquiry. Too ignorant, the brain too sluggish, thought he, in this anguish of a man urged to acts wherein his will stood for nothing, and the reason whereof had disappeared from his mind.

A train again passed by with the flash of its lights, and plunged like a thunderbolt that roars and expires, into the mouth of the tunnel;

and Jacques, as if this anonymous, indifferent, and hasty crowd had been able to hear him, stood up, swallowing his sobs and taking an innocent attitude. How many times at the end of one of his attacks, had he started thus, like the guilty, at the least sound? He only lived tranquil and happy, when detached from the world on his locomotive. When the engine bore him along in the trepidation of its wheels at express speed, when he had his hand on the reversing-wheel, and was entirely engaged in watching the metals and looking out for the signals, he ceased thinking, and took deep draughts of the pure air, which always blew a gale. And this was why he was so fond of his engine.

On leaving the École des Arts et Métiers, he selected this occupation of engine-driver, notwithstanding his bright intelligence, for the solitude and distraction it gave him. Without ambition, having in four years attained the position of driver of the first class, he already earned 2,800 frcs. a year, which, coupled with the gratuities he received for economy in fuel and grease, brought the annual amount of his wages up to more than 4,000 frcs., and that satisfied him. He saw his comrades of the second and third class, those instructed by the company, the engine-fitters they took as pupils, he saw almost all of them marry work-girls, women who kept in the background, whom one only occasionally caught sight of at the hour of departure, when they brought the little baskets of provisions; while the ambitious comrades, particularly those who came from a school, waited until they were heads of depôts to get married, in the hope of meeting with someone of the middle class, a lady who wore a hat. For his part, he avoided women. What did he care? He would never marry. His only future was to roll along alone, to roll along always, always, without stay.

His chiefs pointed him out as a model driver, who did not drink and who did not run after petticoats. His tipsy comrades made fun of his exaggeration of good conduct, and the others were secretly alarmed when they saw him fall into his silent, melancholy fits, with eyes dim and ashy countenance. How many hours did he recollect having passed, all those hours of freedom, shut up like a monk in his cell, in that little room in the Rue Cardinet, whence the depôt at Batignolles, to which his engine belonged, could be seen.

Jacques made an effort to rise. What was he doing there in the grass, on this mild and hazy winter night? The country remained plunged in shadow. There was only light above, where the moon lit up the thin fog, the immense ground-glass-like cupola which concealed it from view, with a pale yellow reflex. Below, the black earth slumbered in the immobility of death. Come! it must be near nine o'clock. The best thing to do would be to return to the house, and go to bed. But, in his torpor, he saw himself back at the Misards, ascending the staircase to the loft, stretching himself on the hay against the plank partition separating him from the room occupied by Flore. She would be there, he would hear her breathing; and, as he was aware that she never locked her door, he would be able to join her. His shivering fit returned. He was racked again with such a violent sob at the image of this girl, that he once more sank to the ground.

He had wanted to kill her—wanted to kill her! Great God! He was choking in anguish at the thought that he would go and kill her in her bed, presently, if he returned to the house. He might well be without a weapon; he might cover his head with his two arms to render himself powerless, but he felt that the male, independent of his own will, would thrust open the door and strangle the girl, urged to the crime by a thirst to avenge the ancient wrong. No, no! He had better pass the night beating about the neighbourhood, than return there. Bounding to his feet he fled again.

Then, once more, for half an hour, he tore across the dark country as if an unchained pack of devils followed howling at his heels. He ascended the hills, he plunged down into the narrow gorges. He went through two streams, one after the other, drenching himself to the hips. A bush, barring his progress, exasperated him. His only thought was to go straight on, further, still further, to flee, to flee from the other one, the mad animal he felt within him; but the beast accompanied him, it flew along as fast as he did. For months he had fancied he had driven it from him; he had pursued the same life as other people; and, now, he had to begin again, he would have to resume the struggle to prevent the brute leaping upon the first woman he chanced to brush against in the street.

Nevertheless, the intense silence and vast solitude appeased him a little, and made him dream of a life as mute and lonely as this desolate land, where he would stroll about always, without ever meeting a soul. He must have turned round without noticing it, for he found himself kicking against the metals on the opposite side of the line, after describing a wide circle among the slopes, bristling with bushes, above the tunnel. He started back in the irritable uneasiness of once more falling upon the living. Then, with the intention of taking a short cut behind a hillock, he lost his way, to find it again before the railway hedge, just at the exit from the tunnel on the down-line, opposite the field where he had been sobbing a short time previously; and, tired to death, he remained motionless, when the thunder of a train issuing from the bowels of the earth, at first slight, but becoming louder and louder every second, attracted his attention. It was the Havre express which had left Paris at 6.30 and passed by there at 9.25; the train he drove every two days.

Jacques first of all saw the dark mouth of the tunnel lit up, like the opening to an oven ablaze with faggots. Then the engine burst out with a tremendous crash amidst the dazzling splendour of its great round eye the lantern in front whose fire bored into the country, illuminating the metals for a long way ahead, with a double line of flame. It came like a thunderbolt; the carriages followed one another immediately afterwards, the small square windows of the doors, brilliant with luminosity, displayed compartments full of travellers, flying past at such a whirling speed, that there afterwards remained a doubt in the mind of the spectator, as to what the eye had seen.

And Jacques, very distinctly, at that precise quarter of a second, perceived through the flaming glass of a coupé window, one man holding another down on the seat, and plunging a knife into his throat; while a dark heap, perhaps a third person, perhaps some articles of luggage fallen from the rack, weighed with all its weight on the convulsed legs of the victim. But the train had already dashed past, and was disappearing in the direction of La Croix-de-Maufras, displaying naught of itself in the dense obscurity, but the three lights at the back—the red triangle.

The young man, riveted to the spot, followed the train with his eyes as its thunder gradually died away, leaving the deathlike peacefulness of the surroundings undisturbed. Was he sure he had seen what he thought? And now he hesitated. He no longer dared affirm the reality of this vision which came and went in a flash. Not one single feature of the two actors in the drama remained vivid. The dark heap must have been a travelling-rug that had fallen across the body of the victim. Nevertheless, he thought he had first of all caught sight of a pale profile beneath waves of thick hair. But all this became confused, and evaporated as in a dream. For an instant, the profile he had evoked reappeared, and then definitely vanished. Doubtless it was nothing more than imagination; and all this gave him an icy chill. It seemed to him so extraordinary, that at last he admitted he must have been the victim of hallucination, due to the frightful crisis he had just passed through.

Jacques walked about for nearly another hour, his head loaded with confused thoughts. He felt broken down, but relief came, and his fever left him. He ended by turning in the direction of La Croix-de-Maufras, but without having decided to do so. Then when he found himself before the house of the gatekeeper, he was determined he would not go in, that he would sleep in the little shed built against one of the walls. But a ray of light passed under the door, and pushing it open, without giving a thought to what he was doing, a strange sight stopped him on the threshold.

Misard had disturbed the butter-jar in the corner, and, on the ground on all fours, a lighted lantern beside him, he was sounding the wall with little taps of the knuckle, searching. The noise made by the door opening, made him stand up, but he did not show the least confusion. He merely remarked in the most natural tone of voice imaginable:

"Some matches have fallen down."

And when he had put the butter-jar back in its place, he added:

"I came to fetch my lantern, because a little while ago, as I came along, I perceived a man stretched across the line, and I believe he's dead."

Jacques, at first struck at the idea of surprising Misard searching for the hoard of Aunt Phasie, which abruptly transformed his doubt respecting the accusations of the latter into certainty, was then so violently upset by this news of the discovery of a corpse, that he forgot the other drama—the one that was being performed there, in this little out-of-the-way dwelling. The scene in the coupé, the brief vision of one man slaughtering another, returned to him in a vivid flash.

"A man on the line!" he exclaimed, turning pale. "Where?"

Misard was about to relate that he was returning with a couple of eels which he had taken from his ground lines, and that he had first of all run home, as fast as he could, to hide them. But he reflected that there was no necessity to confide in this young man, and with a vague gesture he replied:

"Over there, about half a mile away. It requires a light to find out more."

At this moment Jacques heard a thud overhead. He was so nervous that he started.

"It's nothing," said Misard. "It's only Flore moving."

And, in fact, the young man recognised the pit-pat of two naked feet on the floor. She had come to listen at the half-open door.

"I'll go with you," Jacques resumed. "Are you sure he's dead?"

"Well, he looked like it," answered the other. "We shall soon see with the lantern."

"What's your opinion?" inquired Jacques. "An accident?"

"Maybe," replied Misard. "Some chap who's got cut in two, or perhaps a passenger who jumped out of a carriage."

Jacques shuddered.

"Come along quick, quick!" he exclaimed.

Never had he been agitated with such a fever to see and know. Outside the house, while his companion, without any concern, walked along the line swinging his lantern, he ran on ahead, irritated at the delay. It was like a physical desire, the fire within that precipitates the steps of lovers at the hour of meeting. He feared what awaited him yonder, and yet he flew there with all the muscles of his limbs. When he reached the spot, when he almost stumbled over a dark heap lying near the down-line, he remained planted where he stood with a shiver running from his heels to the nape of his neck. And, his anguish at being unable to see distinctly, turned to oaths against the other, who was loitering along, thirty paces behind.

"Come on, come on!" he shouted. "If he's still alive, we may be able to do something for him."

Misard waddled forward in his sluggish way. Then, when he had swung the lantern to and fro, over the body, he muttered:

"Ah! the devil take me! It's all up with him."

The man, no doubt tumbling out of a carriage, had fallen with his face downwards, a couple of feet at the most from the metals. Nothing could be seen of his head but a crown of thick black hair. His legs were apart. His right arm lay as if dislocated, while his left was bent under his chest. He was very well attired in a big, blue cloth overcoat, neat boots, and fine linen. The body bore no trace of having been crushed, but a quantity of blood had run from the throat, and soiled the shirt collar.

"Some gentleman whom they've done for," tranquilly resumed Misard, after a few seconds' silent inspection. Then, turning towards Jacques, who stood motionless and thunderstruck, he continued:

"He must not be touched. It's forbidden. You will have to remain here, and watch over him, while I go to Barentin to tell the station-master about it."

ÉMILE ZOLA

He raised his lantern, and looked at a mile-post.

"Good!" said he. "Just at post 153." And, placing his lantern on the ground beside the corpse, he took himself off at his usual loitering gait.

Jacques, left by himself, did not move, but continued gazing at this inert mass that had fallen there, and which the uncertain light, just above the ground, only revealed indistinctly. The agitation that had made him rush forward, the horrible attraction that held him there, ended in this keen thought which burst from all his being: the other one, the man he had caught sight of with the knife in his hand had dared! He had gratified his desire! He had killed. Ah! what would he give not to be a coward, to be able to satisfy himself at last, to plunge in the knife! He, who had been tortured by this thirst for ten years!

In his fever, he felt contempt for himself, and admiration for the other; and, above all, he felt the necessity to gaze on the victim, the quenchless thirst to feast his eyes on this human remnant, this broken dancing-Jack, this limp rag, which the stab of a knife had made of a creature. What he dreamed of, the other had realised, and it was that. If he killed, he would have that on the ground. His heart beat fit to break. His prurience for murder became violent as concupiscence, at the sight of this tragic corpse. He took a step, approached nearer, after the manner of a child making himself familiar with an object he fears. Yes, he would dare, he would dare in his turn!

But a roar behind his back, made him spring aside. A train arrived which he had not heard, being so taken up with the contemplation of the body. He would have been crushed to pieces had not the warm steam and the formidable puffing of the engine warned him in time. The train flew past in its hurricane of noise, smoke, and flame. This one also carried a great many people. The flood of travellers continued streaming towards Havre, for the fête on the morrow. A child was flattening his nose against a window, looking out at the black country; profiles of men appeared, while a young woman, lowering one of the glasses, threw out a paper stained with butter and sugar. Already the joyous train was flying away in the distance, listless of the corpse its wheels had almost grazed. And the body continued lying there on its face, indistinctly lit up by the lantern, amidst the melancholy peacefulness of night.

Then Jacques had a desire to see the wound, while he was alone. But he hesitated, in the anxiety that if he touched the head, it would, perhaps, be noticed. He reckoned that Misard could not be back with the station-master before three-quarters of an hour; and as the minutes passed, he thought of this Misard, of this puny fellow, so slow, so calm, who also dared, who was killing as tranquilly as possible, with doses of poison. Then it was easy enough to kill? Everybody killed. He drew nearer the corpse, and the idea of looking at the wound stung him so sharply that he was burning all over. He wanted to see how it had been done, and what had run from it, to see the red hole! By carefully putting the head back into its position, nobody would know anything about it. But at the bottom of his hesitation was another fear which he had not owned, the dread of blood. He had still a quarter of an hour to himself, and he was on the point of making up his mind to look, when a slight sound beside him, made him start.

It was Flore, standing gazing at the corpse like himself. She was keen on accidents; as soon as ever the news arrived that an animal had been pounded to atoms, or a man cut in two by a train, she hurried to the scene of disaster. She had just dressed again, and wanted to see the corpse. Unlike Jacques, she did not hesitate. After a first glance, she stooped down, raising the lantern with one hand, while with the other she took the head, and threw it back.

"Mind what you're doing," murmured Jacques; "it's forbidden."

But she shrugged her shoulders. The face appeared in the yellow light, the face of an old man, with a large nose and the blue, wide-open eyes of one formerly fair. A frightful wound was gaping beneath the chin. The throat had been cut with a deep, jagged gash, as if the knife had been twisted round probing it. The right side of the chest was drenched in blood. On the left, in the button-hole of the great coat, the rosette of Commander of the Legion of Honour looked like a clot of blood that had spurted there.

Flore uttered an exclamation of surprise.

"Hullo! the old man!" said she.

Jacques advanced, bending forward as she was doing, mingling his hair with her hair, to see better. He was choking, gorging himself with the sight. Unconsciously he repeated:

"The old man? The old man?"

"Yes, old Grandmorin, the President."

For another moment she examined this livid face, with the distorted mouth and the great, terrifying eyes. Then she let go the head, which was beginning to turn icy cold in cadaverous rigidity, and the wound closed.

"He's done larking with the girls!" she resumed in a lower tone. "It's got something to do with one of them, for sure. Ah! my poor Louisette! Ah! the pig! Serve him right!"

A long silence ensued. Flore, who had set down the lantern, waited, slowly casting glances at Jacques, while he, separated from her by the corpse, did not move. He seemed as if lost, completely prostrated by what he had just seen. It must have been eleven o'clock. The embarrassment due to the scene in the evening prevented him speaking the first. But a sound of voices was heard. It was her stepfather returning with the station-master, and, not wishing to be seen, she made up her mind to break the ice.

"Aren't you going back to bed?" she inquired.

He started, and seemed agitated by an inner struggle. Then, with an effort, with a recoil full of despair, he answered:

"No, no!"

She made no movement, but her look, with her robust arms hanging down beside her, expressed great sorrow. As if to ask pardon for her resistance of a short time before she became very humble, and added:

"Then if you are not going back to the house, I shall not see you again?"

"No, no!" he replied.

The voices approached, and without seeking to press his hand, as he seemed to purposely place this corpse between them, without even giving him the familiar good-bye of their comradeship of childhood, she withdrew, disappearing in the darkness, and breathing hard, as if to stifle her sobs.

The station-master appeared on the scene almost at once, along with Misard and a couple of porters. He also proved the identity: it was President Grandmorin sure enough. He knew him by seeing him get down at his station each time he went to Madame Bonnehon, at Doinville. The body could remain where it had fallen, but he would have it covered with the cloak a man had brought with him. One of the staff had taken the eleven o'clock train at Barentin to inform the Imperial Procurator at Rouen. But they could not count on the latter before five or six o'clock in the morning, for he would have to bring the examining-magistrate, the registrar of the Court, and a doctor with him. And so the station-master arranged for the body to be guarded. The men would take turns throughout the night, one man being constantly there on the watch, with the lantern.

And Jacques, before making up his mind to go and stretch himself under some shed at the Barentin station, whence he would not set out for Havre before 7.20, remained for a long time where he stood, motionless, and worried. Then he became troubled at the idea of the examining-magistrate who was expected, as if he felt himself an accomplice. Should he say what he had seen as the train went by? At first he resolved to speak, as, after all, he had nothing to fear. Moreover, there could be no doubt as to his duty. But, then, he asked himself, what was the good of it? he could not bring one single, decisive fact to bear on the matter, he would not dare affirm any detail respecting the murderer. It would be idiotic to mix himself up in the business, to lose his time, and worry himself, without profit to anyone.

No, no, he would say nothing! At last, he took himself off, but he turned round twice, to see the black heap the body made on the ground, in the circle of yellow light shed by the lantern. Sharper cold fell from the fumy sky, on the desolation of this desert with arid hills. More trains had passed. Another, a very long one, arrived for Paris. All crossed in their inexorable mechanic might, flying to their distant goal, to the future, almost grazing, without taking heed of it, the half-severed head of this man whom another man had slaughtered.

III

The following day, a Sunday, five o'clock in the morning had just struck from all the belfries of Havre, when Roubaud came down under the iron marquee of the station, to resume duty. It was still pitch dark; but the wind, blowing from the sea, had increased, and drove along the haze, smothering the hills which extend from Sainte-Adresse to Tourneville; while westward, above the offing, appeared a bright opening, a strip of sky, where shone the last stars. The gas-lamps under the marquee were still alight, but looking pale in the damp chill of this matutinal hour. Shunters were engaged in making-up the first train for Montivilliers, under the orders of the assistant station-master on night duty. The doors of the waiting-rooms had not yet been opened, and the platforms stretched forward, deserted, in this drowsy awakening of the station.

As Roubaud left his apartments, upstairs, over the waiting-rooms, he found Madame Lebleu, the wife of the cashier, standing motionless in the middle of the central corridor, on which the lodgings of the members of the staff opened. For weeks past this lady had been in the habit of getting up during the night to watch Mademoiselle Guichon, the office-keeper, whom she suspected of carrying on an intrigue with M. Dabadie, the station-master. As a matter of fact, she had never surprised the least thing, not a shadow, not a breath. And, again on this particular morning, she had quickly returned to her own quarters, taking no news back with her, save the expression of her astonishment at what she had caught sight of in the rooms occupied by the Roubauds, during the two or three seconds the husband had required to open and shut the door. There she had seen the beautiful Séverine, who was in the habit of lying abed until nine o'clock in the morning, standing up in the dining-room dressed, combed, and booted. And she had roused Lebleu to tell him of this extraordinary occurrence.

On the previous night they sat up until the arrival of the Paris express at 11.5, burning to learn what had become of the affair with the sub-prefect. But they were unable to read anything in the attitude of the Roubauds, who returned with faces wearing their everyday expression; and in vain did they listen until midnight: not a sound came from the rooms occupied by their neighbours, who must have gone to bed at once, and fallen fast asleep. Their journey could certainly not have been attended with a good result, otherwise Séverine would not have risen at such an early hour. The cashier having inquired how she looked, his wife had been at pains to describe her: very stiff, very pale, with her great blue eyes appearing so bright against her black hair; she was standing quite still, and had the aspect of a somnambulist. But they would find out all about it in the course of the day.

Down below, Roubaud found his colleague Moulin, who had been on duty during the night; and as he took over the service, Moulin walked along with him for a minute or two, posting him up in the few small events that had occurred since the previous evening: some vagrants had been surprised as they were effecting an entrance into the cloakroom; three porters had been reprimanded for indiscipline; a coupling-hook had just broken while the Montivilliers train was being made-up. Roubaud listened in silence, and with calm countenance. He was only a trifle pale, due no doubt to a remainder of fatigue, which was also visible in his heavy eyes. When his colleague ceased speaking, he still seemed to look at him inquiringly, as if he expected something more. But what he had heard was all, and he bent his head, gazing for an instant on the ground.

As the two men walked along the platform they reached the end of the corrugated iron roofing, and on the right stood a coach-house where the carriages in constant use remained, such as came in one day, and served to make up the trains on the morrow. Roubaud raised his head, and was looking fixedly at a first-class carriage with a coupé, bearing the No. 293, which as it happened a gas-lamp lit up with its vacillating glimmer, when Moulin remarked:

"Ah! I forgot—"

The pale face of the other coloured, and he was unable to restrain a slight movement.

"I forgot," repeated Moulin; "that carriage must not leave. Do not put it on the 6.40 express this morning."

A short silence ensued before Roubaud, in a very natural voice said:

"Indeed! Why is that?"

"Because," replied Moulin, "a coupé has been booked for the express of this evening. We are not sure that one will come in during the day, so we may just as well keep this one."

"Certainly," replied Roubaud, staring at his colleague.

But he was absorbed by another thought, and all at once, flying into a rage, he exclaimed:

"It's disgusting! Just see how those fellows do the cleaning! That carriage looks as if it had the accumulated dust of a week on it."

"Ah!" resumed Moulin. "When trains arrive after eleven o'clock at night, there is no fear of the men giving the coaches a brush up. It's as much as they will do to cast a glance inside of them. The other night, they overlooked a passenger asleep on one of the seats, and he only awoke the next morning."

Then, stifling a yawn, he said he was going up to bed. But as he went off, an abrupt feeling of curiosity brought him back.

"By the way, what about your affair with the sub-prefect?" he inquired. "It's all settled, I suppose?"

"Yes, yes," answered Roubaud. "I made a very good journey. I'm quite satisfied."

"Well, so much the better. And bear in mind that the 293 does not start," replied the other.

When Roubaud found himself alone on the platform, he slowly went back towards the Montivilliers train, which was ready. The doors of the waiting-rooms were open, and some passengers appeared: a few sportsmen with their dogs, and two or three families of shop-keepers, taking advantage of the Sunday—only a few people altogether. But when that train had gone, the first of the day, Roubaud had not much time to lose. He immediately had to make up the 5.40 slow train for Rouen and Paris.

At this early hour not many servants of the company were about; and the work of the assistant station-master on duty, was complicated by all sorts of details. When he had superintended the making-up of the train, consisting in each carriage being taken from the coach-house and placed on a truck, which a gang of men pushed along under the marquee, he had to run off to the main building, to give a glance at the ticket office, and the luggage booking department. A quarrel breaking out between some soldiers and one of the staff, necessitated his intervention. For half an hour, in the icy draughts, amid the shivering public, his eyes still heavy with sleep, and in the ill-humour of a man jostled at every moment in the obscurity, he hurried hither and thither without a moment to himself. Then, when the departure of the slow train had cleared the station, he hastened to the box of the pointsman, to make sure that all was right in that quarter. For the through train from Paris, which was behind time, was coming in. He returned to the platform to see the stream of passengers leave the carriages, give up their tickets, and crowd into the omnibuses from the hotels, which in those days entered the station, to wait under the marquee, where they were separated from the line by a mere paling. And then, only, did he find leisure to breathe for a moment, the station having again become silent and deserted.

Six o'clock struck. Roubaud sauntered out of the main building; and, beyond, with space before him, he raised his head and inhaled the fresh air, watching day at last breaking. The wind from the offing had completely driven away the mist. It was the clear morning of a fine day. He looked northward, in the direction of Ingouville, as far as the trees of the cemetery, standing out in a violescent line against the whitening sky. Then, turning towards the south and west, he observed a final flight of light white clouds floating slowly along in a squadron across the sea; while the entire east, the immense opening formed by the mouth of the Seine, began to be embraced in approaching sunrise.

In a casual way, he removed his cap, embroidered with silver, as if to refresh his forehead in the sharp, pure air. This outlook to which he was accustomed, this vast flat sweep of dependencies of the station—the arrival on the left, then the engine depôt, to the right the departure, a regular little town—seemed to appease him, to bring him back to the calmness of his daily occupations which were ever the same. Factory chimneys were smoking above the wall of the Rue Charles Lafitte; and enormous heaps of coal could be seen following the line of the Vauban basin. A hum already began to rise from the other docks. The whistling of the goods trains, the awakening of the town, the briny smell of the sea wafted by the wind, made him think of the fête of the day, of this vessel they were about to launch, and around which the crowd would be crushing.

Roubaud, returning inside the station, found the gang of shunters commencing to make up the 6.40 express; and thinking the men were putting No. 293 on the truck, all the calm that the fresh morning air had brought him, disappeared in a sudden burst of anger. With an oath he shouted:

"Not that carriage! Leave it alone! It is not to go till tonight."

The foreman of the gang explained to him that they were merely pushing the carriage along, to take another from behind it. But, deafened by his own passion, which was out of all proportion, he did not hear.

"You clumsy idiots!" he exclaimed; "when you are told to leave the thing alone, do so!"

Having at length been made to understand, he continued, furious, turning his wrath against the inconvenience of the station, where it was not even possible to turn a carriage round. In fact, the station, one of the first built on the line, was not equal to modern requirements. It was unworthy of Havre, with its old timber coach-house glazed with small panes of glass, and its dismal, naked buildings full of cracks.

"It's a disgrace. I can't comprehend why the company has not knocked it all down."

The shunters looked at him, surprised to hear him speak so freely, he who was generally so well disciplined. Perceiving their attitude, he all at once ceased his remarks, and, silent and stiff, continued to watch the manœuvres. A line of discontent furrowed his low forehead, while his round, coloured face, bristling with the reddish beard, took an expression of intensely strong will.

From that moment, Roubaud was in possession of all his equanimity. He gave active attention to the express, busying himself with every detail connected with it. The couplings appearing to him to be badly attached, he insisted on having them screwed up before his eyes. A mother and two daughters, on terms of intimacy with his wife, wanted him to seat them in the compartment for ladies only. Then, before whistling to give the signal to start, he again made sure that the train was in perfect trim; and he stood watching it, as it moved away, with that clear gaze of a man whose least carelessness might involve the loss of human lives.

He had at once to cross the line, to be present at the arrival of a train from Rouen, which was just entering the station. There he met a man from the Post Office, with whom he every day exchanged news. This was a short rest for him in his busy early hours, and as no immediate duty required his attention, he had time to draw breath. On this morning, as was his habit, he rolled a cigarette, and chatted gaily. Day had broadened, and the gas-lamps under the marquee, had just been extinguished; but the glazing of this extension of the station was so bad, that the light continued gloomy. Outside, the vast stretch of sky on which the building opened, was already ablaze with a fire of sun-rays; while the entire view became rosy, and the smallest objects stood out crisp, in this pure air of a fine winter morning.

M. Dabadie, the station-master, usually came down from his rooms at eight o'clock, when the assistant station-master went to him to make his report. The former was a handsome man, very dark, neat in his attire, with the bearing of a commercial magnate engrossed in business.

Indeed, he willingly left the passenger department of the station to his assistants, so that he might give particular attention to the movement in the docks, to the enormous transit of merchandise; and he was in constant contact with the high commerce of Havre, and of the entire world. Today he came late. Roubaud had already pushed the door of his office ajar twice, without finding him. On the table lay his letters, which had not even been opened. Among them Roubaud had just noticed a telegram. Then, as if drawn to the spot by fascination, he had been unable to leave the threshold, returning, in spite of himself, to cast rapid glances at the table.

At last, at ten minutes past eight, M. Dabadie appeared. Roubaud seated himself without speaking, to allow him to open the telegram. But the chief was in no hurry. Wishing to be pleasant with his subordinate, whom he esteemed, he said:

"I suppose all went well in Paris?"

"Yes, sir, I thank you," replied Roubaud.

He had ended by opening the telegram; but he did not read it. He continued smiling at his assistant, whose voice thickened in the violent effort he was making to get the better of a nervous twitch contracting his chin.

"We are very pleased to keep you here," said the station-master.

"And I, sir, am very glad to remain with you," answered Roubaud.

Then, as M. Dabadie made up his mind to run his eye over the telegram, Roubaud, who felt a slight perspiration moistening his face, watched him. But the agitation which he expected to see on the countenance of his chief, did not appear. The latter placidly continued perusing the telegram, which he eventually threw back on the table. No doubt it had to do with a simple detail connected with the service. He at once began to open his letters, while his assistant, in accordance with daily custom, made his verbal report on the events of the night and morning. Only, on this occasion, Roubaud hesitated, and had to think before he could recall what his colleague had told him about the vagrants caught in the cloakroom. A few more words were exchanged, and when the two deputy chiefs of the docks and slow train departments came in, also to make their reports, the station-master dismissed Roubaud by a gesture. The newcomers brought another telegram, which one of the staff had just handed them on the platform.

"You can go," said M. Dabadie to Roubaud, seeing he had stopped at the door.

But the latter waited with fixed, expectant eyes; and he only went away when the small piece of paper had fallen on the table, put aside with the same indifferent gesture as before. For a few moments, he wandered under the marquee, feeling perplexed and dizzy. The clock pointed to 8.35. The next departure was the slow train at 9.50. He usually took advantage of this hour of rest, to stroll round the station, and he now walked about for a few minutes without knowing where his feet were taking him. Then, as he raised his head, and found himself opposite the carriage numbered 293, he abruptly turned aside in the direction of the engine-house, although he had nothing to attend to in that quarter. The sun was now rising on the horizon, filling the air with golden dust. But he no longer enjoyed the fine morning. He hastened along as if very much occupied, endeavouring to overcome the uneasiness caused by the suspense.

All at once a voice stopped him.

"Good morning, M. Roubaud! Did you see my wife?"

It was Pecqueux, the fireman, a great, thin fellow of three-and-forty, with big bones, and a face tanned by fire and smoke. His grey eyes, under a low forehead, his great mouth, set in a prominent jaw, had the constant, jovial expression of a man addicted to merry-making.

"What! Is that you?" said Roubaud, stopping astonished. "Ah! yes. Your engine met with an accident. I forgot. And so you're not going off again until tonight? Twenty-four hours' holiday. Good business, eh?"

"Good business!" repeated the other, not yet recovered from his libations of the previous evening.

Born at a village near Rouen, he had entered the service of the company quite young, as engine-fitter. Then, at thirty, tired of the workshop, he had wanted to be a fireman so as to become driver. It was then that he married Victoire, who belonged to the same village as himself. But years went by, and he continued fireman. He would never become driver now, being of bad conduct, careless in dress and mode of life, a drunkard, and a runner after petticoats. He would have been dismissed twenty times over, had it not been for the protection of President Grandmorin, and had not his superiors become accustomed to his vices, for which he condoned by his good humour, and his experience as an old workman. He only gave cause for alarm when under the influence of drink, for he then became a real brute, capable of any violence.

"Did you see my wife?" he inquired again, with a broad grin.

"Yes, indeed," answered the assistant station-master; "we saw her.

We even had a very nice lunch in your room. Ah! you've a good wife, Pecqueux; and it's wrong of you to be unfaithful to her."

He gave a broader grin than before.

"Oh! how can you say such a thing?" he exclaimed. "It's she who wants me to enjoy myself!"

This was true. Victoire, who was two years his senior, and who had grown enormously stout, was in the habit of slipping five-franc pieces into his pocket, so that he might amuse himself when away. She had never suffered much from his infidelity; and, now, their mode of life was settled. He had two wives, one at each end of the line. Victoire, who knew everything, accepted the position, and even went so far as to mend his linen, in order that the other one might not be able to say that she allowed their husband to go about in rags and tatters.

"No matter," resumed Roubaud, "it's not at all nice on your part. My wife, who is very fond of her foster-mother, wants to scold you."

But he held his tongue, on seeing a tall, lean woman come from a shed beside which they were standing. She proved to be Philomène Sauvagnat, sister of the chief of the depôt, and the second Madame Pecqueux. The couple must have been talking together in the shed, when Pecqueux came out to call to the assistant station-master. Philomène still looked young in spite of her two-and-thirty years, but was raw-boned, with a flat chest, a long head, and flaming eyes. She had the reputation of drinking. Her occupation consisted in keeping house for her brother, who lived in a cottage near the engine-depôt, which she very much neglected. They came from Auvergne, and the brother, an obstinate man and a strict disciplinarian, greatly esteemed by his superiors, had met with the utmost vexation on account of this sister, even to the point of being threatened with dismissal. And, if the company bore with her, now, on his account, he only kept her with him because of the family tie. But this did not prevent him belabouring her so severely with blows whenever he caught her at fault, that he frequently left her half dead on the floor. She had commenced an intrigue with Pecqueux about a year before; but it was only Séverine, who had fallen out with her, thinking it due to Mother Victoire for her to do so. Having already been in the habit of avoiding her as much as possible, from a feeling of innate pride, she had subsequently ceased to greet her.

"Well, Pecqueux, I shall see you again, later on!" said Philomène saucily. "I'll leave you now, as M. Roubaud has a moral lecture to read you, on behalf of his wife."

Pecqueux, who was a good-natured fellow, continued laughing.

"No, no, stay," he answered. "He's only joking."

"I can't," retorted Philomène. "I must run and take these two eggs from my hens, to Madame Lebleu, to whom I promised them."

She had purposely let fly this name, being aware of the secret rivalry between the wife of the cashier, and the wife of the assistant station-master, affecting to be on the best of terms with the former, so as to enrage the other. But she remained, nevertheless, becoming all at once interested, when she heard the fireman inquiring for news of the affair with the sub-prefect.

"So it's all settled; and you're very glad of it, are you not, M. Roubaud?" inquired Pecqueux.

"Very pleased indeed," answered the assistant station-master.

Pecqueux gave a cunning wink.

"Oh! you had no need to be anxious," said he, "because when one has a big-wig behind one, eh? You know who I mean. My wife also is very grateful to him."

The assistant station-master interrupted this allusion to President Grandmorin, by abruptly remarking:

"And so you only leave tonight?"

"Yes," answered the other; "the repairs to La Lison will soon be finished. They're completing the adjustment of the connecting-rod. And I'm waiting for my driver, who has gone for an airing. Do you know him, Jacques Lantier? He comes from the same neighbourhood as yourself."

Roubaud did not answer for an instant, but stood there as if absent-minded. Then, recovering himself with a start, he exclaimed:

"Eh! Jacques Lantier, the driver? Of course I know him! Oh! you understand, enough to say good-day and good-night. It was here that we came across one another, for he is my junior, and I never saw him down there at Plassans. Last autumn he did my wife a little service, in the form of an errand to some cousins at Dieppe. He's a capable young fellow, according to all I hear."

He spoke at random, with abundance of verbosity. All at once he went off with the remark:

"Good day, Pecqueux. I've got to take a look round here."

It was only then that Philomène moved away at her long stride; while Pecqueux, standing motionless, with his hands thrust into his pockets, laughing at ease at his laziness on this bright morning, was astonished to see the assistant station-master rapidly returning, after limiting his inspection to circumambulating the shed. He had not been long taking his look round. What on earth could he have come to spy out?

Nine o'clock was on the point of striking, as Roubaud returned under the marquee. He walked to the end, near the parcel office, where he gave a look, without appearing to find what he sought; and then, impatiently, strode back again, peering inquiringly at the offices of the different departments, one after the other. The station, at this hour, was quiet and deserted. He alone wandered about, more and more enervated at this peacefulness, in the torment of a man menaced with a catastrophe, who at last ardently hopes for it to come. His composure was exhausted. He found it impossible to remain for a minute in the same place. Now his eyes never quitted the clock. Nine, five minutes past. As a rule he only went up to his rooms for the knife-and-fork breakfast at ten, after the departure of the 9.50 train. But all at once the thought struck him that Séverine must also be waiting there in expectancy; and he proceeded to join her.

In the corridor, Madame Lebleu, at this precise moment, was opening the door to Philomène, who had run round in neighbourly fashion, with untidy hair, and held a couple of eggs in her hand. They remained on the threshold, so that Roubaud had to enter his apartment before their eyes. He had his key, and was as quick as he could be. Notwithstanding, in the rapid opening and closing of the door, they perceived Séverine, seated on a chair in the dining-room, with her hands idle, her profile pale, and her body motionless. And Madame Lebleu, dragging in Philomène and closing her own door, related that she had already seen Séverine in the same state, in the early part of the morning. No doubt the business with the sub-prefect was taking a bad turn. But no; and Philomène explained that she had hastened to make a call because she had news; and she repeated what she had just heard the assistant station-master say himself. The two women were then lost in conjectures. It was the same at each of their meetings—gossiping without end.

"They've had their hair combed, my dear," said Madame Lebleu. "I'd stake my life on it. They're tottering on their pedestals."

"Ah! my dear lady," answered Philomène, "if we could only be rid of them!"

The rivalry between the Lebleus and the Roubauds, which had become more and more envenomed, simply arose from a question of apartments. All the first floor of the main station building, served to lodge members of the staff; and the central corridor, a regular corridor of a second-rate hotel, painted yellow, lighted from above, separated the floor in two, with lines of brown doors to right and left. Only the windows of the apartments on the right, looked on the courtyard facing the entrance, which was planted with old elms, and above these an admirable view spread out in the direction of Ingouville; while the apartments on the left, with semicircular, squatty windows, opened right on the marquee of the station, whose high slanting roof of zinc and dirty glass barred the horizon from view. Nothing could be more gay than the one side, with the constant animation in the courtyard, the verdure of the trees, the broad expanse of country; nothing more dismal than the other, where it was almost impossible to see, and where the sky was shut out as in a prison.

On the front, resided the station-master, the assistant station-master Moulin, and the Lebleus; on the back, the Roubauds and Mademoiselle Guichon, the office-keeper, without counting three rooms reserved to inspectors who made occasional visits. It was an established fact that the two assistant station-masters had always lodged side by side. If the Lebleus were there, it was due to an act of politeness on the part of the gentleman who had been succeeded by Roubaud, and who, being a widower without children, had thought proper to show Madame Lebleu the courtesy of giving up his apartments to her. But should not this lodging have gone to the Roubauds? Was it fair to relegate them to the back of the building, when they had the right to be on the front? So long as the two households had lived in harmony, Séverine had given way to her neighbour, her senior by twenty years, who, moreover, was in bad health, being so stout that she was constantly troubled with fits of choking. War had only been declared, since the day Philomène set the two women at variance, by her abominable tongue.

"You know," resumed the latter, "that they are quite capable of having taken advantage of their trip to Paris, to ask for your ejectment. I am told that they have written a long letter to the manager, setting forth their claim."

Madame Lebleu was suffocating.

"The wretches!" she exclaimed. "And I am sure they have been doing their best to get the office-keeper on their side. For the past fortnight she has hardly greeted me. There is another one who is no better than she should be! But I'm watching her."

She lowered her voice to say that Mademoiselle Guichon must be carrying on an intrigue with the station-master. Their doors faced one another. It was M. Dabadie, a widower, and the father of a grown-up daughter still at school, who had brought this thirty-year-old blonde to the station. Already faded, she was silent, slim, and supple as a serpent. She must have been a sort of governess. And it was impossible to catch her, so noiselessly did she glide along through the narrowest apertures.

"Oh! I shall succeed in finding it out," continued Madame Lebleu. "I will not be ridden down. We are here, and here we remain. All worthy people are on our side. Is it not so, my dear?"

Indeed, all the station was impassioned with this battle of the lodgings. The corridor, particularly, was torn asunder by it. It was only the assistant station-master Moulin, satisfied at being on the front, who did not take much interest in the matter. He was married to a little, timid, delicate woman, whom nobody ever saw, but who presented him with a baby every twenty months.

"Anyhow," concluded Philomène, "if they are tottering on their pedestals, this shock will not bring them down. Be on your guard, for they know someone of great influence."

She still held her two eggs, and she presented them, eggs laid that same morning, which she had just taken from under her hens, and the old lady was effusive in thanks.

"Oh! how kind of you!" said she. "You are spoiling me, I declare. Come and have a chat more frequently. You know that my husband is always in his counting-house; and I have a tedious time of it, riveted here on account of my poor legs! What would become of me, if those wretches were to take away my view?"

Then, as she accompanied her, and opened the door, she placed a finger on her lips.

"Hush! Let us listen," said she.

Both of them remained standing in the corridor for five full minutes, holding their breath, without a movement. They bent their heads, with ears turned towards the dining-room of the Roubauds; but not a sound came from that direction. Deathlike silence reigned within. And, in fear of being surprised, they at last separated, giving each other a nod, without pronouncing a word. While one went off on tiptoe, the other closed her door so gently, that the catch could hardly be heard entering the socket.

At 9.20 Roubaud was again below under the marquee superintending the making-up of the 9.50 slow train; and, in spite of all his efforts

ÉMILE ZOLA

to keep calm, he gesticulated more than ever, stamping his feet, and turning round at every moment to examine the platform from one end to the other. But nothing came, and his hands trembled with impatience.

Then, abruptly, as he was looking behind him, and searching again all over the station, he heard a telegraph boy, out of breath, close to him, saying:

"Monsieur Roubaud, do you know where the station-master, and the commissary of police are? I have got telegrams for them, and have been running after them for the last ten minutes."

He turned round with such a stiffening of all his being, that not a muscle of his face moved. His eyes were fixed on the two telegrams which the lad held in his hand. And this time, from the excited look of the latter, he felt convinced that the catastrophe had come at last.

"Monsieur Dabadie passed by here a short time ago," said he tranquilly.

And never had he felt himself so cool, with an intelligence so bright, prepared for the defence from head to foot.

"Look!" he resumed; "here is Monsieur Dabadie coming towards us."

In fact, the station-master was returning from the goods train department. As soon as he had run his eye over the telegram, he exclaimed:

"There has been a murder on the line. The inspector at Rouen telegraphs to me to that effect."

"What?" inquired Roubaud; "a murder among our staff?"

"No, no," answered the station-master. "The murder of a passenger in a coupé. The body was thrown out almost at the exit from the tunnel of Malaunay at post 153. And the victim is one of our directors, President Grandmorin."

The assistant station-master immediately exclaimed:

"The President! Ah! my poor wife, what a terrible blow it will be for her!"

The tone was so natural, so pitiful, that it for a moment arrested the attention of M. Dabadie.

"Ah! true enough!" said he; "you knew him. Such a worthy man, was he not?"

Then, turning to the other telegram addressed to the commissary of police, he added:

"This must be from the examining-magistrate, no doubt for some formality. And, as it is only 9.25, Monsieur Cauche is not yet here, naturally. Let someone run to the Café du Commerce, on the Cours Napoléon. He will be found there for certain."

Five minutes later M. Cauche arrived, brought to the scene by a porter. Formerly an officer, he looked upon the post he occupied as a sinecure, and never put in an appearance at the station before ten o'clock, when he strolled about for a moment or two, and returned to the café. This drama, which had burst upon him between a couple of games at piquet, had first of all astonished him, for the matters that passed through his hands were not, as a rule, very grave. But the telegram came from the examining-magistrate at Rouen; and, if it arrived twelve hours after the discovery of the body, it was because this magistrate had first of all telegraphed to the station-master at Paris, to ascertain under what circumstances the victim had set out on his journey. Having found out the number of the train, and that of the carriage, he had only then sent orders to the commissary of police to examine the coupé in carriage 293 if it still happened to be at Havre. The ill-humour that M. Cauche displayed at having been disturbed needlessly, as he had at first fancied, at once gave place to an attitude of extreme importance, proportionate to the exceptional gravity that the affair began to assume.

"But," he exclaimed, suddenly becoming anxious, in fear lest the inquiry might escape him, "the carriage will no longer be here, it must have gone back this morning."

It was Roubaud who reassured him in his calm manner.

"No, no, excuse me," he broke in. "There was a coupé booked for this evening. The carriage is there in the coach-house."

And he led the way to the building, followed by the commissary and the station-master. In the meanwhile, the news must have spread, for the porters, slyly leaving their work, also followed; while clerks made their appearance on the thresholds of the offices of the different departments, and ended by approaching one by one. A small crowd had soon assembled.

As they came to the carriage, M. Dabadie remarked:

"But the coaches were examined last night. If any traces had remained, it would have been mentioned in the report."

"We shall soon see," said M. Cauche.

Opening the door, he went up into the coupé. And, forgetting himself, he immediately exclaimed with an oath:

"It looks as if they had been bleeding a pig here!"

A little thrill of horror ran through all who were present, and a number of necks were craned forward. M. Dabadie was one of the first who wished to see. He drew himself up on the step; while behind him, Roubaud, to do like the others, also craned his neck.

The inside of the coupé displayed no disorder. The windows had remained closed, and everything seemed in its proper place. Only, a frightful stench escaped by the open door; and there, in the middle of one of the cushions, a pool of blood had coagulated, a pool so deep, and so large, that a stream had sprung from it, as from a source, and had poured over on the carpet. Clots of blood remained sticking to the cloth. And there was nothing else, nothing but this nauseous gore.

M. Dabadie flew into a rage.

"Where are the men who looked into the carriages last night? Bring them here!"

It so happened that they were there, and they advanced, spluttering excuses: how was it possible to see at night time? Nevertheless, they had passed their hands everywhere. They vowed they had felt nothing on the previous night.

In the meanwhile, M. Cauche, who remained standing up in the compartment, was taking pencil notes for his report. He called Roubaud, with whom he was familiar, being in the habit of smoking cigarettes with him along the platform, in moments of leisure.

"Roubaud," said he, "just come up here, you will be able to help me."

And when the assistant station-master had stepped over the blood on the carpet, so as not to tread in it, the commissary added:

"Look under the other cushion, to see if anything has slipped down there."

Roubaud raised the cushion, feeling with prudent hands, and looks that simply denoted curiosity.

"There is nothing," said he.

But a spot on the padded cloth at the back of the seat, attracted his attention; and he pointed it out to the commissary. Was it not the mark of a finger covered with blood? No; they both came to the conclusion that it was some blood which had spurted there. The crowd had drawn nearer, to watch this inspection of the coupé, sniffing the crime, pressing behind the station-master, who, with the repugnance of a refined man, remained on the step.

Suddenly the latter remarked:

"But, I say, Roubaud, you were in the train, were you not? You returned last night by the express. You can, perhaps, give us some information?"

"Yes, indeed," exclaimed the commissary, "that is true. Did you notice anything?"

Roubaud, for two or three seconds, remained silent. At this moment, he was bending down examining the carpet. But he rose, almost at once, answering in his natural voice, which was a trifle thick:

"Certainly, certainly, I will tell you. My wife was with me. But if what I am going to say is to figure in the report, I should like her to come down, so as to control my recollection by her own."

M. Cauche thought this very reasonable, and Pecqueux, who had just arrived, offered to go and fetch Madame Roubaud. He started off with great strides, and for a moment there was a pause. Philomène, who had joined the crowd with the firemen, followed him with her eyes, irritated that he should undertake this errand. But, perceiving Madame Lebleu hurrying along as fast as her poor swollen legs would carry her, she hastened forward to assist her; and the two women raised their hands to heaven, uttering passionate exclamations at the discovery of such an abominable crime. Although absolutely no details were known, as yet, all kinds of versions of what had occurred, circulated around them, accompanied by excited gestures and looks. Philomène, whose voice could be heard above the hum of the crowd, affirmed, on her word of honour, that Madame Roubaud had seen the murderer, although she had no authority whatever for the statement. And when the latter appeared, accompanied by Pecqueux, there was general silence.

"Just look at her!" murmured Madame Lebleu. "Would anyone take her for the wife of an assistant station-master, with her airs of a princess? This morning, before daybreak, she was already as she is now, combed and laced, as if she were going out on a visit."

Séverine advanced with short, regular steps. She had to walk along the whole length of the platform, facing the eyes watching her approach. But she did not break down. She simply pressed her handkerchief to her eyelids, in the great grief she had just experienced at learning the name of the victim. Attired in a very elegantly fashioned black woollen gown, she seemed to be wearing mourning for her protector. Her heavy, dark hair shone in the sun, for she had come down in such a hurry that she had not found time, in spite of the cold, to put anything on her head. Her gentle blue eyes, full of anguish, and bathed in tears, gave her a most touching appearance.

ÉMILE ZOLA

"She may well cry," said Philomène in an undertone. "They are done for, now that their guardian-angel has been killed."

When Séverine was there, in the middle of all the people, before the open door of the coupé, M. Cauche and Roubaud got out; and the latter immediately began to relate what he knew. Addressing his wife, he said:

"Yesterday morning, my dear, as soon as we arrived at Paris we went to see Monsieur Grandmorin. And it was about a quarter past eleven. That is right, is it not?"

He looked fixedly at her, and she, in a docile tone, repeated:

"Yes, a quarter past eleven."

But her eyes had fallen on the cushion black with blood. She had a spasm, and her bosom heaved with heavy sobs. The station-master, who felt distressed, intervened with much concern:

"If you are unable to bear the sight, madam—We quite understand your grief—"

"Oh! just a few words," interrupted the commissary; "and we will then have madam conducted home again."

Roubaud hastened to continue:

"It was at this visit that Monsieur Grandmorin, after talking of various matters, informed us that he was going next day to Doinville, on a visit to his sister. I still see him seated at his writing-table. I was here, my wife there. That is right, my dear, is it not? He told us he would be leaving on the morrow."

"Yes, on the morrow," said she.

M. Cauche, who continued taking rapid pencil notes, raised his head:

"How is that, on the morrow," he inquired, "considering he left the same evening?"

"Wait a moment," replied the assistant station-master. "When he heard we were returning that night, he had an idea of taking the express with us, if my wife would accompany him to Doinville, to stay a few days with his sister, as had happened before. But my wife, having a great deal to do here, refused. That is so, you refused?"

"Yes, I refused," answered Séverine.

"Then he was very kind," continued her husband. "He had been interesting himself on my behalf. He accompanied us to the door of his study. Did he not, my dear?"

"Yes, as far as the door," said Séverine.

"We left in the evening," resumed Roubaud. "Before seating ourselves in our compartment, I had a chat with Monsieur Vandorpe, the station-master. And I saw nothing at all. I was very much annoyed, because I thought we should be alone, and I found a lady in a corner whom I had not noticed; and the more so, as two other persons, a married couple, got in at the last moment. So far as Rouen, nothing worthy of note occurred. I noticed nothing. But at Rouen, as we left the train to stretch our legs, what was our surprise to see Monsieur Grandmorin standing up at the door of a coupé, three or four carriages away from our compartment. 'What, Mr. President,' said I, 'so you left after all? Ah! well, we had no idea we were travelling with you!' And he explained that he had received a telegram. They whistled, and we jumped into our compartment, which, by the way, we found empty, all our travelling companions having got out at Rouen, and we were not sorry. That is absolutely all, my dear, is it not?"

"Yes, that is absolutely all," she repeated.

This story, simple though it appeared, produced a strong impression on the audience. All awaited the key to the enigma with gaping countenances. The commissary ceasing to write, gave expression to the general astonishment by inquiring:

"And you are sure no one was inside the coupé, along with Monsieur Grandmorin?"

"Oh! as to that, absolutely certain!"

A shudder ran through the crowd. This mystery which required solving inspired the onlookers with fear, and sent a chill down the backs of everyone there. If the passenger was alone, by whom could he have been murdered and thrown from the coupé, three leagues from there, before the train stopped again?

Silence was broken by the unpleasant voice of Philomène:

"It is all the same strange," said she.

And Roubaud, feeling himself being stared at, looked at her, tossing his chin, as if to say that he also considered the matter strange. Beside her, he perceived Pecqueux and Madame Lebleu, tossing their heads as well. All eyes were turned towards him. The crowd awaited something more, sought on his body for a forgotten detail that would throw light on the matter. There was no accusation in these ardently inquisitive looks; and yet, he fancied he noticed a vague suspicion arising, that doubt which the smallest fact sometimes transforms into a certainty.

"Extraordinary," murmured M. Cauche.

"Quite extraordinary," assented M. Dabadie.

Then Roubaud made up his mind.

"What I am, moreover, quite certain of," he continued, "is that the express which runs from Rouen to Barentin without stopping, went along at the regulation speed, and that I noticed nothing abnormal. I mention this, because, as we were alone, I let down the window to smoke a cigarette, and glancing outside several times, had a perfect knowledge of every sound of the train. At Barentin, noticing my successor, the station-master, Monsieur Bessière, on the platform, I called to him, and we exchanged a few words, as he stood on the step, and shook hands. That is so, my dear, is it not? The question can be put to Monsieur Bessière, and he will answer, Yes."

Séverine, still motionless and pale, her delicate face plunged in grief, once more confirmed the statement of her husband.

"Yes, that is correct," said she.

From this moment any accusation was out of the question, if the Roubauds, having returned to their compartment at Rouen, had been greeted, sitting there, by a friend at Barentin. The shadow of suspicion which the assistant station-master had noticed in the eyes of the bystanders, vanished, while the general astonishment increased. The case was assuming a more and more mysterious aspect.

"Come," said the commissary, "are you quite positive that nobody could have entered the coupé at Rouen, after you left Monsieur Grandmorin?"

Roubaud had evidently not foreseen this question. For the first time, he became confused, having no doubt got to the end of his ready answers. He looked at his wife, hesitating.

"Oh! no!" said he; "I do not think so. They were shutting the doors; they had whistled. We only just had time to reach our carriage. And, besides, the coupé was reserved, nobody could get in there, I fancy—"

But the blue eyes of his wife opened wider, and grew so large, that he was afraid to be positive.

"After all," he continued, "I don't know. Yes. Perhaps someone did get into the coupé. There was a regular crush—"

As he continued talking, his voice became distinct again, and a new story began to take shape.

"The crowd, you know, was enormous," he said, "on account of the fêtes at Havre. We were obliged to resist an assault on our own compartment by second and even third-class passengers. Apart from this, the station was badly lighted, one could see next to nothing. People were pushing about in a clamorous multitude, just as the train was starting. Yes, indeed, it is quite possible that someone, not knowing where to find a seat, or, may be, taking advantage of the confusion, actually did force his way into the coupé, at the last second."

And, turning to his wife, he remarked:

"Eh! my dear, that is what must have happened?"

Séverine, looking broken down, with her handkerchief pressed to her swollen eyes, answered:

"That is what happened, certainly."

The clue was now given. The commissary of police and the station-master, without expressing an opinion, exchanged a look of intelligence. The seething crowd swayed to and fro, feeling the inquiry at an end. All were burning to communicate their thoughts; and various conjectures immediately found vent, everyone having his own idea. For a few moments, the business of the station had been at a standstill. The entire staff were there, all their attention taken up by this drama; and it was with general surprise that the 9.38 train was observed coming in, under the marquee. The porters ran to meet it, the carriage doors were opened, and the flood of passengers streamed out. But almost all the lookers-on had remained round the commissary, who, with the scruple of a methodical man, paid a final visit to the gory coupé.

At this moment, Pecqueux, engaged in gesticulating between Madame Lebleu and Philomène, caught sight of his driver, Jacques Lantier, who, having just left the train, was standing motionless, watching the gathering from a distance. He beckoned to him urgently. At first, Jacques did not move; but, afterwards, making up his mind to go, he advanced slowly forward.

"What's it all about?" he inquired of his fireman.

He knew very well, and lent but an inattentive ear to the news of the murder and the rumours that were current respecting it. What surprised, and particularly agitated him, was to tumble into the midst of this inquiry, to again come upon this coupé which he had caught sight of in the obscurity, launched at full speed. He craned his neck, gazing at the pool of clotted blood on the cushion; and, once more, he saw the murder scene, and particularly the corpse, stretched across the line yonder with its throat open. Then, turning aside his eyes, he noticed the Roubauds, while Pecqueux continued relating to him the story of how they were mixed up in the business—their departure from Paris in the same train as the victim, and the last words they had exchanged together at Rouen. Jacques knew Roubaud, from having occasionally pressed his hand since he had been driving the express. As to his wife, he had caught sight of her in the distance, and he had avoided her, like the others, in his unhealthy terror. But, at this moment, he was struck by her, as he observed her weeping and pale, with her gentle, bewildered blue eyes, beneath the crushing volume of black hair. He continued to look at her; and, becoming absent, he asked himself, in surprise, how it was that the Roubauds and he were there? How it was that events had brought them together, before this carriage steeped in crime—they who had returned from Paris on the previous evening, he who had come back from Barentin at that very instant?

"Oh! I know, I know," said he aloud, interrupting the fireman. "I happened to be there, at the exit from the tunnel, last night, and I thought I saw something, as the train passed."

This remark caused great excitement, and everybody gathered round him. Why had he spoken, after formally making up his mind to hold his tongue? So many excellent reasons prompted him to silence! And the words had unconsciously left his lips, while he was gazing at this woman. She had abruptly drawn aside her handkerchief, to fix her tearful eyes, wide-open, on him.

The commissary of police quickly approached.

"Saw what? What did you see?" he inquired.

And Jacques, with the unswerving look of Séverine upon him, related what he had seen: the coupé lit up, passing through the night at full speed, and the fleeting outlines of the two men, one thrown down backwards, the other with a knife in his hand. Roubaud, standing beside his wife, listened with his great bright eyes fixed on Jacques.

"So," inquired the commissary, "you would be able to recognise the murderer?"

"Oh! as to that, no! I do not think so," answered the other.

"Was he wearing a coat, or a blouse?" asked the commissary.

"I can say nothing positively. Just reflect, a train that must have been going at a speed of sixty miles an hour!"

Séverine, against her will, exchanged a glance with Roubaud, who had the energy to say:

"True enough! It would require a good pair of eyes."

"No matter," concluded M. Cauche; "this is an important piece of evidence. The examining-magistrate will assist you to throw light on it all. Monsieur Lantier and Monsieur Roubaud, give me your exact names for the summonses."

It was all over. The throng of bystanders dispersed, little by little, and the business of the station resumed its activity. Roubaud had to run and attend to the 9.50 slow train, in which passengers were already taking their seats. He had given Jacques a more vigorous shake of the hand than usual; and the latter, remaining alone with Séverine, behind Madame Lebleu, Pecqueux, and Philomène, who went off whispering together, had considered himself bound to escort the young woman under the marquee, to the foot of the staircase leading to the lodgings of the staff, finding nothing to say, and yet forced to remain beside her, as if a bond had just been fastened between them.

The brightness of day, had now increased. The sun, conqueror of the morning haze, was ascending in the great expanse of limpid blue sky; while the sea breeze, gaining strength with the rising tide, contributed its saline freshness to the atmosphere. And, as Jacques at last left Séverine, he again encountered those great eyes, whose terrified and imploring sweetness had so profoundly moved him.

But there came a low whistle. It was Roubaud giving the signal to start. The engine responded by a prolonged screech, and the 9.50 train moved off, rolled along more rapidly, and disappeared in the distance, amid the golden dust of the sun.

ÉMILE ZOLA

IV

One day, during the second week in March, M. Denizet, the examining-magistrate, had again summoned certain important witnesses in the Grandmorin case, to his chambers at the Rouen Law Courts.

For the last three weeks, this case had been causing enormous sensation. It had set Rouen upside down; it had impassioned Paris; and the opposition newspapers, in their violent campaign against the Empire, had just grasped it as a weapon. The forthcoming general elections, which occupied the public mind in preference to all other political events, added keen excitement to the struggle. In the Chamber there had been some very stormy sittings; one at which the validity of the powers of two members attached to the Emperor's household, had been bitterly disputed; and another that had given rise to a most determined attack on the financial administration of the Prefect of the Seine, coupled with a demand for the election of a Municipal Council.

The Grandmorin case, coming at an appropriate moment, served to keep up the agitation. The most extraordinary stories were abroad. Every morning, the newspapers were full of assumptions injurious for the Government. On the one hand, the public were given to understand that the victim—a familiar figure at the Tuileries, formerly on the bench, Commander of the Legion of Honour, immensely rich—was addicted to the most frightful debauchery; on the other, the inquiry into the case, having so far proved fruitless, they began to accuse the police and legal authorities, of winking at the affair, and joked about the legendary assassin who could not be found. If there was a good deal of truth in these attacks, they were all the harder to bear.

M. Denizet was fully alive to his heavy responsibility. He, also, became impassioned with the case, and the more so as he was ambitious, and had been burning to have a matter of this importance in his hands, so as to bring into evidence the high qualities of perspicacity and energy with which he credited himself.

The son of a large Normandy cattle-breeder, he had studied law at Caen, but had entered the judicial department of the Government rather late in life; and, his peasant origin, aggravated by his father's bankruptcy, had made his promotion slow. Substitute at Bernay, Dieppe, and Havre, it had taken him ten years to become Imperial Procurator at Pont-Audemer; then, sent to Rouen as substitute, he had been acting as examining-magistrate for eighteen months, and was over fifty years of age.

Without any fortune, a prey to requirements that could not be satisfied out of his meagre salary, he lived in this ill-remunerated dependence of the magistracy, only frankly accepted by men of mediocre capacity, and where the intelligent are eaten up with envy, whilst on the look-out for an opportunity to sell themselves.

M. Denizet was a man of the most lively intelligence, with a very penetrating mind. He was even honest, and fond of his profession, intoxicated with his great power which, in his justice-room, made him absolute master of the liberty of others. It was his interests alone that kept his zeal within bounds. He had such a burning desire to be decorated and transferred to Paris, that, after having at the commencement of the inquiry, allowed himself to be carried away by his love of truth, he now proceeded with extreme prudence, perceiving pitfalls on all sides, which might swallow up his future.

It must be pointed out that M. Denizet had been warned; for, from the outset of his inquiry, a friend had advised him to look in at the Ministry of Justice in Paris. He did so, and had a long chat with the secretary, M. Camy-Lamotte, a very important personage, possessing considerable power over the gentlemen comprising this branch of the civil service. It was, moreover, his duty to prepare the list of promotions, and he was in constant communication with the Tuileries. He was a handsome man, who had started on his career as substitute, like his visitor; but through his connections and his wife, he had been elected deputy, and made grand officer of the Legion of Honour.

The case had come quite naturally into his hands. The Imperial Procurator at Rouen, disturbed at this shady drama wherein a former judge figured as victim, had taken the precaution to communicate with the Minister, who had passed the matter on to the secretary. And here came a coincidence: M. Camy-Lamotte happened to be a schoolfellow of President Grandmorin. Younger by a few years, he had been on such terms of intimacy with him that he knew him thoroughly, even to his vices. And so, he spoke of his friend's tragic death with profound affliction, and talked to M. Denizet of nothing but his warm desire to secure the guilty party. But he did not disguise the fact that they were very much annoyed at the Tuileries, about the stir the business had occasioned, which was quite out of proportion to its importance, and he had taken the liberty to recommend great tact.

In fact, the magistrate had understood that he would do well not to be in a hurry, and to avoid running any risk unless previously approved. He had even returned to Rouen with the certainty that the secretary, on his part, had sent out detectives, wishing to inquire into the case himself. They wanted to learn the truth, so as to be better able to hide it, if necessary.

Nevertheless, time passed, and M. Denizet, notwithstanding his efforts to be patient, became irritated at the jokes of the press. Then the policeman reappeared, sniffing the scent, like a good hound. He was carried away by the necessity of finding the real track, for the glory of being the first to discover it, and reserving his freedom to abandon it if he received orders to do so. And, whilst awaiting a letter, a piece of advice, a simple sign from the Ministry which failed to reach him, he had actively resumed his inquiry.

Not one of the two or three arrests that had been made, could be maintained. But, suddenly, the opening of the will of President Grandmorin aroused in M. Denizet a suspicion, which he felt had flashed through his mind at the first—the possible guilt of the Roubauds. This will, full of strange legacies, contained one by which Séverine inherited the house situated at the place called La Croix-de-Maufras. From that moment, the motive of the crime, sought in vain until then, became evident—the Roubauds, aware of the legacy, had murdered their benefactor to gain possession of the property at once. This idea haunted him the more, as M. Camy-Lamotte had spoken in a peculiar way of Madame Roubaud, whom he had known formerly at the home of the President when she was a young girl. Only, how unlikely! how impossible, materially and morally! Since searching in this direction, he had at every step, encountered facts that upset his conception of a classically conducted judicial inquiry. Nothing became clear; the great central light, the original cause which would illuminate everything, was wanting.

Another clue existed which M. Denizet had not lost sight of, the one suggested by Roubaud himself—that of the man who might have got into the coupé, thanks to the crush, at the moment the train was leaving. This was the famous legendary murderer who could not be found, and in reference to whom the opposition newspapers were making such silly fun. At the outset, every effort had been made to trace this man. At

Rouen, where he had entered the train, at Barentin, where he had left it; but the result had lacked precision. Some witnesses even denied that it could have been possible for the reserved coupé to be taken by assault, others gave the most contradictory information. And this clue seemed unlikely to lead to anything, when the magistrate, in questioning the signalman, Misard, came involuntarily upon the dramatic adventure of Cabuche and Louisette, the young girl who, victimised by the President, had repaired to the abode of her sweetheart to die.

This information burst on him like a thunderbolt, and at once he formulated the indictment in his head. It was all there—the threats of death made by the quarryman against his victim, the deplorable antecedents of the man, an alibi, clumsily advanced, impossible to prove. In secrecy, on the previous night, in a moment of energetic inspiration, he had caused Cabuche to be carried off from the little house he occupied on the border of the wood, a sort of out-of-the-way cavern, where those who arrested the man, found a pair of blood-stained trousers. And, whilst offering resistance to the conviction gaining on him, whilst determined not to abandon the presumption against the Roubauds, he exulted at the idea that he alone had been smart enough to discover the veritable assassin. It was in view of making this a certainty that, on this specific day, he had summoned to his chambers several witnesses who had already been heard immediately after the crime.

The quarters of the examining-magistrate were near the Rue Jeanne d'Arc, in the old dilapidated building, dabbed against the side of the ancient palace of the Dukes of Normandy, now transformed into the Law Courts, which it dishonoured. This large, sad-looking room on the ground floor was so dark, that in winter it became necessary to light a lamp at three o'clock in the afternoon. Hung with old, discoloured green paper, its only furniture were two armchairs, four chairs, the writing-table of the magistrate, the small table of the registrar; and, on the frigid-looking mantelpiece, two bronze cups, flanking a black marble timepiece. Behind the writing-table was a door leading to a second room, where the magistrate sometimes concealed persons whom he wished to have at hand; while the entrance door opened direct on a broad corridor supplied with benches, where witnesses waited.

The Roubauds were there at half-past one, although the subpœnas had only been made returnable for two o'clock. They came from Havre, and had taken time to lunch at a little restaurant in the Grande Rue. Both attired in black, he in a frock coat, she in a silk gown, like a

ÉMILE ZOLA

lady, maintained the rather wearisome and painful gravity of a couple who had lost a relative. She sat on a bench motionless, without uttering a word, whilst he, remaining on his feet, his hands behind his back, strode slowly to and fro before her. But at each turn their eyes met, and their concealed anxiety then passed like a shadow over their mute countenances.

Although the Croix-de-Maufras legacy had given them great joy, it had revived their fears; for the family of the President, particularly his daughter, indignant at the number of strange donations which amounted to half the entire fortune, spoke of contesting the will; and Madame de Lachesnaye, influenced by her husband, showed herself particularly harsh for her old friend Séverine, whom she loaded with the gravest suspicions. On the other hand, the idea that there existed a proof, which Roubaud at first had not thought of, haunted him with constant dread: the letter which he had compelled his wife to write, so as to cause Grandmorin to leave, would be found, unless the latter had destroyed it, and the writing recognised. Fortunately, time passed and nothing happened; the letter must have been torn up. Nevertheless, every fresh summons to the presence of the examining-magistrate, gave them a cold perspiration in their correct attitude of heirs and witnesses.

Two o'clock struck. Jacques in his turn appeared. He came from Paris. Roubaud at once advanced, with his hand extended in a very expansive manner.

"Ah! So they've brought you here as well. What a nuisance this sad business is. It seems to have no end!"

Jacques, perceiving Séverine, still seated, motionless, had stopped short. For the past three weeks, every two days, at each of his journeys to Havre, the assistant station-master had shown him great affability. On one occasion even, he had to accept an invitation to lunch; and seated beside the young woman, he felt himself agitated with his old shivers, and quite upset. Could it be possible that he would want to slay this one also? His heart throbbed, his hands burnt at the mere sight of the white muslin at her neck, bordering the rounded bodice of her gown. And he determined, henceforth, to keep away from her.

"And what do they say about the case at Paris?" resumed Roubaud. "Nothing new, eh? Look here, they know nothing; they'll never know anything. Come and say how do you do to my wife."

He dragged him forward, so that Jacques approached and bowed to Séverine, who, looking a little confused, smiled with her air of a timid child. He did his best to chat about commonplace matters, with the eyes of the husband and wife fixed on him, as if they sought to read even beyond his own thoughts, in the vague reflections to which he hesitated to lend his mind. Why was he so cold? Why did he seem to do his best to avoid them? Was his memory returning? Could it be for the purpose of confronting them with him, that they had been sent for again? They sought to bring over this single witness, whom they feared, to their side, to attach him to them by such firm bonds of fraternity that he would not have the courage to speak against them.

It was the assistant station-master, tortured by uncertainty, who brought up the case again.

"So you have no idea as to why they have summoned us? Perhaps there is something new?"

Jacques gave a shrug of indifference.

"A rumour was abroad just now at the station, when I arrived, that there had been an arrest," said he.

The Roubauds were astounded, becoming quite agitated and perplexed. What! An arrest? No one had breathed a word to them on the subject! An arrest that had been already made, or an arrest about to take place? They bombarded him with questions, but he knew nothing further.

At that moment, a sound of footsteps, in the corridor, attracted the attention of Séverine.

"Here come Berthe and her husband," she murmured.

The Lachesnayes passed very stiffly before the Roubauds. The young woman did not even give her former comrade a look. An usher at once showed them into the room of the examining-magistrate.

"Oh! dear me! We must have patience," said Roubaud. "We shall be here for at least two hours. Sit you down."

He had just placed himself on the left of Séverine, and, with a motion of the hand, invited Jacques to take a seat near her, on the other side. The driver remained standing a moment longer. Then, as she looked at him in her gentle, timid manner, he sank down on the bench. She appeared very frail between the two men. He felt she possessed a submissive, tender character, and the slight warmth emanating from this woman, slowly torpified him from tip to toe.

In M. Denizet's room the interrogatories were about to commence. The inquiry had already supplied matter for an enormous volume of papers, enclosed in blue wrappers. Every effort had been made to follow the victim from the time he left Paris. M. Vandorpe, the station-master, had given evidence as to the departure of the 6.30 express. How the coach No. 293 had been added on at the last moment; how he had exchanged a few words with Roubaud, who had got into his compartment a little before the arrival of President Grandmorin; finally, how the latter had taken possession of his coupé, where he was certainly alone.

Then, the guard, Henri Dauvergne, questioned as to what had occurred at Rouen during the ten minutes the train waited, was unable to give any positive information. He had seen the Roubauds talking in front of the coupé, and he felt sure they had returned to their compartment, the door of which had been shut by an inspector; but his recollection was vague, owing to the confusion caused by the crowd, and the obscurity in the station. As to giving an opinion whether a man, the famous murderer who could not be found, would have been able to jump into the coupé as the train started, he thought such a thing very unlikely, whilst admitting it was possible; for, to his own knowledge, something similar had already occurred twice.

Other members of the company's staff at Rouen, on being examined on the same points, instead of throwing light on the matter, only entangled it by their contradictory answers. Nevertheless, one thing proved was the shake of the hand given by Roubaud from inside his compartment to the station-master at Barentin, who had got on the step. This station-master, M. Bessière, had formally acknowledged the incident as exact, and had added that his colleague was alone with his wife, who was half lying down, and appeared to be tranquilly sleeping.

Moreover, the authorities had gone so far as to search for the passengers who had quitted Paris in the same compartment as the Roubauds. The stout lady and gentleman who arrived late, almost at the last minute, middle-class people from Petit-Couronne, had stated that having immediately dozed off to sleep, they were unable to say anything; and, as to the woman in black, who remained silent in her corner, she had melted away like a shadow. It had been absolutely impossible to trace her.

Then, there were other witnesses, the small fry who had served to identify the passengers who left the train that night at Barentin, the theory being that the murderer must have got out there. The tickets had been counted, and they had succeeded in recognising all the travellers except one, and he precisely was a great big fellow, with his head wrapped up in a blue handkerchief. Some said he wore a coat, and others a short smock. About this man alone, who had disappeared, vanished like a dream, there existed three hundred and ten documents, forming a confused medley, in which the evidence of one person was contradicted by that of another.

And the record was further complicated by the written evidence of the legal authorities: the account drawn up by the registrar, whom the Imperial Procurator and the examining-magistrate had taken to the scene of the crime, comprising quite a bulky description of the spot, on the metal way, where the victim was lying; the position of the body, the attire, the things found in the pockets establishing his identity; then, the report of the doctor, also conducted there, a document in which the wound in the throat was described at length in scientific terms; the only wound, a frightful gash, made with a sharp instrument, probably a knife.

And there were other reports and documents about the removal of the body to the hospital at Rouen, the length of time it had remained there before being delivered to the family. But in this mass of papers appeared but one or two important points. First of all, nothing had been found in the pockets, neither the watch, nor a small pocket-book, which should have contained ten banknotes of a thousand francs each, a sum due to the sister of President Grandmorin, Madame Bonnehon, and which she was expecting.

It therefore would have seemed that the motive of the crime was robbery, had not a ring, set with a large brilliant, remained on the finger of the victim. This circumstance gave rise to quite a series of conjectures. Unfortunately the numbers of the banknotes were missing; but the watch was known. It was a very heavy, keyless watch, with the monogram of the President on the back, and the number, 2516, of the manufacturer, inside. Finally, the weapon, the knife the murderer had used, had occasioned diligent search along the line, among the bushes in the vicinity, where he might have thrown it; but with no result. The murderer must have concealed the knife in the same place as the watch and banknotes. Nothing had been found but the travelling-rug of the victim, which had been picked up at a hundred yards or so from Barentin station, where it had been abandoned as a dangerous article; and it figured among other objects that might assist to convict the culprit.

When the Lachesnayes entered, M. Denizet, erect before his writing-table, was perusing the examination of one of the first witnesses, which his registrar had just routed out from among the other papers. He was a short and rather robust man, clean-shaven, and already turning grey. His full cheeks, square chin, and big nose, had a sort of pallid immobility, which was increased by the heavy eyelids half closing his great light eyes. But all the sagacity, all the adroitness he believed he possessed, was centred in his mouth—one of those mouths of an actor that express the feelings of the owner off the stage. This mouth was extremely active, and at moments, when he became very sharp, the lips grew thin. It was his sharpness that frequently led him astray. He was too perspicacious, too cunning with simple, honest truth. According to the ideal he had formed of his position, the man occupying it should be an anatomist in morals, endowed with second sight, extremely witty; and, indeed, he was by no means a fool.

He at once showed himself amiable towards Madame de Lachesnaye, for he was still a magistrate full of urbanity, frequenting society in Rouen and its neighbourhood.

"Pray be seated, madam," said he.

And he offered a chair to the young woman, a sickly blonde, disagreeable in manner, and ugly in her mourning. But he was simply polite, and even a trifle arrogant, in look, towards M. de Lachesnaye, who was also fair, with a delicate skin; for this little man—judge at the Court of Appeal from the age of thirty-six; decorated, thanks to the influence of his father-in-law, and to the services his father, also on the bench, had formerly rendered on the High Commissions, at the time of the Coup d'Etat—represented in his eyes, the judicial functionary by favour, by wealth, the man of moderate gifts who had installed himself, certain of making rapid progress through his relatives and fortune; whereas he, poor, deprived of protective influence, found himself ever reduced to make way for others. And so he was not sorry to make this gentleman feel all his power in this room—the absolute power that he possessed over the liberty of everyone, to such a point that, by one word, he could transform a witness into an accused, and immediately have him arrested if it pleased him to do so.

"Madam," he continued, "you will pardon me, if I am again obliged to torture you with this painful business. I know that you wish, as ardently as we do, to see the matter cleared up, and the culprit expiate his crime."

By a sign he attracted the attention of the registrar, a big, bilious-looking fellow with a bony face, and the examination commenced.

But M. de Lachesnaye—who, seeing he was not asked to sit down, had taken a seat of his own accord—at the first questions addressed to his wife, did his best to put himself in her place. He proceeded to complain bitterly of the will of his father-in-law. Who had ever heard of such a thing? So many, and such important legacies, that they absorbed almost half the fortune, which amounted to 3,700,000 frcs.—about £148,000! And legacies to persons who for the most part they did not know, to women of all classes! Among them figured even a little violet-seller, who sat in a doorway in the Rue du Rocher. It was unacceptable, and he was only waiting for the inquiry into the crime to be completed, to see if he could not upset this immoral will.

Whilst he complained in this manner, between his set teeth, showing what a stupid he was, an obstinate provincial, up to his neck in avarice, M. Denizet watched him with his great light eyes half closed, and his artful lips assumed an expression of jealous disdain for this nonentity, who was not satisfied with two millions, and whom, no doubt, he would one day, see in the supreme purple of a President, thanks to all this money.

"I think, sir," said he at last, "that you would do wrong. The will could only be attacked if the total amount of the legacies exceeded half the fortune, and such is not the case."

Then, turning to his registrar, he remarked:

"I say, Laurent, you are not writing down all this, I hope."

With the suspicion of a smile, the latter set his mind at ease, like a man who knew his business.

"But, anyhow," resumed M. de Lachesnaye more bitterly, "no one imagines, I suppose, that I am going to leave La Croix-de-Maufras to those Roubauds. A present like that to the daughter of a domestic! And why? for what reason? Besides, if it is proved that they were connected with the crime—"

M. Denizet returned to the murder.

"Do you really think so?" he inquired.

"Well, if they knew what was in the will, their interest in the death of our poor father is manifest. Observe, moreover, that they were the last to speak to him. All this looks very suspicious."

The magistrate, out of patience, disturbed in his new hypothesis, turned to Berthe.

"And you, madam? Do you think your old comrade capable of such a crime?"

Before answering, she looked at her husband. During their few months of married life, they had communicated to one another their ill-humour and want of feeling, which, moreover, had increased. They were becoming vitiated together. It was he who had set her on to Séverine; and, to such a point, that to get back the house, she would have had her old playmate arrested on the spot.

"Well, sir," she ended by saying, "the person you speak about, displayed very bad tendencies as a child."

"What were they? Do you accuse her of having acted improperly at Doinville?"

"Oh! no, sir; my father would not have allowed her to remain."

In this sentence the prudery of the respectable middle-class lady, flared up in virtuous indignation.

"Only," she continued, "when one notices a disposition to be giddy, to be wild—briefly, many things that I should not have thought possible, appear to me positive at the present time."

M. Denizet again showed signs of impatience. He was no longer following up this clue, and whoever continued to do so, became his adversary, and seemed to him to be putting the certainty of his intelligence in doubt.

"But come!" he exclaimed; "one must yield to reason. People like the Roubauds would not kill such a man as your father, in order to inherit sooner; or, at least, there would be indications of them being in a hurry. I should find traces of this eagerness to possess and enjoy, elsewhere. No; the motive is insufficient. It is necessary to find another, and there is nothing. You bring nothing yourselves. Then establish the facts. Do you not perceive material impossibilities? No one saw the Roubauds get into the coupé. One of the staff even thinks he can affirm that they returned to their compartment; and, as they were certainly there at Barentin, it would be necessary to admit of a double journey between their carriage and that of the President, who was separated from them by three coaches, during the few minutes it required to cover the distance, and while the train was going at full speed. Does that seem likely? I have questioned drivers and guards. All replied that long habit, alone, could give sufficient coolness and energy. In any case, the woman could not have been there. The husband must have run the risk without her, and to do what? To kill a protector who had just extricated him from serious embarrassment? No; decidedly no! The presumption is inadmissible. We must look elsewhere. Ah! Supposing a man, who got into the train at Rouen, and left it at the next station, had recently uttered threats of death against the victim—"

In his enthusiasm, he was coming to his new theory. He was on the point of saying too much about it, when the door was set ajar to make way for the head of the usher; but, before the latter could utter a word, a gloved hand sent the door wide open, and a fair lady, attired in very elegant mourning, entered the room. She was still handsome at more than fifty years of age, but displayed the opulent and expansive beauty of a goddess grown old.

"It is I, my dear magistrate. I am behind time, and you must excuse me. The roads are very bad; the three leagues from Doinville to Rouen are as good as six today."

M. Denizet had risen gallantly from his seat.

"I trust your health has been good, madam, since Sunday last?" said he.

"Very good. And you, my dear magistrate, have got over the fright my coachman gave you? The man told me the carriage got almost upset as he drove you back, before he had gone a couple of miles from the château."

"Oh! merely a jolt. I had forgotten all about it. But pray be seated, and, as I just now said to Madame de Lachesnaye, pardon me for awakening your grief with this frightful business."

"Well, as it has to be done——How do you do, Berthe? How do you do, Lachesnaye?"

It was Madame Bonnehon, the sister of the victim. She had kissed her niece, and pressed the hand of the husband. The widow, since the age of thirty, of a manufacturer who had left her a large fortune, and already wealthy in her own right, having inherited the estate at Doinville in the division of property between herself and her brother, she had led a most pleasant existence, full of flirtations. But she was so correct, and so frank in appearance, that she had remained arbiter in Rouennais society.

At times, and by taste, she had flirted with members of the bench. She had been receiving the judicial world, at the château, for the last five-and-twenty years—all that swarm of functionaries at the Law Courts whom her carriages brought from Rouen and carried back in one continual round of festivities. At present, she had not calmed down; she was credited with displaying maternal tenderness for a young substitute, son of a judge at the Court of Appeal, M. Chaumette. Whilst working for the advancement of the son, she showered invitations and acts of kindness on the father. She had, moreover, preserved an admirer of the old days, also a judge, and a bachelor, M. Desbazeilles, the literary glory of the Rouen Court of Appeal, whose cleverly turned sonnets were on every tongue. For years he had a room at Doinville. Now, although more than sixty, he still went to dinner there, as an old comrade, whose rheumatism only permitted him the recollection of his past gallantry. She thus maintained her regal state by her good grace, in spite of threatening old age, and no one thought of wresting it from her. Not before the previous winter had she felt a rival, a Madame Leboucq, the wife of another judge, whose house began to be much frequented by members of the bench. This circumstance gave a tinge of melancholy to her habitually gay life.

"Then, madam, if you will permit me," resumed M. Denizet, "I'll just ask you a few questions."

The examination of the Lachesnayes was at an end, but he did not send them away. His cold, mournful apartment was taking the aspect of a fashionable drawing-room. The phlegmatic registrar again prepared to write.

"One witness spoke of a telegram your brother is supposed to have received, summoning him at once to Doinville. We have found no trace of this wire. Did you happen to write to him, madam?"

Madame Bonnehon, quite at ease, gave her answer as if engaged in a friendly chat.

"I did not write to my brother," said she, "I was expecting him. I knew he would be coming, but no date was fixed. He usually came suddenly, and generally by a night train. As he lodged in a pavilion apart, in the park, opening on a deserted lane, we never even heard him arrive. He engaged a trap at Barentin, and only put in an appearance the following day, sometimes very late, like a neighbour in residence for a long time, who looked in on a visit. If I expected him on this occasion, it was because he had to bring me a sum of 10,000 frcs., the balance of an account we had together. He certainly had the 10,000 frcs. on him. And that is why I have always been of opinion that whoever killed him, simply did so for the purpose of robbing him."

The magistrate allowed a short silence to follow; then, looking her in the face, he inquired:

"What do you think of Madame Roubaud and her husband?"

Madame Bonnehon, making a rapid gesture of protestation, exclaimed:

"Ah! no! my dear Monsieur Denizet, you must not allow yourself to be led astray again, in regard to those worthy people. Séverine was a good little girl, very gentle, very docile even, and, moreover, delightfully pretty, which was no disadvantage. It is my opinion, as you seem anxious for me to repeat what I have already said, that she and her husband are incapable of a bad action."

He nodded in approbation. He triumphed. And he cast a glance towards Madame de Lachesnaye. The latter, piqued, took upon herself to intervene.

"I think you are very easy for them, aunt!" she exclaimed.

"Let be, Berthe," answered the latter; "we shall never agree on this subject. She was gay, fond of mirth; and quite right too. I am well aware of what you and your husband think. But really, the question of interest must have turned your heads, for you to be so astounded at this legacy of La Croix-de-Maufras from your father to poor Séverine. He brought her up, he gave her a marriage portion, and it was only natural he should mention her in his will. Did he not look upon her as his own daughter? Come! Ah! my dear, money counts for very little in the matter of happiness!"

She, indeed, having always been very rich, was absolutely disinterested. Moreover, with the refinement of a beautiful woman who was very much admired, she affected to think beauty and love the only things worth living for.

"It was Roubaud who spoke of the telegram," remarked M. de Lachesnaye drily. "If there was no telegram, the President could not have told him he had received one. Why did Roubaud lie?"

"But," exclaimed M. Denizet with feeling, "the President may have invented this story of the telegram, himself, to explain his sudden departure to the Roubauds! According to their own evidence, he was only to leave the next day; and, as he was in the same train as they were, he had to give some explanation, if he did not wish to tell them the real reason, which we all ignore, for that matter. This is without importance; it leads to naught."

Another silence ensued. When the magistrate continued, he displayed much calm and precaution.

"I am now, madam," said he, "about to approach a particularly delicate matter, and I must beg you to excuse the nature of my questions. No one respects the memory of your brother more than myself. There were certain reports, were there not? It was pretended he had irregular connections."

Madame Bonnehon was smiling again with boundless toleration.

"Oh! my dear sir, consider his age! My brother became a widower early. I never considered I had the right to interfere with what he thought fit to do. He therefore lived as he chose, without my meddling with his existence in any way. What I do know is that he maintained his rank, and that to the end, he mixed in the best society."

Berthe, choking at the idea that they should talk of her father's left-handed connections in her presence, had cast down her eyes; whilst her husband, as uneasy as herself, had moved to the window, turning his back on the company.

"Excuse me if I persist," said M. Denizet; "but was there not some story about a young housemaid you had in your service?"

"Oh! yes, Louisette. But, my dear sir, she was a depraved little creature who, at fourteen, was on terms of intimacy with an ex-convict. An attempt was made to cause a set out against my brother, in connection with her death. It was infamous. I'll tell you the whole story."

No doubt she spoke in good faith. Although she knew all about the President's habits, and had not been surprised at his tragic death, she felt the necessity of defending the high position of the family. Moreover, in regard to this unfortunate business about Louisette, if she thought him quite capable of having made advances to the young girl, she was also convinced of her precocious depravity.

"Picture to yourself a tiny thing, oh! so small, so delicate, blonde and rosy as a little angel, and gentle as well—the gentleness of a saint, to whom one would have given the sacrament without confession. Well, before she was fourteen, she became the sweetheart of a sort of brute, a quarryman, named Cabuche, who had just done five years' imprisonment for killing a man in a wine-shop. This fellow lived like a savage on the fringe of Bécourt forest, where his father, who had died of grief, had left him a hut made of trunks of trees and earth. There he obstinately worked a part of the abandoned quarries, that formerly, I believe, supplied half the stone with which Rouen is built. And it was in this lair that the girl went to join her ruffian, of whom everyone in the district were so afraid that he lived absolutely alone, like a leper. Frequently they were met together, roving through the woods, holding one another by the hand; she so dainty, he huge and bestial—briefly, a depravity one would hardly have believed possible. Naturally, I only heard of all this later. I had taken Louisette into my service almost out of charity, to do a good action. Her family, those Misards, whom

I knew to be poor, were very careful to conceal from me that they had soundly flogged the child, without being able to prevent her running off to her Cabuche, as soon as a door stood open.

"My brother had no servants of his own at Doinville. Louisette and another woman did the housework in the detached pavilion which he occupied. One morning, when she had gone there alone, she disappeared. To my mind, she had premeditated her flight long before. Perhaps her lover awaited her, and carried her off. But the horrifying part of the business was that five days later, came the report of the death of Louisette, along with details of a rape, attempted by my brother, under such monstrous circumstances that the child, out of her mind, had gone to Cabuche, where she had died of brain fever. What had happened? So many different versions were put about that it is difficult to say. For my part, I believe that Louisette, who really died of pernicious fever, for this was established by a doctor, had been guilty of some imprudence, such as sleeping out in the open air, or wandering like a vagabond among the marshes. You, my dear sir, you cannot, yourself, conceive my brother torturing this mite of a girl. It is odious, impossible."

M. Denizet had listened to this version of the business without either approving or disapproving. And Madame Bonnehon experienced some slight embarrassment in coming to an end. But, making up her mind, she added:

"Of course, I do not mean to say that my brother did not joke with her. He liked young people. He was very gay, notwithstanding his rigid exterior. Briefly, let us say he kissed her."

At this word, the Lachesnayes protested in virtuous indignation.

"Oh! aunt, aunt!"

But she shrugged her shoulders. Why should she tell the magistrate falsehoods?

"He kissed her, tickled her, perhaps. There is no crime in that. And what makes me admit this, is that the invention does not come from the quarryman. Louisette must be the falsehood-teller, the vicious creature who exaggerated things, in order to get her lover to keep her with him, perhaps. So that the latter, a brute, as I have told you, ended in good faith by imagining that we had killed his sweetheart. In fact he was mad with rage, and repeated in all the drinking-places that if the President fell into his hands, he would bleed him like a pig."

The magistrate, who had been silent up to then, interrupted her sharply.

"He said that? Are there any witnesses to prove it?"

"Oh! my dear sir, you will be able to find as many as you please. In conclusion, it was a very sad business, and caused us a great deal of annoyance. Fortunately, the position of my brother placed him beyond suspicion."

Madame Bonnehon had just discovered the new clue that M. Denizet was following, and this made her rather anxious. She preferred not to venture further, by questioning him in her turn. He had risen, and said he would not take any further advantage of the civility of the family in their painful position. By his orders, the registrar read over the examinations of the witnesses, before they signed them. They were perfectly correct, so thoroughly purged of all unnecessary and entangling words that Madame Bonnehon, with her pen in her hand, cast a glance of benevolent surprise at this pallid, bony Laurent, whom she had not yet looked at.

Then, as the magistrate accompanied her, along with her niece and nephew-in-law, to the door, she pressed his hands with the remark:

"I shall soon see you again, I hope. You know you are always welcome at Doinville. And, thanks for coming; you are one of my last faithful ones."

Her smile became quite melancholy. But her niece, who had walked out stiffly the first, had only made a slight inclination of her head to the magistrate.

When they were gone M. Denizet breathed for a moment. He remained on his feet, thinking. To his mind the matter was becoming clear. Grandmorin, whose reputation was well known, had certainly acted improperly. This made the inquiry a delicate matter. He determined to be more prudent than ever, until the communication he was expecting from the Ministry reached him. But none the less, he triumphed; anyhow he held the culprit.

When he had resumed his seat at the writing-table, he rang up the usher.

"Bring me the driver Jacques Lantier," said he.

The Roubauds were still waiting on the bench in the corridor, with fixed countenances, as if their protracted patience had set them dozing; but their faces were occasionally disturbed by a nervous twitch, and the voice of the usher, calling Jacques, seemed to make them slightly shudder, as they roused themselves. They followed the driver with expanded eyes, watching him disappear in the room of the magistrate. Then they fell into their former attitude—paler, and silent.

For the last three weeks, Jacques had been pursued by the uncomfortable feeling that all this business might end by turning against him. This was unreasonable, for there was naught he could reproach himself with, not even with keeping silent. And yet he entered the room of the examining-magistrate with that little creeping sensation of a guilty person, who fears his crime may be discovered, and he defended himself against the questions that were put to him; he was cautious in his answers, lest he might say too much. He, also, might have killed; was this not visible in his eyes? Nothing was so repugnant to him as these summonses to the justice-room. He experienced a sort of anger at receiving them, saying he was anxious to be no longer tormented by matters that did not concern him.

But, on this occasion, M. Denizet only dwelt upon the subject of the description of the murderer. Jacques, being the single witness who had caught sight of him, could alone supply precise information. But he did not depart from what he had said at his first examination. He repeated that the scene of the murder had been a vision which had barely lasted a second, a picture that came and went so rapidly that it had remained as if without form, in the abstract, in his recollection. It was merely one man slaughtering another, and nothing more. For half an hour, the judge pestered him with patient persistence, questioning him in every imaginable sense. Was he a big or a small man? Had he a beard? Did he wear his hair long or short? What were his clothes like? To what class of people did he appear to belong? And Jacques, who was uneasy, only gave vague replies.

"Look here," abruptly inquired M. Denizet, staring him full in the eyes, "if he were shown to you, would you recognise him?"

He blinked slightly, seized with anguish under the influence of that piercing gaze, searching in his very brain. His conscience spoke aloud:

"Know him? Yes, perhaps."

But, immediately, his strange fear of unconscious complicity plunged him into his evasive system again, and he continued:

"But no; I don't think so. I should never dare say positively. Just reflect! A speed of sixty miles an hour!"

With a gesture of discouragement, the magistrate was about to send him into the adjoining room to keep him at his disposal, when, changing his mind, he said:

"Remain here. Sit down."

And, ringing for the usher, he told him to introduce M. and Madame Roubaud.

As soon as they were at the doorway and saw Jacques, their eyes lost their brilliancy in a feeling of vacillating anxiety. Had he spoken? Was he detained so as to be confronted with them? All their self-assurance vanished at the knowledge that he was there, and it was in a rather low voice that they began to give their answers. But the magistrate had simply turned to their first examination. They merely had to repeat the same sentences, almost identical, whilst M. Denizet listened with bowed head, without even looking at them. All at once, he turned to Séverine.

"Madam," said he, "you told the commissary of police at the railway station, whose report I have here, that you had the idea, that a man got into the coupé at Rouen, as the train began to move."

She was thunderstruck. Why did he recall that? Was it a snare? Was he about to compare one answer with another, and so make her contradict herself? And, with a glance, she consulted her husband who prudently intervened.

"I do not think my wife was quite so positive, sir," he remarked.

"Excuse me," replied the magistrate, "you suggested the thing was possible, and madam said, 'That is certainly what happened.' Now, madam, I want to know whether you had any particular reasons for speaking as you did?"

She was now completely upset, convinced that if she did not take care, he would, from one answer to another, bring her to a confession. Howbeit, she could not remain silent.

"Oh! no, sir!" she exclaimed; "no reason. I merely said that by way of argument, because, in fact, it is difficult to explain the matter in any other way."

"Then you did not see the man. You can tell us nothing about him?"

"No, no, sir, nothing!"

M. Denizet seemed to abandon this point in the inquiry. But he at once returned to it with Roubaud.

"And you? How is it that you did not see the man, if he really got into the coupé, for, according to your own deposition, you were talking to the victim when they whistled to send the train off?"

This persistence had the effect of terrifying the assistant station-master, in his anxiety to decide what course he ought to take—whether he should set aside his invention about the other man, or obstinately cling to it. If they had proofs against himself, the theory concerning the unknown murderer could hardly be maintained, and might even aggravate his own case. He gained time, until he could understand what was going on, answering in detail with confused explanations.

"It is really unfortunate," resumed M. Denizet, "that your recollection is not more distinct, for you might help us to put an end to suspicions that have spread to several persons."

This seemed such a direct thrust at Roubaud that he felt an irresistible desire to establish his own innocence. Imagining himself discovered, he immediately made up his mind.

"This point is so thoroughly a matter of conscience," said he, "that one hesitates, you understand; nothing is more natural. Supposing I were to confess to you that I really believe I saw the man—"

The magistrate gave a gesture of triumph, thinking this commencement of frankness due to his own ability. He had frequently remarked that he knew, by experience, what strange difficulty some witnesses found in divulging what they knew, and he flattered himself he could make this class of people unburden themselves, in spite of all.

"Go on. How was he? Short, tall, about your own height?"

"Oh! no, no, much taller. At least, that was my sensation, for it was a simple sensation, an individual I am almost sure I brushed against, as I ran back to my own carriage."

"Wait a moment," said M. Denizet.

And, turning to Jacques, he inquired:

"The man you caught sight of, with the knife in his hand, was he taller than Monsieur Roubaud?"

The driver, who was impatient, for he began to be afraid he would not catch the five o'clock train, raised his eyes and examined Roubaud. And, it seemed to him, that he had never looked at him before. He was astonished to find him short, powerful, with a peculiar profile he had seen elsewhere, perhaps in a dream.

"No," he murmured, "not taller; about the same height."

But the assistant station master vehemently protested.

"Oh! much taller! At least a head."

Jacques fixed his eyes, wide open, upon him. And under the influence of this look, wherein he read increasing surprise, Roubaud became agitated, as if to change his own appearance; while his wife also followed the dull effort of memory expressed by the face of the young man. Clearly the latter was astonished. First of all, at certain analogies between Roubaud and the murderer. Then he abruptly became positive that Roubaud was the assassin, as had been reported. He now seemed troubled at this discovery, and stood there with gaping countenance, unable to decide what to do. If he spoke, the couple were lost. The eyes of Roubaud had met his. They penetrated one another to their innermost thoughts. There came a silence.

"Then you do not agree?" resumed M. Denizet, addressing Jacques. "If, in your sight, he appeared shorter, it was no doubt because he was bent in the struggle with his victim."

He also looked at the two men. It had not occurred to him to make use of this confrontation; but, by professional instinct, he felt, at this moment, that truth was flitting away. His confidence was even shaken in the Cabuche clue. Could it be possible that the Lachesnayes were right? Could it be possible that the guilty parties, contrary to all appearance, were this upright employé, and his gentle young wife?

"Did the man wear all his beard, like you?" he inquired of Roubaud.

The latter had the strength to answer in a steady voice:

"All his beard? No, no! I think he had no beard at all."

Jacques understood that the same question was about to be put to him. What should he say? He could have sworn the man had a full beard. After all, he was not interested in these people, why not tell the truth? But as he took his eyes off the husband, he met those of the wife, and in her look he read such ardent supplication, such an absolute gift of all her being, that he felt quite overcome. His old shiver came on him. Did he love her? Was she the one he could love, as one loves for love's sake, without a monstrous desire for destruction? And, at this moment, by singular counter-action in his trouble, it seemed to him that his memory had become obscured. He no longer saw the murderer in Roubaud. The vision was again vague; he doubted, and to such an extent that he mortally regretted having spoken.

M. Denizet put the question:

"Had the man a full beard like Monsieur Roubaud?"

And he replied in good faith:

"Sir, in truth, I cannot say. Once more, it was too rapid: I know nothing. I will affirm nothing."

But M. Denizet proved tenacious, for he wished to clear up the suspicion cast on the assistant station-master. He plied both Roubaud and the driver with questions, and ended by getting a complete description of the murderer from the former: tall, robust, no beard, attired in a blouse—quite the reverse of his own appearance in every particular. But the driver only answered in evasive monosyllables, which imparted strength to the statements of the other. And the magistrate returned to the conviction he had formed at first. He was on the right track. The portrait the witness drew of the assassin was so exact that each new feature added to the certainty. It was the crushing testimony of this unjustly suspected couple, that would lay the head of the culprit low.

"Step in there," said he to the Roubauds and Jacques, showing them into the adjoining room, when they had signed their examinations. "Wait till I call you."

He immediately gave orders for the prisoner to be brought in, and he was so delighted, that he went to the length of remarking to his registrar:

"Laurent, we've got him."

But the door had opened, two gendarmes had appeared bringing in a great, big fellow between twenty-five and thirty. At a sign from the magistrate, they withdrew, and Cabuche, bewildered, remained alone in the centre of the apartment, bristling like a wild beast at bay. He was a sturdy, thick-necked fellow, with enormous fists, and fair, with a very white skin. He had hardly any hair on his face, barely a golden down, curly and silken. The massive features, the low forehead, indicated the violent character of a being of limited brains, but a sort of desire to be tenderly submissive was shown in the broad mouth and square nose, as in those of a good dog.

Seized brutally in his den in the early morning, torn from his forest, exasperated at accusations which he did not understand, he had already, with his wild look and rent blouse, all the suspicious air of a prisoner in the dock—that air of a cunning bandit which the jail gives to the most honest man. Night was drawing in, the room was dark, and he had slunk into the shadow, when the usher brought a big lamp, having a globe without a shade, whose bright light lit up his countenance. Then he remained uncovered, and motionless.

M. Denizet at once fixed his great, heavy-lidded eyes on him. And he did not speak. This was the dumb engagement, the preliminary trial of his power, before entering on the warfare of the savage, the warfare of stratagem, of snares, of moral torture. This man was the culprit, everything became lawful against him. He had now no other right than that of confessing his crime.

The cross-examination commenced very slowly.

"Do you know of what crime you are accused?"

Cabuche, in a voice thick with impotent anger, grumbled:

"No one has told me, but I can easily guess. There has been enough talk about it!"

"You knew Monsieur Grandmorin?"

"Yes, yes; I knew him, only too well!"

"A girl named Louisette, your sweetheart, went as housemaid to Madame Bonnehon?"

The quarryman flew into a frightful rage. In his anger, he was ready to shed blood.

"Those who say that," he exclaimed with an oath, "are liars! Louisette was not my sweetheart."

The magistrate watched him lose his temper with curiosity. And giving a turn to the examination, remarked:

"You are very violent. You were sentenced to five years' imprisonment for killing a man in a quarrel?"

Cabuche hung his head. That sentence was his shame. He murmured:

"He struck first. I only did four years; they let me off one."

"So," resumed M. Denizet, "you pretend that the girl Louisette was not your sweetheart?"

Again Cabuche clenched his fists. Then in a low, broken voice, he replied:

"You must know that when I came back from there, she was a child, under fourteen. At that time everyone fled from me. They would have stoned me; and she, in the forest, where I was always meeting her, approached me, and talked; she was so nice—oh! so nice! It was like that we became friends; we walked about holding each other by the hand. It was so pleasant—so pleasant in those days. Of course she was growing, and I thought of her. I can't say the contrary. I was like a madman I loved her so. She was very fond of me, too, and in the end what you mean would have happened, but they separated her from me by placing her at Doinville with this lady. Then, one night, on coming from the quarry, I found her before my door, half out of her mind, so dreadfully upset that she was burning with fever. She had not dared return to her parents; she had come to die at my place. Ah! the pig! I ought to have run and bled him at once!"

The magistrate pinched his artful lips, astonished at the sincere tone of the man. Decidedly he would have to play a close game, he had to deal with a stronger hand than he had thought.

"Yes," said he, "I know all about the frightful story that you and this girl invented. Only, observe that the whole life of Monsieur Grandmorin places him above your accusations."

Agitated, his eyes round with astonishment, his hands trembling, the quarryman stammered:

"What? What did we invent? It's the others who lie, and we are accused of doing so!"

"Indeed!" observed the examining-magistrate. "Do not try to act the innocent. I have already questioned Misard, the man who married the mother of your sweetheart. I will confront him with you if it be necessary; you will see what he thinks of your tale, and be careful of your answers. We have witnesses, we know all. You had much better tell the truth."

These were his usual tactics of intimidation, even when he knew nothing, and had no witnesses.

"Now, do you deny having shouted out in public, everywhere, that you would bleed Monsieur Grandmorin?" inquired M. Denizet.

"Ah! as to that, yes, I did say it. And I said it from the bottom of my heart; for my hand was jolly well itching to do it!" answered Cabuche.

M. Denizet stopped short in surprise, having expected to meet with a system of complete denial. What! the accused owned up to the threats? What stratagem did that conceal? Fearing he might have been too hasty, he collected himself a moment, then, staring Cabuche full in the face, he abruptly put this question to him:

"What were you doing on the night of the 14th to the 15th of February?"

"I went to bed at dark, about six o'clock," replied the quarryman. "I was rather unwell, and my cousin Louis did me the service to take a load of stones to Doinville."

"Yes, your cousin was seen, with the cart, passing over the line at the level crossing," remarked the magistrate; "but on being questioned, he could only make one reply, namely, that you left him about noon, and he did not see you again. Prove to me that you were in bed at six o'clock."

"Look here, that's stupid," protested Cabuche. "I cannot prove that. I live all alone in a house at the edge of the forest. I was there, I say so, and nothing more."

Then M. Denizet decided on playing his trump card of assertion, which was calculated to impose on the party. His face, by a tension of will, became rigid, whilst his mouth performed the scene.

"I am going to tell you what you did on the night of February 14th," said he. "At three o'clock in the afternoon, you took the train for Rouen, at Barentin, with what object the inquiry has not revealed. You had the intention of returning by the Paris train, which stops at Rouen at 9.3; and while on the platform, amid the crowd, you caught sight of Monsieur Grandmorin in his coupé. Observe that I am willing to admit there was no laying in wait for the victim, that the idea of the crime only occurred to you when you saw him. You entered the coupé, thanks to the crush, and waited until you were in the Malaunay tunnel. But you miscalculated the time, for the train was issuing from the tunnel when you dealt the blow. And you threw out the corpse, and you left the train at Barentin, after having got rid of the travelling-rug as well. That is what you did."

He watched for the slightest ripple on the rosy face of Cabuche, and was irritated when the latter, who had been very attentive at first, ended by bursting into a hearty laugh.

"What's that you're relating?" he exclaimed. "If I'd struck the blow I'd say so."

Then he quietly added:

"I did not do it, but I ought to have done it. Yes, I'm sorry I didn't."

And that was all M. Denizet could get out of him. In vain did he repeat his questions, returning ten times to the same points by different tactics. No; always no! it was not he. He shrugged his shoulders, saying the idea was stupid. On arresting him they had searched the hovel, without discovering either weapon, banknotes, or watch. But they had laid hands on a pair of trousers, soiled with a few drops of blood—an overwhelming proof.

Again he began to laugh. That was another pretty yarn! A rabbit, caught in a noose, had bled down his leg! And it was the magistrate who, in his unswerving conviction of the guilt of the prisoner, was losing ground by the display of too much professional astuteness, by complicating matters, by deposing simple truth. This man of small brains, incapable of holding his own in an effort of cunning, of invincible strength when he said no, always no, almost drove him crazy; for he was positive of the culpability of the man, and each fresh denial made him the more indignant at what he looked upon as obstinate perseverance in savagery and lies. He would force him into contradicting himself.

"So you deny it?" he said.

"Of course I do, because it was not me," said Cabuche. "Had it been, ah! I should be only too proud, I should say it was me."

M. Denizet abruptly rose, and opened the door of the small adjoining room. When he had summoned Jacques, he inquired:

"Do you recognise this man?"

"I know him," answered the driver, surprised. "I've seen him formerly at the Misards."

"No, no," said the magistrate. "Do you recognise him as the man in the coupé, the murderer?"

At once, Jacques became circumspect. As a matter of fact, he did not recognise the man. The other seemed to him shorter, darker. He was about to say so, when it struck him that even this might be going too far. And he continued evasively.

"I don't know, I can't say; I assure you, sir, that I cannot say."

M. Denizet, without waiting, called the Roubauds in their turn, and put the same question to them.

"Do you recognise this man?"

Cabuche continued smiling. He was not surprised. He nodded to Séverine, whom he had known as a young girl when she resided at La Croix-de-Maufras. But she and her husband had felt a pang, on perceiving him there. They understood. This was the man taken into custody, of whom Jacques had spoken, the prisoner who had caused this fresh examination. And Roubaud was astounded, terrified at the resemblance of this fellow to the imaginary murderer, whose description he had invented, the reverse of his own. It was pure chance, but it so troubled him that he hesitated to reply.

"Come, do you recognise him?" repeated the magistrate.

"Sir," answered Roubaud, "I can only say again that it was a simple sensation, an individual who brushed against me. Of course this man is tall, like the other, and he is fair, and has no beard."

"Anyhow, do you recognise him?" asked M. Denizet again.

"I cannot say positively. But there is a resemblance, a good deal of resemblance, certainly."

This time Cabuche began to swear. He had had enough of these yarns. As he was not the culprit, he wanted to be off. And the blood flying to his head, he struck the table with his fists. He became so terrible that the gendarmes, who were called in, led him away. But in presence of this violence, of this leap of the beast who dashes forward

ÉMILE ZOLA

when attacked, M. Denizet triumphed. His conviction was now firmly established, and he allowed this to be seen.

"Did you notice his eyes?" he inquired. "It's by the eyes that I tell them. Ah! his measure is full. We've got him!"

The Roubauds, remaining motionless, exchanged glances. What now? It was all over. As justice had the culprit in its grip, they were saved. They felt a trifle bewildered, their consciences were pricked at the part events had just compelled them to play. But overwhelmed with joy, they made short work of their scruples, and they smiled at Jacques. Considerably relieved, eager for the open air, they were waiting for the magistrate to dismiss all three of them, when the usher brought him a letter.

In a moment M. Denizet, oblivious of the three witnesses, was at his writing-table, perusing the communication. It was the letter from the Ministry containing the indications he should have had the patience to await before resuming the inquiry. What he read must have lessened his feeling of triumph, for his countenance, little by little, became frigid, and resumed its sad immobility. At a certain moment he raised his head, to cast a glance sideways at the Roubauds, as if one of the phrases reminded him of them. The latter, bereft of their brief joy, once more became a prey to uneasiness, feeling themselves caught again.

Why had he looked at them? Had the three lines of writing—that clumsy note which haunted them—been found in Paris? Séverine was well acquainted with M. Camy-Lamotte, having frequently seen him at the house of the President, and she was aware that he had been entrusted with the duty of sorting his papers. Roubaud was tortured by the keenest regret that the idea had not occurred to him to dispatch his wife to Paris, where she might have paid useful visits, and at the least made sure of the support of the secretary to the Ministry, in case the company, annoyed at the nasty rumours in circulation, should think of dismissing him. Thenceforth, neither of them took their eyes off the magistrate, and their anxiety increased as they noticed him become gloomy, visibly disconcerted at this letter which upset all his good day's work.

At last, M. Denizet left the letter, and for a moment remained absorbed, his eyes wide open, resting on the Roubauds and Jacques. Then, submitting to the inevitable, speaking aloud to himself, he exclaimed:

"Well, we shall see! We shall have to return to all this! You can withdraw."

But as the three were going out, he could not resist the desire to learn more, to throw light on the grave point which destroyed his new theory, although he was recommended to do nothing further, without previously coming to an understanding with the authorities.

"No; you remain here a minute," said he, addressing the driver. "I've another question to put to you."

The Roubauds stopped in the corridor. They were free, and yet they could not go. Something detained them there: the anguish to learn what was passing in the magistrate's room, the physical impossibility to depart before ascertaining from Jacques, what the other question was that had been put to him. They turned and turned, they beat time with their worn out legs; and they found themselves again side by side, on the bench where they had already waited for hours. There they sat, downcast and silent.

When the driver reappeared, Roubaud rose with effort.

"We were waiting for you," said he. "We'll go to the station together. Well?"

But Jacques turned his head aside, in embarrassment, as if wishing to avoid the eyes of Séverine which were fixed on him.

"He's all at sea, floundering about," he ended by saying. "Look here, he is now asking me whether there were not two who did the deed. And, as at Havre, I spoke of a black mass weighing on the old chap's legs. He questioned me on the point; he seems to fancy it was only the rug. Then he sent for it, and I had to express an opinion. Well, now, yes, when I come to think, perhaps it was the rug."

The Roubauds shuddered. They were on their track; one word from this man might ruin them. He certainly knew, and he would end by talking. And all three, the woman between the two men, left the Law Courts in silence. In the street the assistant station-master observed: "By the way, comrade, my wife will be obliged to go to Paris, for a day, on business. It would be very good of you, if you would look after her, should she be in need of someone."

V

Precisely at 11.15, the advertised time, the signalman at the Pont de l'Europe, gave the two regulation blows of the horn, to announce the Havre express, which issued from the Batignolles tunnel. Soon afterwards the turn-tables rattled, and the train entered the station with a short whistle, grating on the brakes, smoking, shining, dripping with the beating rain that had not ceased since leaving Rouen.

The porters had not yet turned the handles of the doors, when one of them opened, and Séverine sprang lightly to the platform, before the train had stopped. Her carriage was at the end. To reach the locomotive, she had to hurry through the swarm of passengers, embarrassed by children and packages, who had suddenly left the compartments. Jacques stood there, erect on the foot-plate, waiting to go to the engine-house; while Pecqueux wiped the brasswork with a cloth.

"So it is understood," said she, on tiptoe. "I will be at the Rue Cardinet at three o'clock, and you will have the kindness to introduce me to your chief, so that I may thank him."

This was the pretext imagined by Roubaud: a visit to the head of the depôt at Batignolles, to thank him for some vague service he had rendered. In this manner she would find herself confided to the good friendship of the driver. She could strengthen the bonds, and exert her influence over him.

But Jacques, black with coal, drenched with water, exhausted by the struggle against rain and wind, stared at her with his harsh eyes, without answering. On leaving Havre, he had been unable to refuse the request of the husband to look after her; and this idea of finding himself alone in her company upset him, for he now felt that he was very decidedly falling in love with her.

"Is that right?" she resumed, smiling, with her sweet, caressing look, overcoming her surprise and slight repugnance at finding him so dirty, barely recognisable. "Is that right? I shall rely on your being there."

And, as she raised herself a little higher, resting her gloved hand on one of the iron handles, Pecqueux obligingly interfered:

"Take care, you will dirty yourself," said he.

Then Jacques had to answer, and he did so in a surly tone.

"Yes, Rue Cardinet, unless I get drowned in this abominable rain. What horrid weather!"

She felt touched at his wretched appearance, and added, as if he had suffered solely for her:

"Oh! what a dreadful state you are in! And I was so comfortable. I was thinking of you, you know; and that deluge of rain quite distressed me. I felt very pleased at the idea that you were bringing me up this morning, and would take me back tonight, by the express."

But this familiarity, so tender and so nice, only seemed to trouble him the more. He appeared relieved when a voice shouted, "Back!" Promptly he blew the whistle, while the fireman made a sign to the young woman to stand back.

"At three o'clock!"

"Yes; at three o'clock!"

And as the locomotive moved along, Séverine left the platform, the last of the passengers. Outside, in the Rue d'Amsterdam, as she was about to open her umbrella, she was glad to find it had ceased raining. She walked down to the Place du Havre, where she stood reflecting for an instant, and at last decided that it would be best to lunch at once. It was twenty-five minutes past eleven. She stepped into a little restaurant at the corner of the Rue Saint Lazare, where she ordered a couple of fried eggs and a cutlet. Then, whilst eating very slowly, she fell into reflections that had been haunting her for weeks, her face pale and cloudy, and bereft of its docile, seductive smile.

It was on the previous evening, two days after their examination at Rouen, that Roubaud, judging it dangerous to wait, had resolved to send her on a visit to M. Camy-Lamotte, not at the Ministry, but at his private residence, Rue du Rocher, where he occupied a house close to that of the late President Grandmorin. She knew she would find him there at one o'clock, and she did not hurry. She was preparing what she should say, endeavouring to foresee what he would answer, so as not to get troubled at anything that might transpire.

The evening before, a new cause of anxiety had hastened her journey. They had learnt, from gossip at the station, that Madame Lebleu and Philomène were relating everywhere that the company was going to dismiss Roubaud, who was considered involved. And the worst of it was that M. Dabadie, who had been questioned point blank, had not answered no, which gave considerable weight to the news. From that moment it became urgent that she should hurry off to Paris to plead their cause, and particularly to solicit the protection of the powerful personage in question, as on former occasions she had sought that of the President.

But, apart from this request, which anyhow would serve to explain her visit, there was a more imperative motive—a burning and insatiable hankering to know, that hankering which drives the criminal to give himself away rather than remain ignorant. The uncertainty was killing them, now that they felt themselves discovered, since Jacques had told them of the suspicion which the judicial authorities seemed to entertain of there being an accomplice. They were lost in conjectures: had the letter been found, the facts established? Hour by hour they expected a search would be made at their lodgings, that they would be arrested; and their burden became so heavy, the least occurrence in their surroundings assumed an air of such alarming menace, that in the end they preferred the catastrophe to this constant apprehension, to have a certainty and no longer suffer.

When Séverine had finished her cutlet, she was so absorbed that she awoke almost with a start to reality, astonished to find herself in a public room. Everything seemed bitter. Her food stuck in her throat, and she had no heart to take coffee. Although she had eaten slowly, it was barely a quarter past twelve, when she left the restaurant. Another three-quarters of an hour to kill! She who adored Paris, who was so fond of rambling through the streets, freely, on the rare occasions when she visited the capital, now felt lost, timid, and was full of impatience to have done with the place and hide herself. The pavements were already drying; a warm wind was driving away the last clouds.

Taking the Rue Tronchet, she found herself at the flower-market of the Madeleine, one of those March markets, all abloom with primroses and azaleas, in the dull days of expiring winter. She sauntered for half an hour, amidst this premature spring, resuming her vague reflections, thinking of Jacques as an enemy whom she must disarm. It seemed to her that she had paid her visit to the Rue du Rocher, that all had gone well in that quarter, that the only thing remaining was to ensure the silence of this man; and this was a complicated undertaking that bewildered her, and set her head labouring at romantic plans. But these caused her no worry, no terror; on the contrary she experienced a sweet, soothing feeling. Then, abruptly, she saw the time by a clock at a kiosk: ten minutes past one. She had not yet performed her errand; and, harshly recalled to the agony of reality, she hastened in the direction of the Rue du Rocher.

The residence of M. Camy-Lamotte was at the corner of this street and the Rue de Naples, and Séverine had to pass by the house of

Grandmorin, which stood silent, tenantless, and with closed shutters. Raising her eyes, she hurried on. She recollected her last visit. The great house towered up, terrible, before her, and when a little further on, she instinctively turned round, to look behind, like a person pursued by the shouts of a crowd, she was startled to perceive M. Denizet, the examining-magistrate at Rouen, who was also coming up the street, on the opposite side of the way. The thrill she experienced brought her to a standstill. Had he noticed her casting a glance at the house? He was walking along quietly, and she allowed him to get ahead of her, following him in great trouble. She received another shock when she saw him ring at the corner of the Rue de Naples, at the residence of M. Camy-Lamotte.

She felt terrified. She would never dare enter now. She turned on her heel, cut through the Rue d'Edimbourg, and descended as far as the Pont de l'Europe. It was not until then, that she felt herself secure. And, quite distracted, not knowing where to go nor what to do, she leant motionless against one of the balustrades, gazing below, across the iron sheds, at the vast station, where the trains were constantly performing evolutions. She followed them with her anxious eyes. She thought the magistrate must assuredly have gone to see M. Camy-Lamotte on this business, that the two men were talking about her, and that her fate was being settled at that very minute.

Then, in despair, she was tormented by the desire to cast herself at once under a train rather than return to the Rue du Rocher. Just then a train was issuing from beneath the iron marquee of the main lines. She watched it coming and pass below her, puffing in her face a tepid cloud of white steam. Then the stupid uselessness of her journey, the frightful anguish she would carry away with her, should she fail to have the energy to go and find out something certain, were impressed on her mind with such vigour, that she gave herself five minutes to gain courage.

Engines were whistling. Her eyes followed a small one, branching off a train that served the environs; and, then looking up towards the left, she recognised above the courtyard of the small parcels department, at the very top of the house in the Impasse d'Amsterdam, the window of Mother Victoire—that window on whose rail she again saw herself leaning with her husband, before the abominable scene that had caused their calamity. This brought home to her the danger of her position with such a keen pang of pain, that she suddenly felt ready to encounter anything, to put an end to the business. The blasts of the horn, and the prolonged rumbling noise deafened her, while thick smoke flying over the great, clear, Parisian sky, barred the horizon. And she again took the road to the Rue du Rocher, wending her way with the feelings of a person going to commit suicide, stepping out with precipitation, in sudden fear lest she might find no one there.

When Séverine had touched the bell a renewed feeling of terror turned her icy cold. But a footman, after taking her name, had already offered her a seat in an antechamber; and through the doors, gently set ajar, she very distinctly heard the lively conversation of two voices. Then followed profound and absolute silence. She could distinguish naught but the dull throbbing of her temples. And she said to herself that the magistrate must still be in conference, and that she would no doubt be kept waiting a long time; and this idea of waiting seemed intolerable. All at once, she met with a surprise; the footman came to her, and showed her in. The magistrate had certainly not gone. She conjectured he was there, hidden behind a door.

She found herself in a large study, with black furniture, a thick carpet, and heavy door-hangings, so severe and so completely closed, that not a sound from the outside could penetrate within. Nevertheless, there were some flowers, some pale roses in a bronze corbeil, and this indicated a sort of concealed grace, a taste for amiable life beneath all this severity. The master of the house was on his feet, very correctly attired in a frock-coat; he also looked severe with his pinched face, which his greyish whiskers rendered slightly fuller. But he had all the elegance of a former beau who had remained slim, and a demeanour that one felt would be pleasant, freed from the stiffness that his official position made him assume. In the subdued light of the apartment, he looked very tall.

Séverine, on entering, felt oppressed by the close atmosphere caused by the hangings, and she saw no one but M. Camy-Lamotte, who watched her approach. He made no motion to invite her to be seated, and he was careful not to open his mouth the first, waiting for her to explain the motive of her visit. This prolonged the silence. But, as the result of a violent reaction, she all at once found she was mistress of herself in the peril, and remained very calm, and very prudent.

"Sir," said she, "you will excuse me if I make so bold as to come and solicit your goodwill. You are aware of the irreparable loss I have suffered, and, abandoned as I now am, I have had the courage to think of you to defend us, to continue to give us a little of the same support as your friend, my deeply regretted protector."

M. Camy-Lamotte was then obliged to wave his hand to a seat, for she had spoken in a strain that was perfect, without exaggerated humility or grief, with the innate art of feminine hypocrisy; but he still maintained silence. He had himself sat down, still waiting. Seeing she must explain, she continued:

"Allow me to refresh your memory by reminding you that I have had the honour of seeing you at Doinville. Ah! those were happy days for me! At present, bad times have come, and I have no one but you, sir. I implore you, in the name of him we have lost, you who were his intimate friend, to complete his good work, to take his place beside us."

He listened, he looked at her, and all his suspicions were wavering; she seemed so natural, so charming in her expressions of regret and supplication. It had struck him that the letter he had found among the papers of Grandmorin, those two unsigned lines, could only have come from her, whom he knew to be intimate with the President, and just now the mere mention of her visit had completely convinced him. He had only interrupted his interview with the magistrate, to confirm his conviction. But how could he think her guilty seeing her as she appeared—so quiet and so sweet?

He wished to set his mind at rest. And while maintaining an air of severity, he said:

"Tell me what it is all about, madam. I remember perfectly. I shall only be too happy to be of use to you, if there is no impediment."

Séverine then related, very plainly, that her husband was threatened with dismissal. They were very jealous of him on account of his merit, and of the high patronage which hitherto had covered him. Now, thinking him without support, they hoped to triumph, and redoubled their efforts. Nevertheless, she mentioned no names. She spoke in measured terms in spite of the imminent peril. For her to have decided on making the journey to Paris, she must have been convinced of the necessity of acting as rapidly as possible. Perhaps tomorrow it would be no longer time; it was immediately that she required help and succour. She related all this with such an abundance of logical facts, and good reasons, that it seemed to him really impossible that she should have taken the trouble to come up with any other object.

M. Camy-Lamotte studied her even to the slight, almost imperceptible quiver of her lips, and he struck the first blow.

"But why should the company dismiss your husband? They have nothing grave to reproach him with," said he.

Neither did her eyes leave him. She sat watching the faintest lines on his face, wondering if he had found the letter; and, notwithstanding the apparent innocence of the question, she abruptly became convinced that the letter was there, in one of the pieces of furniture in that study. He knew all about it, for he had set a trap for her, anxious to learn whether she would dare mention the real reasons for his dismissal. Moreover, he had too forcibly accentuated his tone, and she felt herself probed to the innermost recesses of her being, by his sparkless eyes of a worn-out man.

Bravely she advanced to the peril.

"Dear me, sir!" she said; "it sounds very monstrous, but they suspected us of killing our benefactor, on account of that unfortunate will. We had no difficulty in proving our innocence, only there always remains something of these abominable accusations, and the company no doubt fears the scandal."

He was again surprised, thrown off his guard, by this frankness, particularly by the sincerity of her accent. Besides, having at first glance considered her face merely passable, he began to find her extremely seductive, with the complacent submissiveness of her blue eyes, set off by the energy of her raven hair. She was really very charming, very refined, and he allowed the smile of an amateur of feminine charms, no longer interested in such matters, to mingle with the grand, cold manner of the functionary who had such a disagreeable affair on his hands.

But Séverine, with the bravado of the woman who feels her strength, had the imprudence to add:

"Persons like ourselves do not kill for money. There would have been some other motive, and there was none."

He looked at her, and saw the corners of her mouth quiver. It was she. Thenceforth his conviction was absolute. And she understood, immediately, that she had given herself up, at the way in which he had ceased to smile, and at his nervously pinched chin. She felt like fainting, as if all her being was abandoning her. Nevertheless, she remained on her chair, her bust straight. She heard her voice continuing to converse in the same even tone, uttering the words it was necessary to say. The conversation pursued its course; but, henceforth, neither had anything further to learn. He had the letter. It was she who had written it.

"Madam," he at last resumed, "I do not refuse to intercede with the company, if you are really worthy of interest. It so happens that I am expecting the traffic-manager this afternoon, on some other business. Only, I shall require a few notes. Look here, just write me down the name, the age, the record of service, of your husband; briefly, all that is necessary to post me up in regard to your position."

And he pushed a small occasional-table towards her, ceasing to look at her, so as not to frighten her too much. She shuddered. He wanted a page of her handwriting, in order to compare it with the letter. For a moment she despairingly sought a pretext, resolved not to write. Then she reflected: what was the good of that, as he knew? It would be easy to obtain a few lines she had penned. Without any visible discomposure, in the simplest manner in the world, she wrote down what he asked her for; while he, standing up behind her, recognised the writing perfectly, although taller and less shaky than that in the note. And he ended by thinking this slim little woman very brave. He smiled again, now she was unable to see him, with that smile of the man who is no longer touched by anything, save the charm, and whom experience in everything has made insouciant. After all, it was not worth the trouble to be just. He only watched over the decorative part of the régime he served.

"Very well, madam," said he, "give me this. I will make inquiries; I will do the best I can."

"I am very much obliged to you, sir," she answered. "So you will see that my husband is maintained in his position? I may consider the affair arranged?"

"Ah! no, indeed!" he exclaimed; "I bind myself to nothing. I shall have to see, to think the matter over."

In fact he was hesitating. He did not know what course he would follow in regard to the couple. And she was in anguish, since she felt herself at his mercy: this hesitation, this alternative of being saved or ruined by him, without being able to guess the reasons that would influence him in his decision, drove her crazy.

"Oh! sir! think how tormented we are! You will not let me leave without a certainty," she pleaded.

"Indeed, madam, I can do nothing. You must wait," said he.

He led her to the door. She was going away in despair, beside herself, on the point of confessing everything, openly, feeling the immediate necessity of forcing him to say distinctly what he intended doing with them. To remain a minute longer, hoping to find a subterfuge, she exclaimed:

"Ah! I forgot! I wished to ask your advice about that wretched will. Do you think we ought to refuse the legacy?"

"The law is on your side," he prudently answered. "It is a matter of appreciation, and of circumstances."

She was on the threshold of the door, and she made a final effort.

"Sir," said she, "do not allow me to leave thus! Tell me if I may hope."

With a gesture of abandonment, she had seized his hand. He drew it away. But she looked at him with her beautiful eyes so ardent with prayer, that he was stirred.

"Very well, then, return here at five o'clock. Perhaps I may have something to tell you."

She went off. She quitted the house in still greater agony than on entering it. The situation had become clear, her fate remained in suspense. She was threatened with arrest which might take place at once. How could she keep alive until five o'clock? Suddenly she thought of Jacques, whom she had forgotten. He was another who might be her ruin, if they took her in charge! Although it was barely half-past two, she hastened to ascend the Rue du Rocher, in the direction of the Rue Cardinet.

M. Camy-Lamotte, left alone, stood before his writing-table. A familiar figure at the Tuileries, where his functions as chief secretary to the Ministry of Justice, caused him to be summoned almost daily, as powerful as the Minister himself, and even entrusted with more delicate duties, he was aware how irritating and alarming this Grandmorin case proved in high quarters. The opposition newspapers continued to carry on a noisy campaign; some accusing the police of being so busy with political business, that they had no time to arrest murderers; the others, probing the life of the President, gave their readers to understand that he belonged to the Court, where the lowest kind of debauchery prevailed; and this campaign really became disastrous, as the time for the elections approached. And so it had been formally intimated to the chief secretary, that he must bring the business to a termination as rapidly as possible, no matter how. The Minister, having relieved himself of this delicate affair by passing it on to him, he found himself sole arbiter of the decision to be taken, but on his own responsibility, it is true; a matter that required looking into, for he had no idea of paying for the others, should he prove inexpert.

M. Camy-Lamotte, still thinking, went and opened the door of the adjoining room where M. Denizet was waiting. And the latter, who had overheard everything, exclaimed on entering:

"What did I say? It is wrong to suspect those people. This woman is evidently only thinking of saving her husband from possible dismissal. She did not utter a single word that could arouse suspicion."

The chief secretary did not answer at once. All absorbed, his eyes on the magistrate, struck by his heavy, thin-lipped face, he was now thinking of that magistracy, which he held in his hand, as occult chief of its members, and he felt astonished that it was still so worthy in its poverty, so intelligent in its professional torpidity. But really, this gentleman, however sharp he might fancy himself, with his eyes veiled with thick lids, was tenacious in his conviction, when he thought he had got hold of the truth.

"So," resumed M. Camy-Lamotte, "you persist in believing in the guilt of this Cabuche?"

M. Denizet started in astonishment.

"Oh! certainly!" said he; "everything is against him! I enumerated the proofs to you. I may say they are classic, for not one is wanting. I did not fail to look for an accomplice, a woman in the coupé, as you suggested. This seemed to agree with the evidence of a driver, a man who caught a glimpse of the murder scene. But skilfully cross-questioned by me, this man did not persist in his first statement, and he even recognised the travelling-rug, as being the dark bundle he had referred to. Oh! yes; Cabuche is certainly the culprit, and the more so, as, if we cannot fix it on him, we have no one else."

Up to then, the chief secretary had delayed bringing the written proof he possessed to the knowledge of the magistrate; and now that he had formed a conviction, he was still less eager to establish the truth. What was the use of upsetting the false clue of the prosecution, if the real clue was to lead to greater embarrassments? All this would have to be considered in the first instance.

"Very well," he resumed, with that smile of the worn-out man, "I am willing to admit you are right. I only sent for you for the purpose of discussing certain grave points. This is an exceptional case, and it has now become quite political; you feel this, do you not? We shall therefore, perhaps, find ourselves compelled to act as government men. Come, frankly, this girl, the sweetheart of Cabuche, was victimised, eh?"

　　　　　　　　　　　　　　　　　　ÉMILE ZOLA

The magistrate gave the pout of a cunning fellow, whilst his eyes became half lost in his lids.

"If you ask me," said he, "I think the President put her in a great fright, and this will assuredly come out at the trial. Moreover, if the defence is entrusted to a lawyer of the opposition, we may expect a regular avalanche of tiresome tales; for there is no lack of these stories down there, in our part of the country."

This Denizet was not so stupid when free from the routine of the profession, where he soared on high in his unlimited perspicacity and mighty power. He understood why he had been summoned to the private residence of the chief secretary, in preference to the Ministry of Justice.

"Briefly," concluded he, seeing that M. Camy-Lamotte did not open his mouth, "we shall have a rather nasty business."

The chief secretary confined himself to tossing his head. He was engaged in calculating the results of the trial of the Roubauds. It was a dead certainty that if the husband were brought up at the assizes, he would relate all: how his wife had been led astray, she also, when a young girl, and the intrigues that followed, and the jealous rage that had urged him on to murder, without taking into consideration that, in this instance, it was not a question of a domestic and a convicted criminal. This assistant station-master, married to this pretty woman, would mix up a number of people of independent means, and others connected with the railways, in the business. Then, who could tell where the affairs of a man like the President would lead them? They might perhaps fall into unforeseen abominations. No, decidedly; the case against the Roubauds, the real culprits, was more objectionable than the other. He had made up his mind; he put it absolutely aside. If they had to choose between the two, he was in favour of proceeding with the prosecution of the innocent Cabuche.

"I give in to your theory," he at last said to M. Denizet. "There are, indeed, strong presumptions against the quarryman, if so be he had a legitimate vengeance to satisfy; but all this is very sad, and what a quantity of mud will be thrown about! Of course I know that justice should remain indifferent to consequences, and that, soaring above the interests—"

He concluded his phrase with a gesture, while the magistrate, silent in turn, awaited with gloomy countenance, the orders he felt were coming. From the moment they accepted his idea of the truth—that creation of his own intelligence, he was ready to sacrifice the idea of justice to the requirements of the government. But the secretary, notwithstanding his usual dexterity in this kind of transaction, hastened on a little, spoke too rapidly, like a chief in the habit of being obeyed.

"Finally, what is desired is that you should desist from further proceedings," said he. "Arrange matters so that the case may be shelved."

"Excuse me, sir," answered M. Denizet, "I am no longer master of the case; it rests with my conscience."

At once M. Camy-Lamotte smiled, becoming correct again, with an easy and polite bearing that seemed full of mockery.

"No doubt; and it is to your conscience that I appeal. I leave you to take the decision it may dictate, convinced that you will equitably weigh both sides, in view of the triumph of healthy doctrines, and public morality. You know, better than I can tell you, that it is sometimes heroic to accept one evil, rather than fall into another that is worse. Briefly, one only appeals to you as a good citizen, an upright man. No one thinks of interfering with your independence, and that is why I repeat that you are absolute master in the matter, as, for that matter, it has been provided by law."

Jealous of this illimited power, particularly when prepared to make a bad use of it, the magistrate welcomed each of these sentences with a nod of satisfaction.

"Besides," continued the other, redoubling his good grace, with an exaggeration that was becoming sarcastic, "we know whom we address. We have long been watching your efforts; and I may tell you that we should call you without delay to Paris, were there a vacancy."

M. Denizet made a movement. What was this? If he rendered the service required of him, they would not satisfy his great ambition, his dream of a seat at Paris. But M. Camy-Lamotte, who understood, lost no time in adding:

"Your place is marked. It is a question of time. Only, as I have commenced to be indiscreet, I am happy to be able to tell you that your name is down for the cross, on the Emperor's next fête-day."

The magistrate reflected a moment. He would have preferred advancement, for he reckoned that it carried with it an increase of about 166 frcs., or £6 16s., a month in salary. And, in the decent misery in which he lived, this meant greater comfort, his wardrobe renewed, his servant Mélanie better fed, and in consequence better tempered; but the cross, nevertheless, was worth having. Then, he had a promise. And he, who would not have sold himself, nurtured in the tradition of this magistracy, upright and mediocre, he at once yielded to a simple hope, to the vague promise that the administration made to favour him. The judicial function was nothing more than a trade like others, and he bore along the burden of advancement, in the quality of a humble solicitant, ever ready to bend to the orders of authority.

"I feel very much touched at the honour," he murmured. "Kindly say so to the Minister."

He had risen, feeling that anything they might add, would cause uneasiness.

"So," he concluded, his eyes dim, his face expressionless, "I shall complete my inquiry, bearing your scruples in mind. Of course, if we have not absolute proof against this Cabuche, it would be better not to risk the useless scandal of a trial. He shall be set at liberty and watched."

The chief secretary, on the threshold of his study, made a final display of effusive amiability.

"Monsieur Denizet," said he, "we entirely rely on your great tact and high rectitude."

M. Camy-Lamotte, alone again, had the curiosity which, however, was useless, now, to compare the page penned by Séverine with the unsigned note he had found among the papers of President Grandmorin. The resemblance proved complete. He folded up the letter and put it carefully away, for, if he had not breathed a word about it to the examining-magistrate, he nevertheless considered such an arm worth keeping. And as he recalled the profile of this little woman, so delicate, and yet so strong in her nervous resistance, he gave an indulgent, mocking shrug of the shoulders. Ah! those creatures, when they mean it!

When Séverine reached the Rue Cardinet at twenty minutes to three, to keep her appointment with Jacques, she found herself before her time. He occupied a small room right at the top of a great house, to which he only ascended at night for the purpose of sleeping. And he slept out twice a week, on the two nights he passed at Havre, between the evening and morning express. On that particular day, however, drenched with rain, broken down with fatigue, he had gone there and thrown himself on his bed. So that Séverine would perhaps have waited for him in vain, had not a quarrel in an adjoining apartment, a husband brutalising his shrieking wife, awakened him. He had washed and dressed in a very bad humour, having recognised her below, on the pavement, while looking out of his garret window.

"So it's you at last!" she exclaimed, when she saw him issue from the front door. "I was afraid I had misunderstood. You really did tell me at the corner of the Rue Saussure—"

And without awaiting his answer, raising her eyes to the house, she remarked:

"So it's there you live?"

Without telling her, he had made the appointment before his own door, because the depôt where they had to go together, was opposite. But her question worried him. He imagined she was going to take advantage of their good fellowship, to ask him to let her see his room, which was so simply furnished, and in such disorder, that he felt ashamed of it.

"Oh! I don't live there!" he replied; "I perch. Let us be quick, I am afraid the chief may have already gone out!"

And so it happened, for when they presented themselves at the small house which the latter occupied behind the depôt, within the station walls, they did not find him. In vain they went from shed to shed, everywhere they were told to return at about half-past four, if they wished to be sure of catching him at the repairing workshops.

"Very well, we will return," said Séverine.

Then, when she was again outside, alone in the company of Jacques, she remarked:

"If you are free, perhaps you will not mind if I remain and wait with you?"

He could not refuse; and, moreover, notwithstanding the gloomy anxiety she caused, she exercised such a great and ever-increasing charm over him, that the sullen attitude he had made up his mind to observe, vanished at her sweet glances. This one, with her long, tender, timid face, must love like a faithful hound, whom one would not even have the courage to thrash.

"Of course I shall not leave you," he answered, in a less surly tone; "only we have more than an hour to get through. Would you like to go to a café?"

She smiled, delighted to find him more cordial. Vivaciously she protested:

"Oh! no, no; I don't want to shut myself up! I prefer walking on your arm through the streets, anywhere you like."

And gracefully she took his arm of her own accord. Now that he was free from the dirt of the journey, she thought him superior-looking, in his attire of a clerk in easy circumstances, and with his gentlemanly bearing, enhanced by a look of independent pride, due to his life in the open air and the daily habit of facing danger. She had never noticed so distinctly that he was handsome, with his regular, round countenance, and his black moustache on a white skin. His fleeting eyes, those eyes studded with golden sparks, which turned away from her, alone continued to cause her distrust. If he avoided looking her straight in the face, was it because he would not bind himself to anything, because he wished to retain his freedom to act as he pleased, even against her?

From that moment, in her uncertainty as to his intentions, shuddering each time she thought of that study in the Rue du Rocher where her life lay in the balance, she had but one aim—to feel that this man, who gave her his arm, belonged to her entirely; to obtain, that when she raised her head, his eyes should look deeply into her own. Then he would be her property. She did not love him; she did not even think of such a thing. She was simply doing her utmost to make him her creature, so that she need fear him no more.

They walked for a few minutes without speaking, amid the continual stream of passers-by who obstruct this populous quarter. Ever and anon they were compelled to leave the pavement; they crossed the road among the vehicles. Then they found themselves at the Square des Batignolles, which is almost deserted at this time of year. The sky, cleansed by the deluge of the morning, wore a tint of very soft blue, and the lilac-bushes were budding in the gentle March sun.

"Shall we go into the garden?" inquired Séverine. "All this crowd makes me giddy."

Jacques had intended entering the enclosure of his own accord, unconscious of his desire to have her more to himself, far from the multitude of people.

"As you like," said he. "Let us go in."

Slowly they continued walking beside the grass, between the leafless trees. A few women were out with babies in long clothes, and persons were hurrying across the garden to make a short cut. Jacques and Séverine took the brook at a stride, and ascended among the rocks. Then, retracing their steps, not knowing where to go, they passed through a cluster of pines, whose lasting dark green foliage shone in the sun. And there, in this solitary corner, stood a bench hidden from view. They sat down, without even consulting one another this time, as if they had agreed to come to that spot.

"It is lovely weather," she remarked after a silence.

"Yes," he replied; "the sun has made its appearance again."

But their thoughts were elsewhere. He, who fled women, had been reflecting on the events that had drawn him to this one. She sat there, touching him, threatening to invade his existence, and he experienced endless surprise. Since the last examination at Rouen, he no longer had any doubt. This woman was an accomplice in the murder at La Croix-de-Maufras. How was it? As the result of what circumstances? Urged to the crime by what passion, or what interest? He had asked himself these questions, without being able to answer them clearly. Nevertheless, he had ended by arranging a version: the husband, avaricious and violent, yearned to get possession of the legacy; perhaps he feared the will might be altered to their disadvantage; perhaps he wished to attach his wife to him by a sanguinary bond. And he clung to this version. The obscure parts of it interested him without him seeking to elucidate them.

The idea that it was his duty to unbosom himself to justice, had also haunted him. It was this idea, indeed, that had been engaging his attention since he had found himself seated on that bench close to Séverine, so close that he could feel the warmth of her form against his own.

"It's astonishing," he resumed, "to be able to remain out of doors like this, in the month of March, just as in summer."

"Oh!" said she, "as soon as the sun ascends, it is delightful!"

And, on her side, she reflected that this man would have been an idiot, had he not guessed them the culprits. They had been too eager to force themselves on him, and at this very moment she continued to press too close to him. And so, in the silence broken by empty phrases, she followed his reflections.

Their eyes had met. She had just read in his, that he had come to the point of inquiring of himself whether it was not she whom he had seen, weighing with all her weight on the legs of the victim, like a dark bundle. What could she do? what could she say, to bind him to her by an inseverable bond?

"This morning," she remarked, "it was very cold at Havre."

"Without taking into account," said he, "all the rain that fell."

At that instant, Séverine had an abrupt inspiration. She did not reason, she did not think the matter over; it came to her like an instinctive impulse from the obscure depths of her intelligence and heart. Had she thought about it, she would have said nothing. She

ÉMILE ZOLA

simply felt the idea was good, and that by speaking she would conquer him.

Gently she took his hand. She looked at him. The cluster of green trees hid them from the pedestrians in the neighbouring streets. They only heard a distant rumble of vehicles that came deadened to this sunny solitude of the square. Alone, at the bend of the path, a child played in silence, filling a small pail with sand with a wooden spade. Without wavering in her idea, with all her soul, and in a low voice she put this question to him:

"You believe me guilty?"

He slightly trembled, and looked into her eyes.

"Yes," he answered, in the same low, unsteady tone.

Then she pressed his hand, which she had retained, in a tighter clasp. But she did not continue speaking at once. She felt their feverish warmth mingling in one.

"You are mistaken," she resumed; "I am not guilty."

She did not say this to convince him, but simply to warn him that she must be innocent in the eyes of others. It was the avowal of the woman who says no, desiring it to be no, in spite of all, and always.

"I am not guilty," she added. "You will not continue to pain me by believing I am guilty?"

And she was very happy to see his eyes gazing deeply into her own. Without doubt what she had just said, was equivalent to selling herself to him, for she gave herself away, and later on, if he claimed her, she could not refuse. But the bond was tied between them, and could not be severed. She absolutely defied him to speak now. He belonged to her, as she belonged to him. The avowal had united them.

"You will not cause me any more pain?" she asked. "You believe me?"

"Yes, I believe you," he replied, smiling.

What need was there to force her to talk brutally of this frightful event? Later on, she would tell him all about it, if she wished to do so. This way of tranquillising herself by confessing to him, without saying anything, touched him deeply, as a proof of infinite tenderness. She was so confiding, so fragile, with her gentle blue eyes. She appeared to him so womanly, devoted to man, ever ready to submit to him so as to be happy. And what delighted him above all else, while their hands remained joined and their eyes never parted, was to find himself free from his disorder, the frightful shiver that agitated him when beside a woman. Could he love this one, without killing her?

"You know I am your friend, and that you have naught to fear from me," he murmured in her ear. "I do not want to know your business. It shall be as you please, you understand. Make any use of me you like."

He had approached so close to her face that he felt her warm breath in his moustache. That morning, even, he would have trembled at such a thing, in the wild terror of an attack. What could be passing within him, that he barely felt a thrill, attended by the pleasant lassitude of convalescence? This idea that she had killed a fellow creature, which had now become a certainty, made her appear different in his eyes— greater, a person apart. Perhaps she had not merely assisted, but had also struck. He felt convinced of it, without the slightest proof. And, henceforth, she seemed sacred to him, beyond all reasoning.

Both of them now chatted gaily, as a couple just met, with whom love is commencing.

"You should give me your other hand," said he, "for me to warm it."

"Oh! no, not here," she protested. "We might be seen."

"Who by, as we are alone?" he inquired. "And, besides, there would be no harm in it," he added.

She laughed frankly in her joy at being saved. She did not love this man, she thought she was quite sure of that; and, indeed, if she had involved herself, she was already thinking of a way out of the difficulty. He looked nice; he would not torment her; everything could be arranged beautifully.

"We are comrades, that's settled," said she; "and neither my husband nor anyone else shall interfere. Now, let go of my hand, and do not keep on staring at me like that, because you will spoil your eyes!"

But he detained her delicate fingers between his own, and very lowly he stammered:

"You know I love you."

Sharply she freed herself with a slight jerk; and, standing before the bench, where he remained seated, she exclaimed:

"What nonsense, indeed! Conduct yourself properly; someone is coming!"

A wet-nurse appeared, with her baby asleep in her arms. Then a young girl passed along in a great hurry. The sun was sinking, disappearing on the horizon in a violescent mist, and its rays vanished from the grass, dying away in golden dust beside the green patch of pines. A sudden pause came in the continual rumble of vehicles. Five o'clock was heard striking at a neighbouring clock.

"Good heavens!" exclaimed Séverine. "Five o'clock, and I have an appointment in the Rue du Rocher!"

Her joy departed, back came the agony of the unknown awaiting her there, and she remembered she was not yet saved. She turned quite pale, and her lip quivered.

"But you have to see the chief of the depôt," said Jacques.

"It cannot be helped!" she replied; "I must pay him a visit another time. Listen, my friend, I will not keep you any longer. Let me go quickly on my errand. And thanks again, thanks from the bottom of my heart."

She squeezed his hand, and hurried off.

"By-and-bye at the train," he called after her.

"Yes, by-and-bye," she answered.

She was already walking rapidly away, and soon disappeared among the clusters of shrubs; whilst he proceeded leisurely, in the direction of the Rue Cardinet.

M. Camy-Lamotte had just had a long interview in his study, with the traffic-manager of the Western Railway Company. Summoned under pretext of some other business, the latter had ended by admitting that the company felt very much annoyed at this Grandmorin case. First of all, came the complaints of the newspapers, in regard to the little security enjoyed by first-class passengers. Then all the staff were mixed up in the drama. Several of their servants were suspected, without counting this Roubaud, who appeared the most involved, and who might be arrested at any moment. The rumours of the irregular mode of life of the President, who had a seat on the board of directors, seemed to bespatter the whole board. And it was thus that the presumed crime of an insignificant assistant station-master, attributed to some shady, low, and nauseous intrigue, threatened to disorganise the management of an important railway enterprise.

The shock had even been felt in higher places. It had gained the Ministry, menaced the State at a moment of political uneasiness. It was a critical time, when the slightest effervescence might hasten the downfall of the Empire.

So when M. Camy-Lamotte heard from his visitor, that the company had that morning decided to dismiss Roubaud, he energetically opposed the measure. No! no! nothing could be more clumsy! The rumpus in the press would increase, should the writers take it into their heads to set up the assistant station-master as a political victim. Everything would be rent from top to bottom, and heaven only knew what unpleasant revelations would be made about one and another! The scandal had lasted too long, and must be put an end to at once. And the traffic-manager, convinced, had undertaken to maintain Roubaud in his post, and not even to remove him from Havre. It would soon be seen that there were no disreputable people on their staff. It was all over. The matter would be shelved.

When Séverine, out of breath, her heart beating violently, found herself once more in the severe study in the Rue du Rocher, before M. Camy-Lamotte, the latter contemplated her an instant in silence, interested at the extraordinary effort she made to appear calm. He certainly felt sympathy for this delicate criminal with the soft blue eyes.

"Well, madam—" he began.

And he paused to enjoy her anxiety a few seconds longer. But her look was so profound, he felt her casting herself before him in such a burning desire to learn her fate that he had pity.

"Well, madam," he resumed, "I've seen the traffic-manager, and have persuaded him not to dismiss your husband. The matter is settled."

Then, in the flood of joy that overwhelmed her, she broke down. Her eyes were full of tears; but she answered nothing. She only smiled.

He repeated what he had said, laying stress on the phrase, to convey to her all its significance:

"The matter is settled; you can return in tranquillity to Havre!"

She heard well enough: he meant to say that they would not be arrested, that they were pardoned. It was not merely the position maintained, it was the horrible drama forgotten, buried. With an instinctive caressing movement, like a pretty, domestic animal that thanks and fawns, she bent over his hands, kissed them, kept them pressed to her cheeks. And this time, very much troubled himself at the tender charm of her gratitude, he did not withdraw them.

"Only," he continued, trying to resume his severity, "do not forget, and behave properly."

"Oh! sir!" she exclaimed.

In the desire to have them both at his mercy, he alluded to the letter.

"Remember that the papers remain there, and that at the least fault, the matter will be brought up again. Above all, advise your husband not to meddle in politics. On that point we shall be pitiless. I know he has already given cause for complaint; they spoke to me of an annoying quarrel with the sub-prefect. It seems that he passes for a republican, which is detestable, is it not? Let him behave himself, or we shall simply suppress him."

She was standing up, anxious now to be outside, to give room to the joy she felt stifling her.

"Sir," she answered, "we shall obey you; we will do as you please; no matter when, nor where. You have only to command."

He began to smile again, in his weary way, with just a tinge of that disdain of a man who has taken a long draught at the cup of all things, and drained it dry.

He opened the door of his study to her. On the landing, she turned round twice, and with her visage beaming, thanked him again.

Once in the Rue du Rocher, Séverine walked along without giving a thought to where she was going. All at once, she perceived she was ascending the street to no purpose. Turning round, she descended the slope, crossed the road with no object, at the risk of being knocked down. She felt she wanted to move about, to gesticulate, to shout. She already understood why they had been pardoned, and she caught herself saying:

"Of course! They are afraid; there is no fear of them stirring up the business. I was a great fool to give myself all that torture. It was evident they would do nothing. Ah! what luck! Saved, saved for good this time! But no matter, I mean to frighten my husband, so as to make him keep quiet. Saved, saved! What luck!"

As she turned into the Rue St. Lazare, she saw by a clock at the shop of a jeweller, that it wanted twenty minutes to six.

"By Jove! I'll stand myself a good dinner. I have time," said she to herself.

Opposite the station she picked out the most luxurious-looking restaurant; and, seated alone at a small table, with snow-white cloth, against the undraped plate-glass window, intensely amused at the movement in the street, she ordered a nice meal: oysters, filets-de-sole, and the wing of a roast fowl. She was well entitled to make up for a bad lunch. She ate with a first rate appetite, found the bread, made of the finest flour—the pain-de-gruau—exquisite; and she had some beignets soufflés prepared for her, by way of sweets. Then, when she had taken her coffee, she hurried off, for she had only a few minutes left to catch the express.

Jacques, on leaving her, after paying a visit to his room to put on his working-garments, had at once made his way to the depôt, where, as a rule, he never showed himself until half an hour before the departure of his locomotive. He had got into the habit of relying on Pecqueux to inspect the engine, notwithstanding that the latter was in drink two days out of three. But on that particular evening, in his tender emotion, he unconsciously felt a scruple. He wished to make sure, with his own eyes, that all the parts of the engine were in thorough working order; and the more so, as in the morning, on the way from Havre, he fancied he had noticed an increased expenditure of strength, for less work.

Among the other locomotives at rest in the vast engine-house, into which daylight penetrated through tall, dusty windows, the one driven by Jacques was already at the head of a line, and destined to leave the first. A fireman belonging to the depôt, had just made up the fire, and red-hot cinders were falling below into the ash-pit.

It was one of those express engines with double axle-trees coupled together, of delicate elegance, and gigantic build; with its great, light wheels united by steel arms, its broad chest, its elongated and mighty loins, conceived with all that logic and all that certainty, which make up the sovereign beauty of these metal beings—precision with strength. Like the other locomotives of the Western Company, this one bore the name of a railway-station as well as a number, that of Lison, a town in lower Normandy. But Jacques, in affection, had turned the word into a woman's name, by setting the feminine article before it—La Lison, as he called it with caressing gentleness.

And, in truth, he fondly loved his engine, which he had driven for four years. He had been on others, some docile, some jibbers, some courageous, and some lazy. He was well aware that each had its peculiar character, and that some were not worth much. So that if he was fond of this one, it was because it possessed rare qualities, being gentle, obedient, easy to set in motion, and gifted with even and lasting speed, thanks to its good vaporisation.

Some pretended that if this locomotive started off so easily, it was due to its excellent tyres, and particularly to the perfect regulation of its slide-valves; and that if a large quantity of steam could be produced with little fuel, it was owing to the quality of the copper in the tubes, and to the satisfactory arrangement of the boiler.

But he knew there was something else; for other engines, built identically in the same way, put together with the same care, displayed none of the qualities of this one. There was the soul, so to say, to be taken into account, the mystery of the fabrication, that peculiar something which the hazard of the hammer gives to the metal, which the skill of the fitter conveys to the various pieces—the personality of the engine, its life.

So he loved La Lison, which started quickly and stopped sharp, like a vigorous and docile steed; he loved it because, apart from his fixed wages, it earned him cash, thanks to the gratuities on the consumption of fuel. Its excellent vaporisation effected, indeed, considerable economy in coal. It merited but one reproach, that of requiring too much oil. The cylinders, particularly, devoured unreasonable quantities of this liquid. They had a constant appetite which nothing could appease. In vain had he sought to moderate it. The engine lost breath at once. Its constitution required all this nourishment. Ultimately, he had made up his mind to tolerate the gluttonous passion, just as the eyes are closed to a vice in people, who, in other respects, are full of qualities.

Whilst the fire roared, and La Lison was gradually getting up steam, Jacques walked round and round the engine, inspecting it in all its parts, endeavouring to discover why, in the morning, it should have put away more oil than usual. And he found nothing amiss. The locomotive was bright and clean, presenting that delightful appearance which indicates the good, tender care of the driver. He could be seen wiping, and furbishing the metal incessantly, particularly at the end of a journey, in the same manner as smoking steeds are whisked down after a long run. He rubbed it vigorously, taking advantage of its being warm, to remove stains and foam more perfectly.

He never played tricks with his locomotive, but kept it at an even pace, avoiding getting late, which would necessitate disagreeable leaps of speed. And the two had gone on so well together, that not once in four years had he lodged a complaint in the register at the depôt, where drivers book their requests for repairs—the bad drivers, drunkards or idlers, who are ever at variance with their engines. But truly, on this particular evening, he had the consumption of oil at heart; and there was also another feeling, something vague and profound, which he had not hitherto experienced—anxiety, distrust, as if he could not rely on his engine, and wanted to make sure that it was not going to behave badly on the journey.

Pecqueux was not there, and when he at length appeared, with flushed countenance, after lunching with a friend, Jacques flew into a rage. Habitually the two men agreed very well, in that long companionship, extending from one end of the line to the other, jolted side by side, silent, united by the same labour and the same dangers.

Although Jacques was the junior of the other man by more than a decade, he showed himself paternal for his fireman, shielding his vices, allowing him to sleep for an hour when too far gone in drink; and the latter repaid him for this kindness with canine devotedness. Apart from his drunkenness, he was an excellent workman, thoroughly broken to his calling. It must be said, that he also loved La Lison, which sufficed for a good understanding between the two. And Pecqueux, taken aback at being so roughly welcomed, looked at Jacques with increased surprise, when he heard him grumbling his doubts about the engine.

"What is the matter? Why, it goes beautifully!" said the fireman.

"No, no," answered Jacques; "I am uneasy."

And, notwithstanding each part of the locomotive being in good condition, he continued to toss his head. He turned the handles, assured himself that the safety-valve worked well, got on to the frame-plate, and attended to the grease-boxes of the cylinders himself; while the fireman wiped the dome, where a few slight traces of rust remained. Nothing was wrong with the sand-rod. All this should have set his mind at ease.

The fact was, that La Lison no longer stood alone in his heart. Another tenderness was growing there for that slim, and very fragile creature, whom he continued to see beside him on the bench in the garden of the square. A girl so gentle, so caressing, so weak in character, and who needed love and protection. Never, when some involuntary cause had put him behind time, and he had sent his engine along at a speed of sixty miles an hour, never had he thought of the danger the passengers might be incurring. And, now, the mere idea of taking this woman back to Havre, this woman whom he almost detested in the morning, whom he brought up with annoyance, caused him great anxiety, and made him dread an accident, in which he imagined her wounded by his fault, and dying in his arms. The distrusted La Lison would do well to behave properly, if it wished to maintain the reputation of making good speed.

It struck six. Jacques and Pecqueux climbed up to the foot-plate, and the latter, opening the exhaust-pipe at a sign from his chief, a coil of white steam filled the black engine-house. Then, responding to the handle of the regulator which the driver slowly turned, La Lison began to move, left the dépôt, and whistled for the line to be opened. Almost immediately the engine was able to enter the Batignolles tunnel, but at the Pont de l'Europe it had to wait; and it was not until the regulation time that the pointsman sent it on to the 6.30 express, to which a couple of porters firmly secured it.

The train was about to leave; it wanted but five minutes to the time, and Jacques leant over the side, surprised at not perceiving Séverine among the swarm of passengers. He felt certain she would not seat herself without first of all coming to the engine. At last she appeared, behind time, almost running. And, as he had foreseen, she passed all along the train and only stopped when beside the locomotive, her face crimson, exulting with joy.

Her little feet went on tiptoe, her face rose up, laughing.

"Do not be alarmed!" she exclaimed. "Here I am."

He also laughed, happy to see her there, and answered:

"Ah! very good! That's all right."

But she went on tiptoe again, and resumed, in a lower tone:

"My friend, I am pleased, very pleased. I have had a great piece of luck. All that I desired."

He understood perfectly, and experienced great pleasure. Then, as she was running off, she turned round to add, in fun:

"I say, don't you smash me up, now."

And he gaily retorted:

"Oh! what next? No fear!"

But the carriage doors were being slammed. Séverine had only just time to get in. Jacques, at a signal from the chiefguard, blew the whistle, and then opened the regulator. They were off. The departure took place at the same time as that of the tragic train in February, amidst the same activity in the station, the same sounds, the same smoke. Only it was still daylight now, a clear crepuscule, infinitely soft. Séverine, with her head at the window of the door, looked out.

Jacques, standing to the right on La Lison, warmly clothed in woollen trousers and vest, wearing spectacles with cloth sides, fastened behind his head under his cap, henceforth never took his eyes off the line, leaning at every minute outside the cab so as to see better. Roughly shaken by the vibration, of which he was not even conscious, his right hand rested on the reversing-wheel, like that of a pilot on the wheel of the helm; and he manœuvred it with a movement that was imperceptible and continuous, moderating, accelerating the rapidity; while, with his left hand, he never ceased sounding the whistle, for the exit from Paris is difficult, and beset with pitfalls.

He whistled at the level crossings, at the stations, at the great curves. A red light having appeared in the distance, as daylight vanished, he for a long time inquired if the road was free, and then passed like lightning. It was only from time to time that he cast a glance at the steam-gauge, turning the injector-wheel as soon as the pressure reached ten kilogrammes. But it was always to the permanent way that his eyes returned, bent on observing its smallest peculiarities, and with such attention, that he saw nothing else, and did not even feel the wind blowing a tempest. The steam-gauge falling, he opened the door of the fire-box, raising the bars; and Pecqueux, accustomed to a gesture, understood at once. He broke up coal with his hammer, and with his shovel put on an even layer. The scorching heat burnt the legs of both of them. Then, the door once closed again, they had to face the current of icy air.

When night closed in, Jacques became doubly prudent. Rarely had he found La Lison so obedient. He handled the engine as he pleased, with the absolute will of the master; and yet he did not relax his severity, but treated it as a tamed animal that must always be distrusted.

There, behind his back, in the train, whirling along at express speed, he saw a delicate, confiding, smiling face. He felt a slight shiver. With a firmer hand he grasped the reversing-wheel, piercing the increasing darkness with fixed eyes, in search of red lights. After the embranchments at Asnières and Colombes, he breathed a little. As far as Mantes all went well, the line was as a sheet of glass, and the train rolled along at ease.

After Mantes he had to urge La Lison on, so that it might ascend a rather steep incline, almost half a league long. Then, without slackening speed, he ran down the gentle slope to the Rolleboise tunnel, just about two miles in length, which he negotiated in barely three minutes. There remained but one more tunnel, that of La Roule, near Gaillon, before the station of Sotteville—a spot to be feared, for the complication of the lines, the continual shunting proceeding there, and the constant obstruction, made it exceedingly dangerous. All the strength of his being lay in his eyes which watched, in his hand which drove; and La Lison, whistling and smoking, dashed through Sotteville at full steam, only to stop at Rouen, whence it again set out, a trifle calmer, ascending more slowly the incline that extends as far as Malaunay.

A very clear moon had risen, shedding a white light, by which Jacques was able to distinguish the smallest bushes, and even the stones on the roads, in their rapid flight. As he cast a glance to the right, on leaving the tunnel of Malaunay, disturbed at the shadow cast across the line by a great tree, he recognised the out-of-the-way corner, the field full of bushes, whence he had witnessed the murder. The wild, deserted country flew past, with its continuous hills, its raw black patches of copses, its ravaged desolation. Next, at La Croix-de-Maufras, beneath the motionless moon, abruptly appeared the vision of the atrociously melancholy house set down aslant in its abandonment and distress, with its shutters everlastingly closed. And without understanding why, Jacques, this time again, and more vigorously than on previous occasions, felt a tightening at the heart as if he was passing before his doom.

But immediately afterwards, his eyes carried another image away. Near the house of the Misards, against the gate at the level crossing, stood Flore. He now saw her at this spot at each of his journeys, awaiting, on the watch for him. She did not move, she simply turned her head so as to be able to get a longer view of him in the flash that bore him away. Her tall silhouette stood out in black, against the white light, her golden locks alone being illumined by the pale gold of the celestial body.

And Jacques, having urged on La Lison, to make it scale the ascent at Motteville, allowed the engine breathing time across the plateau of Bolbec. But he finally sent it on again, from Saint-Romain to Harfleur, down the longest incline on the line, a matter of three leagues, which the engines devour at the gallop of mad cattle sniffing the stable. And he was broken down with fatigue at Havre, when, beneath the iron marquee, full of the uproar and smoke at the arrival, Séverine, before going up to her rooms, ran to say to him, in her gay and tender manner:

"Thanks. We may see one another tomorrow."

VI

A month passed, and great tranquillity again pervaded the lodging occupied by the Roubauds, on the first floor of the railway station, over the waiting-rooms. With them, with their neighbours in the corridor, with all this little crowd of public servants subjected to an existence regulated by the clock, life had resumed its monotony. And it seemed as if nothing violent or abnormal had taken place.

The noisy and scandalous Grandmorin case was quietly being forgotten, was about to be shelved, owing to the apparent inability of the authorities to discover the criminal. After Cabuche had been locked up a fortnight, the examining-magistrate, Denizet, had ordered his discharge, on the ground that there was not sufficient evidence against him. And a romantic fable was now being arranged by the police: that of an unknown murderer on whom it was impossible to lay hands, a criminal adventurer, who was everywhere at the same time, who was accused of all the murders, and who vanished in smoke, at the mere sight of the officers.

It was now only at long intervals that a few jokes about this fabulous murderer were revived in the opposition press, which became intensely excited as the general elections drew near. The pressure of the government, the violence of the prefects, every day furnished other subjects for indignant articles; and the newspapers were so busy with these matters that they gave no further attention to the case. It had ceased to interest the public, who no longer even spoke on the subject.

What had completed the tranquillity of the Roubauds was the happy way in which the other difficulty, connected with the will of President Grandmorin, had been smoothed over.

On the advice of Madame Bonnehon, the Lachesnayes had at last consented to accept the will, partly because they did not wish to revive the scandal, and also because they were very uncertain as to the result of an action. And the Roubauds, placed in possession of their legacy, had for the past week been the owners of La Croix-de-Maufras, house and garden, estimated to be worth about 40,000 frcs., a matter of £1,600.

They had immediately decided on selling the place, which haunted them like a nightmare, and on selling it in a lump, with the furniture, just as it stood, without repairing it, and without even sweeping out the dust. But, as it would not have fetched anything like its value at an auction, there being few purchasers who would consent to retire to such solitude, they had resolved to await an amateur, and had nailed up an immense board on the front of the house, setting forth that it was for sale, which could easily be read by persons in the frequent trains that passed.

This notice in great letters, this desolation to be disposed of, added to the sadness of the closed shutters, and of the garden invaded with briars. Roubaud, having absolutely refused to go there, even to take a look round, and make certain necessary arrangements, Séverine had paid a visit to the house one afternoon, and had left the keys with the Misards, telling them to show any possible purchasers who might make inquiries, over the property. Possession could be arranged in a couple of hours, for there was even linen in the cupboards.

And from that moment, there being nothing further to trouble the Roubauds, they passed each day in blissful expectation of the morrow. The house would end by being sold, they would invest the money, and everything would go on very well. Besides, they forgot all about it, living as if they were never going to quit the three rooms they occupied: the dining-room, with the door opening on the corridor; the bedroom, fairly large, on the right; the small, stuffy kitchen on the left.

Even the roofing over the platforms, before their windows, that zinc slope shutting out the view like the wall of a prison, instead of exasperating them, as formerly, seemed to bring calm, increasing that sensation of infinite repose, of recomforting peace, wherein they felt secure. In any case, the neighbours could not see them, there were no prying eyes always in front of them peering into their home; and, spring having set in, they now only complained of the stifling heat, of the blinding reflex from the zinc, fired by the first rays of the sun.

After that frightful shock, which for two months had caused them to live in a constant tremble, they enjoyed this reaction of absorbing insensibility, in perfect bliss. They only desired never to move again, happy to be simply alive, without trembling and without suffering.

Never had Roubaud been so exact and conscientious. During the week of day duty, he was on the platform at five in the morning. He did not go up to breakfast until ten, and came down again an hour later, remaining there until five in the evening—eleven hours full of work. During the week of night duty, he had not even the brief rest afforded by a meal at home, for he supped in his office. He bore this hard servitude with a sort of satisfaction, seeming to take pleasure in it, entering into details, wishing to see to everything, to do everything, as if he found oblivion in fatigue; the return of a well-balanced, normal life.

Séverine, for her part, almost always alone, a widow one week out of two, and who during the other week, only saw her husband at luncheon and dinner-time, displayed all the energy of a good housewife. She had been in the habit of sitting down to embroidery, detesting to put her hand to household work, which an old woman, called Mother Simon, came to do, from nine to twelve. But since she had recovered tranquillity at home, and felt certain of remaining there, she had been occupied with ideas of cleaning and arranging things; and she now only seated herself, after rummaging everywhere in the apartment. Both slept soundly. In their rare conversations at meal-times, as on the nights which they passed together, they never once alluded to the case, considering it at an end, and buried.

For Séverine, particularly, life once more became extremely pleasant. Her idleness returned. Again she abandoned the housework to Mother Simon, like a young lady brought up for no greater exertion than fine needlework. She had commenced an interminable task, consisting in embroidering an entire bedcover, which threatened to occupy her to the end of her days. She rose rather late, delighted to remain alone in bed, rocked by the trains leaving and coming in, which told her how the hours fled, as exactly as if her eyes had been on a clock.

In the early days of her married life, these violent sounds in the station—the whistling, the shocks of turn-tables, the rolls of thunder, the abrupt oscillations, like earthquakes, which made both her and the furniture totter—had driven her half crazy. Then, by degrees, she had become accustomed to them; the sonorous and vibrating railway station formed part of her existence; and, now, she liked it, finding tranquillity in all this bustle and uproar.

Until lunch-time, she went from one room to another, talking to the charwoman, with her hands idle. Then, she passed the long afternoons, seated before the dining-room window, with her work generally on her lap, delighted at doing nothing. During the weeks when her husband came up at daylight, to go to bed, she heard him snoring until dark; and these had become her good weeks—those during which she lived as formerly, before her marriage, having the whole bed to herself, enjoying her time after rising, as she thought proper, with the entire day before her, to do as she liked.

She rarely went out. All she could see of Havre, was the smoke of the neighbouring factories, whose great turbillions of black stained the sky above the zinc roof, which shut out the view at a few yards from her eyes.

The city was there, behind this perpetual wall; she always felt its presence, and her annoyance at being unable to see it had, in the end, subsided. Five or six pots of wallflowers and verbenas, which she cultivated in the gutter, gave her a small garden to enliven her solitude. At times she spoke of herself as of a recluse in the depths of a wood. Roubaud, in his moments of idleness, would get out of the window, then, passing to the end of the gutter, would ascend the zinc slope, seating himself on the top of the gable, overlooking the Cours Napoléon. There he smoked his pipe, in the open air, towering above the city that lay spread out at his feet, above the docks planted with tall masts, and the pale green sea, expanding as far as the eye could roam.

It seemed that the same somnolence had gained the other households, near the Roubauds. This corridor, where generally whistled such a terrible gale of gossip, was also wrapt in slumber. When Philomène paid a visit to Madame Lebleu, barely a slight murmur could be heard. Both of them, surprised at the turn matters had taken, now spoke of the assistant station-master with disdainful commiseration, convinced that his wife, to keep him in his post, had been up to her games at Paris.

He was now a man with a slur upon him, who would never free himself of certain suspicions. And, as the wife of the cashier felt convinced that, henceforth, her neighbours would not have the power to take her lodging from her, she simply treated them with contempt, stiffening herself when she passed them, and neglecting to bow. This behaviour even estranged Philomène, who called on her less and less frequently. She considered her too proud, and no longer found amusement in her company.

Madame Lebleu, in order to have something to occupy her, continued to watch the intrigue between Mademoiselle Guichon and the station-master, M. Dabadie, but without ever surprising them. The almost imperceptible brush of his felt slippers along the corridor, could alone be heard. Everything having thus settled down, a month of supreme peacefulness ensued, similar to the great calm that follows great catastrophes.

But one painful, anxious matter remained, to occasionally worry the Roubauds. There was a particular part of the parquetry in the dining-room, whereon their eyes never chanced to rest, without an uncomfortable feeling again troubling them. This spot was to the left of the window. There they had taken up and put in place again, a piece of the pattern in the oak flooring, to hide beneath it the watch, and the 10,000 frcs. (£400) which they had taken from the body of Grandmorin, as well as a purse containing about 300 frcs. (£12) in gold. Roubaud had only drawn the watch and money from the pockets of the victim, to convey the impression that the motive of the crime was robbery.

He was not a thief. He would sooner die of hunger within arms' reach of the treasure, as he said, than profit by a centime, or sell the watch. The money of this old man, to whom he had dealt out justice—money, stained with infamy and blood? No! no! it was not clean enough for an honest man to finger. And he did not even give a thought to the house at La Croix-de-Maufras, which he had accepted as a present. The act of plundering the victim, of carrying off those notes in the abomination of murder, alone revolted him and aroused his conscience to the pitch of making him start back in fright at the idea of touching the ill-gotten gain.

Nevertheless, he had not had the courage to burn the notes; and then, one night, to go and cast watch and purse in the sea. If simple prudence urged him to act thus, inexorable instinct protested against the destruction. Unconsciously, he felt respect for such a large sum of money, and he could never have made up his mind to annihilate it. At the commencement, on the first night, he had thrust it under his pillow, considering no other place sufficiently secure. On the following days, he had exerted his ingenuity to discover hiding-places, changing them each morning, agitated at the least sound, in fear of the police arriving with a search-warrant. Never had he displayed so much imagination.

At last, at the end of artifices, weary of trembling, he one day had the coolness to take the money and watch, hidden the previous evening under the parquetry; and, now, for nothing in the world would he put his hand there. It was like a charnel house, a hole pregnant with terror and death, where spectres awaited him. He even avoided, when moving about the room, to place his feet on that part of the floor. The idea of doing so, caused him an unpleasant sensation, made him fancy he would receive a slight shock in the legs.

When Séverine sat down before the window in the afternoon, she would draw back her chair so as not to be exactly over this skeleton which they kept under their floor. They never spoke of the matter to one another, endeavouring to think they would get accustomed to it; and, at length, they became irritable at remembering the thing again, at feeling it there at every hour, more and more importunate, beneath the soles of their boots. And this uncomfortable sensation was all the more singular, as they in no way suffered from the knife, the beautiful new knife purchased by the wife, and which the husband had stuck into the throat of the sweetheart. It had been simply washed, and lay in a drawer. Sometimes Mother Simon used it to cut the bread.

Amidst the peacefulness in which they were living, Roubaud had just introduced another cause of trouble, which was slowly gaining ground, by forcing Jacques to visit them. The duties of the engine-driver brought him three times a week to Havre. On Monday, from 10.35 in the morning, to 6.20 at night. On Thursday and Saturday, from 11.5 at night, to 6.40 in the morning. And on the first Monday after the journey Séverine had made to Paris, the assistant station-master displayed effusive affability towards him.

"Come, comrade," said he, "you cannot refuse to have a snack with us. The deuce! you were very obliging to my wife, and I owe you some thanks!"

Twice in a month, Jacques had thus accepted an invitation to lunch. It seemed that Roubaud, inconvenienced at the long silence that now prevailed when he met his wife at table, felt a relief as soon as he could place a guest between them. He at once recalled amusing anecdotes, chatted and joked.

"Come as often as possible," said he; "you can see you are not in the way."

One Thursday night, as Jacques, who had washed himself, was thinking of going off to bed, he met the assistant station-master strolling round the depôt; and, notwithstanding the late hour, the latter, disinclined to walk back alone, persuaded the young man to accompany him to the station. Once there he insisted on taking him to his rooms. Séverine was still up, and reading. They drank a glass or two together, and played cards until after midnight.

Henceforth the luncheons on Monday, and the little evening parties on Thursday and Saturday, became a habit. It was Roubaud, himself, when the comrade once missed a day, who kept a look-out for him, and brought him home, reproaching him with his neglect. But he became more and more gloomy, and it was only in the company of his new friend that he was really in good spirits. This man, who had first of all so cruelly alarmed him, whom he should now have held in execration as the witness—the living vision of things he wished to forget—had, on the contrary, become necessary to him, perhaps for the simple reason that he knew what had occurred, and had not spoken. This position took the form of a powerful bond, a sort of complicity between them. The assistant station-master had often looked at the other in a knowing way, pressing his hand with a sudden burst of feeling, and with a violence that surpassed the simple expression of good fellowship.

But it was particularly at home that Jacques became a source of diversion. There, Séverine also welcomed him with gaiety, uttering an exclamation as soon as he entered, like a woman bestirred by a thrill of pleasure. She put aside everything—her embroidery, her book, escaping from the gloomy somnolence, in which she passed her time, in a torrent of words and laughter.

"Ah! how nice of you to have come! I heard the express, and thought of you," she would say.

When he lunched there, it was a fête. She had already learnt his tastes, and went out herself for fresh eggs. And she did this in a very nice way, like a good housewife who welcomes the friend of the family, without giving him any cause to attribute her actions to aught else than a desire to be agreeable, and divert herself.

"Come again on Monday, you know," said she. "We shall have cream."

Only, when at the end of the month, he had made himself at home there, the separation between the Roubauds became more pronounced. Jacques certainly assisted to bring about this informal divorce by his presence, which drew them from the gloom into which they had fallen. He delivered both of them.

Roubaud had no remorse. He had only been afraid of the consequences, before the case was shelved, and his greatest anxiety had been the dread of losing his place. At present, he felt no regret. Perhaps, though, had he to do the business over again, he would not make his wife take a part in it. Women lose their spirit at once. His wife was escaping from him, because he had placed on her shoulders, a load too heavy to bear. He would have remained the master, had he not descended with her to the terrifying and quarrelsome comradeship of crime.

But this was how things were, and it became imperative to put up with them; the more so, as he had to make a regular effort, to place himself again in the same frame of mind, as when, after the confession, he had considered the murder necessary to his existence. It seemed to him, at that time, that if he had not killed this man, he would not have been able to live. At present, his jealous flame having died out, himself freed from the intolerable burn, assailed by a feeling of torpidity, as if the blood of his heart had become thickened by all the blood he had spilt, the necessity for the murder did not appear to him so evident.

He had come to the pass of inquiring of himself, whether killing was really worth the trouble. This was not repentance; it was at most a disillusion, the idea that people often do things they would not own to, in order to become happy, without being any the more so. He, usually so talkative, fell into prolonged spells of silence, into confused reflections, from which he issued more gloomy than before. Every day, now, to avoid remaining face to face with his wife, after the meals, he went on the roof and seated himself on the gable. There, in the breeze from the offing, soothing himself in vague dreams, he smoked his pipe, gazing beyond the city at the steamers disappearing on the horizon, bound to distant seas.

But one evening, Roubaud felt a revival of that savage jealousy of former times. He had been to find Jacques at the depôt, and was bringing him up to his rooms to take a dram, when he met Henri Dauvergne, the headguard, coming down the staircase. The latter appeared confused, and explained that he had been to see Madame Roubaud on an errand confided to him by his sisters. The truth was that for sometime past, he had been running after Séverine, to make love to her.

The assistant station-master violently addressed his wife at the door.

"What did that fellow come up again about?" he roughly inquired. "You know that he plagues me!"

"But, my dear, it was for a pattern of embroidery," she answered.

"Embroidery, indeed!" he rejoined. "I'll give him embroidery! Do you think I'm such a fool as not to understand what he comes here for? And as to you, take care!"

He advanced towards her, his fists clenched, and she stepped back, white as a sheet, astonished at the violence of this anger, in the state of calm indifference for one another, in which they lived. But he was already recovering his self-possession, and, addressing his companion, he said:

"Whoever heard of such a thing? Fellows who tumble into your home with the idea that your wife will immediately fall into their arms, and that the husband, very much flattered, will shut his eyes! It makes my blood boil. Look here, if such a thing did happen, I would strangle my wife, oh! on the spot! And this young gentleman had better not show his face here again, or I'll settle his business for him. Isn't it disgusting?"

Jacques, who felt very uncomfortable at the scene, hardly knew how to look. Was this exaggerated anger intended for him? Was the husband giving him a warning? He felt more at ease when the latter gaily resumed:

"As to you, I know you would very soon fling him out at the door. No matter. Séverine, bring us something to drink out of. Jacques, touch glasses with us."

He patted Jacques on the shoulder, and Séverine, who had also recovered, smiled at the two men. Then they all drank together, and passed a very pleasant hour.

It was thus that Roubaud brought his wife and comrade together, with an air of good friendship, and without seeming to think of the possible consequences. This outburst of jealousy became the very cause of a closer intimacy, and of a great deal of secret tenderness, strengthened by outpourings of the heart, between Jacques and Séverine. For, having seen her again two days after this scene, he expressed his pity that she should have been the object of such brutal treatment; while she, with eyes bathed in tears, confessed, with an involuntary overflow of grief, what little happiness she met with in her home.

From that moment, they had found a subject of conversation for themselves alone, a complicity of friendship wherein they ended by understanding one another at a sign. At each visit, he questioned her with his eyes, to ascertain if she had met with any fresh cause for sadness. She answered in the same way, by a simple motion of the eyelids. Moreover, their hands sought each other behind the back of the husband. Becoming bolder, they corresponded by long pressures, relating, at the tips of their warm fingers, the increasing interest the one took in the smallest incidents connected with the existence of the other.

Rarely did they have the good fortune to meet for a minute, in the absence of Roubaud. They always found him there, between them, in that melancholy dining-room; and they did nothing to escape him, never having had the thought to make an appointment at some distant corner of the station. Up to then, it was a matter of real affection between them; they were led along by keen sympathy, and Roubaud caused them but slight inconvenience, as a glance, a pressure of the hand, sufficed for them to comprehend one another.

ÉMILE ZOLA

The first time Jacques whispered in the ear of Séverine, that he would wait for her on the following Thursday at midnight, behind the depôt, she revolted, and violently withdrew her hand. It was her week of liberty, the week when her husband was engaged on night duty. But she was very much troubled at the thought of leaving her home, to go and meet this young man so far away, in the darkness of the station premises. Never had she felt so confused. It resembled the fright of innocent maids with throbbing hearts. She did not give way at once. He had to beg and pray of her for more than a fortnight, before she consented, notwithstanding her own burning desire to take this nocturnal walk.

It was at the commencement of June. The evenings became intensely hot, and were but slightly refreshed by the sea breeze. Jacques had already waited for her three times, always in the hope that she would join him, notwithstanding her refusal. On this particular night, she had again said no. The sky was without a moon, and cloudy. Not a star shone through the dense haze that obscured everything. As he stood watching in the dark, he perceived her coming along at last, attired in black, and with silent tread. It was so sombre that she would have brushed against him without recognising him, had he not caught her in his arms and given her a kiss. She uttered a little cry, quivering. Then, laughingly, she left her lips on his. But that was all; she would never consent to sit down in one of the sheds surrounding them. They walked about, and chatted in low tones, pressing one to the other.

Just there, was a vast open space, occupied by the depôt and other buildings, all the land that is shut in by the Rue Verte and the Rue François-Mazeline, both of which cut the line at level crossings: a sort of immense piece of waste ground, encumbered with shunting lines, reservoirs, water-cranes, buildings of all sorts—the two great engine-houses, the cottage of the Sauvagnats, surrounded by a tiny kitchen-garden, the workshops, the block where the drivers and firemen slept. And nothing was more easy than to escape observation, to lose oneself, as in the thick of a wood, among those deserted lanes with their inextricable maze of turnings. For an hour, they enjoyed delicious solitude, relieving their hearts in friendly words stored-up there so long. For she would only consent to speak of affection. She had told him, at once, that she would never be his, that it would be too wicked to tarnish this pure friendship, of which she felt so proud, being jealous of her own self-esteem. Then he accompanied her to the Rue Verte, where their lips joined in a long kiss, and she returned home.

At that same hour, in the office of the assistant station-masters, Roubaud began to doze in an old leather armchair, which he quitted twenty times in the course of the night, with aching limbs. Up to nine o'clock, he had to be present at the arrival and departure of the night trains. The tidal train engaged his particular attention: there were the manœuvres, the coupling, the way-bills to be closely scrutinised. Then, when the Paris express had arrived and had been shunted, he supped alone in the office at a corner of the table, off a slice of cold meat between a couple of pieces of bread, which he had brought down from his lodging. The last arrival, a slow train from Rouen, steamed in at half past twelve. The platforms then became quite silent. Only a few lamps remained alight, and the entire station lay at rest, in this quivering semi-obscurity.

Of all the staff there remained but a couple of foremen, and four or five porters, under the orders of the assistant station-master. They slept like tops on the sloping plank platform in the quarters allotted to them; while Roubaud, obliged to rouse them at the least warning, could only doze with his ears open. Lest he should succumb to fatigue, towards daybreak, he set his alarum at five o'clock, at which hour he had to be on his feet, to be present at the arrival of the Paris train. But, occasionally, especially recently, he suffered from insomnia, and turned about in his armchair without being able to close his eyes. Then he would get up and go out, take a look round, walk as far as the box of the pointsman, where he chatted an instant. And the vast black sky, the sovereign peacefulness of the night, ultimately calmed his fever.

In consequence of a struggle with marauders, he had been supplied with a revolver, which he carried loaded in his pocket. And he often walked about in this way, up to daybreak, stopping as soon as he perceived anything moving in the darkness, resuming his walk with a sort of vague feeling of regret at not having had to make use of his weapon. He felt relieved when the sky whitened, and drew the great pale phantom of the station from darkness. Now that day broke as early as three o'clock he went in, and, throwing himself into his armchair, slept like a dormouse, until his alarum brought him, with a start, to his feet.

Séverine met Jacques once a fortnight, on Thursday and Saturday. And, one night, when she had told him about the revolver, they both felt considerably alarmed. As a matter of fact, Roubaud never went so far as the depôt. But this circumstance did not divest their walks of an aspect of danger, which added to their charm. Moreover, they had found a delightful nook, behind the cottage of the Sauvagnats, a sort of alley, between some enormous heaps of coal, which formed the only street in a strange town of great, square, black-marble palaces. There, they were completely hidden.

This girl, who had killed, was his ideal. His cure seemed to him more certain every day, because he had fondled her, his lips upon her lips, absorbing her very soul, without that furious envy having been aroused, to master her by slaughtering her.

And so these happy meetings followed one upon another. The two sweethearts never wearied for a moment of seeking one another, of strolling together in the obscurity, between the great heaps of coal that deepened the darkness around them.

One night in July, Jacques, to reach Havre at 11.5, the fixed time, had to urge on La Lison, as if the stifling heat had made the engine idle. From Rouen, a storm accompanied him on the left, following the valley of the Seine, with great brilliant flashes; and, from time to time, he turned round anxiously, for Séverine was to meet him that night. He feared that if this storm burst too soon, it would prevent her going out. And so, when he had succeeded in attaining the station before the rain, he felt impatient with the passengers, who seemed as if they would never finish leaving the carriages.

Roubaud was on the platform, glued there for the night.

"The deuce!" said he, laughing. "What a hurry you're in to get off to bed! Pleasant dreams!"

"Thanks," answered Jacques.

After driving back the train, he whistled, and made his way to the depôt. The flaps of the immense door were open. La Lison penetrated the engine-house, a sort of gallery with double lines, about sixty yards long, and built to accommodate six locomotives. Within, it was very dark. Four gas-burners did not suffice to dispel the obscurity, which they seemed to deepen into four great moving shadows. But, at moments, the vivid flashes of lightning, set the glazed roof and the tall windows to right and left, ablaze; and one then distinguished, as in a flame of fire, the cracked walls, the timber black with smoke, all the tumble-down wretchedness of this out-of-date building. Two locomotives were already there, cold and slumbering.

Pecqueux at once began to put out the fire. He violently raked it, and, the live coal escaping from the cinder-box, fell into the pit below.

"I'm dying of hunger," said he. "I shall go and have a mouthful. Are you coming?"

Jacques did not reply. In spite of his hurry, he did not wish to leave La Lison before the lights had been extinguished, and the boiler emptied. This was a scruple, the habit of a good driver, wherefrom he never departed. When he had time, he remained there until he had examined and wiped everything, with all the care that is taken to groom a favourite nag.

It was only when the water ran gurgling into the pit, that he exclaimed: "Hurry on, hurry on!"

A formidable flash of lightning interrupted him. This time, the tall windows stood out so distinctly against the flaming sky, that the very numerous broken panes of glass could have been counted. To the left, a thin sheet of iron, which had remained fixed in one of the vices serving for the repairs, resounded with the prolonged vibration of a bell. All the antiquated timber-work of the roof had cracked.

"The devil!" simply said the fireman.

The driver made a gesture of despair. This put an end to his appointment, and the more so, as a perfect deluge was now pouring down on the engine-house. The violence of the rain threatened to break the glazed roof. Up there some of the panes of glass must also have been broken, for big raindrops were falling on La Lison in clusters. A violent wind entered by the doors which had been left open, and anyone might have fancied that the body of the old structure was about to be swept away.

Pecqueux was getting to the end of his work on the locomotive.

"There!" said he; "we shall be able to see better tomorrow. I have no need to tidy it up any more tonight."

And, returning to his former idea, he added:

"I must get something to eat. It's raining too hard to go and stick oneself on one's mattress."

The canteen, indeed, was at hand, against the depôt itself; while the company had been obliged to rent a house—Rue François-Mazeline—where beds had been provided for the drivers and firemen who passed the night at Havre. In such a deluge, they would have got drenched to the skin before arriving there.

Jacques had to make up his mind to follow Pecqueux, who had taken the small basket belonging to his chief, to save him the trouble of carrying it. He knew that this basket still contained two slices of cold veal, some bread, and a bottle of wine that had hardly been touched; and it was simply this knowledge that made him feel hungry. The rain increased. Another clap of thunder had just shaken the engine-house. When the two men went away on the left, by the small door leading to the canteen, La Lison was already becoming cold. The engine slumbered, abandoned, in the obscurity, lit up by the vivid flashes of lightning, with the heavy drops of rain falling on its flanks. Hard by, a water-crane, imperfectly turned off, continued dripping, and formed a pool that ran between the wheels of the locomotive into the pit.

But Jacques wished to wash before entering the canteen. Warm water and buckets were always to be found in an adjoining room. Drawing a piece of soap from his basket, he removed the dirt from his travel-begrimed hands and face; and, as he had taken the precaution to bring a second lot of clothes with him, in accordance with the advice given to the drivers, he was able to change his garments from head to foot, as he was accustomed to do, for that matter, each night on his arrival at Havre, when he had an appointment with Séverine. Pecqueux was already waiting in the canteen, having only just dipped the tip of his nose, and the ends of his fingers, in the water.

This canteen simply consisted of a small, bare room painted yellow, where there was nothing but a stove to warm the food, and a table fixed in the ground, and covered with a sheet of zinc, by way of tablecloth. A couple of forms completed the furniture. The men had to bring their own victuals, and eat off a piece of paper with the points of their knives. Light entered the room through a large window.

"What a vile downpour!" exclaimed Jacques, planting himself before the panes of glass.

Pecqueux had settled himself on a form at the table.

"You are not going to eat then?" he inquired.

"No, mate. Finish my bread and meat, if you care for it. I've no appetite."

The other, without more ado, fell upon the veal, and emptied the bottle. He frequently met with similar luck, for his chief was a poor eater; and he loved him the better, in his canine-like fidelity, for all the crumbs picked up in this way, behind him. With his mouth full, he resumed after a silence:

"The rain! What do we care about that, so long as we're under cover? Only, if it continues, I shall cut you, and be off next door."

He began laughing, for he made no secret of his mode of life; and, no doubt, had told the driver all about his intrigue with Philomène Sauvagnat.

Jacques muttered an oath, as he perceived the deluge of rain increase in violence, after showing signs of abating.

Pecqueux, with the last mouthful of meat at the end of his knife, again gave a good-humoured laugh.

"You must have something to do then, tonight?" said he. "Well, they can't reproach us two with wearing out the mattresses, over there, in the Rue François-Mazeline."

Jacques quickly left the window.

"Why?" he inquired.

"Well, you're just like me. Since the spring, you never turn in till two or three o'clock in the morning," answered the other.

He seemed to know something. Perhaps he had caught them together. In each room the bedsteads were in couples: fireman and driver. The railway authorities sought to bind these men to one another as firmly as possible, on account of their work, which necessitated such a close understanding. And so, Jacques was not astonished that the fireman should have noticed the late hours he kept, particularly as he had formerly been so regular.

"I suffer from headache," remarked the driver, for want of something better to say; "and it does me good to walk out at night-time."

But the fireman was already excusing himself.

"Oh! you know," he broke in, "you are free to do as you please. What I said, was only by way of a joke. And if you should meet with any trouble one of these days, don't mind coming to me, because I'm ready to do anything you like."

Without explaining his meaning more clearly, Pecqueux grasped him by the hand, pressing it fit to crush it, so as to make him understand that he was at his service, body and soul. Then, crumpling up the greasy paper which the meat had been in, he threw it away, and placed the empty bottle in the basket, performing this little service like a careful servant accustomed to the broom and sponge. And, as the rain obstinately continued, although the thunder had ceased, he exclaimed:

"Well, I'm off, and leave you to your own business!"

"Oh!" said Jacques, "as there are no signs of it clearing up, I shall go and lie down on a camp bedstead!"

Beside the depôt was a room with mattresses protected by canvas slips, where the men rested in their clothes when they had only to wait three or four hours at Havre. So, as soon as Jacques saw the fireman disappear in the downpour of rain, he risked it in his turn, and ran to the drivers' quarters. But he did not lie down. He stood on the threshold of the wide-open door, stifled by the oppressive heat within, where another driver, stretched on his back, was snoring with his mouth wide open.

A few more minutes passed, and Jacques could not make up his mind to abandon all hope. In his exasperation against this disgusting rain, he felt an increasing wild desire to gain, in spite of all, the place where he and Séverine were to meet; so as at least to have the pleasure of being there himself, even if he no longer expected to find his sweetheart. With spasmodic precipitation, he at last dashed through the rain. He reached their favourite corner, and followed the dark alley formed by the heaps of coal. And, as the sharp rain whipped his face and blinded him, he went as far as the tool-house, where he and Séverine had already once found shelter. He seemed to think he would be less lonely there.

Jacques was entering the dense obscurity of this retreat when a couple of slender arms entwined him, and a pair of warm lips rested on his own. Séverine was there.

"Goodness gracious! is it you?" he exclaimed.

"Yes," she answered; "I saw the storm approaching, and ran here before the rain came down. What a time you have been!"

"You expected me then?"

"Oh! yes. I waited, waited—"

They had seated themselves on a pile of empty sacks, listening to the pouring rain beating, with increased violence, on the roof. The last train from Paris, which was just coming in, passed by, roaring, whistling, rocking the ground. All at once Jacques rose. On seating himself a few moments before, he had by chance found the handle of a hammer beneath his hand, and he was now deluged with intense joy. It was all over then! He had not grasped that hammer and smashed the skull of his sweetheart. She was his own, without a battle, without that instinctive craving to fling her lifeless on her back, like a prey torn from others.

He no longer thirsted to avenge those very ancient offences, whose exact details escaped his memory, that rancour stored up from male to male since the first deceptions in the depths of caverns. No. This girl had cured him, because he saw she was different from the others, violent in her weakness, reeking with human gore, which encircled her in a sort of cuirass of horror. She predominated over him, he, who had never dared do as she had done.

Séverine was also lost in reflections. Her heart had been pining after love—absolute, constant love; and it was frightful cruelty that these recent events should have cast her, haggard and anxious, into such abominations. Fate had dragged her in mire and blood with such violence that her beautiful blue eyes, though still naïve, had preserved a look of terror-stricken expansion beneath her tragic crest of raven hair.

"Oh! my darling, carry me off, keep me with you!" she exclaimed; "your desires shall be mine."

"No, no, my treasure," replied Jacques, who had again seated himself beside her, "you are mistress. I am only here to love and obey you."

The hours passed. The rain had ceased sometime. The station was plunged in absolute silence, troubled only by a distant and indistinct moan rising from the sea. Suddenly a pistol-shot brought them to their feet with a start. Day was about to break. A pale spot whitened the sky above the mouth of the Seine. What could be the meaning of that shot? Their imprudence, this folly of remaining together so late, made them, in swift imagination, picture to themselves the husband pursuing them with a revolver.

"Don't venture out!" exclaimed Jacques. "Wait! I'll go and see!"

Jacques had prudently advanced to the door, and there, in the dense darkness that still prevailed, he could hear men advancing at the double. He recognised the voice of Roubaud, urging forward the watchmen, shouting to them that the thieves were three in number, that he had distinctly seen them stealing coal. For some weeks not a night had passed without hallucinations of the same kind about imaginary brigands. On this occasion, he had fired haphazard into the gloom.

"Quick! quick!" exclaimed the young man; "let us be off! They will come and search this place. Run as fast as you can!"

She fell into his arms. They stifled one another, lips to lips. Then Séverine tripped lightly through the depôt, protected by the high wall, while he quietly disappeared among the heaps of coal. And it was only just time, for Roubaud, as he had foreseen, insisted on searching the tool-house. He vowed the thieves must be there. The lanterns of the watchmen danced on a level with the ground. There were words, and in the end they all turned back towards the station, irritated at this fruitless chase; while Jacques, with his mind at ease, at last determined to make his way to the Rue François-Mazeline and go to bed.

The meetings between him and Séverine continued throughout the summer. Nor were they interrupted when the cold weather came at the commencement of October. She arrived wrapped in an ample cloak, and, to be screened from the frigid air outside, they barricaded themselves in the tool-house by means of an iron bar that they had found there. In this little retreat they were at home. The November hurricanes could roar, and tear the slates from the roofs, without inconveniencing them.

Jacques no longer had any doubt that he was cured of his frightful hereditary complaint, for since he had known Séverine he had never been troubled by thoughts of murder. Occasionally he suddenly remembered what she had done—that assassination, avowed by her eyes alone, on the bench in the Batignolles Square; but he had no inclination to learn the details. She, on the contrary, seemed more and more tormented by the desire to reveal everything. At times he felt her bursting with her secret; and, in anxiety, he would at once close her mouth with a kiss, sealing up the avowal. Why place this stranger between them? Could they affirm that it would not interfere with their happiness? He suspected danger, and felt his old shiver return at the bare idea of raking up this sanguinary story. And she, no doubt, guessed his thoughts.

Roubaud, since the summer, had grown stouter, and in proportion as his wife recovered her gaiety and the bloom of her twenty years, he grew older and seemed more overcast. In four months he had greatly changed, as she often said. He continued to cordially grasp the hand of Jacques, inviting him to the lodging, never happy but when he had him at his table. Only this diversion no longer sufficed. He frequently took himself off as soon as he had swallowed the last mouthful, sometimes leaving his comrade with his wife, pretending he was stifling, and required fresh air.

The truth was that he now frequented a small café on the Cours Napoléon, where he met M. Cauche, the commissary of police attached to the station. He drank but little, merely a few small glasses of rum; but he had acquired a taste for gambling, which was turning to a passion. He only recovered energy, and forgot the past, when the cards were in his hand, and he found himself engrossed in an interminable series of games at piquet. M. Cauche, a frightful gambler, had suggested having something on the game, and they had made the stake five francs.

From that moment, Roubaud, astonished not to have found himself out before, was burning with a thirst for gain, with that scorching fever brought on by money won which ravages a man to the point of making him stake his position, even his life, on a throw of the dice. So far his work had not suffered. He escaped as soon as free, returning home at three or four o'clock in the morning, on nights when he was off duty. His wife never complained. She only reproached him with coming back more sullen than before; for he was pursued by extraordinary bad luck, and ultimately got into debt.

The first quarrel broke out between Séverine and Roubaud one evening. Without hating him as yet, she had reached the point of enduring him with difficulty, for she felt that he weighed on her existence. She would have been so bright, so happy, had he not burdened her with his presence. She experienced no remorse at deceiving him. Was it not his own fault? Had he not almost thrust her to the brink of the precipice? In the slow process of their disunion, to cure themselves of the uneasiness that upset them, both found consolation after their own hearts. As he had taken to gambling, she could very well have a sweetheart.

But what angered her more than anything, what she would not accept without revolt, was the inconvenience to which they were subjected by the continual losses of her husband. Since the five-franc pieces of the family flew to the café on the Cours Napoléon, she at times did not know how to pay her washerwoman, and was deprived of all sorts of delicacies and little toilet comforts.

On this particular evening, it was about the purchase of a pair of boots which she really required, that they began quarrelling. He, on the point of going out, not finding a knife on the table wherewith to cut himself a piece of bread, had taken the big knife, the weapon lying in a drawer of the sideboard. She kept her eyes on him while he refused the fifteen francs for the boots, not having them, not knowing where to get them; and she obstinately repeated her demand, forcing him to renew his refusal, which, little by little, took a tone of exasperation.

All at once she pointed out to him with her finger, the place in the parquetry where the spectres slumbered, telling him there was money there, and that she wanted some. He turned very pale, and let go the knife, which fell into the drawer. At first she thought he was going to beat her, for he approached her, stammering that the money there might rot, that he would sooner cut off his hand than touch it again. And with fists clenched he threatened to knock her down if she dared, in his absence, to raise the piece of parquetry and steal even a centime. Never! never! It was dead and buried.

She also had lost her colour, feeling faint at the idea of rummaging in that place. No; let poverty come, both would die of hunger close by the treasure. And, in fact, neither of them referred to the subject again, even on days when more than usually pinched. If they happened to place a foot on the spot, they felt such a sharp burning pain that they ended by giving it a wide berth.

Then, other disputes arose, in regard to La Croix-de-Maufras. Why did they not sell the house? And they mutually accused one another of having done nothing that should have been done, to hasten the sale. He always violently refused to attend to the matter, and on the rare occasions when Séverine wrote to Misard on the subject, it was only to receive vague replies: no inquiries had been made by anyone, the fruit had come to nothing, the vegetables would not grow for want of water.

Little by little, the tranquillity that had settled upon the couple after the crisis, became troubled in this manner, and seemed swept away in a terrible return of wrath. All the germs of unrest, the hidden money, the sweetheart introduced on the scene, had developed, parting them and irritating one against the other. And, in this increasing agitation, life was about to become a pandemonium.

As if by a fatal counter-shock, everything was going wrong in the vicinity of the Roubauds. A fresh gust of tittle-tattle and discussions whistled down the corridor. Philomène had just violently broken off all connection with Madame Lebleu, in consequence of a calumny of the latter, who accused the former of selling her a fowl that had died of sickness. But the real reason of the rupture was the better understanding that prevailed between Philomène and Séverine. Pecqueux having one night met Madame Roubaud arm in arm with Jacques, Séverine at once put aside her former scruples and made advances to the secret wife of the fireman; and Philomène, very much flattered at this connection with a lady, who without contestation was considered the adornment and distinction of the railway station, had just turned against the wife of the cashier, that old wretch, as she called her, who was capable of setting mountains at variance.

Philomène now declared that all the fault lay with Madame Lebleu, telling everybody that the lodging looking on the street belonged to the Roubauds, and that it was an abomination not to give it them. Matters, therefore, began to look very bad for Madame Lebleu, and the more so, as her obstinacy in watching Mademoiselle Guichon, in order to surprise her with the station-master, threatened also to cause her serious trouble. She still failed to catch them, but she had the imprudence to get caught herself, her ear on the alert, stuck to the keyhole. And M. Dabadie, exasperated at being spied upon in this manner, had intimated to the assistant station-master, Moulin, that if Roubaud again claimed the lodging, he was ready to countersign the letter. Moulin, who, although as a rule, little given to gossip, having repeated this remark, the lodgers had nearly come to blows, from door to door, all along the corridor, so high ran the excitement that had been thus revived.

Amidst these disturbances, which became more and more frequent, Séverine had but one quiet day in the week, the Friday. In October she had placidly displayed the audacity to invent a pretext for frequently running up to Paris, the first that entered her head, a pain in the knee, which required the attention of a specialist. Each Friday, she left by the 6.40 express in the morning, which was driven by Jacques, and after passing the day with him at the capital, returned by the 6.30 express in the evening.

At first, she had thought it only right to give her husband news of her knee: it was better, it was worse, and so forth. Then, perceiving he turned a deaf ear to what she said, she had coolly ceased speaking to him on the subject. But ever and anon she would cast her eyes on him, wondering whether he knew. How was it that this ferociously jealous man, who, blinded by blood, had killed a fellow being in an idiotic rage, how was it that he had reached the point of permitting her to have a sweetheart? She could not believe it, she simply thought he must be getting stupid.

One icy cold night in December, Séverine was sitting up very late for her husband. The next morning, a Friday, she was to take the express before daybreak; and on such evenings as these, she had the habit of getting a very nice gown ready, and preparing her other garments, so as to be rapidly dressed, immediately she jumped out of bed.

At last, she retired to rest, and ended by falling off to sleep about one o'clock. Roubaud had not returned home. Already, on two occasions, he had only made his appearance at early dawn, his increasing passion for play being such that he could not tear himself away from the café, where a small room at the back was gradually being transformed into a gambling hell. They now played for high stakes at écarté.

Happy to be alone, in a pleasant frame of mind at the prospect of a delightful day on the morrow, the young woman slumbered soundly, in the gentle warmth of the bedclothes. But, as three o'clock was about to strike, she was awakened by a singular noise. First of all she did not understand, she fancied she must be dreaming and went to sleep again. Then came a dull sound, as of someone pushing against something, followed by cracking of wood, as if somebody was trying to force open a door. A sharp rent, more violent than the other sounds, brought her to a sitting posture in bed. She was frightened to death; someone was certainly trying to burst the lock in the corridor. For a minute or two she dared not move, but listened with drumming ears. Then she had the courage to get up, and look. She walked noiselessly across the room with bare feet, and gently set the door ajar, so chilled with cold that she turned quite pale, and the sight that met her eyes in the dining-room, riveted her to the spot in surprise and horror.

Roubaud, grovelling on the ground, raising himself on his elbows, had just torn away the dreaded piece of parquetry with the assistance of a chisel. A candle, set down beside him, afforded light while casting his enormous shadow on the ceiling. And at that moment, with his face bent over the hole which cut the parquetry with a black slit, he was peering with dilated eyes within. His cheeks were flushed, and he wore his assassin-like expression. Brutally he plunged his hand into the aperture, and, in his trembling agitation, finding nothing, he had to bring the candle nearer. Then at the bottom of the hole appeared the purse, notes, and watch.

Séverine uttered an involuntary cry, and Roubaud turned round, terrified. At first he failed to recognise her, and seeing her there, all in white, with a look of horror on her countenance, no doubt took her for a spectre.

"What are you doing there?" she demanded.

Then, understanding, avoiding to answer, he only gave a sullen growl. But he still looked at her, inconvenienced by her presence, wishing to send her back to bed. And not a reasonable word came to his lips. He simply felt inclined to box her ears, as she stood there shivering in her night-dress.

"So," she continued, "you refuse me a pair of boots, and you take the money for yourself because you have lost."

This remark at once enraged him. Was she going to spoil his life again, to set herself in front of his pleasures—this woman whom he no longer cared for? Again he rummaged in the hole, but only took from it the purse containing the 300 frcs. in gold. And when he had fixed the piece of parquetry in its place with his heel, he went and flung these words in her face, through his set teeth:

"Go to the deuce! I shall act as I choose. Am I asking you what you are going to do, by-and-by, at Paris?"

Then, with a furious shrug of the shoulders, he returned to the café, leaving the candle on the floor.

Séverine picked it up, and went back to bed, cold as ice. But, unable to get to sleep again, she kept the candle alight, waiting, with her eyes wide open, until the time came for the departure of the express, and gradually growing burning hot. It was now certain that there had been a progressive disorganisation, like an infiltration of the crime, which was decomposing this man, and which had worn out every bond between them. Roubaud knew.

VII

O n that particular Friday, the travellers who were to take the 6.40 express from Havre, awoke with an exclamation of surprise; snow had been falling since midnight, so thickly and in such large flakes, that the streets were a foot deep in it.

La Lison, attached to a train of seven carriages, three second and four first class, was already puffing and smoking under the span roof. When Jacques and Pecqueux arrived at the depôt at about half-past five to get the engine ready, they uttered a growl of anxiety at the sight of this persistent snow rending the black sky. And now, at their post, they awaited the sound of the whistle, with eyes gazing far ahead beyond the gaping porch of the marquee, watching the silent, endless fall of flakes draping the obscurity in livid hue.

The driver murmured:

"The devil take me if you can see a signal!"

"We may think ourselves lucky if we can get along," said the fireman.

Roubaud was on the platform with his lantern, having returned at the precise minute to resume his service. At moments his heavy eyelids closed with fatigue, without him ceasing his supervision. Jacques having inquired whether he knew anything as to the state of the line, he had just approached and pressed his hand, answering that as yet he had received no telegram; and as Séverine came down, wrapped in an ample cloak, he led her to a first class compartment and assisted her in. No doubt he caught sight of the anxious look of tenderness that the two sweethearts exchanged; but he did not even trouble to tell his wife that it was imprudent to set out in such weather, and that she would do better to postpone her journey.

Passengers arrived, muffled up, loaded with travelling-bags, and there was quite a crush in the terrible morning cold. The snow did not even melt on the shoes of the travellers. The carriage doors were closed as soon as the people were in the compartments where they barricaded themselves; and the platform, badly lit by the uncertain glimmer of a few gas-burners, became deserted. The light of the locomotive, attached to the base of the chimney, alone burnt brightly like a huge eye dilating its sheet of fire far into the obscurity.

Roubaud raised his lantern to give the signal of departure. The headguard blew his whistle, and Jacques answered, after opening the regulator and revolving the reversing-wheel. They started. For a minute the assistant station-master tranquilly gazed after the train disappearing in the tempest.

"Attention!" said Jacques to Pecqueux. "No joking today!"

He had not failed to remark that his companion seemed also worn out with fatigue. Assuredly the consequence of some spree on the previous night.

"Oh! no fear, no fear!" stammered the fireman.

As soon as they left the span roofing of the station, they were in the snow. The wind, blowing from the east, caught the locomotive in front, beating against it in violent gusts. The two men in the cab did not suffer much at first, clothed as they were in thick woollen garments, with their eyes protected by spectacles. But the light on the engine, usually so brilliant at night, seemed swallowed up in the thick fall of snow. Instead of the metal way being illuminated three or four hundred yards ahead, it came into evidence in a sort of milky fog. The various objects could only be distinguished when the locomotive was quite close to them, and then they appeared indistinct, as in a dream.

The anxiety of the driver was complete when he recognised, on reaching the first signal-post, that he would certainly be unable, as he had feared, to see the red lights barring the lines at the regulation distances. From that moment he advanced with extreme prudence, but without it being possible for him to slacken speed, for the wind offered extraordinary resistance, and delay would have been as dangerous as a too rapid advance.

As far as Harfleur, La Lison went along at a good and well-sustained pace. The layer of snow that had fallen did not as yet trouble Jacques, for, at the most, there were two feet on the line, and the snow-blade could easily clear away four. All his anxiety was to maintain the speed, well aware that the real merit of a driver, after temperance, and esteem for his engine, consisted in advancing in an uniform way, without jolting, and at the highest pressure possible.

Indeed, his only defect lay in his obstinacy not to stop. He disobeyed the signals, always thinking he would have time to master La Lison; and so he now and again over-shot the mark, crushing the crackers, the "corns" as they are termed, and, on two occasions, this habit had caused him to be suspended for a week. But now, in the great danger in which he felt himself, the thought that Séverine was there, that he was entrusted with her dear life, increased his strength of character tenfold;

and he maintained his determination to be cautious all the way to Paris, all along that double metal line, bristling with obstacles that he must overcome.

Standing on the sheet of iron connecting the engine with the tender, continually jolted by their oscillation, Jacques, notwithstanding the snow, leant over the side, on the right, to get a better view. For he could distinguish nothing through the cab window clouded with water; and he remained with his face exposed to the gusts of wind, his skin pricked as with thousands of needles, and so pinched with cold that it seemed like being slashed with razors. Ever and anon he withdrew to take breath; he removed his spectacles and wiped them; then he resumed his former position facing the hurricane, his eyes fixed, in the expectation of seeing red lights; and so absorbed was he in his anxiety to find them, that on two occasions he fell a prey to the hallucination that crimson sparks were boring the white curtain of snow fluttering before him.

But, on a sudden, in the darkness, he felt a presentiment that his fireman was no longer there. Only a small lantern lit up the steam-gauge, so that the eyes of the driver might not be inconvenienced; and, on the enamelled face of the manometer, which preserved its clear lustre, he noticed the trembling blue hand rapidly retreating. The fire was going down. The fireman had just stretched himself on the chest, vanquished by fatigue.

"Infernal rake!" exclaimed Jacques, shaking him in a rage.

Pecqueux rose, excusing himself in an unintelligible growl. He could hardly stand; but, by force of habit, he at once went to his fire, hammer in hand, breaking the coal, spreading it evenly on the bars with the shovel. Then he swept up with the broom. And while the door of the fire-box remained open, a reflex from the furnace, like the flaming tail of a comet extending to the rear of the train, had set fire to the snow which fell across it in great golden drops.

After Harfleur began the big ascent, ten miles long, which extends to Saint-Romain—the steepest on the line. And the driver stood to the engine, full of attention, anticipating that La Lison would have to make a famous effort to ascend this hill, already hard to climb in fine weather. With his hand on the reversing-wheel, he watched the telegraph poles fly by, endeavouring to form an idea of the speed. This decreased considerably. La Lison was puffing, while the scraping of the snow-blade indicated growing resistance. He opened the door of the fire-box with the toe of his boot. The fireman, half asleep, understood, and added more fuel to the embers, so as to increase the pressure.

The door was now becoming red-hot, lighting up the legs of both of them with a violet gleam. But neither felt the scorching heat in the current of icy air that enveloped them. The fireman, at a sign from his chief, had just raised the rod of the ash-pan which added to the draught. The hand of the manometer at present marked ten atmospheres, and La Lison was exerting all the power it possessed. At one moment, perceiving the water in the steam-gauge sink, the driver had to turn the injection-cock, although by doing so he diminished the pressure. Nevertheless, it rose again, the engine snorted and spat like an animal over-ridden, making jumps and efforts fit to convey the idea that it would suddenly crack some of its component pieces. And he treated La Lison roughly, like a woman who has grown old and lost her strength, ceasing to feel the same tenderness for it as formerly.

"The lazy thing will never get to the top," said he between his set teeth—he who never uttered a word on the journey.

Pecqueux, in his drowsiness, looked at him in astonishment. What had he got now against La Lison? Was it not still the same brave, obedient locomotive, starting so readily that it was a pleasure to set it in motion; and gifted with such excellent vaporisation that it economised a tenth part of its coal between Paris and Havre? When an engine had slide valves like this one, so perfectly regulated, cutting the steam so miraculously, they could overlook all imperfections, as in the case of a capricious, but steady and economical housewife. No doubt La Lison took too much grease, but what of that? They would grease it, and there was an end of the matter.

Just at that moment, Jacques, in exasperation, repeated:

"It'll never reach the top, unless it's greased!"

And he did what he had not done thrice in his life. He took the oil-can to grease the engine as it went along. Climbing over the rail, he got on the frame-plate beside the boiler, which he followed to the end. It was a most perilous undertaking. His feet slipped on the narrow strip of iron, wet with snow. He was blinded, and the terrible wind threatened to sweep him away like a straw.

La Lison, with this man clinging to its side, continued its panting course in the darkness, cutting for itself a deep trench in the immense white sheet covering the ground. The engine shook him, but bore him along. On attaining the cross-piece in front, he held on to the rail with one hand, and, stooping down before the oil-box of the cylinder on the right, experienced the greatest difficulty in filling it. Then he had to go round to the other side, like a crawling insect, to grease the cylinder on the left. And when he got back to his post, he was exhausted and deadly pale, having felt himself face to face with death.

"Vile brute!" he murmured.

Pecqueux had recovered, in a measure, from his drowsiness, and pulled himself together. He, too, was at his post, watching the line on the left. On ordinary occasions he had good eyes, better than those of his chief, but in this storm everything had disappeared. They, to whom each mile of the metal way was so familiar, could barely recognise the places they passed. The line had disappeared in the snow, the hedges, the houses, even, seemed about to follow suit. Around them was naught but a deserted and boundless expanse, where La Lison seemed to be careering at will, in a fit of madness.

Never had these two men felt so keenly the fraternal bond uniting them as on this advancing engine, let loose amidst all kinds of danger, where they were more alone, more abandoned by the world, than if locked up in a room by themselves; and where, moreover, they had the grievous, the crushing responsibility of the human lives they were dragging after them.

The snow continued falling thicker than ever. They were still ascending, when the fireman, in his turn, fancied he perceived the glint of a red light in the distance and told his chief. But already he had lost it. His eyes must have been dreaming, as he sometimes said. And the driver, who had seen nothing, remained with a beating heart, troubled at this hallucination of another, and losing confidence in himself.

What he imagined he distinguished beyond the myriads of pale flakes were immense black forms, enormous masses, like gigantic pieces of the night, which seemed to displace themselves and come before the engine. Could these be landslips, mountains barring the line against which the train was about to crush? Then, affrighted, he pulled the rod of the whistle, and whistled long, despairingly; and this lamentation went slowly and lugubriously through the storm. Then he was astonished to find that he had whistled at the right moment, for the train was passing the station of Saint-Romain at express speed, and he had thought it two miles away.

La Lison, having got over the terrible ascent, began rolling on more at ease, and Jacques had time to breathe. Between Saint-Romain and Bolbec the line makes an imperceptible rise, so that all would, no doubt, be well until the other side of the plateau. While he was at Beuzeville, during the three minutes' stoppage, he nevertheless called the station-master, whom he perceived on the platform, wishing to convey to him his anxiety about this snow, which continued getting deeper and deeper: he would never be able to reach Rouen; the best thing would be to put on another engine, while he was at a depôt, where locomotives were always ready. But the station-master answered that he had no orders, and that he did not feel disposed to take the responsibility of such a measure on himself. All he offered to do was to give five or six wooden shovels to clear the line in case of need; and Pecqueux took the shovels, which he placed in a corner of the tender.

On the plateau, La Lison, as Jacques had foreseen, continued to advance at a good speed, and without too much trouble. Nevertheless, it tired. At every minute the driver had to make a sign and open the fire-box, so that the fireman might put on coal. And each time he did so, above the mournful train, standing out in black upon all this whiteness and covered with a winding sheet of snow, flamed the dazzling tail of the comet, boring into the night.

At three-quarters of an hour past seven, day was breaking; but the wan dawn could hardly be discerned in the immense whitish whirlwind filling space within the entire horizon. This uncertain light, by which nothing could as yet be distinguished, increased the anxiety of the two men, who, with eyes watering, notwithstanding their spectacles, did their utmost to pierce the distance. The driver, without letting go the reversing-wheel never quitted the rod of the whistle. He sounded it almost continuously, by prudence, giving a shriek of distress that penetrated like a wail to the depths of this desert of snow.

They passed Bolbec, and then Yvetot, without difficulty. But at Motteville, Jacques made inquiries of the assistant station-master for precise information as to the state of the line. No train had yet arrived, and a telegram that had been received merely stated that the slow train from Paris was blocked at Rouen in safety. And La Lison went on again, descending at her heavy and weary gait the ten miles or so of gentle slope to Barentin.

Daylight now began to appear, but very dimly; and it seemed as if this livid glimmer came from the snow itself which fell more densely, confused and cold, overwhelming the earth with the refuse of the sky. As day grew, the violence of the wind redoubled, and the snowflakes were driven along in balls. At every moment the fireman had to take his shovel to clear the coal at the back of the tender between the partitions of the water-tank.

The country, to right and left, so absolutely defied recognition, that the two men felt as if they were being borne along in a dream. The vast flat fields, the rich pastures enclosed in green hedges, the apple orchards were naught but a white sea, barely swelling with choppy waves, a pallid, quivering expanse where everything became white. And the driver erect, with his hand on the reversing-wheel, his face lacerated by the gusts of wind, began to suffer terribly from cold.

When the train stopped at Barentin, M. Bessière, the station-master, himself approached the engine, to warn Jacques that a considerable accumulation of snow had been signalled in the vicinity of La Croix-de-Maufras.

"I believe it is still possible to pass," he added; "but it will not be without difficulty."

Thereupon, the young man flew into a passion, and with an oath exclaimed:

"I said as much at Beuzeville! Why couldn't they put on a second locomotive? We shall be in a nice mess now!"

The headguard had just left his van, and he became angry as well. He was frozen in his box, and declared that he could not distinguish a signal from a telegraph pole. It was a regular groping journey in all this white.

"Anyhow, you are warned," said M. Bessière.

In the meantime the passengers were astonished at this prolonged stoppage, amid the complete silence enveloping the station, without a shout from any of the staff, or the banging of a door. A few windows were lowered, and heads appeared: a very stout lady with a couple of charming, fair young girls, no doubt her daughters, all three English for certain; and, further on, a very pretty dark, young woman, who was made to draw in her head by an elderly gentleman; while two men, one young and the other old, chatted from one carriage to the other, with their bodies half out of the windows.

But as Jacques cast a glance behind him, he perceived only Séverine, who was also looking out and gazing anxiously in his direction. Ah! the dear creature, how uneasy she must be, and what a heartburn he experienced knowing her there, so near and yet so far away in all this danger!

"Come! Be off!" concluded the station-master. "It is no use frightening the people."

He gave the signal himself. The headguard, who had got into his van, whistled; and once more La Lison went off, after answering with a long wail of complaint.

Jacques at once felt that the state of the line had changed. It was no longer the plain, the eternal unfolding of the thick sheet of snow, through which the engine ran along, like a steam-boat, leaving a trail behind her. They were entering the uneven country of hills and dales, whose enormous undulation extended as far as Malaunay, breaking up the ground into heaps; and here the snow had collected in an unequal manner. In places the line proved free, while in others it was blocked by drifts of considerable magnitude. The wind that swept the embankments filled up the cuttings; and thus there was a continual succession of obstacles to be overcome: bits of clear line blocked by absolute ramparts. It was now broad daylight, and the devastated country, those narrow gorges, those steep slopes, resembled in their white coating, the desolation of an ocean of ice remaining motionless in the storm.

Never had Jacques felt so penetrated by the cold. His face seemed bleeding from the stinging flagellation of the snow; and he had lost consciousness of his hands, which were so benumbed and so bereft of sensibility, that he shuddered on perceiving he could not feel the touch of the reversing-wheel. When he raised his elbow to pull the rod of the whistle, his arm weighed on the shoulder as if dead. He could not have affirmed that his legs still carried him, amid the constant shocks of oscillation that tore his inside. Great fatigue had gained him, along with the cold, whose icy chill was attaining his head. He began to doubt whether he existed, whether he was still driving, for he already only turned the wheel in a mechanical way; and, half silly, he watched the manometer going back.

All kinds of hallucinations passed through his head. Was not that a felled tree, over there, lying across the line? Had he not caught sight of a red flag flying above that hedge? Were not crackers going off every minute amidst the clatter of the wheels? He could not have answered. He repeated to himself that he ought to stop, and he lacked the firmness of will to do so. This crisis tortured him for a few minutes; then, abruptly, the sight of Pecqueux, who had fallen asleep again on the chest, overcome by the cold from which he was suffering himself, threw him into such a frightful rage that it seemed to bring him warmth.

"Ah! the abominable brute!" he exclaimed.

And he, who was usually so lenient for the vices of this drunkard, kicked him until he awoke, and was on his feet. Pecqueux, benumbed with cold, grumbled as he grasped the shovel:

"That'll do, that'll do; I'm going there!"

With the fire made up, the pressure rose; and it was time, for La Lison had just entered a cutting where it had to cleave through four feet of snow. It advanced with an energetic effort, vibrating in every part. For an instant it showed signs of exhaustion, and seemed as if about to stand still, like a vessel that has touched a sandbank. What increased the weight it had to draw was the snow, which had accumulated in a heavy layer on the roofs of the carriages.

They continued thus, seaming the whiteness with a dark line, with this white sheet spread over them; while the engine itself had only borders of ermine draping its sombre sides, where the snowflakes melted to run off in rain. Once more it extricated itself, notwithstanding the weight, and passed on. At the top of an embankment, that made a great curve, the train could still be seen advancing without difficulty, like a strip of shadow lost in some fairyland sparkling with whiteness.

But, farther on, the cuttings began again; and Jacques and Pecqueux, who had felt La Lison touch, stiffened themselves against the cold, erect at their posts, which even, were they dying, they could not desert. Once more the engine lost speed; it had got between two talus, and the stoppage came slowly and without a shock. It seemed as if glued there, exhausted; as though all its wheels were clogged, tighter and tighter. It ceased moving, the end had come; the snow held the engine powerless.

"It's all up!" growled Jacques with an oath.

He remained a few seconds longer at his post, his hand on the wheel, opening everything to see if the obstacle would yield. Then, hearing La Lison spitting and snorting in vain, he shut the regulator, and, in his fury, swore worse than ever.

The headguard leant out from the door of his van, and Pecqueux, turning round, shouted to him:

"It's all up! We're stuck!"

Briskly the guard sprang into the snow, which reached to his knees. He approached, and the three men consulted together.

"The only thing we can do is to try and dig it out," said the driver at last. "Fortunately, we have some shovels. Call the second guard at the end of the train, and between us four we shall be able to clear the wheels."

They gave a sign to the other guard behind, who had also left his van. He made his way to them with great difficulty, getting at times half buried in the snow.

But this stoppage in the open country, amid this pallid solitude, this clear sound of voices discussing what must be done, the guard floundering along beside the train with laborious strides had made the passengers uneasy. The windows went down; the people called out and questioned one another; a regular confusion ensued—vague, as yet, but becoming more pronounced.

"Where are we? Why have they stopped? What is the matter? Good heavens! is there an accident?"

The guard found it necessary to allay the alarm; and just as he advanced to the carriages, the English lady, whose fat red face was flanked by the charming countenances of her daughters, inquired with a strong accent:

"Guard, is there any danger?"

"No, no, madam," he replied. "It's only a little snow. We shall be going on at once."

And the window went up again amid the bright twittering of the young girls—that music of English syllables which is so sparkling on rosy lips. Both were laughing, very much amused.

But the elderly gentleman, who was farther on, also called the guard, while his young wife risked her pretty dark head behind him.

"How was it that no precautions were taken? It is unbearable. I am returning from London. My business requires my presence in Paris this morning, and I warn you that I shall make the company responsible for any delay."

"We shall be going on again in three minutes, sir," said the guard.

The cold was terrible; the snow entered the carriages, driving in the heads and bringing up the windows. But the agitation continued within the closed vehicles, where everyone was disturbed by a low hum of anxiety. A couple of windows alone remained down; and two travellers leaning out, three compartments away from each other, were talking. One was an American some forty years of age, and the other a young gentleman from Havre. Both were very much interested in the task of clearing away the snow.

"In America everyone would get down and take a shovel," remarked the former.

"Oh! it is nothing!" answered the other. "I was blocked twice last year. My business brings me to Paris every week."

"And mine every three weeks, or so."

"What! from New York?"

"Yes; from New York."

It was Jacques who directed the labour. Perceiving Séverine at the door of the first carriage, where she always took her seat, so as to be near him, he gave her a look of entreaty; and she, understanding, drew back out of the icy wind that was stinging her face. Then, with her occupying his thoughts, he worked away heartily.

But he remarked that the cause of the stoppage, the embedment in the snow had nothing to do with the wheels, which cut through the deepest drifts. It was the ash-pan, placed between them, that produced the obstruction, by driving the snow along, compressing it into enormous lumps. And he was struck with an idea.

"We must unscrew the ash-pan," said he.

At first the headguard opposed the suggestion. The driver was under his orders, and he would not give his consent to the engine being touched. Then, giving way to argument, he said:

"If you take the responsibility, all right!"

Only it was a hard job. Stretched out beneath the engine, with their backs in the melting snow, Jacques and Pecqueux had to toil for nearly half an hour. Fortunately they had spare screwdrivers in the toolchest. At last, at the risk of burning themselves and getting crushed a score of times over, they managed to take the ash-pan down. But they had not done with it yet. It was necessary to drag it away. Being an enormous weight, it got jammed in the wheels and cylinders. Nevertheless, the four together were able to pull it out, and drag it off the line to the foot of the embankment.

"Now let us finish clearing away the snow," said the guard.

The train had been close upon an hour in distress, and the alarm of the passengers had increased. Every minute a glass went down, and a voice inquired why they did not go on. There was a regular panic, with shouts and tears, in an increscent crisis of craziness.

"No, no, enough has been cleared away," said Jacques. "Jump up, I'll see to the rest."

He was once more at his post, along with Pecqueux, and when the two guards had gained their vans, he turned on the exhaust-tap. The deafening rush of scalding steam melted the remainder of the snow still clinging to the line. Then, with his hand on the wheel, he reversed the engine, and slowly retreated to a distance of about four hundred yards, to give it a run. And having piled up the fire, and attained a pressure exceeding what was permitted by the regulations, he sent La Lison against the wall of snow with all its might and all the weight of the train it drew.

The locomotive gave a terrific grunt, similar to that of a woodman driving his axe into a great tree, and it seemed as though all the powerful ironwork was about to crack. It could not pass yet. It came to a standstill, smoking and vibrating all over with the shock. Twice the driver had to repeat the manœuvre, running back, then dashing against the snow to drive it away. On each occasion, La Lison, girded for the encounter, struck its chest against the impediment with the furious respiration of a giant, but to no purpose. At last, regaining breath, it strained its metal muscles in a supreme effort and passed, while the train followed ponderously behind, between the two walls of snow ripped asunder. It was free!

"A good brute, all the same!" growled Pecqueux.

Jacques, half blinded, removed his spectacles and wiped them. His heart beat hard. He no longer felt the cold. But abruptly he remembered a deep cutting, some four hundred yards away from La Croix-de-Maufras. It opened in the direction of the wind, and the snow must have accumulated there in a considerable quantity. He at once felt certain that this was the rock, marked out, whereon he would founder. He bent forward. In the distance, after a final curve, the trench appeared before him in a straight line, like a long ditch full of snow. It was broad daylight, and the boundless whiteness sparkled amid the unceasing fall of snowflakes.

La Lison skimmed along at a medium speed, having encountered no further obstacle. By precaution, the lanterns had been left burning in front and behind; and the white light at the base of the chimney shone in the daylight like a living Cyclopean eye. The engine rolled along, approaching the cutting, with this eye wide open. Then it seemed to pant, with the gentle short respiration of an affrighted steed. It shook with deep thrills, it reared, and was only impelled forward under the vigorous hand of the driver. The latter had rapidly opened the door of the fire-box for the fireman to put in coal. And now it was no more the tail of a comet illuminating the night, it was a plume of thick black smoke, soiling the great shivering pallidness of the sky.

La Lison advanced. At last it had to enter the cutting. The slopes, to right and left, were deep in snow; and at the bottom not a vestige of the line could be seen. It was like the bed of a torrent filled up with snow from side to side. The locomotive passed in, rolling along for sixty or seventy yards, with exhausted respiration that grew shorter and shorter. The snow it pushed forward formed a barrier in front, which flew about and rose like an ungovernable flood threatening to engulf it. For a moment it appeared overwhelmed and vanquished. But, in a final effort, it delivered itself to advance another forty yards. That was the end, the last pang of death. Lumps of snow fell down covering the wheels; all the pieces of the mechanism were smothered, connected with one another by chains of ice. And La Lison stopped definitely, expiring in the intense cold. Its respiration died away, it was motionless and dead.

"There, we're done for now," said Jacques. "That is just what I expected."

He at once wanted to reverse the engine, to try the previous manœuvre again. But, this time, La Lison did not move. It refused either to go back or advance, it was blocked everywhere, riveted to the ground, inert and insensible. Behind, the train, buried in a thick bed reaching to the doors, also seemed dead. The snow, far from ceasing, fell more densely than before in prolonged squalls. They were in a drift, where engine and carriages, already half covered up, would soon disappear amid the shivering silence of this hoary solitude. Nothing more moved. The snow was weaving the winding sheet.

"What!" exclaimed the chiefguard, leaning out of his van; "has it begun again?"

"We're done for!" Pecqueux simply shouted.

This time, indeed, the position proved critical. The guard in the rear ran and placed fog-signals on the line, to protect the train at the back; while the driver sounded distractedly, with swift breaks, the panting, lugubrious whistle of distress. But the snow loading the air, the sound was lost, and could not even have reached Barentin. What was to be done? They were but four, and they would never be able to clear away such an immense mass—a regular gang of labourers would be necessary. It became imperative to run for assistance. And the worst of it was that the passengers were again in a panic.

A door opened. The pretty dark lady sprang from her carriage in a fright, thinking they had met with an accident. Her husband, the elderly commercial man, followed, exclaiming:

"I shall write to the Minister. It's an outrage!"

Then came the tears of the women, the furious voices of the men, as they jumped from their compartments, amid the violent shocks of the lowered windows. The two young English girls, who were at ease and smiling, alone displayed some gaiety. While the headguard was trying to calm the crowd, the younger of the two said to him in French, with a slight Britannic accent:

"So, it is here that we stop, then, guard?"

Several men had got down, notwithstanding the depth of snow in which their legs entirely disappeared. The American again found himself beside the young man from Havre, and both made their way to the engine, to see for themselves. They tossed their heads.

"It will take four or five hours to get us out of that," said one.

"At least," answered the other, "and even then it will require a score of workmen."

Jacques had just persuaded the headguard to send his companion to Barentin to ask for help. Neither the driver nor the fireman could leave the engine.

The man was already far away, they soon lost sight of him at the end of the cutting. He had three miles to walk, and perhaps would not be back before two hours. And Jacques, in despair, left his post for an instant, and ran to the first carriage where he perceived Séverine who had let down the glass.

"Don't be afraid," said he rapidly; "you have nothing to fear."

She answered in the same tone, avoiding familiarity lest she might be overheard:

"I'm not afraid; only I've been very uneasy about you."

And this was said so sweetly that both were consoled, and smiled at one another. But as Jacques turned round, he was surprised to see Flore at the top of the cutting; then Misard, accompanied by two other men, whom he failed to recognise at first. They had heard the distress whistle; and Misard, who was off duty, had hastened to the spot along with his two companions, whom he had been treating to a morning draught of white wine. One of these men proved to be Cabuche, thrown out of work by the snow, and the other Ozil, who had come from Malaunay through the tunnel, to pay court to Flore, whom he still pursued with his attentions, in spite of the bad reception he met with. She, out of curiosity, like a great vagabond girl, brave and strong as a young man, accompanied them.

For her and her father, this was a great event—an extraordinary adventure, this train stopping, so to say, at their door. During the five years they had been living there, at every hour of the day and night, in fine weather and foul, how many trains had they seen dart by! All were borne away in the same breath that brought them. Not one had even slackened speed. They saw them dash ahead, fade in the distance, disappear, before they had time to learn anything about them. The whole world filed past; the human multitude carried along full steam, without them having knowledge of aught else than faces caught sight of in a flash—faces they were never more to set eyes on, apart from a few that became familiar to them, through being seen over and over again on particular days, and to which they could attach no name.

And here, in the snow, a train arrived at their door. The natural order of things was reversed. They stared to their hearts' content at this little unknown world of people, whom an accident had cast on the line; they contemplated them with the rounded eyes of savages, who had sped to a shore where a number of Europeans had been shipwrecked. Those open doors revealing ladies wrapped in furs, those men who had got out in thick overcoats; all this comfortable luxury, stranded amid this sea of ice, struck them with astonishment.

But Flore had recognised Séverine. She, who watched each time for the train driven by Jacques, had perceived, during the past few weeks, the presence of this woman in the express on Friday morning; and the more readily, as Séverine, on approaching the level crossing, put her head out of the window to take a glance at her property of La Croix-de-Maufras. The eyes of Flore clouded as she noticed her talking in an undertone with the driver.

"Ah! Madame Roubaud!" exclaimed Misard, who had also just recognised her; and at once assuming his obsequious manner, he continued: "What dreadful bad luck! But you cannot remain there, you must come to our house."

Jacques, after pressing the hand of the gateman, supported his invitation.

"He is right," said he. "We may have to wait here for hours, and you will be perished to death."

Séverine refused. She was well wrapped up, she said. Then, the four hundred yards in the snow frightened her a little. Thereupon Flore drew near, and, looking fixedly at her with her great eyes, ended by saying:

"Come, madam, I will carry you."

And before Séverine had time to accept she had caught her in her arms, vigorous as those of a young man, and lifted her up like a little child. She set her down on the other side of the line, at a spot which had been well-trodden, and where the feet no longer sank into the snow. Some of the travellers began to laugh, marvelling at the achievement. What a strapping wench! If they only had a dozen of the same kidney the train would be free in a couple of hours.

In the meanwhile, the suggestion that Misard had been heard to make, this house of the gatekeeper, where they could take refuge, find a fire, and perhaps bread and wine, flew from one carriage to another. The panic had calmed down when the people understood that they ran no immediate danger; only the position remained none the less lamentable: the foot-warmers were becoming cold, it was nine o'clock, and if help tarried they would be suffering from hunger and thirst. Besides, the line might remain blocked much longer than was anticipated. Who could say they would not have to sleep there?

The passengers divided into two camps: those who in despair would not quit the carriages, and installed themselves as if they were going to end their days there, wrapped up in their blankets, stretched out in a peevish frame of mind on the seats; and those who preferred risking the trip, in the hope of finding more comfortable quarters, and, who above all, were desirous of escaping from this nightmare of a train stranded in the snow and being frozen to death. Quite a small party was formed, the elderly commercial man and his young wife, the English lady and her two daughters, the young man from Havre, the American, and a dozen others all ready to set out.

Jacques, in a low voice, had persuaded Séverine to join them, vowing he would take her news, if he could get away. And as Flore continued observing them with her clouded eyes, he addressed her gently, like an old friend:

"All right! It's understood, you will show these ladies and gentlemen the way. I shall keep Misard and the others. We'll set to work and do what we can until help arrives."

Cabuche, Ozil, and Misard, in fact, at once caught hold of shovels to join Pecqueux and the headguard who were already attacking the snow. The little gang strove to clear the engine, digging round the wheels and emptying their shovels against the sides of the cutting. Nobody spoke, nothing could be heard but the sound of their impulsive labour amid the gloomy oppression of the pallid country. And when the little troop

ÉMILE ZOLA

of passengers were far away, they took a last look at the train, which remained alone, showing merely a thin black line beneath the thick layer of white weighing on the top of it. The travellers remaining behind had closed the doors and put up the glasses. The snow continued falling, slowly but surely, and with mute obstinacy, burying engine and carriages.

Flore wanted to take Séverine in her arms again; but the latter refused, wishing to walk like the others. The four hundred yards were painful to get over, particularly in the cutting where the people sank in up to the hips; and on two occasions it became necessary to go to the rescue of the stout English lady who was half smothered. Her daughters, who were delighted, continued laughing. The young wife of the old gentleman, having slipped, consented to take the arm of the young man from Havre; while her husband ran down France with the American. On issuing from the cutting walking became easier; the little band advanced along an embankment in single file, beaten by the wind, carefully avoiding the edges rendered uncertain and dangerous by the snow.

At length they arrived, and Flore took them into the kitchen where she was unable to find a seat for all, as there proved to be quite a score of them crowding the room, which fortunately was fairly large. The only thing she could think of was to go and fetch some planks, and rig up a couple of forms by the aid of the chairs she possessed. She then threw a faggot on the hearth, and made a gesture to indicate that they must not ask her for anything more. She had not uttered a word. She remained erect, gazing at these people with her large greenish eyes, in the fierce, bold manner of a great blonde savage.

Apart from the face of Séverine, those of the American, and the young man from Havre alone, were known to her. These she was familiar with through having frequently noticed them at the windows for months past; and she examined them, now, just as one studies an insect which, after buzzing about in the air, has at length settled on something, and which it was impossible to follow on the wing. They struck her as peculiar. She had not imagined them exactly thus, having caught but a glimpse of their features. As to the other people, they seemed to her to belong to a different race—to be the inhabitants of an unknown land, fallen from the sky, who brought into her home, right into her kitchen, garments, customs, and ideas that she had never anticipated finding there.

The English lady confided to the young wife of the commercial gentleman that she was on her way to join her eldest son, a high functionary in India; and the young woman joked about the ill-luck she had met with, on the first occasion she happened to have the caprice to accompany her husband to London where he went twice a year. All lamented being blocked in this desert. What were they to do for food, and how were they going to sleep? What could be done, good heavens!

Flore, who was listening to them motionless, having caught the eyes of Séverine, seated on a chair before the fire, made her a sign that she wanted to take her into the adjoining room.

"Mamma," said she as they entered, "it's Madame Roubaud. Wouldn't you like to have a chat with her?"

Phasie was in bed, her face yellow, her legs swollen; so ill that she had not been able to get up for a fortnight. And she passed this time in the poorly furnished room, heated to suffocation by an iron stove, obstinately pondering over the fixed idea she had got into her head, without any other amusement than the shock of the trains as they flew past full speed.

"Ah! Madame Roubaud," she murmured; "very good, very good."

Flore told her of the accident, and spoke to her of the people she had brought home, and who were there in the kitchen. But such things had ceased to interest her.

"Very good, very good," she repeated in the same weary voice.

Suddenly she recollected, and raised her head an instant to say:

"If madam would like to see her house, the keys are hanging there, near the wardrobe."

But Séverine refused. A shiver had come over her at the thought of going to La Croix-de-Maufras in this snow, in this livid daylight. No, no, there was nothing she desired to do there. She preferred to remain where she was, and wait in the warmth.

"Be seated, madam," resumed Flore. "It is more comfortable here than in the other room; and, besides, we shall never be able to find sufficient bread for all these people; whereas, if you are hungry, there will always be a bit for you."

She had handed her a chair, and continued to show herself attentive, making a visible effort to attenuate her usual rough manner. But her eyes never quitted the young woman. It seemed as if she wished to read her; to arrive at a certainty in regard to a particular question that she had already been asking herself for sometime; and, in her eagerness, she felt a desire to approach her, to stare her out of countenance, to touch her, so as to know.

Séverine expressed her thanks, and made herself comfortable near the stove, preferring, indeed, to be alone with the invalid in this room, where she hoped Jacques would find means to join her. Two hours passed. Yielding to the oppressive heat, she had fallen asleep, after chatting about the neighbourhood. Suddenly, Flore, who at every minute had been summoned to the kitchen, opened the door, saying in her harsh tones:

"Go in, as she is there."

It was Jacques who had escaped with good news. The man sent to Barentin had just brought back a whole gang, some thirty soldiers, whom the administration, foreseeing accidents, had dispatched to the threatened points on the line; and they were all hard at work with pick and shovel. Only it would be a long job, and the train would, perhaps, not be able to get off again before evening.

"Anyhow, you are not so badly off," he added; "have patience. And, Aunt Phasie, you will not let Madame Roubaud starve, will you?"

Phasie, at the sight of her big lad, as she called him, had with difficulty sat up, and she looked at him, revived and happy, listening to him talking. When he had drawn near her bed, she replied:

"Of course not, of course not. Ah! my big lad, so there you are. And so it's you who have got caught in the snow; and that silly girl never told me so."

Turning to her daughter, she said reproachfully:

"Try and be polite, anyhow. Return to those ladies and gentlemen, show them some attention, so that they may not tell the company that we are no better than savages."

Flore remained planted between Jacques and Séverine. She appeared to hesitate for an instant, asking herself if she should not obstinately remain there, in spite of her mother. But she reflected that she would see nothing; the presence of the invalid would prevent any familiarity between the other two; and she withdrew, after taking a long look at them.

"What! Aunt Phasie!" exclaimed Jacques sadly; "you have taken to your bed for good? Then it's serious?"

She drew him towards her, forcing him even to seat himself at the edge of the mattress; and without troubling any further about the young woman, who had discreetly moved away, she proceeded to relieve herself in a very low voice.

"Oh! yes, serious! It's a miracle if you find me alive. I wouldn't write to you, because such things can't be written. I've had a narrow escape; but now I am already better, and I believe I shall get over it again this time."

He examined her, alarmed at the progress of the malady, and found she had not preserved a vestige of the handsome, healthy woman of former days.

"Then you still suffer from your cramps and dizziness, my poor Aunt Phasie?" said he.

She squeezed his hand fit to crush it, continuing in a still lower tone:

"Just fancy, I caught him. You know, that do what I would, I could not find out how he managed to give me his drug. I didn't drink, I didn't eat anything he touched, and all the same, every night I had my inside afire. Well, he mixed it with the salt! One night, I saw him; and I was in the habit of putting salt on everything in quantities to make the food healthy!"

Since Jacques had known Séverine, he sometimes pondered in doubt over this story of slow and obstinate poisoning, as one thinks of the nightmare. In his turn he tenderly pressed the hands of the invalid, and sought to calm her.

"Come, is all this possible? To say such things you should really be quite sure; and, besides, it drags on too long. Ah! it's more likely an illness that the doctors do not understand!"

"An illness," she resumed, with a sneer; "yes, an illness that he stuck into me! As for the doctors, you are right; two came here, who understood nothing, and who were not even of the same mind. I'll never allow another of such creatures to put a foot in this house again. Do you hear, he gave it me in the salt. I swear to you I saw him! It's for my 1,000 frcs., the 1,000 frcs. papa left me. He says to himself, that when he has done away with me, he'll soon find them. But, as to that, I defy him. They are in a place where nobody will find them. Never, never! I may die, but I am at ease on that score. No one will ever have my 1,000 frcs.!"

"But, Aunt Phasie," answered Jacques, "in your place, if I were so sure as all that, I should send for the gendarmes."

She made a gesture of repugnance.

"Oh! no, not the gendarmes," said she. "This matter only concerns us. It is between him and me. I know that he wants to gobble me up; and naturally I do not wish him to do it. So you see I have only to defend myself; not to be such a fool as I have been with his salt. Eh! Who would ever have thought it? An abortion like that, a little whipper-snapper of a man whom one could stuff into one's pocket, and who, in the long-run, would get the better of a big woman like me, if one let him have his own way with his teeth like those of a rat."

She was seized with a little shiver, and breathed heavily before she could conclude.

"No matter," said she at last, "he will be short of his reckoning again this time. I am getting better. I shall be on my legs before a fortnight. And he'll have to be very clever to catch me again. Ah! yes, I shall be curious to see him do it. If he discovers a way to give me any more of his drug, he will decidedly be the stronger of the two; and then, so much the worse for me. I shall kick the bucket. But I don't want to have any meddling between us!"

Jacques thought it must be her illness that caused her brain to be haunted by these sombre ideas; and, to amuse her, he tried joking, when, all at once, she began trembling under the bedclothes.

"Here he is," she whispered. "I can feel him coming whenever he approaches."

And sure enough, Misard entered a few seconds afterwards. She had become livid, a prey to that indomitable fright which huge creatures feel in presence of the insect that preys upon them. For, notwithstanding her obstinate determination to defend herself single-handed, she felt an increasing terror of him that she would not confess. Misard cast a sharp look at her and the driver, from the threshold, and then, gave himself an air of not having noticed them side by side. With his expressionless eyes, his thin lips, his mild manner of a puny man, he was already showing great attention to Séverine.

"I thought madam would perhaps like to take advantage of the opportunity, to have a look at her property. So I managed to slip away for a moment. If madam wishes I will accompany her."

And as the young woman still refused, he continued in a doleful voice:

"Madam was perhaps surprised in regard to the fruit. It was all wormeaten, and was really not worth packing up. Then we had a gale that did a lot of harm. Ah! it's a pity madam cannot sell the place! One gentleman came who wanted some repairs done. Anyhow, I am at the disposal of madam; and madam may be sure that I replace her here, as if she were here herself."

Then he insisted on giving her bread and pears, pears from his own garden, which were not wormeaten, and she accepted.

As Misard crossed the kitchen he told the passengers that the work of clearing away the snow was proceeding, but it would take another four or five hours. It had struck midday, and there ensued more lamentation, for all were becoming very hungry. Flore had just declared that she would not have sufficient bread for everyone. But she had plenty of wine. She had brought ten quarts up from the cellar, and only a moment before, had set them in a line on the table.

Then there were not enough glasses, and they had to drink by groups, the English lady with her two daughters, the old gentleman with his young wife. The latter had found a zealous, inventful groom in the young man from Havre, who watched over her well-being. He disappeared and returned with apples and a loaf which he had found in the woodhouse. Flore was angry, saying this was bread for her sick mother. But he had already commenced cutting it up, and handing pieces to the ladies, beginning with the young wife, who smiled at him amiably, feeling very much flattered at his attention.

Her husband was not offended; indeed, he no longer paid any attention to her, being engaged with the American in exalting the commercial customs of New York. The two English girls had never munched apples so heartily. Their mother, who felt very weary, was half asleep. Two ladies were seated on the ground before the hearth, overcome by waiting. Men who had gone out to smoke, in front of the house to kill a quarter of an hour, returned perishing and shivering with cold. Little by little the uneasy feeling increased, partly from hunger having only been half satisfied and partly from fatigue, augmented by impatience and absence of all comfort. The scene was assuming the aspect of a shipwrecked camp, of the desolation of a band of civilised people, cast by the waves on a desert island.

And as Misard, going backward and forward, left the door open, Aunt Phasie gazed on the picture from her bed of sickness. So these were the kind of people whom she had seen flash past, during close upon a year that she had been dragging herself from her mattress to her chair. It was now but rarely that she could go on to the siding. She passed her days and nights alone, riveted there, her eyes on the window, without any other company than those trains which flew by so swiftly.

She had always complained of this outlandish place, where they never received a visit; and here was quite a small crowd come from the unknown. And only to think that among them—among those people in a hurry to get to their business—not one had the least idea of the thing that troubled her, of that filth which had been mixed with her salt! She had taken that device to heart, and she asked herself how it was possible for a person to be guilty of such cunning rascality without anybody perceiving it. A sufficient multitude passed by them, thousands and thousands of people; but they all dashed on, not one would have imagined that a murder was calmly being committed in this little, low-roofed dwelling, without any set out. And Aunt Phasie looked at one after the other of these persons, fallen as it were from the moon, reflecting that when people have their minds so occupied with other things, it is not surprising that they should walk into pools of mire, and not know it.

"Are you going back there?" Misard inquired of Jacques.

"Yes, yes," replied the latter; "I'm coming immediately."

Misard went off closing the door. And Phasie, retaining the young man by the hand, whispered in his ear:

"If I kick the bucket, you'll see what a face he'll pull when he's unable to find the cash. That's what amuses me when I think of it. I shall go off contented all the same."

"And then, Aunt Phasie, it'll be lost for everybody," said Jacques. "Won't you leave it to your daughter?"

"To Flore? For him to take it from her? Ah! no, for certain. Not even to you, my big lad, because you also are too stupid, he'd get some of it. To no one; to the earth, where I shall go and join it!"

She was exhausted, and Jacques, having made her comfortable in bed, calmed her by embracing her, and promising to return and see her again shortly. Then, as she seemed to be falling asleep, he passed behind Séverine, who was still seated near the stove, raising his finger with a smile to caution her to be prudent. In a pretty, silent movement she threw back her head offering her lips, and he, bending over, pressed his mouth to them in a deep discreet kiss. Their eyes closed, and when the lids rose again it was to find Flore standing in the doorway gazing at them.

"Has madam done with the bread?" she inquired in a hoarse voice.

Séverine, confused and very much annoyed, stammered out:

"Yes, yes. Thank you."

For an instant Jacques fixed his flaming eyes on the girl. He hesitated, his lips trembling, as if he wanted to speak. Then, with a furious, threatening gesture, he made up his mind to leave. The door was slammed violently behind him.

Flore remained erect, presenting the tall stature of a warrior virgin, coifed with a heavy helmet of fair hair. So she had not been deceived by the anguish she had felt each Friday, at the sight of this lady in the train he drove. She was at last in possession of the absolute certainty she had been seeking since she held them there together. The man she was in love with, would never love her. It was this slim woman, this insignificant creature that he had chosen; and her regret at having refused him a kiss that night when he had brutally attempted to take one, touched her so keenly that she would have sobbed. For, according to her simple reasoning, it would have been she whom he would have embraced now, had she kissed him before the other. Where could she find him alone at this hour, to cast herself on his neck and cry, "Take me, I was stupid, because I did not know!"

But, in her impotence, she felt a rage rising within her against the frail creature seated there, uneasy and stammering. With one clasp of her arms, hard as those of a wrestler, she could stifle her like a little bird. Why did she hesitate to do so? She vowed she would be revenged, nevertheless, being aware of things connected with this rival that would send her to prison, she whom they permitted to remain at liberty; and tortured by jealousy, bursting with anger, she began clearing away the remainder of the bread and pears with the hasty movements of a beautiful untamed girl.

"As madam will take no more, I'll give this to the others," said she.

Three o'clock struck, then four o'clock. The time dragged on, immeasurably long, amidst increasing lassitude and irritation. Here was livid night returning to the vast expanse of white country. Every ten minutes the men who went out to see from a distance how the work was proceeding, returned with the information that the engine did not appear to be cleared. Even the two English girls began weeping in a fit of enervation. In a corner, the pretty dark lady had fallen asleep against the shoulder of the young man from Havre, a circumstance the elderly husband did not even notice, amid the general abandonment that had swept away decorum.

The room was becoming cold. Everyone was shivering, and not a soul thought of throwing some wood on the fire. The American took himself off, thinking he would feel much more comfortable stretched out on one of the seats in a carriage. That was now the general idea.

Everyone expressed regret: they should have remained where they were. Anyhow, had they done so, they would never have been devoured by the anxiety to learn what was going on there. It was necessary to restrain the English lady, who also spoke of regaining her compartment, and going to bed there. When they placed a candle on a corner of the table, to light the people in this dark kitchen, the feeling of discouragement became intense, and everyone gave way to dull despair.

The removal of the snow from the line was nevertheless coming to an end; and while the troop of soldiers, who had set the engine free, were clearing the metals in front, the driver and fireman had ascended to their post.

Jacques, observing that the snow had at last ceased, regained confidence. Ozil, the pointsman, had told him positively, that on the other side of the tunnel, in the neighbourhood of Malaunay, the state of the line was much better. But he questioned him again.

"You came through the tunnel on foot, and were able to enter, and issue from it without any difficulty?" said he.

"When I keep on telling you so," answered the other. "You will get through, take my word for it."

Cabuche, who had been working with the energy of a good giant, was already retiring in his timid, shy manner, which his recent difference with the judicial authorities had only increased; and it became necessary for Jacques to call to him.

"I say, comrade," he shouted, "hand me those shovels that belong to us, over there against the slope, so that if we happen to want them we shall be able to find them again."

And when the quarryman had rendered him this last service he gave him a hearty shake of the hand, to show him that he felt esteem for him in spite of all, having seen him at work.

"You are a good fellow, you are," said he.

This mark of friendship agitated Cabuche in an extraordinary manner.

"Thank you," he answered simply, stifling his tears.

Misard, who had made friends with him again, after accusing him before the examining-magistrate, gave his approval with an inclination of the head, pinching his lips into a slight smile. He had long since ceased working, and, with his hands in his pockets, stood gazing at the train with a bilious look, as if waiting to see whether he would not be able to pick up something lost between the wheels.

At length, the headguard had just decided with Jacques that an attempt could be made to go on again, when Pecqueux, who had got down on to the line, called the driver.

"Come and look!" said he. "One of the cylinders has had a shock."

Jacques, approaching him, also bent down. He had already discovered, on examining La Lison carefully, that it had received a blow at the place indicated. In clearing the engine, the workmen had ascertained that some oak sleepers, left at the bottom of the slope by the platelayers, had been shifted by the action of the snow and wind, so that they rested on the rails; and the stoppage, even, must have been partly due to this obstruction, for the locomotive had run against the sleepers. They could see the scratch on the box of the cylinder, and the piston it enclosed seemed slightly bent; but that was all the visible harm, and the fears of the driver were at first removed. Perhaps there existed serious interior injuries; nothing is more delicate than the complicated mechanism of the slide valves, where beats the heart, the living spirit of the machine.

Jacques got up again, blew the whistle, and opened the regulator to feel the articulations of La Lison. It took a long time to move, like a person bruised by a fall, who has difficulty in recovering the use of his limbs. At last, with a painful puff, it started, gave a few turns of the wheels still dizzy and ponderous. It would do, it could move, and would perform the journey. Only Jacques tossed his head, for he, who knew the locomotive thoroughly, had just felt something singular in his hand—something that had undergone a change, that had grown old, that had been touched somewhere with a mortal blow. It must have got this in the snow, cut to the heart, a death chill, like those strongly built young women who fall into a decline through having returned home one night, from a ball, in icy cold rain.

Again Jacques blew the whistle, after Pecqueux had opened the exhaust pipe. The two guards were at their posts. Mizard, Ozil, and Cabuche, had got on the footboard of the leading van; and the train slowly issued from the cutting between the soldiers, armed with their shovels, who had stood back to right and left along the base of the slopes. Then it stopped before the house of the gatekeeper to pick up the passengers.

Flore was there, in front. Ozil and Cabuche joined her and remained at her side; while Misard was now assiduous in his attentions, greeting the ladies and gentlemen who left his dwelling, and collecting the silver pieces. So at last the deliverance had come. But they had waited too long. All these people were shivering with cold, dying of hunger and exhaustion. The English lady led off her two daughters, who were half asleep; the young man from Havre got into the same compartment as the pretty dark lady, who looked very languid, and made himself most agreeable to the husband. And what with the slush caused by the trampled-down snow, the pushing, the free and easy manners, anyone might almost have imagined himself present at the entraining of a troop in flight, who had lost even the instinct of decent behaviour.

For an instant, Aunt Phasie appeared at the window of her room. Curiosity had bought her from her mattress, and she had dragged herself there to see. Her great hollow eyes of sickness watched this unknown crowd, these passers-by of the world on the move, whom she would never look on again, who were brought there and borne away by the tempest.

Séverine left the house the last. Turning her head she smiled at Jacques, who leant over to follow her to her carriage with his eyes. And Flore, who was on the look-out for them, again turned pale at this tranquil exchange of tenderness. Abruptly she drew nearer to Ozil, whom hitherto she had repelled, as if now, in her hatred, she felt the need of a man.

The headguard gave the signal. La Lison answered with a plaintive whistle; and Jacques this time started off, not to stop again before Rouen. It was six o'clock. Night was completing its descent from the black sky on to the white earth; but a pale, and frightfully melancholy reflex remained nearly level with the ground, lighting up the desolation of the ravaged country. And, in this uncertain glimmer, the house of La Croix-de-Maufras rose up aslant, more dilapidated than ever, and all black in the midst of the snow, with the notice nailed to the shut-up front, "For Sale."

VIII

The train did not reach the Paris terminus before 10.40 at night. There had been a stoppage of twenty minutes at Rouen to give the passengers time to dine; and Séverine had hastened to telegraph to her husband that she would only return to Havre by the express on the following night.

As they left Mantes, Pecqueux had an idea. Mother Victoire, his wife, had been at the hospital for a week, laid up with a severely sprained ankle occasioned by a fall; and, as he could find a bed at the house of some friends, he desired to offer their room to Madame Roubaud. She would be much more comfortable than at a hotel in the neighbourhood, and could remain there until the following night as if she were at home. And, when she approached the locomotive, among the swarm of passengers who at last left the carriages under the marquee, Jacques advised her to accept, at the same time holding out to her the key which the fireman had given him. But Séverine hesitated.

"No, no," said she, "I've a cousin. She will make me up a bed."

Jacques looked at her so earnestly that she ended by taking the key; while he, bending forward, whispered: "Wait for me."

Séverine had only to take a few steps up the Rue d'Amsterdam, and turn into the Impasse, or Blind Alley of the same name. But the snow was so slippery that she had to walk very cautiously. She had the good fortune to find the door of the house still open, and ascended the staircase without even being seen by the portress, who was deep in a game of dominoes with a neighbour. On the fifth floor she opened the door and closed it so softly that certainly none of the neighbours could suspect her there. Crossing the landing on the floor below, she had very distinctly heard laughter and singing at the Dauvergnes; doubtless one of the small receptions of the two sisters, who invited their friends to musical evenings once a week.

And now that Séverine had closed the door, and found herself in the oppressive darkness of the room, she could still distinguish the sound of the lively gaiety of all this youth coming through the boards. For a moment the obscurity seemed to her complete; and she started when the cuckoo clock, amidst the gloom, began to ring out eleven with deep strokes—a sound she recognised. Then her eyes became accustomed to the dimness of the apartment. The two windows stood out in two

ÉMILE ZOLA

pale squares, lighting the ceiling with the reflex of the snow. She was already beginning to find her way about, seeking for the matches on the sideboard in a corner where she recollected having seen them. But she had more difficulty in finding a candle. At last she discovered the end of one at the back of a drawer; and having put a lucifer to it the room was lit up. At once she cast a rapid, anxious glance around, as if to make sure that she was quite alone. She recognised everything: the round table where she had lunched with her husband; the bed draped with red cotton material, beside which he had knocked her down with a blow from his fist. It was there sure enough, nothing had been changed in the room during her absence of six months.

Séverine slowly removed her hat. But, as she was also about to set aside her cloak, she shivered. It was as cold as ice in this room. In a small box near the stove, were coal and firewood. Immediately, without taking off her wraps, she began to light the fire. This occupation amused her, serving as a diversion from the uneasiness she had at first experienced. When the stove began to draw, she busied herself with other household duties, arranging the chairs as it pleased her to see them, looking out clean sheets, and making the bed again, which caused her a deal of trouble, as it was unusually wide. She felt annoyed to find nothing to eat or drink in the sideboard. Doubtless Pecqueux had made a clean sweep of everything during the three days he had been master there. It was the same in regard to the light, there being only this single bit of candle.

And now, feeling very warm and lively, she stood in the middle of the room glancing round to make sure that everything was in order. Then, just as she was beginning to feel astonished that Jacques had not yet arrived, a whistle drew her to one of the windows. It was the 11.20 through train to Havre that was leaving. Below, the vast expanse, the trench extending from the station to the Batignolles tunnel, appeared one sheet of snow where naught could be distinguished save the fan of metals with its black branches. The engines and carriages on the sidings formed white heaps, looking as if they rested beneath coverings of ermine. And between the immaculate glass of the great marquees and the ironwork of the Pont de l'Europe bordered with frets, the houses in the Rue de Rome opposite, in spite of the darkness, could be seen jumbled together in a tint of dirty yellow.

The through train for Havre went along, crawling and sombre, its front lamp boring the obscurity with a bright flame; and Séverine watched it vanish under the bridge, reddening the snow with its three back lights. On turning from the window she gave another brief shiver—was she really quite alone? She seemed to feel a warm breath heating the back of her neck, a brutal blow grazing her skin through her clothes. Her widely opened eyes again looked round. No, no one.

What could Jacques be after, to remain so long as this? Another ten minutes passed. A slight scraping, a sound of finger-nails scratching against wood, alarmed her. Then she understood, and hastened to open the door. It was Jacques with a bottle of Malaga and a cake.

In an outburst of tenderness she threw her arms round his neck, rippling with laughter.

"Oh! you pet of a man to have thought to bring something," she exclaimed.

But he quickly silenced her.

"Hush! hush!" he whispered.

And she, fancying he might be pursued by the portress, lowered her voice. No; as he was about to ring, he had the luck to see the door open to let out a lady and her daughter, who had no doubt come down from the Dauvergnes; and he had been able to come up unperceived. Only there, on the landing, through the door standing ajar, he had just caught sight of the newsvendor woman who was finishing a little washing in a basin.

"Let us make as little noise as possible," said he. "Speak low."

Séverine replied by squeezing him passionately in her arms and covering his face with silent kisses. This game of mystery, speaking no louder than a whisper, diverted her.

"Yes, yes," she said; "you shall see: we will be as quiet as two little mice."

She took all kinds of precautions in laying the table: two plates, two glasses, two knives, stopping with a desire to burst out laughing when one article, set down too hastily, rang against another.

Jacques, who was watching her, also became amused.

"I thought you would be hungry," said he in a low voice.

"Why, I am famished!" she answered. "We dined so badly at Rouen!"

"Well, then, let me run down and fetch a fowl," he suggested.

"Ah! no," said she; "the portress might not let you come up again! No, no, the cake will do."

They immediately seated themselves side by side, almost on the same chair; and the cake was divided and eaten amid the frolics of sweethearts. She said she was thirsty, and swallowed two glasses of Malaga, one after the other, which flushed her cheeks. The stove, reddening behind their backs, thrilled them with warmth. But, as he was kissing her on the neck too loudly, she, in her turn, stopped him.

"Hush! hush!" she whispered.

She made him a sign to listen; and, in the silence, they distinguished a swaying movement to the accompaniment of music, ascending from the Dauvergnes; these young ladies had just arranged a hop. Hard by, the newsvendor was throwing the soapy water from her basin down the sink on the landing. She shut her door. The dancing downstairs had for a moment ceased; and outside, beneath the window, nothing could be heard but a dull rumble, stifled by the snow—the departure of a train, which seemed weeping with low whistles.

"An Auteuil train," murmured Jacques. "Ten minutes to twelve."

She made no answer, being absorbed by thoughts of the past, in her fever of happiness, living over again the hours she had passed there with her husband. Was this not the bygone lunch continuing with the cake, eaten on the same table, amid the same sounds? She became more and more excited, recollections flowed fast upon her. Never had she experienced such a burning necessity to tell her sweetheart everything, to deliver herself up to him completely. She felt, as it were, the physical desire to do so. It seemed to her that she would belong to him more absolutely were she to make her confession in his ear. Past events came vividly to her mind. Her husband was there. She turned her head, imagining she had just seen his short, hirsute hand pass over her shoulder to grasp the knife.

"Hullo! the candle is going out," said Jacques.

She shrugged her shoulders, as if to say she did not care. Then, stifling a laugh, she whispered:

"I've been good, eh?"

"Oh! yes!" he answered. "No one has heard us. We've been exactly like two little mice."

They said no more. The room was in darkness. Barely could the pale squares of glass be distinguished at the two windows; but on the ceiling appeared a ray from the stove, forming a round crimson spot. Both gazed at it with wide open eyes. The music had ceased. There came a slamming of doors; and then all the house fell into the peacefulness of heavy slumber. The train from Caen, arriving below, shook the turn-tables with dull shocks that barely reached them, so far did they seem away.

And now, Séverine again felt the desire to make her confession. She had been tormented by this feeling for weeks. The round spot on the ceiling increased in size, appearing to spread out like a spurt of blood. She had a fit of hallucination by looking at it. The objects round the bedstead took voices, relating the story aloud. She felt the words rising to her lips in the nervous wave passing through her frame. How delightful it would be to have nothing hidden, to confide in him entirely!

"You know, darling—" she began.

Jacques, who had also been steadily watching the red spot, understood what she was about to say. He had observed her increasing uneasiness in regard to this obscure, hideous subject which was present in both their minds, although they never alluded to it. Hitherto he had prevented her speaking, dreading the precursory shiver of his former complaint, trembling lest their affection might suffer if they were to talk of blood together. But, on this occasion, he did not feel the strength to bend his head, and seal her lips with a kiss. He thought it settled, that she would say all. And so, he was relieved of his anxiety, when, appearing to become troubled, she hesitated, then shrank back, and observed:

"You know, darling, my husband suspects we are in love with one another."

At the last second, in spite of herself, it was the recollection of what had passed the night before at Havre, that came to her lips, instead of the confession.

"Oh! Do you think so?" he murmured incredulous. "He seems so nice. He gave me his hand again this morning."

"I assure you he knows," she replied. "I have the proof."

Séverine paused. Then, after a quivering meditation, she exclaimed: "Oh! I hate him! I hate him!"

Jacques was surprised. He had no ill-feeling against Roubaud.

"Indeed! Why is that?" he inquired "He does not interfere with us!"

Without replying, she repeated:

"I hate him! The mere idea of his being beside me is a torture. Ah! If I could, I would run away, I would remain with you!"

Jacques pressed her to him. Then, after another pause, she resumed: "But you do not know, darling—"

The confession was on her lips again, fatally, inevitably. And this time he felt certain that nothing in the world would delay it. Not a sound could be heard in the house. The newsvendor even must have been in deep slumber. Outside, Paris covered with snow was wrapped in silence. Not a rumble of a vehicle could be heard in the streets. The last train for Havre, which had left at twenty minutes after midnight, seemed to have borne away the final vestige of life in the station. The stove had ceased roaring. The fire burning to ashes, gave fresh vigour to the red spot circling on the ceiling like a terrified eye. It was so warm that a heavy, stifling mist seemed to weigh down on them.

"Darling, you do not know—" she repeated.

Then he also spoke, unable to restrain himself any longer:

"Yes, yes, I know," said he.

"No; you may think you do, but you cannot know," she answered.

"I know that he did it for the legacy," he retorted.

She made a movement, and gave an involuntary little nervous laugh.

"Ah! bosh; the legacy!" she remarked.

And, in a very low voice, so low that a moth grazing the window panes, would have made a louder sound, she related her childhood at the house of the sister of President Grandmorin. Gaining courage as she proceeded, she continued in her low tone:

"Just fancy, it was here in this room, last February. You recollect, at the time when he had his quarrel with the sub-prefect. We had lunched very nicely—just as we have supped now—there, on that table. Naturally, he knew nothing, I had not gone out of my way to relate the story. But all of a sudden, about a ring, an old present, about nothing, I know not how it occurred, he understood everything. Ah! my darling! No, no; you cannot imagine how he treated me!"

After a shudder, she resumed:

"With a blow from his fist, he knocked me to the ground. And then he dragged me along by the hair. Next he raised his heel above my face, as if he would crush it. No; as long as I live, I shall never forget that! After this came more blows, to force me to answer his questions. No doubt he loved me. He must have been very much pained when he heard all he made me tell him; and I confess that it would have been more straightforward on my part to have warned him before our marriage. Only, you must understand that this intrigue was old and forgotten. No one but a positive savage would have become so mad with jealousy. You, yourself, my darling, will you cease to love me on account of what you now know?"

Jacques had not moved. He sat inert, reflecting. He felt very much surprised. Never had he a suspicion of such a story. How everything became complicated, when the will sufficed to account for the crime! But he preferred that matters should be as they were. The certainty that the couple had not killed for money, relieved him of a feeling of contempt.

"I! cease to love you. Why?" he inquired. "I do not care a fig about your past. It does not concern me."

After a silence, he added:

"And then, what about the old man?"

In a very low tone, with an effort of all her being, she confessed.

"Yes; we killed him," she answered. "He made me write to the President to leave by the express, at the same time as we did, and not to show himself until he reached Rouen. I remained trembling in my corner, distracted at the thought of the woe into which we were plunging. Opposite me sat a woman in black, who said nothing, and who gave me a great fright. I could not even look at her. I imagined she could distinctly read in our brains what was passing there, that she knew very well what we meant to do. It was thus that the two hours were spent from Paris to Rouen. I did not utter one word. I did not move, but closed my eyes to make believe I was asleep. I felt him beside me, motionless also; and what terrified me was my knowledge of the terrible things that were rolling in his head, without being able to make an exact guess of what he had resolved to do. Ah! what a journey, with that whirling flood of thoughts, amidst the whistling of the locomotive, and the jolting, and the thunder of the wheels!"

"But, as you were not in the same compartment, how were you able to kill him?" inquired Jacques.

"Wait a minute, and you will understand," answered Séverine. "It was all arranged by my husband; but if the plan proved successful, it was entirely due to chance. There was a stoppage of ten minutes at Rouen. We got down, and he compelled me to walk with him to the coupé occupied by the President, like persons who were stretching their legs. And there, seeing M. Grandmorin at the door, he affected surprise, as if unaware of his being in the train. On the platform there was a crush, a stream of people forced their way into the second-class carriages all going to Havre, where there was to be a fête on the morrow.

"When they began to close the doors, the President invited us into his compartment. I hesitated, mentioning our valise; but he cried out that there was no fear of anyone taking it, and that we could return to our carriage at Barentin, as he would be getting down there. At one moment my husband, who was anxious, seemed as if he wanted to run and fetch the valise; but at that same minute, the guard whistled, and Roubaud, making up his mind, pushed me into the coupé, got in after me, closed the door, and put up the glass. How it happened that we were not perceived, I have never been able to comprehend! A number of persons were running, the railway officials appeared to lose their heads, finally not a single witness came forward who had seen anything. At last, the train slowly left the station."

She paused a few seconds, unconsciously living the scene over again, and then resumed:

"Ah! during the first moments in that coupé, as I felt the ground flying beneath me, I was quite dizzy. At the commencement, I thought of nothing but our valise: how were we to recover it? And would it not betray us if we left it where it was? The whole thing seemed to me stupid, devoid of reason, like a murder dreamed of by a child, under the influence of nightmare, which anyone must be mad to think of putting into execution. We should be arrested next day, and convicted. But I sought to calm myself with the reflection that my husband would shrink from the crime, that it would not take place, that it could not. And yet, at the mere sight of him chatting with the President, I understood that his resolution remained as immutable as it was ferocious.

"Still, he was quite calm. He even talked merrily after his usual manner; and it must have been in his intelligible look alone, which ever and anon rested on me, that I read his obstinate determination. He meant to kill him a mile farther on, perhaps two, at the exact place he had settled in his mind, and as to which I was in ignorance. This was certain. One could even see it glittering in the tranquil glances which he cast upon the other who presently would be no more. I said nothing, feeling a violent interior trepidation, which I exerted myself to conceal by smiling when either of them looked at me. How was it that I never even thought of preventing all this? It was only later on, when I sought to understand my attitude, that I felt astonished I did not run to the door and shout out, or that I did not pull the alarm bell. At that time I was as if paralysed, I felt myself radically powerless. When I only think that I have not the courage to bleed a fowl! Oh! what I suffered on that hideous night! Oh! the frightful horror that howled within me!"

"But tell me," said Jacques, "did you help him to kill the old fellow?"

"I was in a corner," she continued without answering. "My husband sat between me and the President, who occupied the other corner. They chatted together about the forthcoming elections. From time to time I noticed my husband bend forward, and cast a glance outside to find out where we were, as if impatient. Each time he acted thus, I followed his eyes, and also ascertained how far we had travelled. The night was not very dark, the black masses of trees could be seen filing past with furious rapidity. And there was always that thunder of wheels, such as I had never heard before, a frightful tumult of enraged and moaning voices, a lugubrious wail of animals howling at death! The train flew along at full speed. Suddenly there came flashes of light, and the reverberating echo of the locomotive and carriages passing betwixt the buildings of a station. We were at Maromme, already two leagues and a half from Rouen. Malaunay would be next, and then Barentin.

"Where would the thing happen? Did he intend waiting until the last minute? I was no longer conscious of time or distances. I abandoned myself like the stone that falls, to this deafening downfall in the gloom, when, on passing through Malaunay, I all at once understood: the deed would be done in the tunnel, less than a mile farther on. I turned towards my husband. Our eyes met: yes; in the tunnel. Two minutes more. The train flew along. We passed the Dieppe embranchment, where I noticed the pointsman at his post. At this spot are some hills, and there I imagined I could distinctly see men with their arms raised, loading us with imprecations. Then, the engine gave a long whistle. We were at the entrance to the tunnel. And when the train plunged into it, oh! How that low-vaulted roof resounded! You know, those sounds of an upheaval of iron, similar to a hammer striking on an anvil, and which I, in this second or two of craziness, transformed into the rumble of thunder."

She shivered, and broke off to say, in a voice that had changed, and was almost merry:

"Isn't it stupid, eh! darling, to still feel the cold in the marrow of one's bones? And yet, I'm warm enough. Besides, you know there is nothing whatever to fear. The case is shelved, without counting that the bigwigs connected with the government are even less anxious than ourselves to throw light on it. Oh! I saw through it all, and am quite at ease!"

Then she added, without seeking to conceal her merriment:

"As for you, you can boast of having given us a rare fright! But tell me, I have often wondered—what was it you actually did see?"

"What I told the magistrate, nothing more," he answered. "One man murdering another. You two behaved so strangely with me that you aroused my suspicions. At one moment I seemed to recognise your husband. It was only later on though, that I became absolutely certain—"

She gaily interrupted him:

"Yes, in the square. The day when I told you no. Do you remember? The first time we were alone in Paris together. How peculiar it was! I told you it was not us, and knew perfectly well that you thought the contrary. It was as if I had told you all about it, was it not? Oh! darling, I have often thought of that conversation, and I really believe it is since that day I love you."

After a pause, she resumed the story of the crime:

"The train flew through the tunnel, which is very long. It takes three minutes to reach the end, as you know. To me it seemed like an hour. The President had ceased talking, in consequence of the deafening clatter of clashing iron. And my husband at this last moment must have lost courage, for he still remained motionless. Only, in the dancing light of the lamp, I noticed his ears become violet. Was he going to wait until we were again in the open country? The crime seemed to me so fatally inevitable, that, henceforth, I had but one desire: to be no longer subjected to this torture of waiting, to have it all over. Why on earth did he not kill him, as the thing had to be done? I would have taken the knife and settled the matter myself, I was so exasperated with fear and suffering. He looked at me. No doubt he read my thoughts on my face. For all of a sudden, he fell upon the President, who had turned to glance through the glass at the door, grasping him by the shoulders.

"M. Grandmorin, in a scare, instinctively shook himself free, and stretched out his arm towards the alarm knob just above his head. He managed to graze it, but was seized again by my husband, and thrown down on the seat with such violence that he found himself doubled up. His open mouth uttered frantic yells, in stupefaction and terror, which were drowned in the uproar of the train; while I heard my husband distinctly repeating the word: Beast! beast! beast! in a passionate hiss. But the noise subsided, the train left the tunnel, the pale country appeared once more with the dark trees filing past. I had remained stiffened in my corner, pressing against the back of the coupé as far off as possible.

"How long did the struggle last? Barely a few seconds. And yet it seemed to me it would never end, that all the passengers were now listening to the cries, that the trees saw us. My husband, holding the open knife in his hand, could not strike the blow, being driven back, staggering on the floor of the carriage, by the kicks of his victim. He almost fell to his knees; and the train flew on, carrying us along full speed; while the locomotive whistled as we approached the level-crossing at La Croix-de-Maufras.

"Without me being able to recall afterwards how the thing occurred, I know it was then that I threw myself on the legs of the struggling man. Yes, I let myself fall like a bundle, crushing his two lower limbs with all my weight, so that he was unable to move them any more. And if I saw nothing, I felt it all: the shock of the knife in the throat, the long quivering of the body, and then death, which came with three hiccups, with a sound like the running-down of a broken clock. Oh! that quivering fit of agony! I still feel the echo of it in my limbs!"

Jacques, eager for details, wanted to interrupt her with questions. But she was now in a hurry to finish.

"No; wait," said she. "As I rose from my seat we flashed past La Croix-de-Maufras. I distinctly perceived the front of the house with the shutters closed, and then the box of the gatekeeper. Another three miles, five minutes at the most, before reaching Barentin. The corpse was doubled-up on the seat, the blood running from it forming a large pool. And my husband, standing erect, besotted as if with drink, reeling in the swaying of the train, gazed on his victim as he wiped the knife with his pocket handkerchief. This lasted a minute, without either of us doing anything for our safety. If we kept this corpse with us, if we remained there, everything perhaps would be discovered when the train stopped at Barentin.

"But my husband had put the knife in his pocket. He seemed to wake up. I saw him search the clothes of the dead man, take his watch, his money, all he could find; and, opening the door, he did his utmost to thrust the body out on the line without taking it in his arms, being afraid of the blood. 'Assist me,' said he; 'push at the same time as I do!' I did not even attempt to try, my limbs were without feeling. With an oath he repeated, 'Will you push with me?'

"The head, which had gone out first, hung down to the step; while the trunk, rolled into a ball, would not pass. And the train flew on. At last, in response to a stronger effort, the corpse turned over, and disappeared amidst the thunder of the wheels. 'Ah! the beast; so it is all over!' said my husband. Then, picking up the rug, he threw that out as well. There were now only us two standing before the pool of blood on the seat, where we dare not sit down. The open door continued beating backward and forward; and broken down and bewildered as I was, I did not at first understand what my husband was doing, when I saw him get out, and in his turn disappear.

"But he returned. 'Come, quick, follow me,' said he, 'unless you want them to cut our heads off!' I did not move. He became impatient. 'Come on,' he repeated with an oath, 'our compartment is empty.' Our compartment empty! Then he had been there? Was he quite certain that the woman in black, who did not speak, whom one could not see, was he quite certain that she had not remained in a corner? 'If you don't come, I'll throw you on the line like the other one!' he threatened. He had entered the carriage, and pushed me as a brute, half mad. I found myself outside on the step, with my two hands clinging to the brass rail. Leaving the coupé after me, he carefully closed the door. 'Go on, go on!' said he. But I did not dare. I stood there, borne along in the whirling flight of the train, beaten by the wind which was blowing a gale. My hair came unbound, and I thought my stiffened fingers would lose their hold on the rail. 'Go on!' he exclaimed with another oath. He continued pushing me, and I had to advance, hand over hand, keeping close to the carriages, with my skirt and petticoats blowing about and embarrassing the action of my lower limbs. Already, in the distance, after a curve, one could see the lights of the Barentin station. The engine began to whistle. 'Go on!' repeated my husband still swearing at me.

"Oh! that infernal riot, that violent vacillation amidst which I walked! It seemed as if I had been caught in a storm that swept me along like a straw, to cast me against a wall. The country flew behind my back, the trees followed me in a furious gallop, turning over and over, twisted, each uttering a short moan as it passed. When I came to the end of the carriage, and had to take a stride to reach the footboard of the next, and grasp the other rod, I stopped, having lost all courage. Never should I have the strength to do it. 'Go on,' said my husband, accompanying the words with his usual imprecation. He was behind, he gave me a push, and I closed my eyes. I know not how it was I continued to advance. Possibly by the force of instinct, as an animal who has planted his claws into something, and means not to fall. How was it, too, that nobody saw us? We passed before three carriages, one of which was a second-class carriage, completely crammed. I remember seeing the heads of the passengers ranged in a line, in the light of the lamp. I believe I should recognise them if I were to meet them one of these days. There was a stout man with red whiskers, and I particularly recollect two young girls who were leaning forward laughing.

"'Go on! Go on!' exclaimed my husband with two frightful oaths. And I hardly remember what followed. The lights at Barentin were drawing near, the locomotive whistled. My last sensation was one of being dragged along, carried anyhow, caught up by the hair. My husband must have grasped hold of me, opened the door over my shoulder, and thrown me into the compartment. I was reclining breathless and half fainting in a corner when we stopped; and, without making a movement, I heard my husband exchange a few words with the station-master. Then, when the train went on again, he sank down on the seat, exhausted also. Between Barentin and Havre neither of us said a word. Oh! I hate him! I hate him, for all those abominations he made me suffer!"

"And so you sank down on his legs, and felt him dying?" inquired Jacques.

The unknown was being revealed to him. A ferocious wave ascended from his inside, filling his head with a crimson vision. His curiosity about the murder returned.

"And then, the knife, you felt the knife go in?" he continued.

"Yes, with a thud," she answered.

"Ah! a thud," said he, "not a rip; you are sure of that?"

"No, no," she replied; "nothing but a shock."

"And then, he quivered, eh?" he suggested.

"Yes; he gave three twitches from top to toe, and they lasted so long that I even felt them in his feet," she said.

"And those twitches stiffened him, did they not?" he persisted.

"Yes," she answered. "The first was very long, the other two weaker."

"And then he died?" he continued. "And what effect did it have on you, when you felt him expire under the knife?"

"On me? Oh! I don't know," she said.

"You don't know! Why tell stories?" he asked her. "Describe to me, describe to me your feeling, quite frankly. Was it pain?"

"No, no, not pain," said she.

"Pleasure?" he inquired.

"Pleasure!" she answered, "Ah! no, not pleasure!"

"What then, my love?" he urged. "I implore you to tell me all. If you only knew—Tell me what one feels."

ÉMILE ZOLA

"Good heavens!" she exclaimed. "How is it possible to describe it? It is frightful. You are borne away. Oh! so far, so far! I lived longer in that one minute than in all my previous life."

The crimson reflex had disappeared from the ceiling, and the fire had died out. The room became cooler in the intense cold outside. Not a sound ascended from Paris, padded with snow. For a moment, the newsvendor in the adjoining room, could be heard snoring, and then the whole house subsided into complete silence. Séverine had succumbed to invincible slumber. The cuckoo clock had just struck three.

Jacques was unable to close his eyes, which a hand, invisible in the obscurity, seemed to keep open. He could now distinguish nothing in the room. Every object had disappeared, stove, furniture, and walls. He had to turn round to find the two pale squares of windows, which appeared motionless and faint as in a dream. Notwithstanding his excessive fatigue, prodigious cerebral activity kept him in a thrill, ceaselessly unwinding the same coil of ideas. Each time that, by an effort of will, he fancied himself slipping off to sleep, the same haunting pictures began filing by again, awakening the same sensations.

And the scene unfolded thus, with mechanical regularity, while his fixed, wide-open eyes became clouded, was that of the murder, detail by detail. It kept returning again and again, identically the same, gaining hold on him, driving him crazy. The knife entering the throat with a thud, the body giving three long twitches, life ebbing away in a flood of warm blood—a crimson flood which he fancied he felt coursing over his hands. Twenty, thirty times, the knife went in, and the body quivered. Oh! if he could but deal a blow like that, satisfy his long craving, learn what one experiences, become acquainted with that minute which is longer than a lifetime!

In spite of his effort to sleep, the invisible fingers kept his eyes open; and in the darkness the murder scene reappeared in all its sanguinary traits. Then, he ceased the struggle and remained a prey to the stubborn vision. He could hear within him the unfettered labour of the brain, the rumble of the whole machine. It came from long ago, from his youth. And yet he had fancied himself cured, for this desire to kill had been dead for months; but, since the story of that crime had been told him just now, he had never felt the feeling so intensely. An intolerable warmth ran up his spine, and at the back of the neck he felt a pricking, as if red-hot needles were boring into him. He became afraid of his hands, and imprisoned them under him, as if he dreaded some abomination on their part, some act that he was determined not to allow them to commit.

Each time the cuckoo clock struck, Jacques counted the strokes. Four o'clock, five o'clock, six o'clock. He longed for daylight, in the hope that dawn would dispel this nightmare. And now, he turned towards the windows, watching the panes of glass. But he could see naught save the vague reflex of the snow. At a quarter to five he had heard the through train arrive from Havre, with a delay of only forty minutes which proved that the line must be clear. And it was not until after seven that he saw the window panes slowly becoming milky white. At length the darkness in the apartment disappeared, to give place to an uncertain glimmer, in which the furniture looked as if floating. The stove, the cupboard, the sideboard reappeared. He was still unable to close his lids. His eyes seemed determined to see.

All of a sudden, before it even became sufficiently light for him to distinguish the object, he had guessed that the knife he had used to cut the cake the previous night lay on the table. He now saw nothing but this knife, a small pointed weapon. And as day grew, all the clear rays from the two windows centred upon this thin blade. In terror of what his hands might do, he thrust them farther under him, for he could feel that they were agitated, in open revolt, more powerful than his own will. Would they cease to belong to him, those hands that came from another, bequeathed to him by some ancestor of the days when man strangled animals in the woods?

So as not to see the knife, Jacques turned towards Séverine, who was sleeping very calmly in her intense fatigue, with the even respiration of a child. Her mass of unbound, black hair made her a sombre pillow, and spread over her shoulders. Beneath her chin, her throat appeared amidst the curls, a throat of cream-like delicacy, faintly tinted with rose. He gazed at her, as if he did not know her. And yet he adored her, carrying her image along with him, impressed on his mind, wherever he went. She was ever in his thoughts, even when he was driving his engine; and so much so, that on one occasion, when he awoke to reality, as from a dream, it was to find himself going at full speed past a station, in defiance of the signals.

But, at the sight of that white throat, he was overcome by a sudden, inexorable fascination; and, with a feeling of horror, of which he still had conscience, he felt the imperious necessity rising within him to take the knife from the table and bury it up to the handle in the flesh of this woman. He heard the thud of the blade entering the throat, he saw the body quake with three spasms, then stiffen in the death agony amidst a crimson flood.

In the struggle to free himself from these haunting thoughts, he every second lost a little of his will. It seemed to be succumbing to the fixed idea, to be reaching that extremity when a man yields, vanquished, to the impulse of instinct. Everything went wrong. His revolted hands, overcoming his effort to conceal them, became unclasped of themselves, and escaped. He then understood that, henceforth, he was not their master, and that they would go, and brutally satisfy themselves if he continued gazing at Séverine.

Although it was now broad daylight, the room appeared to him to be full of reddish smoke, as if it was a dawn of icy fog, drowning everything. He shivered with fever. He had taken the knife, and concealed it up his sleeve, certain of killing one woman, the first he should meet on the pavement outside, when a crumpling of linen, a prolonged sigh, made him turn pale and stop riveted beside the table. It was Séverine waking up.

He felt convinced that if he approached her, with that knife in his sleeve, if he only saw her again, in all her delicate beauty, there would be an end to that will which kept him firmly standing there close to her. In spite of himself, his hand would rise and bury the knife in her neck. Distracted, he opened the door, and fled.

It was eight o'clock when Jacques found himself on the pavement of the Rue d'Amsterdam. The snow had not yet been removed, and the footsteps of the few passers-by could barely be heard. He immediately caught sight of an old woman, but, as she happened to be turning the corner of the Rue de Londres, he did not follow her. Being among men he walked down towards the Place du Havre, grasping the handle of the knife, whose blade disappeared up his sleeve. As a girl about fourteen left a house opposite, he crossed the road, but only reached the other side to see her enter the shop of a baker next door. His impatience was such that he could not wait, but sought farther on, continuing to descend the street.

Since he had quitted the room with this knife, it was no longer he who acted, but the other one, him whom he had so frequently felt stirring in the depths of his being, that unknown party who dated back so very far, who was burning with the hereditary thirst for murder. He had killed in days of yore, he wanted to kill again.

And the objects around Jacques were only things in a dream, for he saw them in the light of his fixed idea. His everyday life was as if abolished. He strode along like a somnambulist, without memory of the past, without forethought for the future, a slave to his necessity. His personality was absent from the body, which took its own direction.

Two women who brushed by, as they advanced ahead of him, caused him to hasten his step; and he had caught them up, when a man stopped them. All three stood laughing and chatting together. This man being in his way, he began following another woman who went by, looking feeble and gloomy, and presenting a poverty-stricken appearance in her thin shawl. She advanced with short steps, on her way, no doubt, to some execrated task, that was hard and meanly remunerated, for she did not hurry, and her face looked despairingly sad.

Nor did he hurry, now that he had found a victim, but waited to select a spot where he could strike her at ease. Probably she perceived him following her, as her eyes turned towards him in unutterable distress, astonished that anybody could wish to have anything to say to her. She had already led him to the middle of the Rue du Havre, where she turned round twice more, each time preventing him plunging the knife, which he drew from his sleeve, into her throat—her eyes looked so full of misery, and so supplicating! He would strike her down over there, as she stepped from the pavement. But, he abruptly turned aside, in pursuit of another woman coming the opposite way. And he acted thus without reason, without will, simply because she happened to be passing at that minute.

Jacques followed her towards the station. This young woman was very lively, and walked with sonorous tread. She looked adorably pretty. She could be no more than twenty, and was plump and fair, with lovely, merry eyes that laughed at life. Apparently in a great hurry, she did not even notice that a man was following her, but briskly ascended the flight of steps in the Cour du Havre the grand hall, along which she almost ran in her haste to reach the ticket-office of the Ceinture line. And as she there asked for a first-class ticket to Auteuil, Jacques took the same. He then accompanied her through the waiting-rooms, on to the platform, and seated himself beside her in the compartment she selected. The train at once started.

"I have plenty of time," thought he; "I'll kill her in a tunnel."

But opposite them, an elderly lady, the only other person there, had just recognised the young woman.

"What! Is it you?" she exclaimed. "Where are you off to so early?"

The other laughed heartily with a comical gesture of despair.

"Only fancy," said she, "one cannot go anywhere without meeting somebody one knows! I hope you will not betray me. Tomorrow is the birthday of my husband; and, as soon as he went away to business, I set out on my errand. I am going to Auteuil to find a florist who has an orchid which my husband has set his mind on. A surprise, you understand."

The elderly lady nodded her head up and down with tender benevolence. "And how is the baby?" she inquired.

"The baby?" answered the young mother. "Oh! she is going on beautifully. You know I weaned her a week ago. You should see her eating her pap. We are all remarkably well. It is perfectly disgraceful."

She laughed louder than ever, displaying the white teeth between her ruby lips. And Jacques, who had seated himself on her right, his knife in his fist, hidden under his leg, said to himself that he was in a first-rate position to deal the blow. He had only to raise his arm, and turn half round, to have her within reach. But in the Batignolles tunnel, the thought of something she wore round her neck stopped him.

"There is a knot which will inconvenience me," he reflected. "I want to be quite sure."

The two ladies continued chatting gaily together.

"So I see you are happy," remarked the older one.

"Happy? Ah! if I could only tell you to what extent," replied the other. "Two years ago I was nobody at all. You remember, there was no amusement at the home of my aunt; and I was without a sou of dowry. When he used to call, I trembled, I had become so fond of him. He was so handsome, so wealthy. And he is mine, my husband, and we have baby between us. I assure you it is too delightful!"

Jacques, in examining the knot of the scarf, perceived a big gold locket underneath, attached to a black velvet band; and he calculated how he would proceed.

"I will grasp her by the neck," thought he, "with my left hand, and thrust aside the locket as I put her head back to have the throat free."

The train stopped, and went on again every few minutes, the stations being so close together. Short tunnels followed one another at Courcelles and Neuilly. Presently would do, one minute would be sufficient.

"Did you go to the seaside last summer?" inquired the old lady.

"Yes," answered the other, "to Brittany, for six weeks, in an out-of-the-way corner, a perfect paradise. Then we passed September in Poitou, at the seat of my father-in-law, who owns extensive woods down there."

"And you are going to the south for the winter?" said the old lady.

"Yes," answered the younger one, "we shall be at Cannes about the 15th. The house is taken. A delightful bit of garden facing the sea. We have sent someone down to prepare the place. Neither of us fear the cold, but then, the sun is so nice! We shall be back in March. Next year we intend to remain in Paris. After two years, when baby is big, we mean to travel. I hardly know what afterwards. It is one constant holiday!"

She was so overflowing with felicity, that yielding to a feeling of expansion, she turned towards Jacques, towards this unknown individual to smile at him. In making this movement the knot of her scarf was displaced, carrying the locket away with it, and revealing the rosy neck with a slight dimple gilded by the shadow.

The fingers of Jacques clutched the handle of the knife, at the same time as he formed an irrevocable resolution.

"That is the spot where I will deal the blow," said he to himself. "Yes, in the tunnel before reaching Passy."

But, at the Trocadero station, a member of the staff got in, who, knowing Jacques, began to talk about a theft of coal that had been brought home to a driver and his fireman. From that moment everything became confused. Later on he was never able to establish the facts, exactly. The laughter continued in such a beam of happiness that he felt as if penetrated and appeased by it. Perhaps he went as far as Auteuil with the two ladies, only he had no recollection of seeing them leave the carriage.

In the end he found himself beside the Seine, without knowing how he came there. But he had the distinct remembrance of casting the knife, which had remained in his hand, with the blade up his sleeve, from the top of the bank into the river. Then he hardly knew what occurred, being half silly, absent from his being, which the other one had also left along with the knife. He must have wandered about for hours through streets and squares, wherever his body chanced to take him. People and houses filed past very faintly. Doubtless, he had gone in somewhere to get food at the end of a room full of customers, for he clearly recalled the white plates. He had also the firm impression that he saw a red broadside on the shutters of a shop. And then, all sank into a black chasm, to nothingness, where there was neither time nor space, where he lay inert, perhaps since centuries.

When Jacques came to himself, he was in his little room in the Rue Cardinet. He had fallen across his bed in his clothes. Instinct had taken him there, just as a lame dog drags himself to his kennel, or his hole. He remembered neither going upstairs, nor going to sleep. He awoke from heavy slumber, scared to suddenly regain self-possession, as if after a long fainting fit. Perhaps he had slept three hours, perhaps three days. All at once his memory returned: the confession Séverine had made of the murder, and his departure like a feline animal in search of blood. He had been beside himself, but he now had full command of his faculties, and felt astounded at what had taken place against his will. Then the recollection of the young woman awaiting him, made him leap to his feet at a bound. He looked at his watch, and saw it was already four o'clock; and, with a clear head, very calm, as if after a copious bleeding, he hastened back to the Impasse d'Amsterdam.

Séverine had been wrapped in profound slumber until noon. Then, waking up, surprised not to see Jacques there, she had lit the fire, and, dying of inanition, had made up her mind, at about two o'clock, to run down and get something to eat at a neighbouring restaurant. When Jacques appeared she had just come up again, after going on a few errands.

"Oh! my darling!" she exclaimed, as he entered the room; "I was most anxious!"

And she hung round his neck, looking into his eyes, quite close.

"What has happened?" she added inquiringly.

He placidly removed her fears, without feeling in the least troubled.

"Oh! nothing," he replied, "a nasty job. When they once get hold of you, they will never let you go."

Then, Séverine, lowering her voice, became very humble and fondling.

"Only think," said she, "I fancied,—oh! an ugly thought, that caused me a great deal of pain!—Yes, I fancied to myself that perhaps after the confession I made, you would have nothing more to do with me; and I imagined you had gone, never, never to return!"

Tears filled her eyes, and she burst into sobs, pressing him distractedly in her arms.

"Ah! my darling," she continued, "if you only knew how I yearn for kindness! Love me, love me fondly, because, you see, it is only your love that can make me forget. Now that I have told you all my trouble, you must not leave me. Oh! I implore you!"

Jacques felt penetrated by this tenderness. An invincible relaxation softened him little by little, and he stammered out:

"No, no, I love you, do not be afraid."

And quite overcome, he also wept, in face of the fatality of that abominable evil which had again taken hold of him, and of which he would never be cured. It was shame, and despair without limit.

"Love me, love me fondly, also," he continued. "Oh! with all your strength, for I have as great a need of love as you."

She shuddered, and wished to know more.

"If you are in grief, you must confide in me," said she.

"No, no," he replied, "not grief, things that do not exist, moments of sadness that make me horribly unhappy, without it being even possible to speak of them."

They strained one another, mingling their frightfully melancholy trouble. It was infinite suffering without any possible oblivion, and without pardon. They wept, and upon them they felt the blind force of life, made up of struggles and death.

"Come," said Jacques, disengaging himself, "it is time to think of leaving! Tonight you will be at Havre!"

Séverine, with clouded brow and vacant eyes, murmured after a silence:

"If I were only free, if my husband were no longer there. Ah! how soon we should forget!"

He gave a violent gesture, and thinking aloud, he muttered:

"Still we cannot kill him!"

She gazed at him fixedly, and he started, astonished at what he had said, for such an idea had never entered his mind. But as he wished to kill someone, why not kill this embarrassing man? And, as he left her to run to the depôt, she again clasped him in her arms, and smothered him with kisses.

"Oh! my darling," she repeated, "love me fondly. I will love you, more and more. We shall be happy, you will see."

IX

During the ensuing days at Havre, Jacques and Séverine, who were alarmed, displayed great prudence. As Roubaud knew all, would he not be on the watch to surprise and wreak vengeance on them in a burst of rage? They recalled his previous angry fits of jealousy, his brutalities of a former porter, when he struck out with his clenched fists; and now, observing him so sour, so mute, with his troubled eyes, they imagined he must be meditating some savage, cunning trick, some stealthy snare to get them in his clutches. So, for the first few months, they were ever on the alert, and in meeting one another took all kinds of precautions.

Still Roubaud absented himself more and more. Perhaps, he merely disappeared for the purpose of returning unexpectedly to find them together. But this fear proved groundless. His spells of absence became so prolonged that he was never at home, running off as soon as he became free, and only returning at the precise minute when the service claimed him. During the weeks he was on day duty, he managed to get through his ten o'clock knife-and-fork breakfast in five minutes, and was not seen again before half-past eleven; and at five o'clock in the evening, when his colleague came down to relieve him, he slipped away again, often to remain out the whole night. He barely allowed himself a few hours' sleep. His behaviour was similar during the weeks he did night duty. Free at five o'clock in the morning, he no doubt ate and slept in the town, as he did not return until five o'clock in the afternoon.

Notwithstanding this disorderly mode of life, he for a long time maintained exemplary punctuality, being invariably at his post at the exact minute, although he was sometimes so worn out that he could hardly keep on his feet. Still he was there, and conscientiously went through his work. Now came interruptions. Moulin, the other assistant station-master, had twice waited an hour for him; and one morning after breakfast, finding he had not returned, he had even in good fellowship sought him out, to save him from a reprimand. All the duty Roubaud had to perform suffered from this slow course of disorganisation.

In the daytime he was no longer the same active man who, when a train went off or came in, examined everything with his own eyes, noting down the smallest details in his report to his chief, as hard for himself as for those under him. At night, he slept like a top in the great armchair in the office. When awake he seemed still sleeping, going and coming along the platform with hands behind his back, giving orders without emphasis, and without verifying their execution. Nevertheless, the work went on satisfactorily, apart from a slight collision, due to his negligence in sending a passenger train on to a shunting-line. His colleagues merely laughed, contenting themselves with saying that he went on the spree.

The truth was that Roubaud, at present, passed all his spare time in a small, out-of-the-way room on the first floor of the Café du Commerce, which little by little had become a gambling-place. It was there the assistant station-master satisfied that morbid passion for play which had commenced on the morrow of the murder through a chance game at piquet, to increase afterwards and become a firmly rooted habit, owing to the absolute diversion and oblivion it afforded. Henceforth, the gambling mania had a firm grip on him, as if it was the sole gratification in which he found contentment. Not that he had ever been tormented through remorse with a desire to forget, but amidst the upheaval at home, amidst his shipwrecked existence, he had found consolation in the diverting influence of this egotistic pleasure, which he could enjoy alone; everything was obliterated by this passion which completed his disorganisation.

Alcohol could not have brought him lighter or swifter moments, so free from every anxiety. He had even released himself from the care of life. He seemed to live with extraordinary, but disinterested intensity, without being touched by any of those annoyances that formerly made him burst with rage. And, apart from the fatigue of sitting-up all night, he enjoyed very good health. He even put on fat, a heavy yellow kind of fat, and his lids hung wearily above his troubled eyes. When he went home with his slow, sleepy gestures, it was to display supreme indifference for everything.

On the night that Roubaud returned to his lodgings to take the 300 frcs. in gold from under the parquetry, he wanted to pay M. Cauche, the commissary of police at the station, several successive losses he had made. Cauche, who was an old gambler, showed magnificent composure, which rendered him redoubtable. Compelled by his duties to keep up the appearances of an old military man, who, having remained bachelor, spent all his time at the café as a quiet, regular customer, he averred that he only played for pleasure; which did not prevent him passing the whole night at cards and pocketing all the money of the others. Rumours had got abroad that, owing to his inexactitude in the discharge of his functions, it had become a question of forcing him to resign. But matters dragged on, and there being so little to do, it seemed unnecessary to exact greater zeal. So he continued to confine himself to appearing for an instant on the platform of the station, where everyone bowed to him.

Three weeks after the payment of the first debt, Roubaud owed nearly another 400 frcs. to M. Cauche. He explained that the legacy to his wife put them quite at their ease; but he added, with a laugh, that she kept the keys of the safe, which explained his delay in discharging his gambling liabilities. Then, one morning, when alone and tormented, he again raised the piece of parquetry, and took a 1000-franc-note from the hiding-place. He trembled in all his limbs. He had not experienced such emotion on the night he helped himself to the gold. Doubtless, in his mind, that was only odd change come across by chance, whereas the theft began with this note. It made his flesh creep when he thought of this sacred money, which he had vowed never to touch.

Formerly he had sworn he would sooner die of hunger, and yet he touched it, and he could not explain how he had got rid of his scruples. Doubtless he had lost a portion of them day by day in the slow fermentation of the murder. At the bottom of the hole he fancied he felt something damp, something flabby and nauseous, which gave him horror. Quickly replacing the piece of parquetry, he once more swore that he would cut off his hand rather than remove it again. His wife had not seen him. He drew a breath of relief, and drank a large glass full of water to compose himself. Now his heart beat with delight at the idea of his debt being paid, and of all this sum he would be able to risk on the gambling-table.

But when it became a question of changing the note, the vexations of Roubaud began again. Formerly he was brave, he would have given himself up had he not committed the folly of involving his wife in the business; while now the mere thought of the gendarmes made him shiver. It served him but little to know that the judicial authorities were not in possession of the numbers of the notes that had disappeared, and that the criminal proceedings were at rest, shelved for ever in the cardboard boxes; as soon as he formed the project of going somewhere to ask for change, he was seized with terror.

For five days he kept the note about him, and got into the habit of constantly touching it, of changing its place, of even keeping it with him at night. He built up some very complicated plans, but always to encounter unforeseen apprehensions. At first he thought of getting rid of it at the station: why should not a colleague in charge of one of the paying-in offices take it from him? Then, when this struck him as extremely dangerous, he conceived the idea of going to the other end of Havre without his uniform cap, to purchase the first thing that entered his head. Only, would not the shopman be astonished to see him offer such a big note in payment of so small a purchase? And he had then made up his mind to present the note at the shop of a tobacconist on the Cours Napoléon, where he went daily. Would this not be the most simple course of all? It was known he had inherited the legacy, and the shopkeeper could not be surprised.

He walked to the door, but feeling himself falter he went down to the Vauban dock to muster up courage. After walking about for half an hour, he returned without yet being able to do as he had decided. But in the evening, at the Café du Commerce, as M. Cauche happened to be there, a sudden feeling of bravado made him pull the note from his pocket and beg the hostess to change it; but as she did not happen to have sufficient gold, she had to send a waiter to the tobacco shop. Everyone made fun about the note, which seemed quite new, although dated ten years back. The commissary of police, taking it in his hand, turned it over and over, with the remark that it must certainly have been lying in some out-of-the-way place, which made another person relate an interminable story about a hidden fortune being discovered under the marble top of a chest of drawers.

Weeks passed, and this money which Roubaud had in his hands sufficed to send his passion to fever heat. It was not that he played for high stakes, but he was pursued by such constant dismal bad luck that the small daily losses, added together, totalled up to a large amount. Towards the end of the month he found himself without a sou, besides being a few louis in debt, and so ill that he hardly dared touch a card. Nevertheless, he struggled on, and almost had to take to his bed. The idea of the nine notes remaining there under the floor of the dining-room preyed on his mind at every minute. He could see them through the wood, he felt them heating the soles of his boots. If he chose he could take another! But this time he had formally sworn he would rather thrust his hand in the fire than rummage there again. But one night, when Séverine had gone to bed early, he again raised the piece of parquetry, yielding with rage and distracted with such grief that his eyes filled with tears. What was the use of resisting thus? It was only needless suffering, for he could see that he would now take all the notes, one by one, until the last.

Next morning Séverine chanced to notice a chip, quite fresh, at the spot where the treasure lay concealed. Stooping down, she found the trace of a dent. Her husband evidently continued taking money, and she was astonished at the anger that got the better of her, for as a rule she was not grasping; and besides, she also fancied herself resolved to die of hunger rather than touch one of those blood-stained notes. But did they not belong to her as much as to him? Why should he avoid consulting her and dispose of them on the sly? Until dinner-time she was tormented by the desire to be positive, and she would in her turn have taken up the parquetry to look, had she not felt a little cold shiver in her hair at the thought of searching there all alone. Would not the dead rise from this hole? This childish fear made the dining-room seem so unpleasant that she took her work and shut herself up in her bedroom.

Then, in the evening, as the two were silently eating the remains of a stew, she again became irritated at seeing him cast involuntary glances at the spot where the money was hidden.

"You've been helping yourself to some more?" she said interrogatively.

He raised his head in astonishment.

"Some more what?" he inquired.

"Oh! do not act the innocent," she continued; "you understand very well. But listen: I will not have you do it again, because it is no more yours than mine, and it upsets me to know that you touch it."

Habitually he avoided quarrels. Their life in common had become the mere obligatory contact of two beings bound one to the other, passing entire days without exchanging a word; and, henceforth, going and coming like indifferent and solitary strangers. So he refused to give any explanation, and contented himself with shrugging his shoulders.

But she became very excited. She meant to finish with the matter, with the question of this money hidden there, which had made her suffer since the day of the crime.

"I insist on you answering me!" she exclaimed. "Dare to say that you have not touched it!"

"What does it matter to you?" he asked.

"It matters to me, this much," she replied,—"that it makes me ill. Again today I was afraid. I could not remain here. Every time you go to that place I have horrible dreams three nights in succession. We never mention the subject. Then remain quiet, and do not force me to speak about it."

He contemplated her with his great staring eyes, and repeated in a weighty tone:

"What does it matter to you if I touch it, so long as I do not force you to do so? It is my own business, and concerns me alone!"

She was about to make a violent gesture, which she repressed. Then, quite upset, with a countenance full of suffering and disgust, she exclaimed:

"Ah! indeed! I do not understand you! And yet you were an honest man. Yes, you would never have taken a sou from anyone. And what you did might have been forgiven, for you were crazy, and made me the same. But this money! Ah! this abominable money! which should not exist for you, and which you are stealing sou by sou for your pleasure. What has happened? How could you have fallen so low?"

He listened to her, and in a moment of lucidity he also felt astonished that he should have arrived at thieving. The phases of the slow demoralisation were becoming effaced, he was unable to re-join what the murder had severed around him, he failed to understand how another existence, how almost a new being had commenced, with his home destroyed, his wife standing aside, and hostile. But the unavoidable subject at once came uppermost in his mind. He gave a gesture, as if to free himself from troublesome reflections, and growled:

"When there is no pleasure at home, one seeks diversion outside. As you no longer love me—"

"Oh! no, I have no more love for you," she interrupted.

He looked at her, gave a blow with his fist on the table, and the blood rushed to his face.

"Then leave me alone!" he exclaimed. "Do I interfere with your amusements? Do I sit in judgment on you? There are many things an upright man would do in my place, and which I do not do! To begin with, I ought to kick you out at the door. After that I should perhaps not steal."

She had become quite pale, for she also had often thought that when a man, and particularly a jealous man, is ravaged by some internal evil to the point of allowing his wife a sweetheart, there exists an indication of moral gangrene invading his being, destroying the other scruples, and entirely disorganising his conscience. But she struggled inwardly, refusing to hold herself responsible, and in an unsteady voice she exclaimed:

"I forbid you to touch the money!"

He had finished eating, and, quietly folding up his napkin, he rose, saying in a bantering tone:

"If you want to share the cash, let us do so."

He was already bending down as if to take up the piece of parquetry, and she had to rush forward and place her foot on it.

"No, no!" she pleaded. "You know I would prefer death. Do not open it. No, no! not before me!"

That same night Séverine had an appointment with Jacques behind the goods station. When she returned home after twelve o'clock, the scene with her husband in the evening recurred to her, and she double-locked herself in her bedroom. Roubaud was on night duty, and she had no anxiety lest he should return and come to bed, a circumstance that very rarely happened, even when he had his nights to himself. But with bedclothes to her chin, and the lamp turned down, she failed to get to sleep. Why had she refused to share?

And she found that her ideas of honesty were not so keen as before, at the thought of taking advantage of this money. Had she not accepted the legacy of La Croix-de-Maufras? Then she could very well take the money also. Now the shivering fit returned. No, no, never! Money she would have taken. What she dared not touch, without fear of literally burning her fingers, was this money stolen from a dead body, this abominable money of the murder! She again recovered calm, and reasoned with herself: if she had taken the money, it would not have been to spend it; on the contrary, she would have hidden it somewhere else, buried it in a place known to her alone, where it would have remained eternally; and, at this hour even, half the amount would still be saved from the hands of her husband. He would not enjoy the triumph of having it all, he would not be able to gamble away what belonged to her.

When the clock struck three she felt mortally sorry that she had refused to share. A thought, indeed, came to her, still confused, and far from being determined on: supposing she were to get up, and search beneath the parquetry, so that he might have nothing more. Only she was seized with such icy coldness that she would not dream of it. Take all, keep all, without him daring to complain! And this plan, little by little, gained on her; while a will stronger than her resistance arose from the unconscious depths of her being. She would not do it; and yet she abruptly leapt from the bed, for she could not restrain herself. Turning up the lamp, she passed into the dining-room.

From that moment Séverine ceased trembling. Her terror left her, and she proceeded calmly, with the slow and precise gestures of a somnambulist. She had to fetch the poker, which served to raise the piece of parquetry, and failing to see when the hole was uncovered, she brought the lamp near it. But then, bending forward, motionless, she became riveted to the spot in stupor: the hole was empty. It appeared evident, that while she had gone to her appointment with Jacques, Roubaud had returned, tormented by the same desire as herself to take all and keep all, a desire that had come to him before attacking her; and at one stroke he had pocketed all the banknotes that were left. Not a single one remained. She knelt down, but only perceived the watch and chain at the back of the hiding-place, where the gold sparkled in the dust of the joists. Frigid rage kept her there an instant, rigid and half nude, repeating aloud, a score of times over:

"Thief! thief! thief!"

Then, with a furious movement, she grasped the watch, while a great black spider, which she had disturbed, fled along the plaster. Replacing the piece of parquetry with blows from her heel, she returned to bed, standing the lamp on the night-table. When she had become warm, she looked at the watch which she held in her hand, turning it over and examining it for a long time. The two initials of the President, interlaced on the back of the case, interested her. Inside, she read the number of the manufacturer, 2516. It was a very dangerous piece of jewelry to keep, for the judicial authorities knew the number. But, in her anger at being unable to save anything but this, she had no fear. She even felt there would be an end to her nightmares, now that the skeleton had disappeared from under the floor. At last she would be able to tread at home in peace, wherever she pleased. So, slipping the watch beneath her pillow, she turned out the lamp and fell asleep.

Next day Jacques, who was free, had to wait until Roubaud had settled down at the Café du Commerce in accordance with his habit, to run up and lunch with Séverine. Occasionally, when they dared, they treated themselves to these little diversions. And on that day, as she was eating, still all of a tremble, she spoke to him about the money, relating how she had found the hiding-place empty. Her rancour against her husband was not appeased, and the words she had used the previous night came incessantly to her lips:

ÉMILE ZOLA

"Thief! thief! thief!"

Then she brought the watch, and insisted on giving it to Jacques in spite of his repugnance to take it.

"But you see, my darling," she said, "no one will ever think of searching for the thing at your place. If it remains with me, he will get possession of it. And rather than that should happen I would let him tear me to pieces. No, he has had too much already. I did not want the money; it gave me horror. I would never have spent a sou of it. But had he the right to take it? Oh! I hate him!"

She was in tears, and persisted with so many supplications, that Jacques ended by placing the watch in his waistcoat pocket.

An hour had passed when Roubaud, who had his own key, opened the door and stepped in. She was at once on her feet, while Roubaud stopped short, and Jacques, who was stupefied, remained seated. Séverine, without troubling to give any sort of explanation, advanced towards her husband, and passionately repeated:

"Thief! thief! thief!"

Roubaud hesitated for a second. Then, with that shrug of the shoulders, which served to brush everything aside now, he entered the bedroom and picked up a note-book connected with the railway, which he had forgotten. But she followed him, giving free play to her tongue.

"You have been there again," she said. "Dare to deny that you have been there again! And you have taken it all! Thief! thief! thief!"

He crossed the dining-room without a word. It was only at the door that he turned round to embrace her in his leaden glance, and say:

"Just let me have peace, eh!"

He was gone, and the door did not even bang. He appeared not to have seen, and made no allusion to the sweetheart seated there.

From that day Séverine and Jacques enjoyed perfect freedom, without troubling any further about Roubaud. But if the husband ceased to cause them anxiety, it was not the same with the eavesdropping of Madame Lebleu, the neighbour ever on the watch. She certainly had the idea that something irregular was going on. Jacques might well muffle the sound of his footsteps. At each visit he noticed the opposite door imperceptibly come ajar, and an eye staring at him through the chink. It became intolerable. He no longer dared ascend the staircase; for if he ran the risk, she knew he was there; and her ear went to the keyhole, so that it became impossible to take a kiss, or even to converse at liberty.

It was then that Séverine, in exasperation, resumed her former campaign against the Lebleus, to gain possession of their lodging. It was notorious that an assistant station-master had always lived there. But it was not now for the superb view afforded by the windows opening on the courtyard at the entrance, and stretching to the heights of Ingouville, that she desired it; her sole motive, anent which she never breathed a word, was that the lodging had a second entry—a door opening on a back staircase. Jacques could come up and go out that way without Madame Lebleu having even a suspicion of his visits. At last they would be free.

The battle was terrible. This question, which had already impassioned all the corridor, began afresh, and became envenomed from hour to hour. Madame Lebleu, in presence of the menace, desperately defended herself, convinced in her own mind that she would die if shut up in the dark lodging at the back, with the view barred by the roofing of the marquee, and as sad as a prison. How could she live in that black hole— she, who was accustomed to her beautifully bright room opening on the vast expanse of country, enlivened by the constant coming and going of travellers? And the state of her lower limbs preventing her going out for a walk, she would never have aught but the zinc roof to gaze upon; she might just as well be killed straight off.

Unfortunately these were mere sentimental reasons, and she was forced to own that she held the lodging from the former assistant station-master, predecessor of Roubaud, who, being a bachelor, had ceded it to her from motives of courtesy; and it appeared that there even existed a letter from her husband, undertaking to vacate the rooms should any future assistant station-master claim them; but as the letter had not yet been found, she denied that it had ever been written. In proportion as her case suffered, she became more violent and aggressive. At one moment she had sought to involve the wife of Moulin, the other assistant station-master, in the business, and so gain her over to her side by saying that this lady had seen men kiss Madame Roubaud on the stairs. Thereupon Moulin became angry; for his wife, a very gentle and insignificant creature, whom no one ever saw, vowed, in tears, that she had neither seen nor said anything.

For a week all this tittle-tattle swept like a tempest, from one end of the corridor to the other. But the cardinal mistake of Madame Lebleu, and the one destined to bring about her defeat, consisted in constantly irritating Mademoiselle Guichon, the office-keeper, by obstinately spying on her. It was a mania on the part of Madame Lebleu, a firm conviction, that this spinster was carrying on an intrigue with the station-master. And her anxiety to surprise them had become a malady, which was all the more intense as she had had her eye on them for three years, without surprising anything whatever, not even a breath.

So Mademoiselle Guichon, furious that she could neither go out nor come in without being watched, now exerted herself to have Madame Lebleu relegated to the back; a lodging would then separate them, and anyhow, she would no longer have her opposite, nor be obliged to pass before her door. Moreover, it was evident that M. Dabadie, the station-master, who hitherto had avoided meddling in the struggle, was becoming more and more unfavourable to the Lebleus every day, which was a grave sign.

Besides, the situation became complicated by quarrels. Philomène, who now brought her new-laid eggs to Séverine, displayed great insolence every time she ran across Madame Lebleu; and as the latter purposely left her door open, so as to annoy everybody, spiteful remarks were continually being exchanged between the two women.

This intimacy of Séverine and Philomène having drifted into confidences, the latter had ended by taking messages from Jacques to his sweetheart when he did not dare run upstairs himself. Arriving with her eggs, she altered the appointments, said why he had been obliged to be prudent on the previous evening, and related how long he had stayed at her house in conversation. Jacques, at times, when an obstacle prevented him meeting Séverine, found no displeasure in passing his time in this way at the cottage of Sauvagnat, the head of the engine depôt. He accompanied Pecqueux, his fireman, there, as if for the purpose of distraction, for he dreaded staying a whole evening alone. But when the fireman disappeared, to go from one to another of the drinking resorts frequented by sailors, he called on Philomène alone, entrusted her with a message, then, seating himself, he remained there sometime. And she, becoming little by little mixed-up in this love affair, began to be smitten. The small hands and polite manners of this sad lover seemed to her delightful.

One evening she unbosomed herself to him, complaining of the fireman, an artful fellow, said she, notwithstanding his jovial manner, quite capable of dealing a nasty blow when intoxicated. Jacques noticed that she now paid more attention to her personal appearance, drank less, and kept the house cleaner. Her brother Sauvagnat, having one night overheard a male voice in the room, entered with his hand raised ready to strike; but recognising the visitor talking to her, he contented himself with uncorking a bottle of cider. Jacques, who was well received, shook off his fainting fits, and apparently amused himself. Philomène, for her part, displayed warmer and warmer friendship for Séverine, and made no secret of her feelings for Madame Lebleu, whom she alluded to everywhere as an old hag.

One night, meeting the two sweethearts at the back of her garden, she accompanied them in the dark to the shed, where they usually concealed themselves.

"Ah! well," said she, "it is too good of you. As the lodging is yours, I would drag her out of it by the hair of her head. Give her a good hiding!"

But Jacques was opposed to a scandal.

"No, no," he broke in, "M. Dabadie has the matter in hand. It will be better to wait until it can be properly settled."

"Before the end of the month," affirmed Séverine, "I mean to sleep in her room, and we shall then be able to see one another whenever we please."

Philomène left them to return home, but, hidden in the shadow a few paces away, she paused and faced round. She felt considerable emotion at the knowledge that they were together. Still, she was not jealous; she simply felt the need of loving and of being loved in this same way.

Jacques became more and more gloomy every day. On two occasions when he could have met Séverine, he invented excuses not to do so, and sometimes when he remained late at the cottage of the Sauvagnats, it was also for the purpose of avoiding her. Nevertheless, he still loved her. But now the frightful evil had returned. He suffered from terrible swimming in the head, he turned icy cold. In terror, he perceived he was no longer himself, and that the animal was there ready to bite.

He sought relief in the fatigue of long journeys, soliciting additional work, remaining twelve hours at a stretch erect on his engine, his body racked by the vacillation, his lungs scorched by the wind. His comrades complained of this hard life of a driver, which did for a man, said they, in a score of years. He would have liked to be done for at once. He was never sufficiently tired. Never did he feel so happy as when borne along by La Lison, thinking no more, and with eyes only for the signals. On reaching the end of the run sleep overpowered him, before he had even time to wash. Only, when he awoke, the torment of the fixed idea returned.

He had also endeavoured to resume his former affection for La Lison. Again he passed hours cleaning it, exacting from Pecqueux that the steel should shine like silver. The inspectors who got up beside him on the way, paid him compliments. But he only shook his head in dissatisfaction, for, he knew very well, that since the stoppage in the snow, it was not the same efficient, valiant engine as formerly. Doubtless, in the repairs to the pistons and slide-valves, it had lost some of its principal motive power—that mysterious equilibrium, due to the hazard of building. This decay caused him suffering which turned to bitter vexation, and to such a pitch that he pursued his superiors with unreasonable complaints, asking for unnecessary repairs, and suggesting improvements that were impracticable. These being refused, he became more gloomy, convinced that La Lison was out of order, and that henceforth he could do nothing decent with the engine. His affection in consequence became discouraged; what was the good of loving anything, as he would kill all he loved?

Séverine had not failed to observe the change, and she was grieved, thinking his sadness due to her, since he knew all. When she perceived him shudder on her neck, avoid her kiss by abruptly drawing back, was it not because he remembered, and she caused him horror? Never had she dared resume the conversation on the subject. She repented of having spoken, and was surprised at the way her confession had burst from her. As if satisfied at present to have him with her, at the bottom of this secret, she forgot how long she had felt the need to confide in him. She loved him more passionately since he knew everything. She only lived for Jacques, and her one dream was that he might carry her away and keep her with him.

Of the hideous drama she had merely retained the astonishment of being mixed up in it, and she would not even have felt angry with her husband, had he not been in her way. But her execration for this man increased in proportion with her passion for the other. Now that her husband was aware of her intrigue and had absolved her, the sweetheart was the master, the one she would follow, and who could dispose of her as he pleased. She had made him give her his portrait, and she took it to bed with her, falling asleep with her lips glued to the image. And she felt very much pained since she saw him unhappy, without being able to exactly understand what caused him such suffering.

Nevertheless, they continued to meet outside, until they could see one another at her home, in the new, conquered lodging. Winter approached its term, and the month of February proved very mild. They prolonged their walks, sauntering for hours over the open ground adjoining the station. Séverine continued to make her trip to Paris every Friday; and now she did not offer her husband the slightest explanation. For the neighbours, the old pretext, a bad knee sufficed; and she also said that she went to see her wet-nurse, Mother Victoire, who was a long time getting through her convalescence at the hospital. Both Séverine and Jacques still took great pleasure in these journeys. He showed himself particularly attentive to his locomotive; she, delighted to see him less gloomy, found amusement in looking out of the window, notwithstanding that she began to know every little hill and clump of trees on the way.

From Havre to Motteville were meadows, flat fields separated by green hedges and planted with apple-trees; then as far as Rouen came a stretch of irregular, desert land. After Rouen, the Seine streamed by. They crossed it at Sotteville, at Oissel, at Pont-de-l'Arche. Now it constantly reappeared, expanding to great breadth across the vast plains. From Gaillon it was hardly once lost to view. It ran on the left, slackening in speed between its low banks, bordered with poplars and willows. The train, darting along a hillside, abandoned the river at Bonnières to abruptly meet it once more on issuing from the Rolleboise tunnel at Rosny. It seemed like a friendly companion on the journey, and was crossed three times again before reaching Paris.

As the train sped gaily on its way, Mantes appeared with its belfry amidst the trees, Triel with its white limekilns, Poissy, which the line severed in twain, in the very heart of the town. Next came the two green screens of Saint Germain forest, the slope of Colombes, bursting with lilac, and they were in the outskirts of Paris. The city could be perceived from the bridge at Asnières; the distant Arc de Triomphe, towering above sordid buildings, bristling with factory chimneys. The engine plunged beneath Batignolles, and the passengers streamed from the carriages on to the platform of the echoing station.

Until night Séverine and Jacques were free, and belonged to one another. On the return journey, it being dark, she closed her eyes, enjoying her happiness over again. But morning and night, each time she passed La Croix-de-Maufras, she advanced her head; and, without discovering herself, cast a furtive glance outside the carriage, certain

ÉMILE ZOLA

that she would there find Flore, erect before the gate of the level-crossing, presenting the flag in its case, and embracing the train with her flaming eyes.

Since the snowy day when this girl had caught them kissing one another, Jacques had warned Séverine to be careful of her. He was no longer ignorant of that passion of a wild creature wherewith she had pursued him from her earliest years. He felt that she was jealous, and that she possessed virile energy, as well as unbridled and deadly rancour. Moreover, she must be well-informed in regard to matters concerning Séverine, for he remembered her allusion to the intimacy of the President with a certain young lady whom no one suspected, and for whom he had found a husband. If she knew this, she must assuredly have penetrated the mystery of the crime. Doubtless, she would be talking or writing, so as to avenge herself by a denunciation.

But days and weeks passed without anything happening. He still found her there, planted rigidly at her post beside the line, with her flag. Far away, as soon as she was able to catch sight of the locomotive, he felt the sensation of her burning eyes. She saw him, notwithstanding the smoke, and embraced all his frame in her glance, following him in the lightning flash amidst the thunder of the wheels.

And the train was scrutinised at the same time, pierced through and through, inspected from the first carriage to the last; she always discovered the other one, the rival, whom she now knew to be there every Friday. And Séverine might well advance her head but a trifle, impelled by the imperious necessity to look. She was seen. Their eyes crossed like rapiers. The train was already far away, devouring space; and one person remained on the ground, powerless to follow it, raging at the happiness it bore along. Flore seemed to be growing. Jacques found her taller at each journey, and felt uneasy at her taking no action, wondering what plan would ripen in the head of this great, gloomy girl, whose motionless apparition he could not avoid.

There was also one of the servants of the company, that headguard, Henri Dauvergne, who inconvenienced Séverine and Jacques. He happened to be in charge of this Friday train, and he displayed importunate amiability towards the young woman. The attentions of Henri became so apparent, that Roubaud observed them with sneering countenance on the mornings when he was on duty at the departure from Havre. The headguard was in the habit of reserving an entire compartment for his wife, and took pains to see she was comfortable there, feeling the foot-warmer to make sure the water was hot, and so forth. On one occasion the husband, while continuing a chat with Jacques, attracted his notice to the proceedings of the young man with a wink, as if to inquire whether he permitted that kind of thing.

In the family quarrels, Roubaud flatly accused his wife of making love to the pair. And Séverine imagined, for an instant, that Jacques also had this belief, which was the cause of his sadness. In a burst of tears, she protested her innocence, telling him to kill her if she were unfaithful. But he merely laughed, and, turning very pale, embraced her, saying he was convinced of her fidelity, and that he sincerely hoped he would never kill anybody.

The first evenings of March were frightful, and they were obliged to interrupt their meetings. The trips to Paris, the few hours of freedom sought so far away, were no longer enough for Séverine. She experienced an increasing desire to have Jacques with her, always with her, to live together, without ever leaving one another. And her execration for her husband increased. The mere presence of this man threw her into an unhealthy and intolerable state of excitement. She so docile, with all the complacence of a tender-hearted woman, became irritated as soon as it was a question of Roubaud, flying into a passion at the least opposition he made to her will.

On such occasions the shade of her raven hair seemed to darken the limpid blue of her eyes. She became fierce, accusing him of having so thoroughly spoilt her existence that henceforth it would be impossible to live together. Had not he done it all? If they were no longer as man and wife, if she had a sweetheart, was it not his own fault? His sluggish tranquillity, the look of indifference with which he met her anger, his round shoulders, his enlarged stomach, all that dreadful fat, resembling happiness, completed her exasperation, she who suffered. Her one thought, now, was to break with him, to get away, to go and begin life again elsewhere. Oh! could she but commence again, wipe out the past, return to the life she led previous to all these abominations, find herself as she was at fifteen, and love, and be loved, and live as she dreamed of living then!

For a week, she courted the idea of taking flight: she would leave with Jacques, they would conceal themselves in Belgium, where they would set up housekeeping as a hard-working young couple. But she had not spoken to him on the subject. Obstacles had at once come in the way: their irregular position, the constant anxiety in which they

ÉMILE ZOLA

would find themselves, and particularly the annoyance of leaving her fortune to her husband—the money, La Croix-de-Maufras.

By a donation to the survivor of the pair—which is possible in France, and cannot be revoked without the consent of both parties—they had willed everything away; and she found herself in his power, in that legal tutelage of a wife which tied her hands. Rather than leave, and abandon even a sou, she would have preferred to die there. One day when he came up, livid, to say that crossing the line in front of a locomotive he had felt the buffer graze his elbow, she reflected that if he had been killed, she would have been free. She observed him with her great staring eyes; why on earth did he not die, since she had ceased to love him, and he was now in the way of everyone?

From that moment the dream of Séverine changed: Roubaud had been killed in an accident, and she left with Jacques for America. But they were married. They had sold La Croix-de-Maufras, and realised all the fortune. Behind them they left nothing they were afraid of. If they emigrated, it was to be born again in the arms of one another. Over there, naught would exist of the events she wished to forget, and she could imagine she was beginning a new life. As she had made a mistake, she would engage in the experience of happiness again at the commencement. He would find employment; she could undertake something else. They would make their fortune. Perhaps children might come, and there would be a new existence of labour and felicity.

As soon as she was alone in bed in the morning, and while engaged on her embroidery in the daytime, she resumed the construction of this castle in the air, modifying, enlarging, ceaselessly adding delightful details to it, and ended by imagining herself overwhelmed with joy and riches. She, who formerly went out so rarely, had now a passion for going to see the mail-steamers put to sea: she ran down to the jetty, leant over the balustrade, followed the smoke of the vessel until it became lost in the haze of the offing; and she fancied herself on deck with Jacques, already far from France, steaming for the paradise of her dreams.

One evening in the month of March, Jacques having taken the risk of going up to see her, related that he had brought one of his old schoolfellows in his train from Paris, who was leaving for New York, to bring out a new invention, a machine for making buttons; and, as he wanted an engineer as partner, he had offered to take the driver with him. Oh! it was a magnificent enterprise, only requiring the investment of 30,000 frcs., a matter of £1,200, and in which there were perhaps millions to be made. Jacques merely mentioned the subject casually, and concluded by saying that he had of course refused the offer. Nevertheless, he felt a bit sorry, for it is hard to turn the back on fortune when it comes to one.

Séverine, on her feet, listened to him with vacant eyes. Was not this her dream which was going to be realised?

"Ah!" murmured she at last, "we would start tomorrow—"

He raised his head in surprise, and interrupted her with the inquiry:

"What do you mean by we would start?"

"Yes, if he were dead," she replied.

She had not named Roubaud, but he understood, and gave a vague gesture to say that, unfortunately, he was not dead.

"We would set out," she resumed in her slow, deep voice, "and we should be so happy over there! I could get the 30,000 frcs. by selling the property, and I should still have enough to enable us to settle down. You could turn the cash to account; I would arrange a little home, where we would love one another with all our might. Oh! it would be so nice, so nice!"

And she added, very low:

"Far from all recollection of the past, and only new times ahead of us!"

He felt deeply affected. Their two hands joined, and pressed one another instinctively. Then came a pause, both Séverine and Jacques being rapt in this hope. It was she who broke the silence.

"All the same, it would be best for you to see your friend again before his departure, and ask him not to take a partner without letting you know," she suggested.

Once more he was surprised.

"What is the use of that?" he inquired.

"Good heavens! Who knows?" she answered. "The other day, with that locomotive! Another second and I was free. One is alive in the morning, and dead at night. Is it not true?"

Looking at him fixedly, she repeated:

"Ah! if he were only dead!"

"But you don't want me to kill him, do you?" he inquired, trying to smile.

Thrice she answered no; but her eyes said yes—those eyes of a tender-hearted woman, who had abandoned herself to the inexorable cruelty of her passion. As he had killed another, why should not he

ÉMILE ZOLA

be killed himself? This idea had abruptly begun to assert itself as a consequence of the crime, a necessary termination to the difficulty. Kill him and go away: nothing could be more simple. When he was once dead, everything would be over, and she could begin again. She saw no other solution possible, and her resolution was irrevocably taken; but, not having the courage of her violence, she continued, in slightly wavering tones, to say no.

Jacques, standing with his back to the sideboard, still affected to smile. He had just caught sight of the knife lying there.

"If you want me to kill him," said he, his smile broadening into a laugh, "you must give me the knife. I already have the watch, and this will help to make me a small museum."

"Take the knife," she gravely answered.

And when he had put it in his pocket, as if to carry on the joke to the end, he kissed her.

"And now, good-night," he said. "I shall go and see my friend at once, and tell him to wait. If it does not rain next Saturday, come and meet me behind the cottage of Sauvagnat, eh? Is that understood? And rest assured that we will kill no one. It's only a joke."

Nevertheless, in spite of the late hour, Jacques went down towards the port to find the comrade leaving on the morrow. He spoke to him of a legacy he might receive, and asked for a fortnight before giving a definite answer. Then, on his way back towards the station by the great dark avenues, he thought the matter over, and felt astonished at what he had just done. Had he then resolved to kill Roubaud, since he was disposing of his wife and money? No, indeed, he had come to no decision, and if he took these precautions, it was no doubt in case he should decide. But the recollection of Séverine entered his mind, the burning pressure of her hand, her fixed eyes saying yes, while her lips said no. She evidently wanted him to kill her husband. He felt very much troubled. What should he do?

When Jacques returned to the Rue François-Mazeline and lay down in his bed, beside that of Pecqueux, who was snoring, he could not sleep. Do what he would, his brain set to work on this idea of murder, this web of a drama that he was arranging, and whose most far-reaching consequences he calculated. He thought. He weighed the reasons for, and the reasons against. Summing up calmly, without the least excitement, after reflection, everything was in favour of the crime. Was not Roubaud the sole obstacle to his happiness? With Roubaud dead, he would marry Séverine, whom he adored. Besides, there was the money—a fortune.

He would give up his hard handicraft, and in his turn become an employer of labour, in that America of which he heard his comrades talk as of a country where engine-men shovelled in the gold. His new existence, over there, would unfold like a dream: a wife who passionately loved him, millions to be earned at once, a grand style of living, unlimited scope for ambition; in fact, anything he pleased. And to realise this dream he had only to make a movement, only to suppress a man, the insect, the plant in your way on the path, and which you trample on. He was not even interesting, this man who had now grown fat and heavy, who was plunged in that stupid passion for cards, which had destroyed his former energy. Why spare him? There was nothing, absolutely nothing to plead in his favour. Everything condemned him, because in response to each question, came the answer that it was to the interest of others he should die. To hesitate would be idiotic and cowardly.

Jacques bounded in his bed, starting at a thought, at first vague, and then abruptly so piercing that he felt it like a prick in his skull. He, who from childhood desired to kill, who was ravaged to the point of torture by the horror of that fixed idea, why did he not kill Roubaud? Perhaps, on this selected victim, he would for ever assuage his thirst for murder; and, in that way, he would not only do a good stroke of business, but he would be cured as well. Cured, great God! He became bathed in perspiration. He saw himself with the knife in his hand, striking at the throat of Roubaud as the latter had struck the President, and become satisfied and appeased in proportion as the wound bled upon his hands. He would kill him. He was resolved to do so, for that would give him his cure, as well as the woman he adored, and fortune. As he had to kill somebody, since he must kill, he would kill this man, with the knowledge at all events that what he did was done rationally, by interest and logic.

Three o'clock in the morning had just struck, when this decision was arrived at, and Jacques endeavoured to sleep. He was already dozing off when a violent start brought him up in his bed in a sitting posture, choking. Kill this man! Great God! had he the right? When a fly pestered him he crushed it with a smack. One day when a cat got between his legs he broke its spine by a kick, without wishing to do so, it is true. But this man, his fellow creature! He had to resume all his

ÉMILE ZOLA

reasoning to prove to himself that he had a right to commit murder—the right of the strong who find the weak in their way and devour them. It was he whom the wife of the other one loved at this hour, and she wanted to be free to marry him and bring him what she possessed.

When two wolves met in the wood, and a she-wolf was there, did not the stronger rid himself of the other with his fangs? And in ancient times, when men found refuge in the caverns, like the wolves, did not the coveted woman belong to that man in the band who could win her in the blood of his rivals? Then, as this was the law of life, it should be obeyed, apart from the scruples invented later on to regulate existence in common.

Little by little his right appeared to him absolute, and he felt his resolution affirmed. On the morrow he would select the spot and hour, and make preparations for the deed. Doubtless it would be best to stab Roubaud at night on the station premises, during one of his rounds, so as to convey the impression that he had fallen a victim to some thieves he had surprised. He knew a good place, over there behind the coal heaps, if Roubaud could only be attracted to the spot. In spite of his desire to sleep, he could not help arranging the scene then, debating in his mind where he would place himself, how he would strike, so as to stretch his victim at his feet; and insensibly, invincibly, as he went into the smallest details, his repugnance returned, inner protestation gained the upper hand.

No, no, he would not deal the blow! It appeared to him monstrous, a thing that could not be done, impossible. The civilised man within him, influenced by the power acquired through education, by the slowly erected and indestructible edifice of ideas handed down to him, revolted. Kill not! He had taken in that law at the breast, with the milk of generations. His refined brain, furnished with scruples, repelled the thought of murder with horror, as soon as he began to reason about it. Yes, kill by necessity, instinctively, in a fit of passion; but kill deliberately, by calculation and interest, no, he could never, never do it!

Dawn was breaking when Jacques succeeded in dozing off, but his sleep was so light that the debate continued confusedly in his mind, causing him abominable suffering. The ensuing days were the most painful of his existence. He avoided Séverine. Dreading her look, he sent her word not to come to the appointment on the Saturday. But the following Monday he was obliged to meet her; and, as he had feared, her great blue eyes, so soft and deep, filled him with anguish. She did not refer to the subject, she did not make a sign, nor say a word to urge him on, only her eyes were full of the thing, questioning, imploring him. He hardly knew which way to turn to avoid their impatient and reproachful gaze. He always found them fixed on his own eyes, in an expression of astonishment that he could hesitate to be happy.

When he kissed her at parting, he abruptly strained her to him, to give her to understand that he had resolved to act. And so, indeed, he had, until he reached the bottom of the stairs and found himself struggling with his conscience again. When he saw her, two days later, he was pale with confusion, and had the furtive look of a coward who hesitates in face of a necessary action. She burst into sobs without saying a word, weeping with her arms round his neck, horribly unhappy; and he, quite unhinged, felt the utmost contempt for himself. He must put an end to it.

"On Thursday, over there, will you?" she inquired in a low voice.

"Yes, on Thursday I will wait for you," he answered.

On that particular Thursday the night was very dark, a starless sky, opaque and heavy, loaded with mist from the sea. Jacques, as usual, arrived the first, and, standing behind the cottage of the Sauvagnats, watched for Séverine. But the gloom was so intense, and she hurried along so lightly, that she brushed against him before he caught sight of her, making him start. She was already in his arms, and alarmed at feeling him tremble, she murmured:

"Did I frighten you?"

"No, no," he replied, "I was expecting you. Let us walk on; no one can see us."

And with their arms round the waists of one another, they strolled slowly over the vacant ground. There were but few gas-lamps on this side of the depôt. In some gloomy quarters there were none at all; whereas they swarmed in the distance, near the station, like a quantity of bright sparks.

Jacques and Séverine walked about for a long time without a word. She had rested her head on his shoulder, and raised it ever and anon to kiss him on the chin; while he, bending down, returned the kiss on her forehead at the roots of her hair. The grave, solitary stroke of one o'clock in the morning, had just resounded from air the distant churches. If they failed to speak, it was because they felt they were both thinking. They were thinking of nothing but that one subject. It was impossible for them to be together now without finding themselves beset by it. The mental debate continued. What was the use of saying useless words aloud, as it was necessary to act? When she raised herself against him for a caress, she felt the knife, which formed a lump in his pocket. Could it be possible that he had made up his mind?

But her thoughts were too much for her, and her lips parted in a murmur that was scarcely audible:

"Just now he came upstairs; I was wondering what for. Then I saw him take his revolver, which he had forgotten. He is certainly going to make a round."

They resumed silence, and it was only twenty paces further on that he, in his turn, remarked:

"Last night some thieves took away the lead from here. He will come along presently for sure."

She gave a little shudder; both became silent, and they walked on more slowly. Then she had a doubt: was it really the knife that formed the lump in his pocket? Twice she stooped down knocking against it to get a better idea. Then, being still uncertain, she let her hand drop, and felt. It was the knife sure enough. And Jacques, understanding her thoughts, suddenly strained her to him stammering into her ear:

"He will come, and you shall be free."

The murder was decided. They no longer seemed to be walking. It appeared to them that some strange force sent them along just above the ground. Their senses had, all at once, become extremely acute, particularly the touch, for their hands, resting one in the other, were in pain, and the slightest brush of the lips was like a scratch. They also heard sounds which were lost a moment before—the rumble, the distant puffs of the engines, the muffled shocks, footsteps wandering in the depth of the obscurity. And they could see into the night; they distinguished the black spots of objects as if a mist had been removed from their eyes, they were able to follow the sharp curves described in the air by a passing bat. They stopped, motionless, at the corner of a heap of coal, ears and eyes on the alert, and with all their beings in a state of tension; they now spoke in whispers.

"Did you hear that?" she inquired. "Over there, somebody calling."

"No," he replied, "they're putting a carriage into the coach-house."

"But there, someone is walking on our left," said she. "I heard the sound on the gravel."

"No, no," he answered, "rats are running over the coal heaps, and some of the pieces rolled down."

Several minutes passed. Suddenly it was she who strained him to her more closely.

"There he is!" she exclaimed.

"Where? I can't see him," said he.

"He has turned round the shed of the slow-train goods department," she continued. "He is coming straight towards us. Look at his shadow, passing along the white wall!"

"Do you think it is? That dark spot? Then he must be alone," he said.

"Yes, alone. He is alone," she repeated.

And at this decisive moment she passionately threw herself on his neck, she pressed her burning lips to his. It was a prolonged embrace, in which she would have wished to have conveyed her own blood to him. How she loved him! and how she execrated the other! Ah! had she but dared, twenty times over she would have done the business herself, to spare him the horror; but her hands were unequal to the effort, she felt herself too feeble, it required the fist of a man. And this kiss, which was without end, was all she could breathe to him of her own courage.

A locomotive whistled in the distance, casting to the night a melancholy lamentation of distress. At regular intervals they could hear the loud strokes of a colossal hammer coming from an undeterminable direction. The vapour ascending from the sea sailed across the sky in chaotic confusion, while drifting shreds seemed at moments to extinguish the bright sparks of the gas-lamps. When Séverine at length removed her mouth from his, it seemed as if she had ceased to exist, as if all her soul had passed into him.

Jacques abruptly opened the knife. But with a stifled oath, he exclaimed:

"It's all up! He's off!"

And so it was. The moving shadow, after approaching to within fifty paces of them, had just turned to the left, and was retreating with the even step of a night watchman who had no cause for alarm.

Then she pushed him.

"Go on, go on!" said she.

And they both started. He ahead; she close at his heels. They glided behind the man, hunting him down, careful not to make a noise. Then as they took a short cut across a shunting-line, they found him twenty paces at the most away. They had to take advantage of every bit of wall for shelter. One false step would have betrayed them.

"We shall never reach him," said he, in a hollow voice. "If he attains the box of the pointsman he will escape."

She continued, repeating behind him:

"Go on, go on!"

At this minute, surrounded by the vast flat waste ground plunged in obscurity, amidst the nocturnal desolation of a great railway station, he was resolved to act, as in that solitude which is the natural attendant on assassination. And while he stealthily hastened his steps, he became excited, reasoning with himself, supplying himself with arguments that were to make this murder a wise, legitimate action, logically debated and decided on. It certainly was a right that he would be exercising, the right even of life, as this blood of another was indispensable to his own existence. He had merely to plunge this knife into the man to win happiness.

"We shall not get him, we shall not get him," he repeated furiously, observing the shadow pass beyond the box of the pointsman. "It's all up! There he is, going off."

But Séverine abruptly caught him by the arm with her nervous hand, and brought him to a standstill against her.

"Look!" she exclaimed, "he's coming back!"

Roubaud, indeed, was retracing his steps. He had gone to the right, then he returned. Perhaps, behind him, he had felt the vague sensation of the murderers on his track. Nevertheless, he continued to walk at his usual tranquil pace, like a conscientious watchman, who will not retire to his quarters without having taken a glance everywhere.

Jacques and Séverine, pulled up short in their race, no longer moved. Chance had placed them right at the angle of the heap of coal. They pressed their backs so closely to it that they seemed to form part of the black mass. There, without a breath, they watched Roubaud advancing towards them. They were barely separated from him by thirty yards. Each stride lessened the distance, regularly, as if timed by the inexorable pendulum of destiny. Another twenty, another ten paces, and Jacques would have the man before him. He would raise his arm in such a manner and plunge the knife in the throat of Roubaud, drawing it from right to left so as to stifle his shriek. The seconds seemed interminable. Such a flood of thoughts ran through the blank in his skull that the measure of time no longer existed. All the reasons that had brought him to his determination filed past once more. He again distinctly saw the murder, the causes and the consequences. Another five steps. His resolution, strained fit to break, remained firm. He wanted to kill; he knew why he would kill.

But at two paces, at one pace, came a downfall; everything gave way within him at a single stroke. No, no! he would not, he could not kill a defenceless man in this way. Reasoning would never suffice for murder; it required the instinct to bite, the spring that sends the destroyer on the prey, the hunger or passion that makes him tear it to pieces. What matter if conscience were merely made up of ideas transmitted by a slow heredity of justice! He did not feel that he had the right to kill, and do what he would, he was unable to persuade himself that he could take it.

Roubaud passed slowly by. His elbow almost grazed the other two in the coal. A breath would have betrayed them; but they remained as dead. The arm did not rise; it did not plunge in the knife. No quiver disturbed the dense obscurity, not even a shudder. Roubaud was already far, ten paces off; but they were still standing there motionless, their backs riveted to the black heap. Both were without breath, in terror of this man, alone and unarmed, who had just brushed past them so peacefully.

Jacques, choking with rage and shame, gave a sob.

"I cannot do it! I cannot do it!" he repeated.

He wanted to take Séverine to him again, to press against her, with the desire to be excused and consoled. She escaped without a word. He had stretched out his hands, but only to catch her skirt, which slipped from his fingers; and he heard nothing, save her light, fleeting footsteps. Her sudden disappearance completely undid him, and he pursued her for an instant or two; but in vain. Was she then so very angry at his weakness? Did she despise him? Prudence prevented him rejoining her. When he found himself alone on this extensive flat land, studded with small yellow flames of gas, he felt overwhelmed with despair, and hastened to leave it, to go and bury his head in his pillow, there to forget the abomination of his existence.

It was a matter of ten days later, towards the end of March, that the Roubauds at last triumphed over the Lebleus. The railway company had recognised their appeal, supported by M. Dabadie, as just; and the more easily did they arrive at this conclusion as the famous letter from the cashier, undertaking to give up the lodging if a new assistant station-master claimed it, had been found by Mademoiselle Guichon, while looking over some old accounts in the archives of the station. And

Madame Lebleu, exasperated at her defeat, at once spoke of moving; as they wanted to kill her, she might just as well die now without waiting.

For three days this memorable removal kept the corridor in a fever. Little Madame Moulin, herself usually so retiring, whom no one ever saw come in or go out, became implicated in the business by carrying a work-table from one lodging to the other. But it was particularly Philomène who breathed the breath of discord. She had arrived there, to assist, from the very commencement, doing up packages, jostling the furniture, invading the lodging on the front before the tenant had left; and it was she who pushed her out, amidst the going and coming of the two sets of household goods, which had got mixed together, in wild confusion, in the course of transport. When Philomène had carried off the last chair the doors banged; but perceiving a stool, which the wife of the cashier had forgotten, she opened again, and threw it across the corridor. That was the end.

Philomène had reached the point of displaying such excessive zeal for Jacques and all he loved, that Pecqueux was astonished. Feeling suspicious, he asked her, in his nasty, sly manner, with his air of a vindictive drunkard, whether she was now smitten with his driver, warning her that he would settle the account of both of them if he ever caught them together. Her fancy for the young man had increased, and she acted as a sort of servant to him and his sweetheart, in the hope of gaining a little of his affection by placing herself between them.

Life slowly resumed its monotonous course. While Madame Lebleu, at the back, riveted to her armchair by rheumatism, was dying of spleen, with great tears in her eyes because she could see nothing but the zinc roof of the marquee shutting out the sky, Séverine worked at her interminable bed-covering beside one of the windows on the front. Below, she had the lively activity of the courtyard, the constant stream of pedestrians and carriages. The forward spring was already turning the buds of the great trees that lined the pavements green, and beyond, the distant hills of Ingouville displayed their wooded slopes, studded with the white spots of country houses.

But she felt astonished to find so little pleasure in the realisation of this dream at last, to be there, in this coveted apartment, with space, daylight, and sun before her. When her charwoman, Mother Simon, grumbled, furious at finding herself disturbed in her habits, she lost patience, and at times regretted her old hole, as she termed it, where the dirt could not be so easily seen.

Roubaud had simply let matters take their course. He did not seem to be aware that he had changed his abode. He frequently made mistakes, and only perceived his error on finding that his new key would not enter the old lock. He absented himself more and more. The irregularity of his life continued. Nevertheless, at one moment he seemed to brighten up under the influence of a revival of his political ideas. Not that they were very clear or very ardent, but he had at heart that trouble with the sub-prefect, which had almost cost him his position.

Now that the Empire, which had met with a severe shock at the general elections, was passing through a terrible crisis, he triumphed, and he repeated that those people would not always be the masters. But a friendly warning from M. Dabadie, who heard about the matter from Mademoiselle Guichon, in whose presence the revolutionary remark had been made, sufficed to calm him. As the corridor was quiet, and everyone lived at peace, now that Madame Lebleu was drooping with sadness, why cause fresh annoyance on the subject of the government? Roubaud simply shrugged his shoulders. He cared not a fig about politics, nor anything else! Growing fatter and fatter, day by day, and free from remorse, he moved along with heavy tread and an air of indifference.

The feeling of constraint had increased between Séverine and Jacques, since they were able to meet at any time. Nothing now interfered with their happiness. He ran up to see her by the other staircase whenever he pleased, without fear of being spied upon. But the recollection of the thing that had not been realised, of the deed that both had consented to, and wished to see done, and which he failed to perform, had created an uneasiness, an insurmountable barrier between them. He, coming with the shame of his weakness, found her on each occasion more depressed, sick at waiting uselessly. Their lips no longer even sought one another, for they had exhausted this semi-felicity; what they desired was complete happiness—the departure, the marriage over there, the other life.

One night Jacques found Séverine in tears, and when she perceived him, she did not stop, but sobbed louder, hanging round his neck. She had already wept like this, but he had appeased her with an embrace; whereas now, with her to his heart, he felt her ravaged with increasing despair the more he pressed her to him. He was quite unhinged. At last, taking her head between his two hands, and looking at her quite close, into her streaming eyes, he made a vow, thoroughly understanding that if she despaired to this extent, it was because she felt herself a woman, and in her passive gentleness, dared not strike with her own hand.

"Forgive me!" said he; "wait a little longer. I swear to you that I will do it shortly, as soon as I can."

She immediately pressed her lips to his, as if to seal this oath, and they enjoyed one of those deep kisses in which they mingled one with the other, in the communion of their flesh.

X

Aunt Phasie died, in a final convulsion, at nine o'clock on Thursday evening; and Misard, standing at the bedside, tried in vain to close her lids. The eyes obstinately remained open. The head had become rigid, and was slightly inclined over the shoulder, as if looking about the room, while a contraction of the lips seemed to have curled them upward in a jeering smile. A single candle, stuck on the corner of a table near her, lighted the surroundings; and the trains passing by, full speed, in ignorance of the corpse being there, made it quiver for a second or two in the vacillating light.

Misard, to get rid of Flore, at once sent her off to Doinville to apprise the authorities of the decease. She could not be back until eleven o'clock, so that he had two hours before him. He first of all quietly cut himself a slice of bread, for he felt hungry, having gone without his dinner on account of the death agony, which seemed interminable. And he ate standing up, going and coming, arranging one thing and another about the room. Fits of coughing brought him to a standstill, bent him double. He was half dead himself. So thin, so puny, with his leaden eyes and discoloured hair, that he did not seem likely to enjoy his victory for long.

No matter, he had devoured this buxom wife, this tall, handsome woman, as the insect eats down the oak. She was on her back, polished off, reduced to nothing, and he still lasted. But why had she been so obstinate? She had tried to be cunning; so much the worse for her. When a married couple play the game of seeing which shall bury the other, without putting anyone in the secret, it is necessary to keep a sharp look out. He was proud of his achievement, and chuckled to himself as if it were a good joke.

At that instant an express train swept by, enveloping the low habitation in such a gust of tempest, that in spite of his habit, he turned towards the window with a start. Ah! yes, that constant flood, that mass of people coming from every quarter, who knew nothing about what they crushed on the road, and did not care, in such a hurry were they to go to the devil! And turning round again, in the oppressive silence, he met the two wide open eyes of the corpse, whose steady pupils seemed to follow each of his movements, while the corners of the mouth curled upward in a smile.

ÉMILE ZOLA

Misard, usually so phlegmatic, made a slight movement of anger. He thoroughly understood; she was saying to him: "Search! search!" But surely she could not have taken her 1,000 frcs. away with her; and now that she no longer existed, he would end by finding them. Ought she not to have given them up willingly? It would have prevented all this annoyance. The eyes followed him everywhere. Search! search!

He now ferreted all over this room, which he had not dared rout out so long as she lived. First of all, in the cupboard. He took the keys from under the bolster, upset the shelves loaded with linen, emptied the two drawers, pulled them out even, to ascertain if they concealed a hiding-place. No, nothing! After that, he thought of the night-table. He unglued the marble top and turned it over, but to no purpose. With a flat rule he probed behind the chimney glass, one of those thin glasses sold in the fairs, that was fastened to the wall by a couple of nails; but only to draw out a cobweb black with dust. Search! search!

Then to escape those wide-open eyes which he felt resting on him, he sank down on all fours, tapping lightly on the tiles with his knuckles, listening whether some resonance would not reveal a hole. Several tiles being loose, he tore them up. There was nothing, still nothing! When he rose to his feet again, the eyes once more caught him. He wheeled round, wishing to stare straight into the fixed orbs of the dead woman, who, from the corners of her curled-up lips, seemed to accentuate her terrible laugh. There could be no doubt about it, she was mocking him. Search! search!

He began to feel feverish. A suspicion came upon him, a sacrilegious idea, that made his livid countenance grow paler still, and he approached the corpse. What had made him think that she could surely not have taken her 1,000 frcs. away with her? Perhaps, after all, she was carrying them off. And he had the courage to uncover, to undress, and search the body, as she told him to search. He looked beneath her, behind the nape of her neck, everywhere. The bedding was all upset. He buried his arm in the paillasse up to the shoulder, and found nothing. Search! search! And the head of the dead woman fell back on the pillow, which was all in disorder, with the pupils of her bantering eyes still observing him.

As Misard, furious and trembling, tried to arrange the bed, Flore came in, on her return from Doinville.

"It will be for the day after tomorrow, at eleven o'clock," said she.

She spoke of the burial. She understood at a glance what kind of work had made Misard lose his breath during her absence, and she made a gesture of disdainful indifference.

"You may just as well give it up," said she. "You'll never find them."

Imagining she also was braving him, he advanced towards her with set teeth.

"She gave them you, or you know where they are?" said he inquiringly.

The idea that her mother could have given her 1,000 frcs. to anyone, even to her daughter, made her shrug her shoulders.

"Ah! to blazes! gave them," she replied; "yes, gave them to the earth! Look, they are there! You can search."

And, with a broad gesture, she indicated the entire house, the garden with its well, the metal way, all the vast country. Yes, somewhere about there, at the bottom of a hole, in a place where none would ever find them. Then, while Misard, beside himself with anxiety, began twisting and turning the furniture about again, sounding the walls, without showing any constraint at her presence, the young girl, standing before the window, continued in a subdued voice:

"Oh! it is so mild outside. Such a lovely night! I walked quick. The stars make it like broad daylight. Tomorrow, how beautiful it will be at sunrise!"

Flore remained for an instant at the window, with her eyes on the serene country, stirred by this first gentle warmth of April, from which she had just returned thoughtful, and suffering more acutely from her vivified torment. But when she heard Misard leave the apartment, and continue his tenacious search in the adjoining rooms, she, in her turn, approached the bed, seating herself with her eyes on her mother. The candle continued burning at the corner of the table, with a long, motionless flame. A passing train jolted the house.

Flore had resolved to remain there all night, and she sat pondering. First of all, the sight of the dead woman drew her from her fixed idea, from the thing that haunted her, which she had been debating in her mind beneath the stars, in the peaceful obscurity, all the way from Doinville. Surprise now set her suffering at rest. Why had she not displayed more grief at the death of her mother? And why, at this moment even, did she not shed tears?

Indeed, she loved her well, notwithstanding her shyness of a great, silent girl, who was for ever breaking away beating about the fields, as soon as released from duty. Twenty times over during the last crisis which was to kill her mother, she had come and sat there to implore her to call in a doctor; for she guessed what Misard was after, and was in hopes that fear would stop him. But she had never been able to obtain anything more from the invalid than a furious No. It seemed as if her mother took pride in accepting no assistance in the struggle, certain of the victory in spite of everything, as she carried off the cash; and then Flore ceased to interfere. Beset by her own chagrin, she disappeared, careering hither and thither to forget.

Assuredly this was what barred her heart. When a person has too keen a trouble, there is no room for another. Her mother had gone; she saw her there, destroyed, and so pallid, without being able to feel any more sad, notwithstanding her efforts. Call in the gendarmes! Denounce Misard! What would be the use of it, as there was about to be a general upheaval? And, little by little, invincibly, although her eyes remained fixed on the dead body, she ceased to perceive it. She returned to her own inner vision, occupied entirely by the idea that had planted itself in her brain, alive to nothing but the heavy shock of the trains, whose passage told her the time.

The approaching thunder of a slow train from Paris could be heard for an instant or two in the distance. When the locomotive at last flew by before the window, with its light, there came a flash, a perfect blaze in the room.

"Eighteen minutes past one," thought Flore. "Seven hours more. This morning at 8.16 they will come past."

Every week for months she had been worried by this expectation. She knew that on Friday morning the express driven by Jacques also took Séverine to Paris, and tortured by jealousy, she only lived, as it were, to watch them. Oh! that train flying along, and the abominable sensation she felt at being unable to cling on to the last carriage, so as to be also borne away! She fancied that all these wheels were cutting up her heart. She suffered so keenly that one night, having hidden herself, she prepared to write to the judicial authorities; for it would be all over if she could get this woman arrested. But, with the pen in her hand, she could never set the matter down. And, besides, would the authorities listen to her? All those fine people must be working together. Perhaps they would even put her in prison, as they had done with Cabuche.

No; she wanted to avenge herself, and she would do so alone, without the assistance of anyone. It was not even a thought of vengeance, as she understood the word, the idea of doing injury to cure herself. She felt the need of finishing with the matter, of upsetting everything, as if thunder and lightning had swept the couple away. Being very proud, more solidly built, and handsomer than the other, she felt convinced of her firm right to be loved; and when she went off alone along the paths of this abandoned district, with her heavy helmet of light hair, ever bare, she would have liked to come face to face with that other one, so as to settle their quarrel at the corner of a wood, after the manner of two hostile warrior women. Never yet had a man touched her; she thrashed the males, and that constituted her invincible strength. Therefore, she would be victorious.

The week before, this idea had suddenly been planted, driven into her head as by the blow of a hammer, come from she knew not where: kill them, so that they might no longer pass by, no longer go there together. She did not reason, she obeyed the savage instinct of destruction. When a thorn entered her flesh, she plucked it out. She would have cut off her finger. Kill them, kill them the first time they passed; and to do that, upset the train, drag a sleeper across the line, tear up a rail, smash everything. He, on his engine, would certainly remain there, stretched out; the woman, always in the first carriage, so as to be nearer to him, could not escape; as for the others, that constant stream of passengers, she had not even a thought. They did not count, she did not know them! And at every hour she was beset by this idea of destroying the train, of making this huge sacrifice of lives. What she desired was an unique catastrophe, sufficiently great, sufficiently deep in human gore and suffering, for her to bathe therein her enormous heart swollen with tears.

Nevertheless, on the Friday morning, she had given way, not having yet decided at what spot nor in what manner she would remove a rail. But the same night, being off duty, she had an idea, and went prowling through the tunnel as far as the Dieppe embranchment. This was one of her walks, this trip through the subterranean passage, a good half league in length, along this vaulted avenue, quite straight, where she felt the emotion of trains with their blinding lights rolling over her. Each time, she had a narrow escape of being cut to pieces, and it must have been the peril that attracted her there in a spirit of bravado.

But on this particular night, having escaped the vigilance of the watchman and advanced to the middle of the tunnel, keeping to the left, so as to make sure that any train coming towards her would pass on her right, she had the imprudence to face about, just to follow the lights of a train on the way to Havre; and when she resumed walking, a false step having made her swing round again, she lost all knowledge of the direction in which the red lights had just disappeared.

Notwithstanding her courage, she stopped, still dizzy with the clatter of the wheels, her hands cold, her bare hair starting up in a breath of terror. She now imagined that when another train came along, she would not know whether it was an up or a down train. With an effort she endeavoured to retain her reason, to remember, to think the matter over. Then, all at once, terror sent her along, haphazard, straight before her, at a frantic pace. No, no! she would not be killed before she had killed the other two!

Her feet were caught in the rails, she slipped, fell, rose up, and ran faster than before. She became affected with tunnel madness. The walls seemed drawing close to one another to squeeze her, the vaulted roof echoed imaginary sounds, menacing utterances, formidable roars. At every moment she turned her head, fancying she felt the burning steam of an engine on her neck. Twice the sudden conviction that she had made a mistake, that she would be killed from the end she was fleeing to, made her at a bound change the direction of her flight.

And she was tearing onward, onward, when in front of her, in the distance, appeared a star, a round flaming eye, increasing in size. But she resisted the intense temptation to again retrace her steps. The eye became a lighted brazier, the mouth of a devouring furnace. Blinded, she sprang to the left, at hazard; and the train passed, like a clap of thunder, doing nothing more than beat her cheek with its tempestuous blast of wind. Five minutes later, she issued from the Malaunay end of the tunnel safe and sound.

It was then nine o'clock, a few minutes more and the Paris express would be there. She immediately continued her excursion at a walking pace, to the Dieppe embranchment, a matter of two hundred yards or so further on, examining the metals in search of something that might serve her purpose. It so happened that her friend Ozil had just switched a ballast train on to the Dieppe line, which was undergoing repair, and it was standing there. In a sudden flash of enlightenment she conceived a plan: simply prevent the pointsman from putting the switch-tongue back on the Havre line, so that the express would dash into the ballast train.

She felt a friendship for this Ozil since the day she had nearly broken his head with a blow from a stick, and she was fond of paying him unexpected visits like this, running through the tunnel after the fashion of a goat escaped from its mountain. An old soldier, very thin and little talkative, a slave to duty, his eyes ever on the look-out, day and night, he had not yet been guilty of a single act of negligence. Only this wild creature, who had beaten him, sturdy as a young man, could make him do what she pleased merely by beckoning to him with her little finger.

And so, on this particular night, when she approached his box in the dark, calling him outside, he went to her, forgetting everything. She made his head swim as she led him out into the country, relating complicated tales about her mother being ill, and that she would not remain at La Croix-de-Maufras if she lost her. Her ear caught the roar of the express in the distance, leaving Malaunay, approaching at full speed. And when she felt it hard by, she turned round to look. But she had been reckoning without the new connecting apparatus: the locomotive, in passing on to the Dieppe line, had itself just caused the danger signal to be displayed; and the driver was able to stop at a few paces from the ballast train.

Ozil, with the shout of a man awakened in a house tumbling down, regained his box at a run; while Flore, stiff and motionless, watched the manœuvre necessitated by the accident in the darkness of night. Two days later, the pointsman, who had been removed, having no suspicion of her duplicity, called to bid her farewell, imploring her to join him as soon as she lost her mother. So her plot came to nothing, and she would have to think of something else.

At this moment, under the influence of the recollection she had evoked, the mist of reverie clouding her eyes disappeared, and again she perceived the corpse in the light of the yellow flame of the candle. Her mother was no more. Should she leave, and wed Ozil, who wanted her, and would perhaps make her happy? All her being revolted at the idea. No, no. If she had the cowardice to allow the other two to live and to live herself, she would prefer to tramp the roads, to take a situation as servant, rather than belong to a man she did not love. And a sound, to which she was unaccustomed, having caused her to listen, she understood that Misard with a mattock was engaged in excavating the beaten earth floor of the kitchen. He was going mad in his search for the hoard; he would have gutted the house. No, she would not remain with this one either. What was she going to do? There came a blast of wind, the walls vibrated, and on the pallid countenance of the corpse passed the reflex of a furnace, conveying a blood-like hue to the open eyes, and to the ironic rictus of the lips. It was the last slow train from Paris, with its ponderous, sluggish engine.

Flore had turned her head, and looked at the stars shining in the serenity of this spring night.

"Ten minutes past three," she murmured. "Another five hours, and they will pass."

She would begin over again; her suffering was too great. To see them like this each week was more than her strength could bear. Now that she was sure of not having Jacques to herself alone, she preferred that he should no longer exist, that there should be nothing. And the aspect of this lugubrious room, where she sat watching, imbued her with mournful suffering, and made her feel an increasing need to annihilate everything. As there remained no one who loved her, the others could go with her mother. As for corpses, there would be more and more still, and they could carry them all away at the same time. Her sister was dead, her mother was dead, her love was dead. What could she do? Remain alone? Whether she stayed or left, she would always be alone, while the others would be two together. No, no! let everything go to smash rather than that. Let death, who was there in this room, blow on the line and sweep the people away.

Then, with her mind made up after this long debate with herself, she proceeded to think out the best way of putting her design into execution. And she returned to the idea of removing a rail. This would be the surest and most practical plan, and could be easily carried out; she had only to drive away the chairs with a hammer, and then raise the rail from the sleepers. She had the tools. Nobody would see her in this deserted district. A good spot to select would certainly be beyond the cutting, on the way to Barentin, at the curve which crossed a dale on an embankment thirty or thirty-five feet high. There the train would for sure run off the line, and the fall would be terrible.

But the calculation of time, which then occupied her, made her anxious. On the up-line, before the Havre express came by at 8.16, there was only a slow train at 7.55. This would therefore give her twenty minutes to do the work, which was sufficient. Only, between the regular trains, they often dispatched others that were unforeseen, loaded with goods, particularly at moments when quantities of cargo arrived. Then what a useless risk she would be incurring! How could she tell beforehand whether it would be the express that would come to smash there? For a long time she turned the probabilities over in her head. It was still night. The candle continued to burn, bathed in tallow, with a long, smutty wick which she had ceased to snuff.

Just as a goods train arrived from Rouen, Misard returned. His hands were covered with dirt, for he had been rummaging in the woodhouse, and he was out of breath, distracted at his vain efforts to lay hands on the treasure. He had become so feverish with impotent rage, that he renewed his search under the articles of furniture, up the chimney, everywhere. There was no end to the interminable train, with the regular fracas of its great wheels, which at each shock jolted the dead woman in her bed. Misard, stretching out his arm to take down a small picture, hanging against the wall, again met the open eyes following his motions, while the lips seemed to move with their laugh.

He became livid. He was shivering, and stuttered out in terrific anger:

"Yes, yes; search! search! Never mind, I shall find it, even if I have to turn over every stone in the house, and every clod of ground in the neighbourhood!"

The black train had passed by in the obscurity, with painful slowness, and the dead woman, who had become motionless again, continued looking at her husband so jeeringly, so certain of conquering, that he disappeared a second time, leaving the door open. Flore, wandering in her reflections, had risen and closed the door, so that this man might not return to disturb her mother; and she felt astonished to hear herself saying aloud:

"Ten minutes beforehand will do."

In fact, she would have time in ten minutes. If no train was signalled ten minutes before the express, she could set to work. The matter being now settled, certain, her anxiety ceased, and she was very calm.

Day broke at about five o'clock, a fresh dawn, of pure limpidity. In spite of the slightly sharp cold, she set the window wide open, and the delicious morning air entered the lugubrious room, full of smoke and an odour of the dead. The sun was still below the horizon, behind a hillock crowned by trees; but it appeared with a rosy tint, streaming over the slopes, pouring into the deep roads, amidst the lively gaiety of the earth at each new spring. She had not been mistaken on the previous evening: it would be fine on that particular morning, one of those days of youth and radiant health on which one delights in life. How lovely it would be to set out along the goat paths at her own free will, in this deserted country among the continuous hills cut up by narrow dales! And when she turned round, facing the room, she was surprised to see the candle looking almost as if gone out, and with naught but a pale tear forming a spot in the broad daylight. The dead woman seemed now to be gazing on the line where the trains continued crossing one another, without even noticing this wan glimmer of a taper beside the corpse.

It was not until daylight that Flore resumed duty, and she only quitted the room for the slow train from Paris at 6.12. Misard, at six o'clock, had also relieved his colleague, the night signalman. It was at the sound of his horn that she had come and placed herself before the gate, the flag in her hand. She followed the train an instant with her eyes.

"Another two hours," thought she aloud.

Her mother had no further need of anybody, and henceforth she experienced invincible repugnance to return to the room. It was all over, she had kissed her, and now she could dispose of her own existence and the lives of others. Usually, between the trains, she escaped and disappeared; but on this particular morning a feeling of interest seemed to keep her at her post near the gate on a bench—a simple plank that happened to be beside the line. The sun was ascending on the horizon, a warm shower of gold fell into the pure air; and she did not move, but sat there wrapped in this sweetness, in the midst of the vast country all thrilling with the sap of April.

For a moment she watched Misard in his wooden hut, on the other side of the line. He was visibly agitated, not having had his customary sleep. He went out, went in, worked his apparatus with a nervous hand, casting constant glances towards the house, as if his spirit had remained there and was still searching. Then she forgot him, was unaware even of him being there. She was all expectant, absorbed, her lips speechless, her face rigid, her eyes fixed on the end of the line in the direction of Barentin. And over there, in the gaiety of the sun, a vision must have risen up for her, on which the stubborn savageness of her look obstinately dwelt.

Minutes slipped away, but Flore did not move. At last, at 7.55, when Misard with a couple of blasts from his horn signalled the slow train from Havre on the up-line, she rose, closed the gate, and planted herself before it, her flag in her fist. The train was already fading away in the distance, after sending a tremor through the ground; and it could be heard plunging into the tunnel, where the sound ceased. She had not gone back to the bench, but remained on her feet again counting each minute. If no goods train was signalled within ten minutes, she would run over there beyond the cutting, and remove a rail.

She was very calm, only her chest felt a little tight under the enormous weight of the deed. But, at this moment, the thought that Jacques and Séverine were approaching, that they would pass by again if she did not stop them, sufficed to make her inexorably blind and deaf in her resolution, without even giving the matter any further consideration; it was the irrevocable, the blow from the paw of the she-wolf that breaks the back of the prey on the way. In the egotism of her vengeance, she saw only the two mutilated bodies, without troubling about the crowd, that stream of unknown people who had been filing past before her for years. There would be dead bodies, blood, the sun would perhaps be obscured by them, that sun whose tender gaiety irritated her.

Two minutes more, one minute more, and she would be starting. Indeed, she was starting, when some heavy jolting on the Bécourt road stopped her. A cart, no doubt a stone dray; the carter would ask her to let him through. She would have to open the gate, engage in conversation, and remain there: it would be impossible for her to act, and she would miss her chance. With an enraged gesture of indifference, she ran off, leaving her post, abandoning the carter with his dray to do the best he could. But the lash of a whip cracked in the matutinal air, and a voice cried out gaily:

"Hey! Flore!"

It was Cabuche. She stopped short, in her first spring, before the gate itself.

"What's up?" he continued. "Are you still asleep with this beautiful sun shining? Quick! let me get through before the express!"

She was completely undone. It was all over. The other two would proceed to their happiness without her being able to find any means to crush them here. And as she slowly opened the old, half-rotten gate, whose ironwork grated in its rust, she looked about her furiously for an object, something she could cast across the line; and she was in such despair, that she would have stretched her own self there, had she thought her bones hard enough to send the engine off the metals.

But her glance had just fallen on the dray, a heavy, low conveyance, loaded with two blocks of stone, which five strong horses found difficulty in drawing. These two enormous masses, high and broad, a colossal lump fit to bar the line, stood there before her; and abruptly a look of covetousness came into her eyes, accompanied by a mad desire

ÉMILE ZOLA

to take and place them on the rails. The gate was wide open, the five steaming, panting cattle were there waiting.

"What is the matter with you this morning?" resumed Cabuche. "You look quite funny."

Then Flore spoke.

"My mother died last night," said she.

He uttered a friendly exclamation of grief, and putting down his whip, took both her hands and pressed them in his own.

"Oh! my poor Flore!" he sighed. "It is only what one might have expected for a long time, but it is hard all the same. Then she is there. I will go and look at her, for we should have ended by agreeing, but for this misfortune."

He walked slowly with her to the house, but on the threshold he cast a glance towards his horses. In one sentence she set his mind at rest.

"There is no fear of them moving," she said. "And, besides, the express is a long way off."

She lied. Her experienced ear had just caught, in the gentle rustle of the country, the sound of the express leaving Barentin station. Another five minutes, and it would be there. It would issue from the cutting at a hundred yards from the level crossing.

While the quarryman stood in the room of the dead woman, feeling very much affected, with his thoughts adverting to Louisette and oblivious of everything else, Flore remained outside, in front of the window, listening to the distant regular puffing of the engine as it approached nearer and nearer. Suddenly she remembered Misard: he would see her, he would prevent her; and she felt a pang in the chest when, turning round, she could not perceive him in his box. But she discovered him on the other side of the house, digging up the ground at the foot of the masonry round the well, unable to overcome his searching mania, and doubtless all at once taken with the conviction that the hoard must be there. Entirely absorbed by his blind, sullen passion, he searched, searched. And this was her last excitation. Events themselves urged her on. One of the horses began to neigh, while the locomotive, at the other end of the cutting, puffed very loudly, like a person hastening along in a hurry.

"I'll go and keep them quiet," said Flore to Cabuche. "Don't be afraid."

She sprang forward, grasped the leader of the team by the bit, and pulled with all her strapping strength of a wrestler. The horses strained.

For an instant the dray, heavy with its enormous load, oscillated without advancing; but, as if she had harnessed herself to it like an extra animal, it at last moved and came across the line. It was right on the rails as the express, a hundred yards away, issued from the cutting. Then to stop the dray, lest it should pass over, she arrested the further progress of the team with a sudden jerk requiring a superhuman effort that made her joints crack.

She who, it will be remembered, had her legend, of whom people related extraordinary feats of strength—the truck shooting down an incline, which she had brought to a standstill as it ran, the cart she had pushed across the metals, and thus saved from a train—she accomplished this action now. In her iron grip she held back those five horses, rearing and neighing with the instinct of peril.

Barely ten seconds passed, but they were seconds of inconceivable terror. The two colossal stones seemed to bar the view. The locomotive came gliding along with its pale brass and glittering steel, arriving at its smooth, fulminating pace in the golden beams of the beautiful morning. The inevitable was there, nothing in the world could now prevent the smash. And the interval seemed interminable.

Misard, who had bounded back to his box, yelled with his arms in the air, shaking his fists in the senseless determination to warn the driver and stop the train. Cabuche, who had quitted the house at the sound of the wheels and the neighing of the horses, rushed forward, also yelling, to make the animals go on. But Flore, who had flung herself on one side, restrained him, which saved his life. He fancied that she had not been strong enough to master the horses, that it was they who had dragged her along. And he taxed himself with carelessness, sobbing in a splutter of despairing terror; while she, motionless, standing at her full height, her eyes like live coal and wide open, looked on. At the same moment, as the front of the engine was about to touch the blocks of stone, when there remained perhaps only three feet to run, during this inappreciable time, she distinctly saw Jacques, with his hand on the reversing-wheel. He had turned towards her, and their eyes met in a gaze that she found inordinately long.

On that particular morning Jacques had smiled at Séverine, when she came down on to the platform at Havre for the express. What was the use of spoiling his life with nightmares? Why not take advantage of the happy days when they came? All would perhaps come right in the end. And, resolved to enjoy himself on this day, at all events, he was making plans in his head, dreaming of taking her to lunch at a restaurant. And so, as she cast him a sorrowful glance, because there was not a first-class carriage at the head of the train, and she was forced to find a seat a long way off him at the end, he wished to console her by smiling merrily. They would arrive together, and make up for being separated. Indeed, after leaning over the rail to see her enter a compartment right at the extremity of the train, he had pushed his good humour so far as to joke with the headguard, Henri Dauvergne, whom he knew to be in love with her.

The preceding week he fancied he had noticed that the guard was becoming bold, and that she encouraged him, by way of diversion, requiring relief from the atrocious existence she had formed for herself. And Jacques inquired of Henri who it was he had been sending kisses to in the air on the previous evening, when hiding behind one of the elms in the entrance yard. This elicited a loud laugh from Pecqueux, engaged in making up the fire of La Lison, which was smoking, and all ready to set out.

The express ran from Havre to Barentin at its regular speed and without incident. It was Henri who first signalled the dray across the line, from his look-out at the top of his box, on issuing from the cutting. The van next to the tender was crammed with luggage, for the train carried a large number of passengers, who had landed from a mail-boat the previous evening. The headguard, very badly off for space, in the midst of this huge pile of trunks and portmanteaux, swaying to and fro in the vibration, had been standing at his desk classing way-bills; and the small bottle of ink, suspended from a nail, never ceased swinging from side to side.

After passing the stations where he put out luggage, he had four or five minutes' writing to do. Two travellers had got down at Barentin, and he had just got his papers in order, when, ascending and seating himself in his look-out, cast a glance back and front along the line in accordance with his custom. It was his habit to pass all his spare time seated in this glazed sentry-box on the watch. The tender hid the driver, but thanks to his elevated position, he could often see further and sooner than the latter. And so, whilst the train was still bending round in the cutting, he perceived the obstacle ahead. His astonishment was such that, in his terror, he lost command of his limbs, and, for an instant, even doubted what he saw. A few seconds were in consequence lost. The train was already out of the cutting, and a loud cry arose from the engine, when he made up his mind to pull the cord of the alarm-bell dangling in front of him.

Jacques, at this supreme moment, with his hand on the reversing-wheel, was looking without seeing, in a minute of absent-mindedness. He was thinking of confused and distant matters, from which the image of Séverine, even, had faded. The violent swinging and riot of the bell, the yells of Pecqueux behind him, brought him back to reality.

Pecqueux, who had raised the rod of the ash-pan, being dissatisfied with the draught, had caught sight of the scene on ahead as he leant over the rail to make sure of the speed. And Jacques, pale as death, saw and understood everything: the stone dray across the line, the engine tearing along, the frightful shock; and he witnessed it all with such penetrating distinctness, that he could even distinguish the grain in the two stones, while he already felt the concussion of the smash in his bones. He had violently turned round the reversing-wheel, closed the regulator, tightened the brake. He had reversed the engine, and was hanging unconsciously with one hand to the whistle handle, in the furious, but impotent determination to give warning, to have the colossal barricade in front removed.

But in the middle of this terrible scream of distress that rent the air, La Lison refused to obey. It continued its course in spite of all, barely slackening in speed. Since it had lost its power of starting off smoothly and its excellent vaporisation, in the snowstorm, it was no longer the docile engine of former days. It had now become whimsical and intractable, like an old woman with her chest ruined by a chill. It panted, resisted the brake, and still went on and on, in the ponderous obstinacy of its huge mass. Pecqueux, maddened with fright, sprang off. Jacques waited, inflexible, at his post, with the fingers of his right hand clutching the reversing-wheel, and those of his left resting on the whistle handle, unaware of what he was doing. And La Lison, smoking, puffing, amidst this piercing screech that never ceased, dashed against the stone dray with the enormous weight of the thirteen carriages it dragged behind it.

Then, eighty feet distant, beside the line, where they stood riveted in terror, Misard and Cabuche with their arms in the air, Flore with her eyes starting from her head, witnessed this frightful scene: the front part of the train rising up almost perpendicularly, seven carriages ascending one on the top of the other, to fall back with an abominable crash in a confused downfall of wreckage. The first three carriages were reduced to atoms, the four others formed a mountain, an entanglement of staved-in roofs, broken wheels, doors, chains, buffers, interspersed with pieces of glass. And what had been heard particularly, was the pounding of the machine against the stones—a heavy crash terminating in a cry of agony. La Lison, ripped open, toppled over to the left, on the other side of the stone dray; while the stones, split asunder, flew about in splinters as in the explosion of a mine, and four out of the five horses, bowled over and dragged along the ground, were killed on the spot. The back half of the train, comprising six carriages, remained intact. They had come to a standstill without even leaving the metals.

Cries arose from the wreckage, appeals in words that were drowned by inarticulate howls, like those of wild beasts.

"Help! help! Oh! my God! I am dying! Help! help!"

In the midst of the riot and confusion of the smash, nothing could be heard or seen distinctly. La Lison, thrown over on the side, the under part rent open, was losing steam in rumbling puffs, similar to a furious rattle in the throat of a giant, at places where taps had been torn away, and where pipes had burst. An inexhaustible white cloud of vapour rolled round and round just on a level with the ground; while the embers, red as blood, fallen from the fire-box, added their black smoke. The chimney, in the violence of the shock, had entered the ground. At the place where it had stood, the frame was broken, bending the two frame-plates; and with the wheels in the air, similar to a monstrous steed, torn open by some formidable rip of a horn, La Lison displayed its twisted connecting-rods, its broken cylinders, its slide valves and their eccentrics flattened out—one huge, frightful wound, gaping in the open air, whence vitality continued issuing with the fracas of enraged despair. Beside the locomotive lay the horse, which had not been killed at once, with his two fore hoofs cut off and his belly ripped up. By his erect head, the neck stiffened in a spasm of atrocious pain, he could be perceived rattling the death agony with a terrible neigh, which failed to reach the ear in the thunder of the agonising engine.

The cries were stifled, unheard, lost, wafted away.

"Save me! Kill me! I am suffering too atrociously. Kill me! Kill me at once!"

In this deafening tumult, and blinding smoke, the doors of the carriages remaining intact opened, and a swarm of bewildered travellers sprang out. Falling down on the line, they struggled with feet and fists to rise again. Then as soon as they found themselves on firm ground, with the open country before them, they fled as fast as they could run, clearing the hedge, cutting across country, ceding to the sole instinct of getting far away from the danger, very, very far. Howling women and men disappeared in the depths of the woods.

Séverine, trampled under foot, with her hair about her back and her gown in shreds, at last got free; but she did not flee. Running towards the roaring engine, she found herself face to face with Pecqueux.

"Jacques! Jacques! He is safe, is he not?" she inquired.

The fireman, who, by a miracle, had not even sprained a joint, was hurrying in the same direction, his heart swelling with pity at the idea of his driver being beneath that heap of wreckage. They had journeyed, they had suffered so much together in the continual fatigue of the high winds! And their engine, their poor engine, the good friend so cherished by both, which lay there on its back, losing its last breath of steam!

"I jumped off," he stammered, "and know nothing, nothing at all. Come on, come on, quick!"

Beside the line they ran up against Flore, who had been watching them advancing towards her. Stupefied at the act she had committed, at the massacre she had accomplished, she had not yet moved. It was all over, and it was well. Her only feeling was one of relief at having performed a necessity, without the least thought of pity for the pain of the other victims, whom she did not even notice. But when she recognised Séverine, her eyes opened immeasurably wide, and a cloud of frightful suffering darkened her pale countenance. Eh? what? this woman lived, when he was certainly dead! This piercing grief at her assassinated love, at this stab which she had given herself right in the heart, abruptly revealed to her all the abomination of her crime. She had done this, she had killed him, she had killed all these people! A loud cry lacerated her throat, she twisted her arms, she ran madly forward, exclaiming:

"Jacques, oh! Jacques! He is there. He was thrown backward, I saw him. Jacques, Jacques!" she called.

The death rattle of La Lison had become subdued. It had taken the form of a hoarse moan which grew weaker and weaker, and the increasing clamour of the wounded could now be heard in tones more and more heartrending. The smoke remained thick. The enormous heap of wreckage, whence issued the voices of the tortured and terrified beings, seemed enveloped in a black cloud of dust that remained motionless in the sun. What could be done? Where commence? How could these wretched victims be reached?

"Jacques!" Flore continued calling. "I tell you he looked at me," she added, "and that he was thrown off there, under the tender. Come along quickly! Help me!"

Cabuche and Misard had just picked up Henri, the headguard, who at the last second had also leapt from the train. He had dislocated his ankle, and they seated him on the ground against the hedge, where, half-stunned and mute, he watched the rescue of the passengers without appearing to suffer.

"Cabuche, come and help me!" cried Flore; "I tell you, Jacques is under there!"

The quarryman did not hear her. He ran to the assistance of the other wounded, and carried away a young woman whose legs were dangling down broken.

It was Séverine who rushed forward to answer the appeal of Flore.

"Jacques, Jacques?" said she inquiringly. "Where is he? I will help you."

"That's it, help me, you!"

Their hands met. Together they tugged at a broken wheel. But the delicate fingers of Séverine could do nothing, while the other with her sturdy fists broke through the obstacles.

"Be careful!" said Pecqueux, who also began to assist in the work.

And he sharply stopped Séverine just as she was going to tread on an arm cut off at the shoulder, which was still clothed in a blue cloth sleeve. She started back in horror. And yet she did not recognise the sleeve. It was an unknown arm that had rolled there from a body they would doubtless find elsewhere. This gave her such a fit of trembling that she seemed as if paralysed, standing weeping, watching the others working, incapable even of removing the splinters of glass which cut her hands.

Then the rescue of the dying, the search for the dead proved full of anguish and danger, for the live coal had set the pieces of wood alight, and to put a stop to this commencement of a fire it became necessary to throw shovels of earth over them. While someone ran to Barentin to ask for assistance, and a telegram left for Rouen, the removal of the wreckage proceeded as briskly as possible, everyone putting a hand to the work with great courage. Many of the runaways had returned, ashamed of their panic. But the relief party had to advance with infinite precautions, the transfer of each bit of wreckage requiring the utmost care, for fears were entertained lest the heap might perchance collapse and finish off the poor wretches in its midst. Some of the wounded emerged from the pile, still buried up to their chests, crushed as if in a vice, and howling. The rescuers laboured a quarter of an hour to deliver one victim as white as a sheet, who, far from complaining, said he felt no pain, and had nothing the matter with him; but when he had been extricated, he was found to be without his legs, and expired immediately, having neither seen nor felt the horrible mutilation in his fit of fright.

An entire family were dragged from a second-class compartment that had caught fire: the father and mother wounded in the knees, the grandmother with a broken arm; but neither did they feel their injuries. They were sobbing and calling their little girl who had disappeared in the smash—a fair-headed mite, barely three years old, who was discovered safe and sound under a strip of roofing with a merry, smiling face. Another little girl drenched in blood and with her poor, tiny hands crushed, had been carried aside pending the discovery of her parents. She remained alone and unknown, breathing with such difficulty that she could not utter a word; but her face was convulsed into an expression of ineffable terror as soon as anyone approached her.

The shock having twisted the iron-fittings of the carriage doors, it was found impossible to open them, and it became necessary to enter the compartments through the broken glass. Four corpses had already been taken out and placed side by side along the line. About ten wounded extended on the ground, were waiting near the dead bodies, there being no doctor to dress their wounds, and no assistance of any kind. The clearance of the wreckage had barely commenced, and a new victim was found under each bit of lumber, while the heap, streaming and palpitating with this human butchery, never seemed to decrease.

"But I tell you that Jacques is under there!" cried Flore, relieving herself by obstinately repeating this expression, which she uttered without reason, as the lamentation of her despair. "He is calling. There, there! Listen!" she added.

The tender lay buried beneath the carriages, which after running one atop of the other, had then tumbled over; and, in fact, since the locomotive had been making less noise, a heavy masculine voice could be distinguished roaring in the midst of the pile. As the work advanced the clamour of these agonising tones became more subdued, but they revealed such atrocious pain that the rescue party, unable to bear them any longer, gave way and called out themselves. Then, at last, when the

ÉMILE ZOLA

excavators reached the victim whose legs they had liberated, and whom they were dragging towards them, the roar of suffering ceased. The man was dead!

"No," said Flore, "it is not Jacques. He is lower down. He is underneath."

And with her arms of a warrior woman, she raised the wheels and cast them to a distance, she twirled the zinc of the roofs, broke the doors, tore away the bits of chain. And as soon as she came to a corpse or a person who was wounded, she called for someone to remove the body, determined not to slacken for a second in her maddening search.

Cabuche, Pecqueux, and Misard worked behind her, while Séverine, enfeebled by standing so long on her feet, had just seated herself on the bench of a shattered carriage. But Misard, gentle and indifferent, again overcome by his sluggishness, anxious to avoid too much fatigue, was always ready to carry away the bodies. And both he and Flore looked at the corpses, as if they hoped to recognise them from among the multitude of thousands and thousands of faces who, in ten years, had filed past before their eyes at full steam, leaving only the confused recollection of a crowd conveyed there and borne away in a flash.

No; it was still that unknown wave of the advancing world, as anonymous in brutal, accidental death, as in that hasty life which brought it tearing past them onward to the future; and they could not name, they could give no information about the heads, furrowed with horror, of these poor creatures struck down on their road, trampled under foot, similar to those soldiers whose bodies fill the trenches in opposing the charge of an enemy ascending to the assault. Nevertheless, Flore fancied she had found one person to whom she had spoken on the day the train was blocked in the snow: that American whose profile she had at last come to know familiarly, without being aware of his name, or anything about him or his. Misard carried him along with the other dead bodies, come no one knew whence, bound for no one knew where, and stopped there.

Then came a heartrending scene: in a first-class compartment turned topsy-turvy they had just discovered a young couple, doubtless newly married, thrown one upon the other in such an unfortunate position that the woman, who was uppermost, crushed the man, and could not make a movement to relieve him. He was choking, he already had the death rattle in his throat; while she, in terror, with her mouth free, her heart rent asunder at the thought that she was killing him, distractedly implored the relief party to make haste. And when they had delivered both, it was she who all at once breathed her last, a blow from one of the buffers having ripped open her side. And the man, coming to himself again, clamoured with grief, kneeling beside the dead body whose eyes remained full of tears.

A dozen corpses and about thirty wounded passengers had now been removed. The workers were setting the tender free. Flore paused, ever and anon, thrusting her head among the splintered wood, the twisted iron, searching ardently with her eyes to see if she could perceive the driver. Suddenly she uttered a loud cry.

"I can see him!" she exclaimed. "He is under here. Look! There is his arm, with his blue woollen jacket. He doesn't move; he doesn't breathe!"

And, rising from her recumbent position, she swore like a man.

"Be quick!" she shouted with an oath. "Get him out from there!"

She made a fruitless effort with both hands to tear away a plank belonging to one of the carriages, which other pieces of wreckage prevented coming towards her. So, running off, she returned with the hatchet that served to chop the wood at home; and brandishing it as a woodcutter wields his axe in the middle of an oak-tree forest, she fell upon the plank with a volley of furious blows. The men, standing aside, allowed her to do as she would, while shouting to her to be careful. But Jacques was the only wounded person there, and he lay sheltered under an entanglement of axle-trees and wheels. Moreover, she paid no attention to what was said. Her spirit being fairly roused, certain of herself, she proceeded with irresistible determination. Each stroke battered down the wood, cut through an obstacle. With her fair hair streaming free, her bodice torn open displaying her bare arms, she resembled some terrible reaper cleaving a way through the destruction she had wrought. The final blow falling upon an axletree, broke the iron of the hatchet in two. Then, assisted by the others, she put aside the wheels which had protected the young man from being crushed to death, and she was the first to seize him and bear him away in her arms.

"Jacques, Jacques!" she cried. "He is alive; he is breathing. Ah! Great God! he lives. I knew I saw him fall, and that he was there!"

Séverine, who was distracted, followed her. Between them they laid him down at the foot of the hedge beside Henri, who continued gazing, stupefied, as if not understanding where he was, nor what went on around him. Pecqueux, who had approached, remained standing before his driver quite unhinged at seeing him in this deplorable state; while the two women, now kneeling down, one to the right the other to the left, supported the head of the poor fellow, watching in anguish for the slightest shiver on his face.

At length Jacques opened his lids. His troubled look fell upon Flore and Séverine, one after the other, but he did not appear to recognise them. They failed to arouse his interest. But his eyes having encountered the expiring locomotive, a few feet away, first of all assumed a wild expression, then, settling on the object, vacillated with increasing emotion.

He recognised La Lison well, and the sight brought everything back to him: the two blocks of stone across the rails, the abominable shock, the crushing sensation he had experienced, at the same moment, within both the engine and himself, and from which he had emerged alive, while the locomotive had assuredly come to an end. It was not the fault of the engine if it had been intractable; for it had always felt the effects of the accident in the snow; without counting, that age makes limbs heavy and joints stiff, which is as applicable to machinery as to living creatures. And so, overwhelmed with grief at seeing La Lison direfully wounded, in the last throes of death, he readily forgave.

Poor La Lison had but a few minutes more. It was becoming cold. The live coal in the fire-box was turning into cinders, the steam that had escaped in such violence from its open flanks, was exhausting itself with the low moan of a weeping child. The locomotive always so bright, now lay on its back in a black bed of coal, soiled with earth and foam. It had met with the tragic end of a costly animal struck down in the public street. At one moment, it had been possible to perceive its mechanism at work through its shattered plates: the pistons beating like twin-hearts, the steam circulating in the slide valves as the blood of its veins; but the connecting-rods merely moved in a jerky fashion, after the manner of convulsive human arms, and constituted the final efforts of life.

Its spirit was ebbing away along with the power that gave it life, that huge breath whereof it could not absolutely free itself. The eviscerated giantess sank lower still, passing little by little into very gentle slumber, and ended by emitting not a sound. La Lison was dead. And the heap of iron, steel, and copper, lying there, this pounded colossal mass with the barrel ripped asunder, the scattered limbs, the interior mechanism smashed, exposed to broad daylight, displayed the frightfully mournful aspect of some enormous human corpse, of a whole world that had lived, and from which life had just been torn in anguish.

Then Jacques, understanding that La Lison was no more, closed his eyes, desiring to die also; moreover, he was so weak that he fancied himself borne away in the final little puff of the engine; and tears, trickling from his closed lids, drenched his cheeks. This was too much for Pecqueux who had remained there motionless with a lump in his throat. Their dear friend had gone, and here was his driver wishing to follow. So the happy family of three was at an end. All over those journeys of hundreds of leagues they made together without exchanging a word, and yet all three understanding one another so well, that they had no need to make even a sign to comprehend. Ah! poor La Lison, as gentle as strong, so beautiful when sparkling in the sun! And Pecqueux, who, nevertheless, had not been drinking, burst into violent sobs, unable to master the hiccoughs that agitated his huge frame.

Séverine and Flore were also in despair at this fresh fainting fit of Jacques. The latter of the two women running home, returned with camphorated spirit, and began to friction him for the sake of doing something. But amidst their anguish they were exasperated by the interminable death agony of the horse, who had his two fore-hoofs cut off, the only survivor of the team of five. He lay close to them, uttering a constant neigh, a cry that sounded almost human. It was so shrill and so expressive of frightful pain, that two of the wounded gained by the contagion, also began howling like animals.

Never had a death-cry rent the air in such a deep, ever memorable complaint. It made the blood run icy cold. The torture became atrocious. Voices, trembling with pity and anger, inveighed against it, beseeching the rescue party to put an end to the misery of this wretched horse, who was in such terrible suffering, and whose endless death rattle, now that the engine had expired, continued like the final lamentation of the catastrophe. Then Pecqueux, still sobbing, picked up the hatchet with the shattered steel head, and at a single blow, right in front of the skull, pole-axed him. Silence now fell on the scene of massacre.

Assistance came at last, after waiting a couple of hours. In the shock of the collision the carriages had all been thrown to the left, so that the down-line could be cleared in a few hours. A train from Rouen, consisting of three carriages and a pilot-engine, had just brought the chief-secretary to the Prefect and the Imperial Procurator, along with some engineers and doctors of the company—quite a swarm of active, busy personages; while M. Bessière, the station-master at Barentin, was already attacking the wreckage with a gang of workmen.

Extraordinary bustle and excitement prevailed in this out-of-the-way place, usually so silent and deserted. The travellers, who had issued from the accident safe and sound, had not yet lost the frenzy of their panic, which asserted itself in a febrile necessity to keep on the move. Some, terrified at the idea of again seating themselves in a railway carriage, endeavoured to hire vehicles; others, seeing it was impossible to find even a wheel-barrow, already became anxious about eating and sleeping. Everybody wished to send off telegrams, and several people set out for Barentin on foot taking messages with them.

While the representatives of the government, assisted by the servants of the railway company, commenced an inquiry, the doctors hastily proceeded to dress the wounds of the injured. Many had lost consciousness and lay in pools of blood. Others, tortured by tweezers and needles, murmured in feeble voices. Altogether there were fifteen passengers killed and thirty-two seriously hurt. The corpses remained in a row on the ground at the foot of the hedge, with their faces to the sky pending identification.

No one, save a little substitute, a fair and rosy young man full of zeal, troubled about them. And he searched their pockets to see if he could find any papers, visiting-cards, or letters, which would enable him to ticket each of them with a name and address. Meanwhile, a gaping crowd had gathered about him; for, although there was no house within a league around, a number of idlers had arrived, no one could say whence—some thirty men, women, and children, who simply stood in the way without lending any assistance. And the black dust, the veil of smoke and vapour that had enveloped everything, having dispersed, the radiant April morning burst triumphant upon the scene of massacre, bathing the dead and dying, the ripped-up La Lison, and the pile of wreckage, in gentle, gay streams of bright sun; while the gang of workmen engaged in clearing the line reminded one of ants repairing the damage done to their hill by the feet of a thoughtless passer-by.

Jacques continued unconscious, and Séverine, stopping a doctor as he came along, besought his assistance. The latter examined the young man without discovering any visible wound, but fearing internal lesions on account of the thin streaks of blood that appeared between his lips, he declined to express a formal opinion, but advised that Jacques should be removed as speedily, and with as little jolting as possible, and put to bed.

Jacques, at the touch of hands passing over him, had again opened his eyes with a suppressed exclamation of pain. This time he recognised Séverine, and stammered in a wandering manner:

"Take me away—take me away!"

Flore bent forward, and Jacques moving his head recognised her also. His eyes at once took the terrified expression of a child, and he turned back towards Séverine, shrinking from the other with a look of hatred and horror.

"Take me away, immediately, immediately!" said he.

Then Séverine, troubling no more about Flore than if she had not been present, inquired in a most affectionate tone:

"Will you let me take you to La Croix-de-Maufras? It is just opposite; and if you consent we shall be at home there."

And still agitated, with his eyes fixed on the other, he acquiesced.

"Anywhere you please, immediately," said he.

Flore, who remained motionless, turned pale as death at his look of terrified execration. And so, in this carnage of innocent people, she had not succeeded in killing them, neither the one nor the other: the woman had come out of it without a scratch; and now he would perhaps escape. She had only succeeded in throwing them together all alone in this solitary house. She saw them comfortable there, the sweetheart recovered, convalescent; the girl full of attention, recompensed for her vigils by continual caresses, both prolonging the honeymoon of the catastrophe in absolute liberty and far from the world. She turned icy cold, and cast her eyes on the dead she had slaughtered to no purpose.

At this moment, Flore, in the glance she had given to the butchery, perceived Misard and Cabuche, who were being questioned by some gentlemen—the judicial authorities assuredly. In fact, the Imperial Procurator and the chief secretary to the Prefect were endeavouring to ascertain how this stone dray had got across the line. Misard maintained that he had not left his post, while at the same time, he was unable to give any precise information as to what had happened. He really knew nothing, so he pretended he had been busy with his apparatus, and had his back turned.

Cabuche, who had not yet recovered his composure, related a long, confused story about how he had committed the imprudence of leaving his team, in order to take a look at the corpse of the dead woman, how the horses had moved on alone, and how the young girl had been unable to stop them. Embroiling himself, he began again without succeeding in making himself understood.

A mad desire for liberty, again caused the frozen blood of Flore to flow warm. She wished for freedom of action, freedom to reflect and come to a decision of her own accord, having never required the assistance of anyone to get into the right path. What was the good of waiting to be annoyed with questions, perhaps to be arrested? For, apart from the crime, there had been neglect of duty, and she would be held responsible. Nevertheless, she remained where she was, feeling unable to quit the spot so long as Jacques stayed there.

Séverine had so begged and prayed of Pecqueux to procure a stretcher, that he at last secured one, and returned from his errand with a comrade, to carry off the injured driver. The doctor had persuaded the young woman to allow Henri, the headguard, to be accommodated at her house also. He merely seemed to be suffering from swimming in the head, as if momentarily struck senseless by the shock. He would be removed after the other one.

As Séverine bent forward to unbutton the collar of Jacques which was troubling him, she kissed him openly on the eyes, wishing to give him courage to support being moved.

"Never mind," she murmured; "we shall be happy."

He returned her kiss smiling. And to Flore this was the supreme rent that tore him from her for ever. It seemed to her that her blood, also, was now flowing from an incurable wound. She fled when they carried him away; but, in passing before the low habitation, she perceived the death-chamber through the window, with the pale spot formed by the candle burning in broad daylight, beside the body of her mother. During the accident the corpse of the dead woman had remained alone, with the head half turned aside, the eyes wide open, the mouth twisted, as if she were watching all these people whom she did not know, being crushed to death.

Flore dashed away, and immediately turning the corner formed by the Doinville road, struck out to the left among the bushes. She was familiar with every innermost corner of the district, and she could now defy the gendarmes to catch her should they happen to be in pursuit. So she abruptly ceased running, continuing at a slow walk towards a hiding-place—an excavation above the tunnel, where she loved to conceal herself on days when she felt sad. Raising her eyes, she saw by the sun that it was noon. When she was in her den, she stretched herself on the hard rock, and remained motionless with her hands clasped behind her neck reflecting. It was not until then that she felt a frightful void within her. A sensation of being dead gradually numbed her limbs. This was not remorse at having uselessly slaughtered all these people, for it required an effort on her part to experience regret and horror at what she had done.

No, but she was now certain that Jacques had seen her holding back the horses; and she had just understood, as she noticed him shrink away, that he felt the same terrified repulsion for her as one has for monsters. He would never forget. However, when you miss doing away with other people, you must not commit the same blunder with yourself. By-and-by, she would put an end to her existence. She had no other hope. She felt the absolute necessity of resorting to this extremity, since she had been there, recovering calm and reasoning. Her fatigue and complete prostration alone prevented her rising to seek a weapon, and die there and then.

And yet, from the midst of the invincible somnolence that settled on her, again came the love of life, a craving for felicity, a final dream of being happy also, considering she had left the other two to the bliss of living freely together. Why not await night, to run off and join Ozil, who adored her and would very well know how to defend her? Then her thoughts became gentle and confused, and she fell into a sound sleep, free from dreams.

When Flore awoke, night had completely set in. Not knowing where she was, she felt about her, and at once remembered everything, on touching the naked rock whereon she lay. Then the implacable necessity presented itself like a thunderbolt: she must die. It seemed as if that cowardly sensation of gentleness, that faltering when life seemed still possible, had vanished with the fatigue. No, no; death alone was good. She could not live in the midst of all this blood, with her tattered heart, and execrated by the only man she cared for, who belonged to another. Now that she had the strength, she must die.

Flore rose, and left the hole in the rocks. She did not hesitate, for instinct had just told her where she should go. Looking towards the stars, she could see it was close on nine o'clock. As she reached the railway, a train flew by at full speed, on the down-line, which seemed to give her pleasure: all would be well. Evidently they had cleared this line, whereas the other, no doubt, was still blocked, for the trains did not seem to be running. Now she followed the hedge amidst the deadly silence of the wild surroundings. There was no hurry, there would be no train before the Paris express, and that would not be there until 9.25.

She continued her walk in the dense darkness very calmly, and at short strides, as if she had been making one of her usual excursions by the deserted pathways of the neighbourhood.

Nevertheless, before coming to the tunnel, she made her way through the hedge, and advanced along the metals themselves, at her dawdling gait, walking to meet the express. She had to keep her wits about her, so as not to be seen by the watchman, as was her custom each time she ran over on a visit to Ozil. And, in the tunnel, she continued walking, still, still advancing. But it was not as on the last occasion. She was no longer afraid, should she turn round, of losing the exact notion of the direction she wished to take. The tunnel folly was not beating in her skull, obliterating all idea of time and space, amidst the thunder of the sounds crashing beneath the vault. What mattered it to her? She did not reason, she did not even think, she had but one fixed resolution: to walk, walk before her until she met the train, and then to still walk on, straight to the lantern, as soon as she should see it flaming in the night.

Nevertheless, Flore felt astonished, for she fancied she had been going along thus for hours. What a distance it was, this death that she desired! The idea that she would not encounter it, that she would walk leagues and leagues without striking against it, caused her momentary despair. Her feet were becoming weary. Would she then be obliged to sit down, and wait for death? To lie across the rails? But this struck her as unworthy. With the instinct of a virgin and warrior woman, she wished to walk on to the end, to die erect. And this thought aroused her energy. She gave another spurt forward, and, in the far distance, perceived the light of the express, looking like a little star, twinkling and alone, in the midst of an inky sky.

The train was not yet beneath the vault. No sound announced its coming. Nothing was visible but this very bright, gay light, increasing little by little in volume. Drawn up to her full, tall height, in all the suppleness of her build, evenly balanced on her strong lower limbs, she now advanced at a long stride, but without running, as if going to meet a friend to whom she wished to spare a part of the distance separating them. But the train had just entered the tunnel, the frightful roar approached, shaking the ground with a tempestuous blast; while the star had become an enormous eye, ever expanding, bursting out as if from its orbit of gloom.

Then, under the empire of an inexplicable sentiment, perhaps to die quite alone, she emptied her pockets without pausing in her heroic, obstinate march, and placed quite a little pile of articles beside the line: a pocket-handkerchief, some keys, some string, a couple of knives; she even removed the fichu tied round her neck, leaving her bodice unhooked and torn half open.

The eye changed into a brazier, into the mouth of an oven vomiting fire. The breath of the monster already reached her, damp and warm, in the roll of thunder that became more and more deafening. And she continued to walk on, going straight towards the furnace so as not to miss the engine, fascinated like some night insect attracted by a flame. And in the frightful shock, in the embrace, she still drew herself up, as if stirred by the final revolt of a wrestler woman, she sought to clasp the giant, and lay him low. Her head went full into the lantern which was extinguished.

It was more than an hour afterwards that a party came to pick up the corpse of Flore. The driver had distinctly seen the tall, pale-faced figure of this girl advancing towards the engine, with all the strange aspect of a terrifying apparition, in the deluge of vivid light that streamed upon her; and, when the lantern abruptly went out, and the train rolled along with its peal of thunder in dense obscurity, he shuddered as he felt death pass by. On issuing from the tunnel he did his best to inform the watchman of the accident, by shouting to him. But only at Barentin could he relate that somebody had just been cut in two down the line. It was certainly a woman for female hair, mingled with bits of skull, still remained sticking to the broken glass of the lamp.

And when the men sent to look for the body discovered it, they started to find it so white—as white as marble. It was lying on the up-line, thrown there by the violence of the shock: the head all pulp, the limbs without a scratch, and half bare, displaying admirable beauty in their purity and strength. The men wrapped up the corpse in silence. They had recognised it. She had certainly done away with herself in a fit of craziness, to escape the terrible responsibility weighing on her.

At midnight the corpse of Flore rested in the little, low habitation beside that of her mother. A mattress had been spread on the ground, and a candle lighted between the two bodies. The great fixed eyes of Aunt Phasie, whose head remained inclined on her shoulder, and whose twisted mouth still bore its hideous grin, seemed now to be gazing at her daughter; while all around in the solitude, amid the profound silence could be heard the grim labour—the panting efforts of Misard, who had resumed his search.

And at the prescribed intervals, the trains flew by, crossing one another on the two lines, the traffic having just been completely restored. They passed inexorably and indifferently with their all-powerful mechanism, ignorant of these dramas and these crimes. What mattered the unknown of the multitude fallen on the road, crushed beneath the wheels? The dead had been removed, the blood washed away, and the trains started off again for yonder, towards the future.

XI

The scene shifted to the bedroom at La Croix-de-Maufras, the room hung in red damask, with the two high windows looking on the railway line a few yards away. From the bedstead—an old four-poster facing the windows—the trains could be seen passing. And not an object had been removed, not a piece of furniture disturbed for years.

Séverine had the wounded Jacques, who was unconscious, carried up to this apartment; while Henri Dauvergne was left in a smaller bedroom on the ground floor. For herself, she kept a room close to the one occupied by Jacques, and only separated from it by the landing. A couple of hours sufficed to make everything sufficiently comfortable, for the house had remained fully set up, and even linen was stowed away in the cupboards. Séverine, with an apron over her gown, found herself transformed into a lady nurse. She had simply telegraphed to Roubaud not to expect her, as she would no doubt remain at the house a short time, attending to the wounded she had put up there.

On the following day, the doctor announced that he thought he could answer for Jacques, indeed he hoped to put him on his feet again in a week; his case proved a perfect miracle, for he had barely received some slight internal injury. But the doctor insisted on the greatest care being taken of him, and on absolute rest. So when the invalid opened his eyes Séverine, who watched over him as over a child, begged him to be good and to obey her in everything. Still very weak, he promised with a nod.

He was in possession of all his faculties. He recognised the room which she had described on the night of her confession. He was lying on the bed. There were the windows through which, without even raising his head, he could see the trains flash past, suddenly shaking the whole house. And he felt by the surroundings, that this house was just as he had so often seen it, when he went by on his engine. He saw it again now in his mind, set down aslant beside the line, in its distress and abandonment, with its closed shutters. The aspect had become more lamentable and dubious, since it had been for sale, with the immense board adding to the melancholy appearance of the garden overgrown with briars. He recalled the frightful sadness he had felt each time he passed the place, the uneasiness with which it haunted him as if it stood at this spot to be the calamity of his existence. And now, as he lay so weak in this room, he seemed to understand it all, there could be no other solution to the matter—he was assuredly going to die there.

As soon as Séverine perceived he was in a condition to understand her, she hastened to set his mind at ease in regard to a subject which she fancied might be worrying him, whispering in his ear as she drew up the bedclothes:

"You need not be anxious. I emptied your pockets, and took the watch."

He gazed at her with wide open eyes, making an effort to remember.

"The watch! Ah! yes! the watch," he murmured.

"They might have searched you," she resumed. "And I have hidden it among my own things. Don't be afraid."

He thanked her with a pressure of the hand. Turning his head, he caught sight of the knife lying on the table. This had also been found in one of his pockets, but there was no need to conceal it, for it was just like many another knife.

The following day, Jacques already found himself stronger, and began to hope he would not die there. He experienced real pleasure when he noticed the presence of Cabuche, who did all he could to make himself useful, and was at great pains to avoid making a noise on the floor with his heavy, giant-like tread. The quarryman had not quitted Séverine since the accident, and it seemed as if he also was under the influence of an ardent desire to show his devotedness. He abandoned his own occupation, and came every morning to assist in the housework, serving her with canine-like fidelity, and with eyes ever fixed on her own. As he remarked: she was a splendid woman, in spite of her slim appearance. One might well do something for her, considering she did so much for others. And the two sweethearts became so accustomed to him that they did not trouble if he happened to surprise them talking affectionately to one another, or even kissing, when he chanced to pass discreetly through the apartment, making as little as he could of his burly frame.

What astonished Jacques was the frequent absence of Séverine from the room. On the first day, in obedience to the orders of the doctor, she had said nothing about Henri being below, feeling that the idea of absolute solitude would act as a sort of soothing draught on her patient.

"We are alone here, are we not?" he inquired.

"Yes, my darling, alone, all alone," she answered. "You can sleep in peace."

But she disappeared at every moment, and the next day he overheard footsteps and whispering on the ground floor. Then, on the following day, he distinguished a lot of stifled merriment, bursts of clear laughter, two fresh, youthful voices that never ceased.

"What is it? Who is there?" he asked. "So we are not alone?"

"Well, no, my darling," she replied. "Down below, just under your room, is another injured man to whom I have given hospitality."

"Ah!" he exclaimed. "Who is it?"

"Henri, you know, the headguard!" said she.

"Henri! Ah!" he exclaimed again.

"And this morning," she continued, "his two sisters arrived. It is they that you hear; they laugh at everything. As he is much better they are going back again tonight, on account of their father who cannot do without them; and Henri is to remain two or three days longer to get quite well. Just fancy, he leapt from the train without breaking a single bone; only he was like an idiot; but his reason has returned."

Jacques made no remark, but he fixed such a penetrating look on her, that she added:

"You understand, eh? If he was not there, people might gossip about us two. So long as I am not alone with you, my husband can say nothing and I have a good pretext for remaining here. You understand?"

"Yes, yes," he replied; "that is all right."

And Jacques, until evening, listened to the laughter of the little Dauvergnes, which he recollected having heard in Paris, ascending in the same manner from the lower floor into the room where Séverine had made her confession to him. With darkness came silence, and he could only distinguish the light footsteps of Séverine going from him to the other wounded man. The door below closed, and the house fell into profound silence. Feeling thirsty, he had to knock twice on the floor with a chair for her to come up to him. When she arrived, she was all smiles and very assiduous, explaining that she could not get away before because it was necessary to keep a compress of cold water on the head of Henri.

On the fourth day, Jacques was able to get up, and pass a couple of hours in an armchair before the window. By bending forward a little he could see the strip of garden inclosed by a low wall and invaded by briars with their pale bloom, a slice of which had been taken by the railway. And he remembered the night when he stood on tiptoe to look over the wall. He again saw the rather large piece of ground at the back of the house shut in by a hedge only, the hedge he had gone through to run up against Flore seated at the entrance to the dilapidated greenhouse, cutting up stolen cord with scissors. Ah! that abominable night full of the terror of his complaint! That Flore, with the tall, supple stature of a fair warrior woman, her flaming eyes fixed straight on his, was ever present since the recollection of it all returned to him more and more distinctly.

At first he had not opened his lips respecting the accident, and no one about him alluded to it, out of prudence. But every detail came back to him, and he pieced it all together again. He thought of nothing else, and his mind was so continuously occupied with the subject, that now, at the window, his sole occupation consisted in looking for traces of the collision, in watching for the actors in the catastrophe. How was it that he did not see Flore there at her post as gatekeeper with her flag in her fist? He dared not ask the question, and this increased the uneasiness he felt in this lugubrious dwelling, which seemed to him to be peopled with spectres.

Nevertheless, one morning, when Cabuche was there assisting Séverine, he ended by making up his mind.

"And where is Flore?" he inquired. "Is she ill?"

The quarryman, taken unawares, misunderstood a gesture the young woman made, and, thinking she was telling him to speak out, he answered:

"Poor Flore is dead."

Jacques looked at them shuddering, and it then became necessary to tell him all. Together they related to him the suicide of the young girl, how she had been cut in two in the tunnel. The burial of the mother had been delayed until the evening, so that her daughter might be carried away at the same time; and they now slept side by side in the little cemetery at Doinville, where they had gone to join the first who had made the journey, the younger sister, that gentle but unfortunate Louisette. Three miserable creatures among those who fall on the road, who are crushed and disappear, as if swept away by the terrible blast of those passing trains.

"Dead! great God!" repeated Jacques very lowly. "My poor Aunt Phasie, and Flore, and Louisette!"

At the last name, Cabuche, who was assisting Séverine to push the bed, instinctively raised his eyes to her, troubled at the recollection of his tender feelings for another in presence of the budding passion which he felt had gained him; he, a soft-hearted creature of limited intelligence, was without defence, like an affectionate dog who is conquered by the first caress. But Séverine who knew all about his tragic love episode remained grave, looking at him with sympathetic eyes, so that he felt very much touched; and his hand having unintentionally grazed her hand, as he was passing her the pillows, he felt like suffocating, and it was in a stammering voice that he replied to the next question Jacques put to him.

"Did they accuse her, then, of causing the accident?" asked the latter.

"Oh! no, no! Only it was her fault, you understand?" answered Cabuche.

In disjointed sentences he related all he knew. For his own part, he had seen nothing as he was in the house when the horses moved on to drag the stone dray across the line. This, indeed, was what caused him silent remorse. The judicial gentlemen had harshly reproached him with leaving his team. The frightful misfortune would not have occurred had he remained with them. The inquiry, therefore, resulted in showing that there had been simple negligence on the part of Flore; and as she had punished herself atrociously, nothing further was done. The company did not even remove Misard, who, with his air of humility and deference, had got out of the scrape by accusing the dead girl: she always did as she liked; he had to leave his box at every minute to close the gate. The company, for their part, were compelled to recognise that on this particular morning he had performed his duty perfectly. And, in the interval that would elapse before he married again, they had just authorised him to take as gatekeeper an old woman of the neighbourhood, named Ducloux, formerly a servant at an inn, who lived on money she had economised in her younger days.

When Cabuche left the room, Jacques detained Séverine by a glance. He looked extremely pale.

"You know very well that it was Flore who pulled on the horses, and barred the line with the blocks of stone," said he.

Séverine in her turn grew pallid.

"Darling, what on earth are you saying?" she answered. "You are getting feverish; you must go to bed again."

"No, no, I am not wandering. Do you hear? I saw her, as I see you," he continued. "She held the cattle, and with her firm fist, prevented the dray advancing."

On hearing this, Séverine, losing her legs, sank down on a chair opposite him.

"Good heavens! good heavens!" she exclaimed. "It strikes terror into one. It is monstrous. I shall never be able to get any sleep."

"Of course," he resumed, "the thing is clear. She attempted to kill us both in the general slaughter. She had been making me advances for a long time, and she was jealous. Coupled with this, she was half off her head, and had all manner of rum ideas. Only think such a number of murders at one stroke—quite a multitude plunged in gore! Ah! the wretch!"

His eyes grew wide open, a nervous twitch drew down his lip, and he held his tongue. They remained looking at one another for fully a minute without speaking. Then, tearing himself from the abominable vision that had risen up between them, he continued in a lower tone:

"Ah! she is dead! So that is why her ghost is here! Since I recovered consciousness she seems to be always present. Again this morning, I turned round thinking her at the head of my bed. Still she is dead, and we are alive. Let us hope she will not avenge herself now!"

Séverine shuddered.

"Hold your tongue, hold your tongue!" said she. "You will drive me crazy."

She left the room, and he heard her go downstairs to the other invalid.

Jacques, who had remained at the window, was again lost in the contemplation of the line, of the small habitation of the gatekeeper, with its great well, of the signal-box, that wooden hut where Misard seemed to be dozing over his regular, monotonous work. Jacques became absorbed by these things now for hours, as if poring over some problem he could not solve, and the solution of which, nevertheless, concerned his safety.

He never felt tired of watching Misard, that puny creature, gentle and pallid, everlastingly disturbed by a nasty little cough, who had poisoned his wife, who had got the better of that strapping woman, like a rodent insect obstinately pursuing its passion. He could certainly not have had any other idea in his head for years, day and night, during the twelve interminable hours he remained on duty. At each electric tinkle, announcing a train, he blew the horn; then, when the train had passed and he had blocked the line, he pressed an electric knob to warn the next signalman of its arrival, afterwards touching a second knob to open the line at the preceding signal-box. These simple mechanical movements had, in the end, entered into his vegetative life, as bodily habits.

Untutored and obtuse he never read anything, but between the calls of his apparatus remained with his arms hanging down beside him, and his eyes gazing vaguely into space. Being almost always seated in his box, he had no other diversion than that of dawdling as long as possible over his lunch. When this was finished he fell into his doltishness again with a skull quite empty, without a thought; and he was particularly tormented with terrible drowsiness, sometimes sleeping with his eyes open. At night-time, if he wished to avoid giving way to this irresistible torpor, he had to get up and walk with unsteady legs like a drunken man. And it was thus that the struggle with his wife, that secret combat as to who should have the concealed 1,000 frcs. after the death of the other, must for months and months have been the sole reflection in the benumbed brain of this solitary being.

When he blew his horn; when he manœuvred his signals, watching in automatic fashion over the safety of so many lives, he thought of the poison; and when he waited with idle arms, his eyes moving from side to side with sleep, he still thought of it. Of nothing did he think but that: he would kill her, he would search, it was he who would have the money.

At present, Jacques was astonished to find Misard had not changed. It was possible then to kill without any trouble, and life continue as before. After the feverishness, attending the first rummages for the money-bag, he had just resumed his usual indifference, the cunning, gentle manner of a feeble being who shunned a shock. As a matter of fact, he might well have put an end to his wife, but she triumphed notwithstanding; for he was beaten. He had turned the house upside down without discovering anything, not a centime; and his looks alone, those anxious ferreting looks, revealed on his sallow countenance how busy was his mind.

Everlastingly he saw the wide open eyes of the dead woman, the hideous smile on her lips which seemed to repeat: "Search! search!" He sought. He could not give his brain one minute of rest now. It worked, worked incessantly in quest of the spot where the treasure was buried, thinking over the possible hiding-places, rejecting those where he had already rummaged, bursting into feverish excitement as soon as he imagined a new one; and then, burning with such haste,

ÉMILE ZOLA

that he abandoned everything to run off there to no purpose. This, in the end, became an intolerable torment, an avenging torture, a sort of cerebral insomnia which kept him awake, stupid and reflecting in spite of himself, in the tic-tac of the pendulum of his fixed idea.

When he blew his horn, once for the down-trains, twice for the up trains, he sought; when he answered the ringing, when he pressed the knobs of his apparatus, closing, opening the line, he sought. He sought, sought, bewilderingly, ceaselessly. In the daytime, during the long period of waiting, heavy with idleness; at night, tormented with sleep as if exiled to the other end of the world, in the silence of the great black country. And the woman Ducloux, who at present looked after the gate, actuated by the desire to become his wife, showed him every possible attention, and was alarmed to see that he never closed his eyes.

One night, Jacques, who began to take a few steps in his room, had got up and approaching the window, saw a lantern moving to and fro at the house of Misard: assuredly the man was searching. But the following night, the convalescent being again on the look out, was astounded to recognise a great dark form, which proved none other than Cabuche, who was standing in the road beneath the window of the adjoining room where Séverine slept. And this sight, without him being able to understand why it should be so, instead of irritating him, filled him with commiseration and sadness: another unfortunate fellow, this great brute, planted there like a bewildered faithful animal.

In truth, Séverine, who was so slim and not handsome, when examined in detail, must possess a very powerful charm with her raven hair and deep blue eyes for even savages, giants of limited intelligence, to be so smitten with her as to pass the night at her door, like little trembling youths! He recalled certain things that he had noticed: the eagerness of the quarryman to assist her, and the look of servility with which he offered his help. Yes, Cabuche was certainly in love with her. And Jacques, having kept his eye on him, the next day noticed him furtively pick up a hair-pin that had fallen from her hair as she made the bed, and keep it in his closed hand so as not to restore it. Jacques thought of his own torment, of all he had suffered through his love, of all the trouble and fright returning with health.

Two more days passed. The week was coming to an end, and the injured men, as the doctor had foreseen, would be able to resume duty. One morning, the driver being at the window, saw a brand new engine pass with his fireman Pecqueux, who greeted him with his hand as if calling him. But he was in no hurry, an awakening of passion detained him there, a sort of anxious expectation as to what would happen next.

That same day, in the lower part of the house, he again heard fresh youthful laughter, a gaiety of grown up girls, filling the sad habitation with all the racket of a ladies' school in the playground. He recognised the voices of the little Dauvergnes, but he did not say a word on the subject to Séverine who absented herself nearly the entire day, unable to remain with him for five minutes at a time. In the evening, the house having fallen into deathlike silence, and as Séverine, looking grave and slightly pale, loitered in his room, he looked at her fixedly, and remarked inquiringly:

"So he has gone? His sisters have taken him away?"

She briefly answered:

"Yes."

"And we are at last alone, quite alone?" he continued.

"Yes, quite alone," said she. "Tomorrow we shall have to quit one another. I shall return to Havre. We have been camping long enough in this desert."

He continued looking at her in a smiling but constrained manner, and at length made up his mind to speak.

"You are sorry he has gone, eh?" he inquired.

And as she started and wished to protest, he interrupted her:

"I am not seeking a quarrel with you," he said. "You know well enough that I am not jealous. One day you told me to kill you if you were unfaithful to me, did you not? I do not look like a man who is going to kill his sweetheart. But really you were always below, it was impossible to have you to myself for a minute. It recalled to my mind a remark your husband one day made, that you would be as likely as not to listen to that young fellow without taking any pleasure in the experiment, simply to begin something new."

She ceased defending herself, and slowly repeated, twice over:

"To begin something new, to begin something new."

Then, in an outburst of irresistible frankness, she continued:

"Well, listen, what you say is true. We two can tell one another everything. We are bound closely enough together. This man has pursued me for months. And, when I found him below, he spoke to me again. He repeated that he loved me to distraction, and in a manner so thoroughly imbued with gratitude for the care I had taken of him, with such gentle tenderness, that, it is true, I for a moment dreamed

ÉMILE ZOLA

of loving him also, of beginning something new, something better, something very sweet. Yes, something without pleasure perhaps, but which would have given me calm—"

She paused, and hesitated, before continuing:

"For the road in front of us two," she resumed, "is now barred. We shall advance no further. Our dream of leaving France, the hope of wealth and happiness over there in America, all the felicity that depended on you, is impossible, because you were unable to do the thing. Oh! I am not making you any reproach! It is better that it was not done; but I want to make you understand that with you I have nothing to hope for; tomorrow will be like yesterday, the same annoyances, the same torments."

He allowed her to speak, and only questioned her when he saw her silent.

"So that is why you gave way to the other?" he suggested.

She had taken a few steps in the room, and returning, she shrugged her shoulders.

"No, I did not give way to him," said she. "I tell you so, simply; and I am sure you believe me, because henceforth there is no reason why we should lie to one another. He kissed my hand, but he did not kiss my lips, and that I swear. He expects to meet me at Paris later on because, seeing him so miserable, I did not wish to drive him to despair."

She was right. Jacques believed her. He saw she was not telling untruths. And his old feeling of anguish began again, in the rekindling flame of their passion, that frightful trouble of the growing mania, at the thought that he was now shut up alone with her, far from the world. Wishing to escape, he exclaimed:

"But then, the other one! For there is another one! This Cabuche!"

Abruptly turning round, she went back to him, and said:

"Ah! So you noticed him! So you know that, too! Yes, it is a fact. There is also this one. I cannot imagine what has come to them all. Cabuche has never said a word to me. But I can see he is beside himself, when he observes us kissing; and when I address you affectionately, he goes off to whimper in out-of-the-way corners. And then he robs me of all sorts of things, my own private belongings. Gloves and even pocket-handkerchiefs disappear, and he carries them over there to his cavern as if they were treasures. Only you need not imagine that I am likely to fall in love with this savage. He is too coarse, he would frighten me to death. Moreover, his love is passive. No, no, when those great brutes are timid, they die of love, without seeking to gratify their passion. You might leave me a month in his keeping, and he would not touch me with the tips of his fingers, no more than he touched Louisette, I can answer for that now."

At this remembrance, they looked at one another, and silence ensued. Past events came to their minds: their meeting before the examining-magistrate at Rouen; then their first trip to Paris, so full of charm; and their love-making at Havre, and all that followed, good and terrible. She drew nearer to him, coming so close that he felt the warmth of her breath.

"No, no," she resumed; "still less with that one than with the other. With nobody in fact do you understand. And do you want to know why? Ah! I feel it at this hour! I am sure I make no mistake: it is because you have taken entire possession of me; there is no other word. Yes, taken, as one takes an object with both hands and walks off with it. Before I knew you I belonged to no one. I am now yours and shall remain yours, even against your own wish, even if I do not desire to do so myself. I cannot explain this to you; it was to that end that we met. Ah! it is you alone that I love! I can love no one but you!"

She put forward her arms to have him to herself, to rest her head on his shoulder, her mouth on his lips. But he grasped her hands, he held her back aghast, terrified at the sensation of the old shiver ascending his limbs, with the blood beating on his brain. Then came the buzzing in the ears, the strokes of a hammer, the clamour of a multitude, as in his former severe attacks. For sometime past he had been almost unable to kiss her in broad daylight or even by the flame of a candle, in terror lest he should go mad if he saw her. And a lamp stood there lighting them both up brilliantly. If he trembled as he did, if he felt himself going crazy, it must be because he perceived the white rotundity of her bosom through her open dressing-gown.

"Our existence may well be barred," she continued. "Let it be! Although I can hope for nothing more from you; although I know that tomorrow will bring us the same worries and the same torments, I do not care; I have nothing to do but to let my life drag along and suffer with you. We shall return to Havre, and things may go on as they will, so long as I have an hour in your company from time to time."

Jacques, in the fury of madness, excited by her caresses, and having no weapon, had already stretched out both his hands to strangle her, when she, turning round, extinguished the lamp of her own accord. Then, seating herself, she said:

"Oh! my darling, if you could only have done it, how happy we should have been over there! No, no, I am not asking you to do what you cannot do; only I'm so sorry our dream has not been realised. I was afraid just now; I do not know how it is, but it seems as if something menaces me. It is no doubt childishness, but at every moment I turn round as though something was there ready to strike me; and I have only you, my darling, to defend me. All my joy depends on you. It is for you alone that I live."

Without answering he strained her to him, putting into this pressure what he did not say: his emotion, his sincere desire to be good to her, the violent love she had never ceased to inspire in him. And yet he had again wanted to kill her that very night; for if she had not turned round and extinguished the lamp he would have strangled her. That was certain; never would he be cured. The attacks came back by the hazard of circumstances without him even being able to discover or discuss the causes. Thus, why did he wish to kill her on that night, when he found her faithful, and imbued with a more expansive and confiding passion? Was it because the more she loved him, the more he wished to make her his, even to destroying her in the terrifying gloom of male egotism? Did he want to have possession of her dead as the earth?

"Tell me, my darling," she murmured, "why am I afraid? Do you know of anything threatening me?"

"No, no," answered Jacques; "rest assured that there is nothing threatening you."

"But at moments," said she, "all my body is in a tremble. Behind me lurks a constant danger which I do not see, but which I feel very distinctly. How is it that I am afraid?"

"No, no," he repeated, "there is no cause for alarm. I love you, and will allow no one to do you any harm. See how nice it is to be as we are, one in body and soul!"

A delicious silence followed, which was broken by Séverine.

"Ah! my darling," she resumed, in her low, caressing whisper, "if we could only always be as we are now. You know we would sell this house, and set out with the money to join your friend in America, who is still expecting you. I never pass a day without making plans for our life over there. But you cannot do it I know. If I speak to you on the subject, it is not to annoy you, it is because it comes from my heart in spite of myself."

Jacques abruptly took the same decision he had so often taken before:

to kill Roubaud in order that he might not kill her. On this occasion, as previously, he fancied he possessed the absolutely firm will to do so.

"I could not before," he murmured in response, "but I might be able to now. Did I not make you a promise that I would?"

She feebly remonstrated.

"No; do not promise, I implore you," said she. "It makes us sick afterwards, when you have lost courage. And then it is horrible. It must not be done. No, no! It must not be done."

"Yes," answered Jacques, "it must, on the contrary as you know. It is because it is necessary that I shall find strength to do it, I wanted to speak to you on the subject, and we will talk about it now, as we are here alone, and so quiet that one could hear a pin drop."

She had already become resigned, and she was sighing, her heart swelling, beating with violent throbs.

"Oh dear! oh dear!" she murmured. "So long as the thing was not to be, I wanted it done. But now that it becomes serious I shall not be able to exist."

This weighty resolution caused another silence. Around them they felt the desert, the desolation of the savage district. Suddenly she resumed her low murmur:

"We must have him here. Yes, I could send for him on some pretext; which, I do not know. We can settle that later on. Then you will be waiting for him in concealment, do you see? And the thing will go on by itself, for we are sure not to be disturbed here. That is what we must do, eh?"

With docility he answered:

"Yes, yes."

But she, lost in reflection, weighed every detail; and little by little, as the plan developed in her head, she discussed and improved it.

"Only, my darling," she went on, "it would be foolish not to take our precautions. If we are to be arrested on the morrow, I prefer to remain as we are. Look here, I have read this somewhere, I have forgotten where, in a novel for sure: the best thing would be to make believe that he committed suicide. For sometime back he has been very peculiar, not quite right in his head, and so gloomy that no one would be surprised to suddenly learn that he came here and killed himself. But then, we must arrange matters in such a way that the idea of suicide will seem probable. Is it not so?"

"Without a doubt," he replied.

After a pause, Séverine, who had been thinking, resumed:

"Eh! Something to hide the trace. I say, here is an idea that has just struck me! Supposing he got that knife in his throat, we should only have to carry him together over there and lay him across the line. Do you understand? We could place him with his neck on a rail, so that he would be decapitated by the first train that passed. After that they could make their investigations. With his head and neck crushed, there would no longer be a hole, nothing! Do you agree? Answer!"

"Yes, I agree," said he; "it is capital."

Both became animated. She was almost gay, and quite proud of her faculty of imagination.

"But, my darling," she continued, "I have just been thinking, there is something more. If you remain here with me, the suggestion of suicide will certainly be viewed with suspicion. You must go away. Do you understand? You will leave tomorrow, openly, in the presence of Cabuche and Misard, so that the fact of your departure may be well established. You will take the train at Barentin, and leave it at Rouen, on some pretence or other; then, as soon as it is dark, you will return, and I will let you in the back way. It is only four leagues, and you can be here in less than three hours. This time everything is settled, and, if you like, it is agreed."

"Yes," he answered; "I am willing, and it is agreed."

It was now he who reflected, and there came a long silence. All at once, she broke out:

"Yes; but what about the pretext for bringing him here? In any case, he could only take the eight o'clock at night train, after coming off duty, and would not get here before ten o'clock, which is all the better. Hi! that person who wishes to see the house, with a view to purchasing it, of whom Misard spoke to me, and who is coming the day after tomorrow morning! That will do. I will send my husband a wire the first thing, to say his presence is absolutely necessary. He will be here tomorrow night. You will leave in the afternoon, and will be able to get back before he arrives. It will be dark, no moon, nothing to interfere with us. Everything dovetails in perfectly."

"Yes," said he approvingly, "perfectly."

When they at last went to sleep, it was not daylight, but a streak of dawn began to whiten the gloom that had hidden them from one another, as if both had been wrapped in a black mantle. He slept like a top until ten o'clock, without a dream; and, when he opened his eyes, he was alone. Séverine was dressing in her own apartment, on the other side of the landing. A sheet of clear sun entered through the window of the room occupied by Jacques, showing up the red curtains of the bedstead, the red paper on the walls, all that red with which the place was flaming; while the house tottered in the thunder of a train that had just sped past. It must have been this train that awakened him. Bedazzled by the glare of light, he looked at the sun, at the streaming crimson surroundings amidst which he found himself; then he recollected: the matter was settled, it was the next night that he would kill, when this great sun had disappeared.

The day passed as had been arranged by Séverine and Jacques. Before breakfast, she requested Misard to take the telegram for her husband to Doinville; and at about three o'clock, as Cabuche was there, Jacques openly made his preparations for departure. As he was leaving to catch the 4.15 train from Barentin, Cabuche, having nothing to do, feeling himself drawn to the other by his secret passion, happy to find in the sweetheart something in common with the woman he was in love with himself, accompanied the driver to the station. Jacques reached Rouen at 4.40, and, getting down, found accommodation at a small inn near the railway kept by a woman from the same neighbourhood as himself. He spoke of looking up his comrades on the morrow, before proceeding to Paris to resume duty. But he said he felt very tired, having presumed too much on his strength; and, at six o'clock, he went off to bed, in a room he had taken on the ground floor, which had a window opening on a deserted alley. Ten minutes later, he was on the road to La Croix-de-Maufras, having got out of this window without being seen, and taken good care to close the shutters, so as to be able to secretly return the same way.

It was not until a quarter after nine that Jacques found himself before the solitary house standing aslant beside the line, in the distress of its abandonment. The night was very dark, not a glimmer could be distinguished on the hermetically closed front. And Jacques again felt that painful blow in his heart, that feeling of frightful sadness which seemed like the presentiment of the evil that awaited him there.

As had been arranged with Séverine, he threw three small pebbles against a shutter of the red room; then he went to the back of the house where a door at last silently opened. Having closed it behind him, he followed the light footsteps that went feeling their way up the staircase. But when he reached the bedroom, and by the light of a large

ÉMILE ZOLA

lamp burning on the corner of a table perceived the bed in disorder, the clothes of the young woman thrown on a chair, and herself in a dressing-gown, with her volume of hair arranged for the night, coiled on the top of her head, leaving her neck bare, he stood motionless with surprise.

"What!" he exclaimed; "you had gone to bed?"

"Of course," she answered, "that is much better. An idea struck me. You see, when he arrives and I go down, as I am to open the door to him, he will have still less cause to be distrustful. I shall tell him I have a headache. Misard already knows I am not well. And this will permit me to affirm that I never left this room when they find him tomorrow, down there, on the line."

But Jacques shuddered, and lost his temper.

"No, no," said he, "dress yourself. You must be up. You cannot remain as you are."

She was astonished, and began to laugh.

"But why, my darling?" she inquired. "Do not be anxious, I can assure you I do not feel at all cold. Just see how warm I am!"

She advanced towards him in a caressing manner, to take him by the shoulders, and in raising her arms displayed her bosom through the dressing-gown she had neglected to fasten, and the night-dress that had come undone. But as he drew back, in increasing irritation, she became docile.

"Do not be angry," said she, "I will get between the sheets again, and then you will have no reason to be afraid that I shall catch cold."

When she was in bed, with the clothes up to her chin, he seemed more calm. And she continued talking quietly, explaining how she had arranged everything in her head.

"As soon as he knocks," she said, "I shall go down and open the door. First of all, I had the idea of letting him come up here, where you would be in waiting for him. But to get his body below again, would have caused complications; and, besides, this room has a parquetry floor, whereas the vestibule is tiled, and I shall easily be able to wash it if there should be any spots. Just before you came, as I was undressing, I thought of a novel I had read, in which the author relates that one man to kill another stripped himself. Do you understand? A wash afterwards, and the clothes are free from any spots. What do you say? Supposing we were to do the same?"

He looked at her in bewilderment. But she had her gentle face, her clear eyes of a little girl, and was simply thinking of arranging the plan perfectly, in order to ensure success. All this passed through his head. But her suggestion, the idea of being bespattered with the blood of the murder, brought on his abominable shiver which shook him to the bones.

"No, no!" he answered. "Do you wish us to act like savages? Why not devour his heart as well? How you must hate him!"

Her face suddenly became clouded. This remark took her from her thoughts of prudent preparation, to reveal to her the horror of the deed. Her eyes filled with tears, and she said:

"I have suffered too much for the last few months, to have much affection for him. I have repeated a hundred times over: anything rather than remain another week with this man. But you are right. It is frightful to come to that, we really must want to be happy together. Anyhow, we will go down without a light. You will stand behind the door, and when I have opened, and he has come in, you will do what you like. If I interfere, it is only to help you; it is so that you may not have all the trouble yourself. I am arranging the thing as well as I can."

He went to the table where he saw the knife, the weapon that had already been used by the husband, and which she had evidently placed there, so that he might strike him in his turn with it. The wide open blade shone beneath the lamp. Jacques took it up and examined it. She watched him, but said nothing. As he held the weapon in his hand there was no need to speak to him about it. And she only opened her lips when he had laid it down again on the table.

"Listen, my darling," she continued, "I am not urging you on to it, am I? There is still time. Go away, if you do not feel you can do it."

But he became obstinate, and with a violent gesture exclaimed:

"Do you take me for a coward? This time it is settled. I have sworn."

At that moment, the house was set rocking by the thunder of a train, which passed like a thunderbolt, and so close to the room that it seemed to go through it in its roar, and Jacques added:

"There is his train. The through train to Paris. He got down at Barentin, and will be here in half an hour."

Neither Jacques nor Séverine made any further remark for sometime. In their minds they saw this man advancing through the night along the narrow paths. Jacques had begun to walk up and down the room, as if counting the steps of the other whom each stride brought a little nearer. Another, another; and, at the last one, he would be in ambush behind the vestibule door, and would drive the knife into his neck the moment he entered. Séverine, still with the bedclothes up to her chin, lying on her back, with her great eyes motionless, watched him going and coming, her mind lulled by the cadence of his walk, which reached her like the echo of distant footsteps over there. They came without pause, one after the other, and nothing would now stop them. When the sufficient number had been taken, she would spring out of bed, and go down to open the door, with bare feet and without a light. "Is it you, my dear? Come in, I went to bed!" she would say. And he would not even answer. He would sink down in the obscurity with his throat gashed open.

Again a train went by. One on the down-line this time, the slow train which passed La Croix-de-Maufras five minutes after the other. Jacques stopped in his walk, surprised. Only five minutes had expired! How long the half hour would be! He experienced the necessity of keeping on the move, and resumed striding from one end of the room to the other. He began to feel anxious, and was already communing with himself: would he be able to do it? He was familiar with the progress of the phenomenon within him, from having followed it on more than ten different occasions; first of all a certainty, an absolute resolution to kill; then a weight in the hollow of the chest, a chill in feet and hands; and all at once the loss of vigour, the impotence of the will to act upon the muscles which had become inert.

In order to gain energy by reasoning, he repeated what he had said to himself so often: it was his interest to suppress this man—the fortune awaiting him in America, the possession of the woman he loved. The worst of it was, that on finding the latter so scantily clothed a few moments before, he verily believed the enterprise would again come to naught; for, as soon as the old shiver returned, he ceased to have command over himself. For an instant he had trembled in presence of the temptation which became too great: she offering herself, and the open knife lying there. But now he felt strong, girded for the effort. He could do it. And he continued waiting for the man, striding up and down the apartment from door to window, passing at each turn beside the bed which he would not look at.

Séverine continued to lie still in that bed. With her head motionless on the pillow, she now watched him come and go in a seesaw motion of the eyes. She also felt anxious, agitated with the fear that this night his courage again would fail him. Polish off this business and begin anew, that was all she wanted. She was entirely for the one who held her, and heartless for the other whom she had never cared for. They were getting rid of him because he was in the way. Nothing could be more natural; and she had to reflect, to be touched by the abomination of the crime. As soon as the vision of blood and the horrible complications disappeared, she resumed her smiling serenity with her innocent, tender, and docile face.

Nevertheless, she, who thought she knew Jacques, was astonished at what she observed. He had his round head of a handsome young man, his curly hair, his coal black moustache, his brown eyes sparkling with gold; but his lower jaw advanced so prominently, with a sort of biting expression, that it disfigured him. He had just now looked at her as he passed, as if in spite of himself; and the brilliancy of his eyes became deadened with a ruddy cloud, while at the same time he started backward in a recoil of all his frame.

Why did he avoid her? Could it be because he was losing his courage, once more? Latterly, ignorant of the constant danger of death threatening her while in his company, she had attributed her instinctive fright, for which there was no apparent cause, to the presentiment of an approaching rupture. The conviction abruptly took firm hold of her, that if presently he found himself unable to strike, he would flee never to return. After that she made up her mind that he would kill, and that she would know how to give him strength, should he need it.

At this moment another train passed: an interminably long goods train, whose extensive string of trucks seemed to be rolling on for ever in the oppressive silence that reigned in the apartment. And, leaning on her elbow, she waited until this tempestuous disturbance became lost in the depth of the slumbering country.

"Another quarter of an hour," said Jacques, aloud. "He has passed Bécourt Wood and is half-way. Ah! how long it is to wait!"

But, as he returned towards the window, he found Séverine standing in front of the bed.

"Suppose we go down with the lamp?" she suggested. "You can see the spot where you will place yourself. I will show you how I shall open the door, and the movement you will have to make."

He drew back, trembling.

"No, no!" he exclaimed. "No lamp!"

"But just listen," she continued, "we will hide it afterwards. You see we must form an idea of the position."

"No, no!" he repeated. "Get into bed again."

Instead of obeying, she advanced towards him with the invincible, despotic smile of the woman who knows herself to be all powerful. When she held him in her arms, he would give way, he would do as she desired; and she continued talking in a caressing voice to conquer him.

"Come, my darling," she said, "what is the matter with you? One would think you were afraid of me. As soon as I approach you seem to avoid me. But if you only knew how much I need to lean on you at this time, to feel you there, that we are absolutely of the same mind for ever and ever. Do you understand?"

She at last made him retreat with his back to the table, and he could not flee further. He looked at her in the bright light of the lamp. Never had he seen her as she was then, with the front of her night-dress in disorder, and her hair coiled up so high that her neck was quite bare. He was choking, struggling, already in a fury, quite giddy with the flood of blood that rushed to his head, at the same moment as the abominable shiver fell upon him. And he remembered that the knife was there behind him, on the table. He instinctively felt it there, he had only to stretch out his hand.

By an effort he still managed to stammer:

"Go back to bed, I implore you."

But she continued to approach until she came close to him.

"Kiss me," she exclaimed, "kiss me with all the love you feel for me! That will give us courage. Ah! yes, courage, we are in need of it! We must love in a different way to others, stronger than others to do what we are about to do. Kiss me with all your heart, with all your soul!"

He no longer breathed. He felt as if he was being strangled. The clamour of a multitude in his brain prevented him from hearing; while biting fire behind the ears burnt holes in his head, gained his arms, his legs, drove him from his own body, in the frantic rush of that other one—the invading brute. His hands were about to escape from his control in the frenzy excited by this feminine semi-nudity. The bare bosom pressing against his clothes, the neck so white, so delicate, extended in irresistible temptation, at last plunged him into a state of furious giddiness, over-powering, tearing away, annihilating his will.

"Kiss me, my darling," she repeated, "while we have still a minute left. He will be here, you know. He might knock from one moment to another, now, if he has walked quick. As you will not go downstairs to arrange matters beforehand, do not fail to bear this in mind: I shall let him in. You will be behind the door; and do not wait, do it at once! Oh! at once, to get it over! I love you so fondly, we shall be so happy! He is nothing but a wicked man, who makes me suffer, and who is the sole obstacle to our happiness. Kiss me, oh! so hard, so hard! Kiss me as if you were going to devour me, so that nothing may remain of me beyond yourself!"

Jacques, feeling behind him with his right hand, had secured the knife without turning round. And for a moment he remained in the same position tightening his grasp on the weapon. Could the feeling that had come over him be a return of that thirst to avenge those very ancient offences, the exact recollection of which escaped him, that rancour amassed from male to male since the first deception in the depths of the caverns? He fixed his wild eyes on Séverine. He now only required to lay her dead on her back, like a prey torn from others. The gate of terror opened on the dark sexual chasm. Love, even unto death. Destroy, to have more absolute possession.

"Kiss me, kiss me!" she pleaded.

She presented her submissive face in imploring tenderness, displaying her bare neck at the part where it voluptuously met the bosom. And he, seeing her white skin as in a burst of flame, raised his fist armed with the knife. But she perceived the flash of the blade and started back, gaping in surprise and terror.

"Jacques, Jacques!" she cried; "me? Good God! Why?"

With set teeth and answering not a word, he pursued her. A brief struggle brought her again beside the bed. She shrank from him, haggard, without defence, her night-dress in shreds.

"Why? good God! Why?" she continued asking.

His fist came down, and the knife stuck the inquiry in her throat. In striking, he twisted the blade round in a frightful compulsion of the hand which satisfied itself. It was the same blow as President Grandmorin had received, inflicted at the same place, and with the same fury. Did she shriek? He never knew. The Paris express flew by at this moment with such violence and rapidity that it shook the floor; and Séverine was dead, as if struck down in this tempestuous blast.

Jacques, standing motionless, now looked at her, stretched at his feet before the bed. The riot of the train was dying away in the distance as he gazed upon her in the oppressive silence of the red bedroom. On the ground, amidst those red hangings, those red curtains, she bled profusely. A crimson stream trickled down between her breasts, spreading over the abdomen to one of the lower limbs, whence it fell in great drops upon the floor. Her night-dress, rent half asunder, was drenched with it. He could never have believed she had so much blood.

But what retained him there, haunted, was the abominable look of terror that the face of this pretty, gentle, docile woman took in death. The black hair stood on end as a helmet of horror, dark as night. The blue eyes, immeasurably wide open, were still inquiring, aghast, terrified at the mystery. Why? Why had he murdered her? And she had just been reduced to nothing, carried off in the fatality of murder, a creature irresponsible, whom life had rolled from vice into blood, and who had remained tender and innocent notwithstanding, for she had never understood.

Jacques was astonished. He heard the sniffing of animals, the grunting of wild boars, the roaring of lions; and he became calm, it was himself breathing. At last! at last! he had gratified his thirst—he had killed! Yes; he had done that. He felt elevated by ungovernable joy, by intense delight at the full satisfaction of his everlasting desire. He experienced surprising pride, an aggrandisement of his male sovereignty. He had slaughtered the woman. He possessed her as he had so long desired to possess her, entirely to the point of destroying her. She had ceased to belong, she never would belong any more to anybody. And a bitter recollection recurred to him, that of the other murdered victim, the corpse of President Grandmorin which he had seen on that terrible night five hundred yards from the house. This delicate body before him, so white, striped with red, was the same human shred, the broken puppet, the limp rag that a knife makes of a creature.

Yes, that was it. He had killed, and he had this thing on the ground. She had just been hurled down like the other; but on her back, the left arm doubled under her right side, twisted, half-torn from her shoulder. Was it not on the night when the body of the President was found that with heart beating fit to burst, he had sworn to dare in his turn, in a prurience for murder which exasperated him like a concupiscence at the sight of the slaughtered man? Ah! if he could only have the pluck, satisfy himself, drive in the knife! This had germinated and developed within him obscurely. For a year, not an hour had gone by without him having advanced towards the inevitable result. Even with his arms about the neck of this woman, and amidst her kisses, the secret work was approaching its termination; and the two murders had become united. Did not the one show the logic of the other?

The clatter of a house falling down, a jolting of the floor drew Jacques from his gaping contemplation of the dead woman. Were the doors flying into splinters? Had people arrived to arrest him? He looked around, but only to find dull, silent solitude. Ah! yes; another train! But the man who would be knocking at the door below, the man whom he wished to kill! He had completely forgotten him. If he regretted nothing, he already judged himself an idiot. What! what had happened? The woman he loved, who loved him passionately, was lying on the floor with her throat cut; while the husband, the obstacle to his happiness, was still alive, and still advancing step by step in the obscurity. He had been unable to wait for this man, who for months had been so sparing of the scruples of his education, and of the ideas of humanity slowly acquired and transmitted; with contempt for his own interest, he had just been carried away by the heredity of violence, by that craving to commit murder, which in the primitive forests threw animal upon animal.

Does anyone kill as the result of reasoning? People only kill by an impulse of blood and nerves—the necessity to live, the joy of being strong. He now merely experienced the lassitude of one satiated. Then he became scared and endeavoured to understand, but without finding anything else than astonishment and the bitter sadness of the irreparable as a result of his gratified passion.

The sight of the unfortunate creature, who still gazed at him with her look of terrified interrogation, became atrocious. Wishing to turn away his eyes, he abruptly felt the sensation of another white form rising up at the foot of the bed. Could this be the double of the murdered woman? Then he recognised Flore. She had already returned, while he had the fever after the accident. Doubtless she was triumphant, at this moment, at being avenged.

He turned icy cold with terror. He asked himself what he could be thinking of, to loiter thus in this room. He had killed, he was gorged, satiated, intoxicated with the dreadful wine of crime. Stumbling against the knife which had remained on the ground, he fled, rolling down the stairs. He opened the front door giving on the perron, as if the small one would not have been sufficiently wide, and dashed out into the pitch-dark night where his furious gallop became lost. He never turned round. The dubious-looking house, set down aslant at the edge of the line, remained open and desolate behind him, in its abandonment of death.

Cabuche, that night as on the others, had found his way through the hedge, and was prowling under the window of Séverine. He knew very well that Roubaud was expected, and was not astonished at the light filtering through a chink in one of the shutters. But this man bounding from the top of the steps, this frantic gallop like that of an animal tearing away into the country, struck him dumbfounded with surprise. It was already too late to pursue the fugitive, and the quarryman remained bewildered, full of uneasiness and hesitation before the open door, gaping upon the black hole formed by the vestibule. What had occurred? Should he enter? The heavy silence, the absolute stillness while the lamp continued burning in the upper room, gave him pangs of anguish.

At last, making up his mind, he groped his way upstairs. Before the door of the red bedroom, which had also been left open, he stopped. In the placid light, he seemed to perceive in the distance a heap of petticoats lying at the foot of the bedstead. No doubt Séverine was undressed. He called gently to her, feeling alarmed, while his veins began throbbing violently. Then he caught sight of the blood, and understood. With a terrible cry that came from his lacerated heart, he sprang forward. Great God! It was she, assassinated, struck down there in her pitiful nudity. He thought her still rattling, and felt such despair, such painful shame at seeing her quite nude in her agony; that he lifted her in a fraternal transport, in his open arms, and, placing her on the bed, drew the sheet over her.

But in this clasp, the only tenderness between them, he covered his chest and both his hands with blood. He was streaming with her gore; and at this moment he saw that Roubaud and Misard were there. Finding all the doors open, they also had just decided to come upstairs. The husband arrived late, having stopped to talk with the gatekeeper, who had then accompanied him, continuing the conversation on the way. Both, in stupefaction, turned their eyes on Cabuche, whose hands were dripping with blood like those of a butcher.

"The same stroke as for the President," said Misard at last, while he examined the wound.

Roubaud wagged his head up and down without answering, unable to take his eyes off Séverine, off that look of abominable terror, with the hair standing on end above the forehead, and the blue eyes immeasurably wide open, inquiring: Why?

XII

Three months later, on a warm June night, Jacques was driving the Havre express that had left Paris at 6.30. His engine, No. 608, was quite new, and he began to know it thoroughly. It was not easy to handle, being restive and capricious, after the manner of those young nags which require to be broken in by hard work before they take kindly to harness. He often swore at it, and regretted La Lison. Moreover, he had to watch this new locomotive very closely, and to constantly keep his hand on the reversing-wheel. But on this particular night the sky was so delightfully serene, that he felt inclined to be indulgent, and allowed the engine to travel along as it would, while he found enjoyment in inhaling great draughts of fresh air. Never had he been blessed with such splendid health. He was untroubled with remorse, and presented the appearance of a man relieved of anxiety, and who was perfectly tranquil and happy.

He who, as a rule, never spoke on the journey, began to joke with Pecqueux, whom the management had left with him as fireman.

"What has come to you?" he inquired. "You've got your eyes about you like a man who has been drinking nothing but water."

Pecqueux, in fact, contrary to his habit, seemed to have taken nothing and to be very gloomy.

"It is necessary to have your eyes about you," he answered in a harsh voice, "when you want to see what is going on."

Jacques looked at him in distrust, like a man who has not a clear conscience. The week before he had been making love to the sweetheart of his comrade, that terrible Philomène, who for sometime past had been purring round him like a lean, amorous cat. He had no affection for her, but wanted to ascertain whether he was cured, now that he had satisfied his frightful craving. Could he make love to this one without plunging a knife into her throat? On two occasions when he had been out with her, he had felt nothing, no uncomfortable feeling, no shiver. His great joy, his appeased and smiling manner must be due, without his being aware of it, to the happiness he experienced at being like any other man.

Pecqueux having opened the fire-box of the engine to throw in coal, Jacques stopped him.

"No, no," said he, "do not make up too much fire. It is going along very well."

The fireman in a grumbling tone uttered some abusive remarks about the locomotive in reply, and Jacques, so as not to get angry, avoided answering him. But he felt that the former cordial understanding of three, no longer existed; for the good friendship between him, his comrade, and the engine had vanished with the destruction of La Lison. They now quarrelled about trifles, about a nut screwed up too tight, about a shovel of coal carelessly laid on the bars. And he determined to be more prudent in regard to Philomène, not wishing to come to open warfare on the narrow foot-plate, which afforded him and his fireman standing room as they were borne onward.

So long as Pecqueux played the part of an obedient dog, devoted to such a point that he was ready to strangle an enemy in gratitude for the kind treatment he received, for being permitted to take his little naps, and to polish off the remains in the provision basket, the pair lived like brothers, silent in the daily danger, and, indeed, having no need of words to understand one another. But it would become a pandemonium if they ceased to agree, pent-up side by side, and swayed to and fro in the oscillation of the engine while struggling together. It so happened that the preceding week, the company had been compelled to separate the driver and fireman on the Cherbourg express, because having been set at variance by a woman, the driver had taken to bullying his fireman, who no longer obeyed him. From words they went to blows, until regular stand-up fights occurred on the journey, without a thought for the long tail of passengers rolling along behind them full speed.

Pecqueux opened the fire-box twice more and threw on coal in disobedience to orders, thereby seeking, no doubt, a quarrel; but Jacques, with an air of having all his attention centred on his driving, feigned not to notice him, merely taking the precaution to turn the wheel of the injector on each occasion, to reduce the pressure. It was so mild, the gentle fresh breeze as they cut through space was so pleasant on this warm July night. At 11.5, when the express reached Havre, the two men polished up the engine with an appearance of being on the same good terms as formerly.

As they left the depôt to go to bed, in Rue François-Mazeline, they heard a voice calling them.

"Why are you in such a hurry to be off? Step in for a minute."

It was Philomène, who, from the doorstep of the cottage of her brother, must have been looking out for Jacques. She had made a movement of lively annoyance on perceiving Pecqueux; and if she determined to hail them together, it was for the pleasure of enjoying a chat with her new friend, in spite of having to support the presence of the other.

"Just leave us alone, will you?" growled Pecqueux. "Go to blazes! We're sleepy."

"How amiable he is!" gaily resumed Philomène. "But Monsieur Jacques is not like you. He'll take a dram. Will you not, Monsieur Jacques?"

The driver was going to refuse, out of prudence, when the fireman abruptly accepted, influenced by the idea of watching them, and so making quite sure of their feelings towards one another. Entering the kitchen they seated themselves at the table, on which Philomène placed glasses and a bottle of brandy, saying in a low tone:

"Try not to make too much noise, because my brother is asleep upstairs, and he is not very pleased when I receive friends."

Then, as she filled their glasses, she immediately added:

"By the way, you know that Mother Lebleu pegged out this morning? Oh! as to that I said so: it will kill her, I said, if they put her in that lodging on the back—a regular prison! Still she lasted four months, chewing the cud of bitterness, because she could see nothing but zinc. And what gave her the finishing stroke, when she found it impossible to move from her armchair, was assuredly the knowledge that she would never more be able to keep watch on Mademoiselle Guichon and Monsieur Dabadie. It was a habit she had got. Yes, she was enraged at never having been able to catch them, and she died of it."

Philomène paused to toss off a thimbleful of brandy, and resumed with a laugh:

"Of course there is something going on between them. Only they are too sharp! It is quite a puzzle! All the same, I think little Madame Moulin saw them one night. But there is no fear of her talking, she is too stupid; and, besides, her husband, the assistant station-master—"

Again she broke off to exclaim:

"I say, it is next week that the Roubaud case comes on for trial at Rouen!"

Until then, Jacques and Pecqueux had listened to her without putting in a word. The latter simply thought her very talkative. Never had she exerted her conversational powers to such an extent with him; and he kept his eyes on her, becoming little by little heated by jealousy at seeing her so excited in the presence of his chief.

"Yes," answered the driver, in a perfectly tranquil manner, "I received the summons."

Philomène drew nearer to him, delighted at being able to graze his elbow.

"So have I," she, said. "I am a witness. Ah! Monsieur Jacques, when I was questioned about you, for you know the examining-magistrate wished to ascertain the real truth in regard to your acquaintance with this poor lady; yes, when he questioned me, I said to him: But, monsieur, he adored her, it is impossible that he can have done her any harm! Is not that right? I had seen you together and was in a fit position to speak."

"Oh!" said the young man, with a gesture of indifference; "I was not anxious. I could say hour for hour how I passed my time. If the company have kept me, it is because there is not the slightest thing they can reproach me with."

A pause followed, and all three slowly drank their brandy.

"It makes one shudder," continued Philomène. "Just fancy, that ferocious brute Cabuche whom they arrested still covered with the blood of that poor lady! What an idiot a man must be to kill a woman because he is in love with her, as if that would help him, when the woman no longer existed! And what I shall never forget so long as I live, was when Monsieur Cauche, over there on the platform, came and arrested Monsieur Roubaud as well. I was there. You know this did not happen until a week afterwards, when Monsieur Roubaud, the day following the burial of his wife, resumed his duty with an air of perfect tranquillity. So then, Monsieur Cauche tapped him on the shoulder, saying he had orders to take him to prison. What do you think of that? Those two who never left one another, who gambled together night after night till daybreak! But when you are a commissary of police you must take even your father and mother to the guillotine if it is your duty to do so. Monsieur Cauche does not care a fig! I caught sight of him at the Café du Commerce a little while ago shuffling the cards, without troubling any more about his friend than the great Mogul!"

Pecqueux, clenching his teeth, struck his fist on the table, and exclaimed with a violent oath:

"If I were in the place of that Roubaud I'd—"

Then, breaking off and turning to Jacques, he added: "What! you make love to his wife, another man kills her, and they take him off to the assizes. No; it's enough to make one burst with rage!"

"But, you great donkey," said Philomène, "it is because they accuse him of having urged the other to rid him of his wife. Yes, in connection with money matters, or something else! It appears that the watch belonging to President Grandmorin, was found in the hut of Cabuche. You remember, the gentleman who was murdered in a railway carriage eighteen months ago. Then they hooked that nasty job on to the one of the other day, and made a long story of it, as black as ink. I cannot explain it all to you, but it was in the newspaper where it filled at least two columns."

Jacques, who was absent-minded, did not even seem to be listening.

"What is the use of puzzling our brains about it?" he murmured. "What does it matter to us? If the judicial authorities do not know what they are doing, how can we expect to know?"

Then, with eyes lost in space, and pallid cheeks, he murmured:

"In all this there is only that poor girl who excites pity! Ah! the poor, poor girl!"

"As for me," concluded Pecqueux, "if anyone took it into his head to interfere with my wench, I should begin by strangling them both. After that, they might cut off my head. I should not care a straw."

Another silence ensued. Philomène, who was filling up the glasses a second time, affected to shrug her shoulders and chuckle; but, in reality, she felt quite upset, and gave Pecqueux a searching look sideways. He had neglected his personal appearance considerably, and looked very dirty and ragged since Mother Victoire, as a result of her accident, had become impotent, and had been obliged to relinquish her post at the station to enter an almshouse. She was no longer there, tolerant and maternal, to slip pieces of silver into his pocket, to mend his clothes, so that the other one at Havre might not accuse her of keeping their man untidy. And Philomène, bewitched by the smart, clean look of Jacques, put on an expression of disgust.

"Do you mean that you would strangle your Paris wench?" she inquired in bravado. "There is no fear of anybody carrying her off!"

"That one or another!" he growled.

But she was already touching glasses in a joking vein.

"Look here! to your health!" she exclaimed. "And bring your linen to me, so that I may have it washed and mended, for really you no longer do honour, to either of us. To your health, Monsieur Jacques!"

The latter started, as if disturbed in a dream. Notwithstanding the complete absence of remorse and the feeling of relief and physical comfort, in which he had been living since the murder, Séverine sometimes passed before his eyes as now, moving his gentle inner self to tears. And he touched glasses, remarking precipitately to hide his trouble:

"You know that we are going to war?"

"Can it be possible?" exclaimed Philomène. "Who with?"

"Why, with the Prussians," answered Jacques. "Yes, on account of one of their princes, who wishes to be King of Spain. Yesterday in the Chamber they were occupied with nothing else."

Then she was in despair.

"Ah! well! That's a nice thing," said she. "They bothered us enough with their elections, their plebiscite, and their riots at Paris! I say, if they do fight, will they take away all the men?"

"Oh! as to us, we are shunted! They cannot disorganise the railways. Only we shall have a warm time, on account of the transport of troops and provisions! Anyhow, if it happens, everyone will have to do his duty."

Thereupon, he rose, noticing that she was becoming too familiar, and that Pecqueux perceived it. Indeed, the face of the latter had become crimson, and he was already clenching his fists.

"It is time for bed," said Jacques. "Let us be off."

"Yes, that will be the better thing to do," stammered the fireman.

He had grasped the arm of Philomène, and squeezed it fit to break it. Restraining a cry of agony, she contented herself with whispering in the ear of the driver, while the other finished his glass in a fury:

"Be on your guard. He is a regular brute when he has been drinking."

But heavy footsteps could now be heard coming downstairs, and Philomène looked scared.

"It is my brother," said she. "Slip out quick! slip out quick!"

The two men were not twenty paces from the house when they heard slaps followed by yells. Philomène was being abominably chastised, like a little girl caught in the act, with her nose in the jam-pot. The driver stopped, ready to run to her assistance, but the fireman held him back.

"What are you going to do?" he inquired; "it is no business of yours. Ah! the slut! if he could only beat her to death!"

On reaching the Rue François-Mazeline, Jacques and Pecqueux went to bed without exchanging a word. The two bedsteads almost touched in the small room, and for a long time the men remained awake with their eyes open, listening to the breathing of one another.

It was on the Monday that the Roubaud trial was to commence

at Rouen. This case proved a triumph for the examining-magistrate, Denizet, for there was no lack of praise in the judicial world as to the way in which he had brought the complicated and obscure business to a satisfactory issue. It was a masterpiece of clever analysis, said they; a logical substitution for the truth; in a word, a genuine creation.

First of all, M. Denizet had caused Cabuche to be arrested as soon as he had visited the house at La Croix-de-Maufras a few hours after the murder of Séverine. Everything pointed openly to this man as author of the crime: the blood trickling down him, the overwhelming evidence of Roubaud and Misard, who related how they had surprised him, alone with the corpse, and in a state of bewilderment. Questioned, pressed, to say in what manner and for what purpose he found himself in this room, the quarryman stammered out a story, which appeared so silly, and so like the usual run of such stories, that the examining-magistrate received it with a shrug of the shoulders.

He had been expecting this story, which was always the same, the tale of an imaginary murderer, the invented culprit, whom the real culprit pretended he had heard fleeing across the dark country. This bugbear must be a long way off, must he not, if he should still happen to be running? Besides, on Cabuche being asked what he was doing in front of the house at such a time, he became troubled, refused to answer, and ended by saying he was walking about. This was childish. How could anyone believe in the existence of this mysterious unknown, who came and committed a murder, and then ran off, leaving all the doors wide open without having searched a single article of furniture, or carried even a pocket-handkerchief away with him? Where did he come from? Why had he killed?

Nevertheless, the examining-magistrate having heard at the commencement of the inquiry, of the intimacy between the victim and Jacques, took measures to ascertain how the latter had passed his time on the day of the murder; but, apart from the accused acknowledging that he had accompanied Jacques to Barentin, to catch the 4.14 train in the afternoon; the innkeeper at Rouen took her solemn oath that the young man, who had gone to bed immediately after his dinner, did not leave his room until the next morning at about seven o'clock. And, moreover, a lover does not slaughter without any reason, a sweetheart whom he adores, and with whom he has never had the slightest quarrel. It would be absurd. No, no; only one murderer was possible, a murderer who was evident, the liberated convict found there red-handed, with the knife at his feet, that brute beast who had related a rigmarole to the representative of justice, fit to send him off to sleep.

But when M. Denizet reached this point he for a moment felt embarrassed, notwithstanding his conviction and his scent, which, said he, gave him better information than proofs. In a first search made at the hovel of the accused, on the outskirts of the forest of Bécourt, absolutely nothing had been found. It having been impossible to prove robbery, it became necessary to discover another motive for the crime. All at once, in the hazard of an examination, Misard put him on the track, by relating that he had one night seen Cabuche scale the wall of the property to look through the window of the room occupied by Madame Roubaud who was going to bed.

Jacques, on being questioned in his turn, quietly related what he knew: the mute adoration of the quarryman for the wife of the assistant station-master, his ardent desire to be of service to her, ever running after her as if fastened to her apron strings. No room, therefore, remained for doubt: bestial passion alone had urged him to the crime. Everything became quite clear: the man returning by the door to which he might have a key, leaving it open in his excitement, then the struggle which had brought about the murder.

Nevertheless, one final objection to this theory occurred to the examining-magistrate. It appeared singular that the man, aware of the imminent arrival of the husband, should have chosen the very hour when Roubaud might surprise him. But on careful consideration this circumstance turned against the accused, and completely overwhelmed him by establishing that he must have acted under the influence of a supreme crisis, driven crazy by the thought that if he failed to take advantage of the time when Séverine was still alone, he would lose her for ever, as she would be leaving on the morrow. From that moment, the conviction of the examining-magistrate was complete and unalterable.

Harassed by interrogations, taken and retaken through the skein of clever questions, careless of the traps laid for him, Cabuche obstinately abided by his first version. He was passing along the road, breathing the fresh night air, when an individual brushed against him as he tore headlong away. The fugitive dashed by him so rapidly in the obscurity, that he could not even say which way he fled.

Then, seized with anxiety and having cast a glance at the house, he perceived that the door stood wide open, and he ended by making up his mind to enter and go upstairs. There he found the dead woman, who was still warm, and who looked at him with her great eyes. In lifting her on the bed, thinking her still alive, he covered himself with blood. That was all he knew, and he repeated the same tale, never varying in a single detail, with an air of confining himself to a story arranged beforehand. When an effort was made to make him say something more, he looked wild, and remained silent, after the fashion of a man of limited intelligence who did not understand.

The first time M. Denizet addressed questions to him on the subject of his intense passion for the deceased, he became very red, like some lad reproached with his first love affair; and he denied, he resisted the accusation of having thought of becoming intimate with this lady, as if it was something very wicked and unavowable, a delicate and also a mysterious matter, buried in the innermost recess of his heart, and which he was not called upon to unbosom to anyone. No, no! He did not love her. He never desired any intimacy with her. They would never make him speak of what seemed to him a profanation, now that she was dead.

But this obstinacy in denying a fact that several of the witnesses affirmed, turned against him. Naturally, according to the theory of the prosecution, it was to his interest to conceal his furious passion. And when the examining-magistrate, assembling all the proofs, sought to tear the truth from him by striking a decisive blow, accusing him point blank of murder and rape, he flew into a mad rage of protestation. He do that! he who respected as a saint! The gendarmes who were called in, had to put restraint on him; while he, with great oaths, talked of strangling the whole show. The examining-magistrate put him down as a most dangerous, cunning scoundrel, but whose violence broke out in spite of all, and proved a sufficient avowal of the crimes he denied.

Each time the murder was brought up, Cabuche flew into a fury, shouting that it was the other one, the mysterious fugitive, who had committed the crime. The inquiry had gone so far when M. Denizet, by chance, made a discovery which suddenly transformed the case, and gave it ten times more importance. He scented out the truth, as he remarked. Influenced by a sort of presentiment, he searched the hovel occupied by Cabuche, a second time, himself; and behind a beam, came upon a hiding-place where he found ladies' gloves and pocket-handkerchiefs, while beneath them lay a gold watch, which he recognised with great delight. This was the watch belonging to President Grandmorin which the examining-magistrate had so ardently endeavoured to trace formerly.

ÉMILE ZOLA

It was a strong watch with two initials entwined, and inside the case it bore the number of the maker, 2516. The whole business stood out illuminated, as in a flash of lightning, the past became connected with the present, and when he had joined the chain of facts together again, their logic enchanted him.

But the consequences would stretch so far that, without alluding to the watch, he at first questioned Cabuche about the gloves and pocket-handkerchiefs. The accused for an instant had the avowal ready on the lips; yes, he adored her to such an extent as to kiss the gowns she had worn, to pick up, to steal behind her, anything she happened to let fall: bits of laces, hooks, pins. Then a feeling of shame and invincible modesty made him silent. When the judge, making up his mind, thrust the watch before his eyes, he looked at it bewildered. He remembered perfectly; he had been surprised to find the watch tied up in the corner of a pocket-handkerchief that he had taken from under a bolster and carried away with him as a prize. Then it had remained in his hut, while he racked his brain thinking how he could return it.

Only what would be the use of relating all this? He would have to own to the other thefts—those odds and ends, the linen that smelt so nice, and of which he felt so ashamed. Already, everything he said was disbelieved. Besides, his power of understanding began to fail him, his simple mind became confused, and what went on around him commenced to take the aspect of a horrible dream. He no longer flew into a rage when accused of murder, but looked as if he had lost his senses, repeating in answer to every question put to him that he did not know. In regard to the gloves and handkerchiefs, he did not know. In regard to the watch, he did not know. The examining-magistrate plagued him to death. He had only to leave him in peace and guillotine him at once.

The following day, M. Denizet had Roubaud arrested. Strong in his almighty power, he had issued the warrant in one of those moments of inspiration, when he put faith in the genius of his perspicacity, and even before he had a sufficiently serious charge against the assistant station-master. In spite of the many obscure points that still remained, he guessed this man to be the pivot, the source of the double crime; and he triumphed at once when he seized a document making everything over to the survivor of the two, which Roubaud and Séverine had executed before Maître Colin, notary at Havre, a week after coming into possession of La Croix-de-Maufras.

From that time the whole business became clear to his mind, with a certainty of reasoning, a strength of evidence which conveyed to the framework of the prosecution such indestructible solidity that the truth itself would have seemed less true, less logical, and tainted with more imagination. Roubaud was a coward, who, on two occasions, not daring to kill with his own hand, had made use of this violent brute Cabuche. The first time, being impatient to inherit from President Grandmorin, the terms of whose will he knew, and aware, moreover, of the rancour of the quarryman for this gentleman, he had pushed him into the coupé at Rouen, after arming him with a knife. Then, when the 10,000 frcs. had been shared, the two accomplices would perhaps never have met again, had not murder engendered murder.

And it was here the examining-magistrate displayed that deep knowledge of criminal psychology which was so much admired, for he now declared that he had never ceased to keep an eye on Cabuche, his conviction being that the first murder would mathematically bring about another. Eighteen months had sufficed for this: the Roubauds were at sixes and sevens. The husband had lost the 5,000 frcs. at cards, while the wife had come to the point of taking a sweetheart to amuse herself. Doubtless she refused to sell La Croix-de-Maufras, in fear lest he should squander the money; perhaps in their continual quarrels she threatened to give him up to justice. In any case, the evidence of numerous persons established the absolute disunion of the couple, and here at last appeared the distant consequence of the first crime. Cabuche now comes forward again with his brutish instincts, and the husband, in the background, arms this man with the knife, to definitely ensure possession of this accursed house, which had already cost one human life, for himself.

That was the truth, the appalling truth, everything led up to it: the watch discovered in the hut of the quarryman, and particularly the two corpses, both struck with the same identical blow in the throat, by the same hand, with the same weapon—that knife picked up in the room. Nevertheless, the prosecution had a doubt on this point. The wound of the President appeared to have been inflicted by a sharper and smaller blade.

Roubaud, in the drowsy, heavy manner now peculiar to him, at first answered Yes or No to the questions of M. Denizet. He did not seem surprised at his arrest, for in the slow disorganisation of his being, everything had become indifferent to him. To get him to talk, the examining-magistrate gave him a warder who never left him. With this man he played cards from morning to night, and was perfectly happy. Besides, he was convinced of the gilt of Cabuche, who alone could be the murderer. Interrogated as to Jacques, he shrugged his shoulders with a laugh, thereby showing that he was aware of the intimacy that had existed between the driver and Séverine. But when M. Denizet, after sounding him, ended by developing his system, inciting him, confounding him with his complicity, endeavouring to wrench an avowal from him, he, in his confusion at finding himself discovered, became remarkably circumspect.

What was this that was being related to him? It was no longer he, it was the quarryman who had killed the President just as he had killed Séverine; yet in both instances he, Roubaud, was the guilty one, because the other had struck on his account and in his place. This complicated legend stupefied and filled him with distrust. Assuredly this must be a trap. The lie was advanced, to force him to confess his part in the first crime. From the moment of his arrest he felt convinced that the old business was coming to the surface again.

Confronted with Cabuche, he declared he did not know him. Only, when he repeated he had found him red with blood before the corpse, the quarryman flew into a rage, and a violent scene, full of extreme confusion ensued, embroiling matters more than ever. Three days passed, and the examining-magistrate plied the prisoners with question upon question, convinced that they had arrived at an understanding to play the farce of being hostile to one another. Roubaud, who felt very weary, had made up his mind to refrain from answering, but all at once, in a moment of impatience, eager to end the business, he gave way to a secret impulse that had been troubling him for months, and burst out with the truth, the whole truth, nothing but the truth.

It so happened that on this particular day, M. Denizet was exerting his cunning to the utmost. Seated at his writing-table, veiling his eyes with their heavy lids, while his mobile lips grew thin in an effort of sagacity, he had been exhausting himself for an hour in endeavouring, by clever artifices, to ensnare this incrassated prisoner, covered with unhealthy yellow fat, whom he considered remarkably crafty, notwithstanding his ponderous frame. And he thought he had tracked him step by step, enlaced him on all sides, caught him in the trap at last, when Roubaud, with the gesture of a man driven to extremities, exclaimed that he had had enough of the business, and that he preferred to confess so that he might be tormented no further. As there appeared to be a desire to make him out guilty in spite of all, let it at least be for something he had really done.

But, as he unfolded his story, his wife led astray by Grandmorin, his jealous rage on hearing of this abomination, and how he had killed, and why he had taken the 10,000 frcs., the eyelids of the examining-magistrate rose to the accompaniment of a frown of doubt, while irresistible incredulity, professional incredulity, caused his lips to distend in a jeering pout. He smiled outright when Roubaud came to the end. The rascal was cleverer than he had thought: to take the first crime for himself, make it a purely passionate crime, free himself from all premeditation of theft, particularly of any complicity in the murder of Séverine was certainly a hardy manœuvre which gave proof of unusual intelligence and determination. Only, the thing did not hold together.

"Come, Roubaud," said M. Denizet, "you must not take us for children. So you pretend that you were jealous, and that it was in a transport of jealousy that you committed the murder?"

"Certainly," answered the other.

"And, if we admit what you relate," resumed the examining-magistrate, "you knew nothing about the intimacy of your wife with the President at the time you married her. Does that appear likely? In your case everything tends to prove, on the contrary, that the speculation was suggested to you, discussed, and accepted. You are given a young girl, brought up like a young lady, she receives a marriage portion, her protector becomes your protector, you know that he leaves you a country house in his will, and you pretend you had no suspicion, absolutely none at all! Get along with you. You knew everything, otherwise your marriage would be incomprehensible. Besides, the verification of one simple fact will suffice to confound you. You are not jealous. Dare to say again that you are jealous!"

"I say the truth," answered Roubaud. "I killed him in a fit of jealous rage."

"Then," said the examining-magistrate, "after killing the President, on account of an intimacy that dated back sometime, which was of a vague nature and which for that matter you invent, explain to me how it was that you allowed your wife to have a sweetheart. Yes; that strapping fellow Jacques Lantier! Everybody has spoken to me about this acquaintance. You, yourself, have not attempted to conceal from me that you were aware of it. You freely allowed them to do what they pleased. Why?"

Roubaud, overcome and with troubled eyes, looked fixedly into space without finding an explanation, and ended by stammering:

"I do not know. I killed the other; I did not kill this one."

"Then," concluded the examining-magistrate, "do not tell me, again, that you are a jealous man who avenges himself. And I do not advise you to repeat this romance to the gentlemen of the jury, for they would only shrug their shoulders. Believe me, change your system. Truth alone can save you."

Henceforth, the more Roubaud stubbornly told this truth, the greater liar he was proved to be. Besides, everything went against him, and to such a point that his previous examination, on the occasion of the first inquiry in connection with the Grandmorin murder, which should have served to support his new version of the crime, because he had denounced Cabuche, became, on the contrary, the proof of a remarkably clever understanding between them.

The examining-magistrate refined the psychology of the affair with a veritable passion for his calling. Never, said he, had he penetrated so thoroughly to the bottom of human nature; and it was by divination rather than observation, for he flattered himself he belonged to the school of far-seeing and fascinating judges, those who have the power of upsetting a man by a glance. Besides, proofs were no longer wanting, and conjointly formed a crushing charge. Henceforth, the prosecution were in possession of a solid basis to work upon, and the certainty of the guilt of the prisoners burst forth in dazzling brightness like the light of the sun.

And what added to the glory of M. Denizet was the way in which he brought out the double crime in one lump, after having patiently pieced it all together in the most profound secrecy. Since the noisy success of the plebiscite, the country continued in a state of feverish agitation, similar to that vertigo which precedes and ushers in great catastrophes. Among the society of this expiring Empire, in political circles, and particularly in the Press, a feeling of unceasing anxiety was manifest, coupled with an exaltation in which joy even took the form of sickly violence. So when it was ascertained, after the murder of a woman in the solitude of that isolated house at La Croix-de-Maufras, with what a stroke of genius the examining-magistrate at Rouen had just disinterred the old case of Grandmorin and connected it with the new crime, the news was hailed by an explosion of triumph among the newspapers intimately connected with the Government.

From time to time there still appeared all sorts of jokes in the opposition news-sheets about that legendary assassin, who remained undiscovered—an invention of the police put forward to conceal the turpitude of certain high and mighty personages who found themselves involved. The response was about to be decisive. The murderer and his accomplice had been arrested, the memory of President Grandmorin would stand out intact. Then the bickering began again, and the excitement at Paris and Rouen increased from day to day. Apart from this hideous romance which haunted the imagination of everyone, people became impassioned with the idea that, as the irrefutable truth had at length been discovered, the State would be consolidated thereby.

M. Denizet, summoned to Paris, presented himself at the private residence of M. Camy-Lamotte in the Rue du Rocher. He found the chief secretary to the Minister of Justice on his feet in the centre of his severe-looking study, with a face more emaciated and fatigued than on the former occasion; for he was on the decline, and a prey to sadness, notwithstanding his scepticism. It seemed as if he felt a presentiment that the downfall of the régime he served was about to happen in the full splendour of its apotheosis. For the two previous days, he had been the victim of an inner struggle. He had not yet been able to decide what use he would make of the letter from Séverine to the President which he still had by him. This letter would upset all the system of the prosecution, by bringing irrefutable proof to bear upon the version put forward by Roubaud.

But on the previous evening, the Emperor had told him that this time he insisted on justice being done, apart from any influence whatsoever, even if his Government suffered thereby. This was simply a straightforward utterance, or maybe the result of a superstitious idea that a single act of injustice after the acclamation of the country, might change its destiny. And if the chief secretary had no conscientious scruples, having reduced the things of this world to a mere matter of mechanism, he nevertheless felt troubled at the command he had received, and was asking himself whether he ought to love his master to the point of disobeying him?

M. Denizet at once burst into an exclamation of triumph.

"Well," said he, "my scent did not deceive me! It was Cabuche who murdered the President. Only there was some truth, I acknowledge, in the other clue, and I felt myself that the case against Roubaud looked suspicious. Anyhow, we have them both now."

M. Camy-Lamotte fixed his pale eyes on him.

"So all the facts in the bundle of papers sent me," he said, "are proved, and you are absolutely convinced?"

"Oh! absolutely!" answered M. Denizet, without the slightest hesitation. "The evidence forms a perfect chain. I do not remember a single case in which the crime followed a more logical course, and one more easy to determine in advance."

"But Roubaud protests," observed M. Camy-Lamotte; "he takes the first murder on his own shoulders; he relates a tale about his wife having been led astray, and how he, mad with jealousy, killed his victim in a fit of blind rage. The opposition newspapers relate all this."

"Oh! yes, they relate it as gossip, without daring to put faith in it. Jealous! this Roubaud who facilitates the meetings of his wife and her sweetheart! Ah! he may repeat this story at the assize court, but he will not succeed in raising the scandal he desires. Why not give some proof? But he produces nothing. It is true that he speaks of a letter he made his wife write, and which should have been found among the papers of the President. You, sir, sorted those papers, I believe, and you would have come across it, would you not?"

M. Camy-Lamotte did not reply. It was a fact that the scandal would finally be buried, by allowing the examining-magistrate to proceed with his system, the memory of the President would be freed from an abominable taint, and the Empire would benefit by this noisy rehabilitation of one of its creatures. Besides, as this Roubaud acknowledged himself guilty, what mattered it for the purpose of justice whether he was condemned for one version or the other? It was true that there remained Cabuche; but, if this man had nothing to do with the first murder, he appeared to be really the author of the second. Then justice itself was but a final illusion! Is not the idea of wishing to be just a snare, when truth is clouded in such dense obscurity? It would be much better to be wise, and prop up this society on the wane, that threatened ruin.

"That is so, is it not?" inquired M. Denizet. "You did not find this letter?"

Again M. Camy-Lamotte raised his eyes to him; and, being himself master of the position, he took on his own conscience the remorse that had disturbed the Emperor, and quietly answered:

"I found absolutely nothing."

Then, all smiles and with great affability, he showered congratulations on the examining-magistrate. Barely a slight pleat at the corners of his mouth indicated an expression of invincible irony. Never had an inquiry been conducted with so much penetration; and it was decided in the proper quarter that he should be summoned to Paris as counsellor after the vacation. And in this manner M. Camy-Lamotte conducted his visitor to the landing.

"You alone have seen clearly through the whole business," said he, in conclusion; "and your perspicacity is really admirable. From the moment truth speaks, nothing can stop it, neither personal interest, nor even State-policy. Proceed. Let the case take its course, whatever the consequences may be."

"That is absolutely the duty of the magistracy," added M. Denizet, who bowed and took his departure beaming with delight.

When M. Camy-Lamotte was alone, he first of all lighted a candle; then he went and took the note, written by Séverine, from the drawer where he had placed it. The candle was burning very high. He unfolded the letter, wishing to read the two lines; and the remembrance came back to him of this delicate criminal with blue eyes, who had formerly stirred him with such tender sympathy. Now she was dead, and he saw her again in tragedy. Who knew the secret she must have carried away with her? Certainly truth and justice were illusions! And as he approached the letter to the flame and it caught alight, he felt very sad, as if he had the presentiment of misfortune. What was the good of destroying this proof, of loading his conscience with this action if the Empire was destined to be swept away, like the pinch of black ash fallen from his fingers?

M. Denizet concluded the inquiry in less than a week. He found the Western Railway Company extremely willing to give him assistance. All the papers he desired, as well as all the evidence likely to be useful, were placed at his disposal; for the company, also, had the keenest desire to see the end of this deplorable scandal connected with one of its staff which, ascending through the complicated machinery of its organisation, had threatened to disturb even its board of directors. It became necessary to remove the mortified limb with all speed. And so, M. Dabadie, Moulin, and others from Havre again filed through the room of the examining-magistrate, giving the most disastrous details in regard to the bad conduct of Roubaud; next came M. Bessière, the station-master at Barentin, as well as several of the servants of the company at Rouen, whose evidence proved of decisive importance, in respect to the first murder; then, M. Vandorpe, the station-master at Paris, Misard, the signalman, and the headguard, Henri Dauvergne— the two last being particularly affirmative concerning the complacent conjugal easiness of the accused. Henri, whom Séverine had looked after at La Croix-de-Maufras, even ventured to relate that one night while still weak he believed he heard Roubaud and Cabuche concerting together under the window. This went a long way towards explaining matters, and upset the system of the two accused, who pretended they were unknown to one another. The entire staff of the company raised a cry of reprobation. Everyone pitied the unfortunate victims, that poor young woman for whose shortcomings there was so much excuse; that upright old gentleman, whose memory was now cleared of the ugly stories which had been circulated respecting him.

But it was in the Grandmorin family, particularly, that this new trial had aroused the passions again, and if M. Denizet still met with powerful support from this quarter, he had to struggle to maintain the integrity of his system. The Lachesnayes chaunted victory, for, exasperated at the legacy of La Croix-de-Maufras, bleeding with avarice, they had never ceased insisting on the guilt of Roubaud. So when the case came to the surface again, the only thing they saw in it was an opportunity to attack the will; and as there existed but one way of obtaining the revocation of the legacy, that of depriving Séverine under a judgment of forfeiture by reason of ingratitude, they accepted, in part, the version of Roubaud; namely, that his wife was an accomplice who had assisted him to kill the President, although not out of vengeance for an imaginary infamy, but for the purpose of robbing him. The examining-magistrate therefore entered into a conflict with them, particularly with Berthe, who showed herself very bitter against her old friend, the murdered woman, whom she charged abominably; while he defended her with heat, flying into a temper when anyone touched his masterpiece—that edifice of logic, so well erected, as he proudly said himself, that if one piece were removed it would all tumble down.

In this connection a very lively scene occurred in his private room, between the Lachesnayes and Madame Bonnehon. The latter, who, on the former occasion, had supported the Roubauds, had found herself compelled to abandon the husband; but she continued to stand up for his wife, by reason of a sort of tender complicity, being very tolerant in regard to beauty and matters of the heart, and she was quite agitated with this tragic romance bespattered with blood.

She spoke out very plainly, and was full of disdain for money. Was her niece not ashamed to return to this question of the legacy? To pronounce Séverine guilty would be to accept the pretended confession of Roubaud in its entirety, and taint the memory of the President afresh. Had not the inquiry so ingeniously established the truth, it would have been necessary to invent it, for the honour of the family. And she spoke rather bitterly about Rouennais society, which made such a fuss anent the matter; that society she no longer reigned over now that age had come, and she was losing even her opulent blonde beauty of a goddess of ripe years. Yes; again on the previous evening, at the house of Madame Leboucq, the wife of the counsellor, that tall, elegant brunette who had dethroned her, the guests whispered broad anecdotes together: the adventure of Louisette, and everything public malignity could invent.

At this moment, M. Denizet intervened to inform her that M. Leboucq would sit as assessor at the coming assizes, and the Lachesnayes, who felt uneasy, held their tongues with an air of giving in. But Madame Bonnehon allayed their alarm, remarking that she was certain justice would be done; the assizes would be presided over by her old friend M. Desbazeilles, whose rheumatism only permitted him the recollection of the past, in the matter of gallantry; and the second assessor would be M. Chaumette, the father of the young substitute who was under her protection. She therefore had no anxiety, although a melancholy smile played on her lips when she mentioned this gentleman, whose son had latterly been noticed as a visitor at the house of Madame Leboucq, where she herself had sent him, so that there might be no impediment to his future.

When the famous trial at last began, the rumour of approaching war and the agitation that spread all over France, prevented a good deal of the reverberation that the proceedings would otherwise have occasioned. Rouen, nevertheless, was for three days in a high state of fever. A regular crush occurred at the entrance to the court, and the reserved seats were invaded by ladies of the town.

Never had the ancient palace of the Dukes of Normandy accommodated such an affluence of people since it had been fitted up as a Palace of Justice. The trial took place in the last days of June. The afternoons were warm and sunny, and the bright light lit up the ten stained-glass windows, bathing in luminosity the oak woodwork, the white stone crucifix, which stood out at the end of the room against the red hangings sprinkled with bees, as well as the celebrated ceiling of the time of Louis XII with its carved squares gilded in very old and softly toned gold.

The public were already stifling before the proceedings commenced. Women stood on tiptoe to see the various incriminating articles lying spread out on the table: the watch belonging to Grandmorin, the blood-stained night-dress of Séverine, and the knife that had served for the two murders. The gentleman defending Cabuche, an advocate from Paris, was also a centre of interest. In the jury-box sat twelve stout and grave Rouennais buttoned up in their frock-coats. And when the judges entered, there was so much pushing among the public who were standing, that the President at once had to threaten that he would have the court cleared.

At last the case was called on, and the jury sworn. Reading over the names of the witnesses caused another stir among the crowd who were burning with curiosity. At those of Madame Bonnehon and M. de Lachesnaye the heads swayed from side to side; but Jacques particularly impassioned the ladies, who followed him with their eyes. As soon as the accused were brought in, each between two gendarmes, the public never ceased looking at them; and, criticising their appearance, found that they both looked low and ferocious, like a couple of bandits. Roubaud, in his dark jacket, with a necktie arranged after the manner of a person neglectful of his appearance, caused surprise by his prematurely old manner, and his stupid-looking face bursting with fat. As to Cabuche, he was as everyone expected to find him. Wearing a long blue blouse he seemed the very type of an assassin, with enormous fists, and a carnivorous jaw. Just one of those fellows whom you would not care to knock up against at the corner of a wood on a dark night.

The examination of the prisoner confirmed this bad impression, and some of his replies aroused violent murmurs. To all the questions addressed to him by the President, Cabuche answered that he did not know. He did not know how it was that the watch had got to his hut, he did not know why he had allowed the real assassin to run away. He persevered in his story of this mysterious unknown, whose flight he had heard in the impenetrable darkness.

Questioned as to his bestial passion for his unfortunate victim, he began stammering in such a sudden, violent fit of anger, that the two gendarmes seized him by the arms. No, no; he did not love her, he did not want her; all these tales were falsehoods. The mere thought would have been an infamy—she who was a lady, whereas he had been in prison and lived like a savage! Then, when he became calm, he fell into doleful silence, confining himself to monosyllables, indifferent to the verdict and sentence that might ensue.

Roubaud, in the same way, kept to what the accusation called his system. He related how and why he had killed Grandmorin, and denied all participation in the murder of his wife; but he did so in broken and almost incoherent phrases, with sudden failures of memory, and with eyes so troubled, and a voice so thick, that at times he seemed to search for and invent the details. But as the President urged him on, pointing out the absurdities in his narrative, he ended by shrugging his shoulders and refused to answer. What was the use of speaking the truth, since lies were logic?

This attitude of aggressive disdain for the bench did him the utmost injury. Everyone also observed the profound unconcern of the two accused for one another, which seemed to be a proof that they had come to an understanding beforehand, and carried it out with extraordinary strength of will. They pretended they were strangers, and even accused each other, solely for the purpose of embarrassing the bench. When the examination of the two prisoners came to an end the case was already tried, so cleverly had the President put his questions. Roubaud and Cabuche had fallen head over ears into the traps set for them, whilst appearing to deliver themselves up. A few witnesses of no importance were also heard on that day. Towards five o'clock the heat had become so unbearable that two ladies fainted.

Great sensation was caused on the morrow by the examination of certain other witnesses. Madame Bonnehon had a genuine success of superiority and tact. The members of the staff of the railway company, M. Vandorpe, M. Bessière, M. Dabadie, and particularly M. Cauche were listened to with interest. The commissary of police proved extremely prolix, relating how he knew Roubaud very well from having frequently played a game with him at the Café du Commerce. Henri Dauvergne repeated his overwhelming testimony respecting his conviction of having, in his feverish drowsiness, overheard the two prisoners concerting together in low voices. Questioned as to Séverine, he displayed great discretion giving it to be understood that he had been in love with her, but finding she had a sweetheart, he had loyally effaced himself.

So when this same sweetheart, Jacques Lantier, at length came forward, a buzz ascended from the crowd. Some people stood up to get a better view of him, and even the jury bestirred themselves in a movement of deep attention. Jacques, who was very calm, leant with both hands on the iron bar in front of him in the attitude he usually took when driving his engine. His appearance in court, which should have troubled him profoundly, left him absolute lucidity of mind. It seemed as if the case did not concern him in any way. He was about to give his testimony as a stranger and an innocent man. Since the crime he had not felt a single shiver, nor did he even think of these matters, which were banished from his recollection. His organs were in a state of equilibrium, and his health was perfect. Here again, at this bar, he experienced neither remorse nor scruple, being absolutely unconscious.

He immediately cast a clear glance at Roubaud and Cabuche. He knew the first to be guilty, but he gave him a slight nod, without reflecting that everybody was aware at present that he had been the sweetheart of his wife. Then, he smiled at the other, the innocent man, whose place in the dock he should have occupied: a good brute at the bottom, in spite of his look of a bandit, a strapping fellow whom he had seen at work, and whose hand he had grasped.

Jacques gave his evidence with perfect ease, answering in short, clear sentences the questions that were put to him by the President, who, after interrogating him at length about his intimacy with the victim, made him relate his departure from La Croix-de-Maufras a few hours before the murder: how he had gone to take the train at Barentin and how he had slept at Rouen. Cabuche and Roubaud listened to him, confirming his answers by their attitude.

At this moment, an unspeakable feeling of sadness took possession of these three men. Deathlike silence reigned in the room, and the jury experienced an emotion occasioned they knew not by what, which caused a lump to rise in their throats. It was truth that was passing mute.

In reply to a question of the President, who desired to know what Jacques thought of the unknown figure, who, according to the story of the quarryman, had vanished in the obscurity, he contented himself by shaking his head, as if he did not wish to overload a prisoner.

An incident then occurred which completely upset the public. Tears welled in the eyes of Jacques, and overflowing, trickled down his cheeks. Séverine, as he had already seen her once before, had just risen up before him—that wretched, murdered woman, whose image he had carried away with him, with her blue eyes, immoderately wide open, and her black hair standing on end on her forehead like a helmet of terror. He still adored her, and seized with immense pity, he wept abundant tears, unconscious of his crime, forgetful of being amidst this crowd. Some of the ladies, affected by this display of tenderness, began to sob. The grief of the sweetheart, while the husband remained unmoved, was considered extremely touching. The President, having inquired of the defence whether they desired to ask the witness any questions, the advocates thanked him and answered No; while the prisoners, whose countenances bore a doltish expression, followed Jacques with their eyes, as he returned to his seat amidst the general sympathy of the public.

The third day of the trial was entirely taken up by the address of the Imperial Procurator, and the pleadings of the advocates on behalf of the accused. First of all the President delivered his summing-up of the case, in the course of which, under an appearance of absolute impartiality, the charge of the prosecution was aggravated. The Imperial Procurator, who followed, did not seem to be in the enjoyment of all his powers. He usually displayed more conviction, a deeper eloquence. This was attributed to the heat, which was really most oppressive. The advocate from Paris, who pleaded for Cabuche, on the contrary, afforded great pleasure without convincing his hearers; while the eminent member of the Rouen bar, who defended Roubaud, also made the most he could of a bad case. The Imperial Procurator, who felt fatigued, did not even reply.

When the jury retired to their room it was only six o'clock. Broad daylight still entered the court by the six windows, and a final ray lit up the arms of the towns of Normandy, decorating the imposts. A loud sound of voices rose to the old gilded ceiling, and the swaying of an impatient crowd shook the iron grating that separated the reserved seats from the public standing up. But silence was restored as soon as the jury returned. The verdict, which was guilty, admitted extenuating circumstances; and the two men were sentenced to hard labour for life. The result caused great surprise. The public streamed out of court in a tumult, and a few shrill whistles were heard as at the theatre.

That same evening throughout Rouen the sentence gave rise to endless comments. According to general opinion, it was a blow for Madame Bonnehon and the Lachesnayes. Nothing short of a death sentence, it appeared, would have satisfied the family; and adverse interests must certainly have made themselves felt. People already spoke in an undertone of Madame Leboucq, three or four of whose faithful slaves were on the jury. No doubt there had been nothing incorrect in the attitude of her husband as assessor; and yet an impression seemed to prevail, that neither M. Chaumette, the other assessor, nor even M. Desbazeilles, the President, felt themselves such absolute masters of the proceedings as they would have wished.

Perhaps it was simply that the jury full of scruples, in according extenuating circumstances, had ceded to that uneasy feeling of doubt that had for a moment swept through the room—the silent flight of melancholy truth. After all, the case remained a triumph for M. Denizet, the examining-magistrate, whose masterpiece nothing could impair. The family lost a good deal of sympathy when a rumour got abroad that M. de Lachesnayes, contrary to all idea of jurisprudence, spoke of bringing an action in revocation, in spite of the death of the donee, to regain possession of La Croix-de-Maufras, which caused astonishment considering he was a judge.

On leaving the law courts, Jacques was joined by Philomène, who had remained as witness, and who now took possession of him. He would only resume duty on the morrow, and he invited her to dinner at the inn near the station, where he pretended he had passed the night of the crime. He did not intend to sleep there, being absolutely obliged to return to Paris by the 12.50 train in the morning.

"What do you think," said she, as she proceeded on his arm towards the inn, "I could swear that I met one of our acquaintances just now! Yes, Pecqueux, who told me, again and again the other day, that he would not put his foot in Rouen for the case. At one time I turned round, and a man, whose back only I could see, slipped into the middle of the crowd."

The driver, with a shrug of the shoulders, interrupted her:

"Pecqueux is in Paris, on the spree," said he; "only too delighted at the holiday that my absence from duty procures him."

"That may be possible," she answered. "But, nevertheless, let us be on our guard, for he is a most abominable brute when he is in a rage."

She pressed against him, adding with a glance behind her:

"And do you know the man who is following us?"

"Yes," he replied. "Do not bother about him. Perhaps he wants to ask me something."

It was Misard, who had in fact been following them at a distance from the Rue des Juifs. He had given his evidence in his usual drowsy manner; and had remained hovering around Jacques, unable to make up his mind to put a question to him, which was visibly on his lips. When the couple disappeared in the inn, he entered in his turn, and called for a glass of wine.

"Hullo! Is that you, Misard?" exclaimed the driver. "And how are you getting on with your new wife? All right?"

"Yes, yes," grumbled the signalman. "Ah! the wretch, she took me in. Eh? I told you about that when I was here on the last occasion."

This story amused Jacques immensely. The woman Ducloux, the former servant of dubious antecedents whom Misard had taken as gatekeeper, had soon perceived, on noticing him rummaging in the corners, that he must be searching for a hoard, hidden by the defunct; and to make him marry her, she had conceived the ingenious idea of giving him to understand by sudden reticences and little laughs that she had found it herself. First of all he was on the point of strangling her; then, reflecting that the 1,000 frcs. would again escape him, if he were to suppress her like the other, before he had them, he became very flattering and amiable. But she repelled him. She would not allow him to touch her. No, no; when she became his wife he should have both her and the money. And when he had married her, she simply laughed at him, remarking that he was a great stupid to believe everything that was told him. The beauty of the whole business, was that when she heard all about it, she caught the fever from him, and henceforth sought for the money in his company, being quite as much enraged as himself to find it. Ah! those undiscoverable 1,000 frcs., they would certainly ferret them out one of these days, now that they were two! And they sought, sought.

"So you have no news?" inquired Jacques, in a bantering tone. "But does not Ducloux assist you?"

Misard fixed his eyes on him, and at last said what he had been wanting to say.

"If you know where they are," he exclaimed, "tell me."

But the driver became angry.

"I know nothing at all," he replied. "Aunt Phasie did not give me anything. You do not mean to accuse me of stealing, I suppose?"

"Oh! She gave you nothing that is certain," he answered. "You see I am ill, and if you know where they are, tell me."

"Go to blazes!" retorted Jacques; "and mind I do not say too much. Just take a look in the salt-box to see if they are there."

Misard continued looking at him with pallid face and burning eyes. Then came a sudden flash of enlightenment.

"In the salt-box?" he remarked. "By Jove that is an idea! Underneath the drawer there is a place where I have not looked."

Hastily settling for his glass of wine, he ran off to the railway station, to see if he could catch the 7.10 train. And yonder in the little low habitation he sought eternally.

In the evening after dinner, while waiting for the 12.50 train, Philomène insisted on taking Jacques for a walk down the dark alleys, and out into the adjoining country. The atmosphere was extremely heavy—a hot, moonless July night, that filled her bosom with heavy sighs. On two occasions she fancied she heard footsteps behind them, but on turning round could perceive no one, owing to the dense obscurity.

Jacques suffered considerably from this oppressive heat. Notwithstanding his tranquil equilibrium of mind and the perfect health that he enjoyed since the murder, he had just experienced at table a return of that distant uneasiness, each time that this woman grazed him with her wandering hands. This was no doubt due to fatigue, to enervation caused by the heavy atmosphere. The anguish now returned more keenly and was full of secret terror. And yet was he not thoroughly cured? Nevertheless, his excitement became such that in dread of an attack, he would have disengaged his arm had not the darkness surrounding him removed his fears; for never, even on days when he felt the effects of his complaint the most sharply, would he have struck without seeing. All at once, as they came to a grassy slope beside a solitary pathway and sat down, the monstrous craving began again. He flew into a fit of madness, and at first searched in the grass for a weapon, for a stone, to smash her head. Then he sprang to his feet, and was already fleeing in distraction, when he heard a male voice uttering oaths, and making a great disturbance.

"Ah! you strumpet!" shouted Pecqueux. "I have waited to the end; I wanted to make sure!"

"It is false," answered Philomène. "Let me go!"

"Ah! It is false!" said Pecqueux. "He may run, the other one. I know who he is, and shall be able to come up with him. Look there, dare to say again that it is not true!"

Jacques tore along in the darkness, not fleeing from Pecqueux whom he had just recognised, but running away from himself, mad with grief.

Eh! what! one murder had not sufficed! He was not satiated with the blood of Séverine as he had thought, even in the morning. He was now beginning again. Another, and then another, and then still another! A few weeks of torpor after being thoroughly gorged, and his frightful craving returned. He required the flesh of women then, without end, to satisfy him. It was now no longer necessary to set eyes on this element of seduction, the mere sensation of feeling the glow of a woman sufficed. This put a stop to all enjoyment in life. Before him was nothing but the dark night, through which he fled, and boundless despair.

A few days passed, Jacques had resumed his duty, avoiding his comrades, relapsing into his former anxious unsociableness. War had just been declared after some stormy scenes in the Chamber; and there had already been a little fight at the outposts, attended by a satisfactory result it was said. For a week past, the departure of troops had overwhelmed the servants of the railway companies with fatigue. The regular service had become upset through the long delays occasioned by the frequent extra trains; without counting that the best drivers had been requisitioned to hasten the concentration of troops. And it was thus that Jacques, one night at Havre, had to drive an enormously long train of eighteen trucks absolutely crammed with soldiers, instead of his usual express.

On that night, Pecqueux arrived at the depôt very drunk. The day after he had surprised Philomène and Jacques, he had accompanied the latter on the engine 608 as fireman; and since then, although he made no allusion to the matter, he was gloomy and seemed as if he dared not look his chief in the face. But the latter found him more and more rebellious, refusing to obey, and greeting every order he received with a surly growl. As a result, they had entirely ceased speaking to one another.

This moving plate, this little bridge which formerly bore them along in unity, was naught at this hour but the narrow, dangerous platform on which their rivalry clashed. The hatred was increasing, they were on the verge of devouring one another on these few square feet as they flew onward full speed, and from which the slightest shock would precipitate them. On this particular night, Jacques, seeing Pecqueux drunk, felt distrustful; for he knew him to be too artful to get angry when sober; wine alone released the inner brute.

The train which should have left at six o'clock was delayed. It was already dark when they entrained the soldiers into cattle-trucks like sheep. Planks had simply been nailed across the vehicles in form of benches, and the men were packed there by squads, cramming the trucks beyond measure; so that while some were seated one upon another a few stood up, so jammed together that they could not move a limb. On reaching Paris another train was in readiness to take them to the Rhine. They were already weighed down with fatigue in the confusion of departure. But as brandy had been distributed among them, and many had visited drinking-places in the vicinity of the station, they were full of heated and brutal gaiety, very red in the face, and with eyes starting from their heads. As soon as the train moved out of the station, they began to sing.

Jacques immediately gazed at the sky, where storm-clouds hid the stars. The night would be very dark, not a breath of wind stirred the burning air, and the wind of the advance, generally so fresh, proved tepid. In the sombre outlook ahead, appeared no other lights than the bright sparks of the signals. He increased the pressure to ascend the long slope from Harfleur to Saint Romain. In spite of the study he had made of the engine No. 608 for some weeks, he had not yet got it perfectly in hand. It was too new, and its caprice, its errors of youth astonished him.

On that night the locomotive proved particularly restive, whimsical, ready to fly away if only a few more pieces of coal than necessary, were placed on the bars. And so, with his hand on the reversing-wheel, he watched the fire, becoming more and more anxious at the behaviour of his fireman. The small lamp, lighting the water-level in the gauge-glass, left the foot-plate in a penumbra, which the red-hot door of the fire-box rendered violescent. He distinguished Pecqueux indistinctly, but on two occasions he had felt a sensation in the legs like the graze of fingers being exercised to grip him there. Doubtless this was nothing more than the clumsiness of a drunkard, for above the riot of the train he could hear Pecqueux sneering very loudly, breaking his coal with exaggerated blows of the hammer, and knocking with his shovel. Each minute he opened the door of the fire-box, flinging fuel on the bars in unreasonable quantities.

"Enough!" shouted Jacques.

The other, pretending not to understand, continued throwing in shovel upon shovel of coal; and as the driver grasped him by the arm, he turned round threateningly, having at last brought on the quarrel he had been seeking, in the increasing fury of his drunkenness.

"If you touch me I shall strike!" yelled Pecqueux. "It amuses me to go quick!"

The train was now rolling along full speed across the plain from Bolbec to Motteville, and was to go at one stretch to Paris without stopping, save at the places indicated to take in water. The enormous mass, the eighteen trucks loaded, crammed with human cattle, crossed the dark country in a ceaseless roar; and these men who were being carted along to be massacred sang, sang at the pitch of their voices, making such a clamour that it could be heard above the riot of the wheels.

Jacques closed the door of the fire-box with his foot. Then, manœuvring the injector, he still restrained himself.

"There is too big a fire," said he. "Go to sleep if you are drunk!"

Pecqueux immediately opened the door again, and obstinately threw on more coal, as if he wanted to blow up the engine. This was rebellion, orders disregarded, exasperated passion that took no further heed of all these human lives. And Jacques, having leant over to lower the rod of the ash-pan himself, so as to at least lessen the draught, the fireman abruptly caught him round the body, and tried to push him, to throw him on the line with a violent jerk.

"You blackguard!" exclaimed Jacques. "So that is your game, is it? And then you would say that I tumbled over! You artful brute!"

He clung to the side of the tender, and both slid down. The struggle continued on the little iron-bridge, which danced violently. They ceased speaking, and with set teeth each did his utmost to precipitate the other through the narrow opening at the side which was only closed by an iron bar. But this did not prove easy. The devouring engine rolled on, and still rolled on. Barentin was passed, the train plunged into the tunnel of Malaunay, and they continued to hold each other tightly, grovelling in the coal, striking their heads against the side of the water-tank, but avoiding the red-hot door of the fire-box, which scorched their legs each time they extended them.

At one moment, Jacques reflected that if he could raise himself he would close the regulator, and call for assistance, so that he might be freed of this furious madman, raging with drink and jealousy. Smaller in build than Pecqueux, he was becoming weak, and now despaired of finding sufficient strength to fling his aggressor from the locomotive. Indeed, he was already vanquished, and felt the terror of the fall pass through his hair. As in a supreme effort, he groped about with his hand, the other understood, and, stiffening his loins, raised him like a child.

"Ah! You want to stop! Ah! you took my girl! Hah! hah! You will have to go over the side!"

The engine rolled onward, onward. The train issued from the tunnel with a great crash, and continued its course through the barren, sombre country. Malaunay station was passed in such a tempestuous blast that the assistant station-master, standing on the platform, did not even see the two men endeavouring to slaughter one another as the thunderbolt bore them away.

At last, Pecqueux with a final spurt, precipitated Jacques from the engine; but the latter, feeling himself in space, clung so tightly in his bewilderment to the neck of his antagonist, that he dragged Pecqueux along with him. There were a couple of terrible shrieks, which mingled one with the other and were lost. The two men falling together, cast under the wheels by the counter shock, were cut to pieces clasping one another in that frightful embrace—they, who so long had lived as brothers. They were found without heads, and without feet, two bleeding trunks, still hugging as if to choke each other.

And the engine, free from all guidance rolled on and on. At last the restive, whimsical thing could give way to the transports of youth, and gallop across the even country like some unbroken filly escaped from the hands of its groom. The boiler was full of water, the coal which had just been renewed in the fire-box, was aglow; and during the first half-hour the pressure went up tremendously, while the speed became frightful. Probably the headguard, overcome with fatigue, had fallen asleep. The soldiers, whose intoxication increased through being packed so closely together, suddenly became amused at this rapid flight of the train, and sang the louder. Maromme was passed in a flash. The whistle no longer sounded as the signals were approached, and the stations reached. This was the straight gallop of an animal charging, head down and silent, amidst the obstacles. And it rolled on and on without end, as if maddened more and more by the strident sound of its breath.

At Rouen the engine should have taken in water; and the people at the station were struck with terror when they saw this mad train dart by in a whirl of smoke and flame; the locomotive without driver or fireman, the cattle-trucks full of soldiers yelling patriotic songs. They were going to the war, and if the train did not stop it was in order that they might arrive more rapidly yonder, on the banks of the Rhine. The railway servants stood gaping, agitating their arms. Immediately there was one general cry, this train let loose, abandoned to itself, would never pass without impediment through Sotteville station, which was always blocked by shunting manœuvres and obstructed by carriages and engines like all great depôts. And there was a rush to the telegraph-office to give warning.

At Sotteville a goods train, occupying the line, was shunted just in time. Already the rumble of the escaped monster could be heard in the distance. It had dashed into the two tunnels in the vicinity of Rouen, and was arriving at its furious gallop like a prodigious and irresistible force that naught could now stay; and Sotteville station was left behind. It passed among the obstacles without touching anything, and again plunged into the obscurity where its roar gradually died away.

But now, all the telegraphic apparatus on the line was tinkling, all hearts were beating at the news of the phantom train which had just been seen passing through Rouen and Sotteville. Everyone trembled with fear, an express on ahead would certainly be caught up. The runaway, like a wild boar in the underwood, continued its course without giving any attention either to red lights or crackers. It almost ran into a pilot-engine at Oissel and terrified Pont-de-l'Arche, for its speed showed no signs of slackening. Again it had disappeared, and it rolled on and on in the obscure night, going none knew where—yonder.

What mattered the victims the engine crushed on the road! Was it not advancing towards the future in spite of all, heedless of the blood that might be spilt? Without a guide, amidst the darkness, like an animal blind and dumb let loose amidst death, it rolled on and on, loaded with this food for cannon, with these soldiers already besotted with fatigue and drink, who were singing.

THE END

A NOTE ABOUT THE AUTHOR

Émile Zola (1840–1902) was a French novelist, journalist, and playwright. Born in Paris to a French mother and Italian father, Zola was raised in Aix-en-Provence. At 18, Zola moved back to Paris, where he befriended Paul Cézanne and began his writing career. During this early period, Zola worked as a clerk for a publisher while writing literary and art reviews as well as political journalism for local newspapers. Following the success of his novel *Thérèse Raquin* (1867), Zola began a series of twenty novels known as *Les Rougon-Macquart*, a sprawling collection following the fates of a single family living under the Second Empire of Napoleon III Zola's work earned him a reputation as a leading figure in literary naturalism, a style noted for its rejection of Romanticism in favor of detachment, rationalism, and social commentary. Following the infamous Dreyfus affair of 1894, in which a French-Jewish artillery officer was falsely convicted of spying for the German Embassy, Zola wrote a scathing open letter to French President Félix Faure accusing the government and military of antisemitism and obstruction of justice. Having sacrificed his reputation as a writer and intellectual, Zola helped reverse public opinion on the affair, placing pressure on the government that led to Dreyfus' full exoneration in 1906. Nominated for the Nobel Prize in Literature in 1901 and 1902, Zola is considered one of the most influential and talented writers in French history.

A NOTE FROM THE PUBLISHER

bookfinity™

Discover more of your favorite classics with Bookfinity™.

- Track your reading with custom book lists.
- Get great book recommendations for your personalized Reader Type.
- Add reviews for your favorite books.
- AND MUCH MORE!

Visit **bookfinity.com** and take the fun Reader Type quiz to get started.

Enjoy our classic and modern companion pairings!

Printed in the USA
CPSIA information can be obtained
at www.ICGtesting.com
JSHW022208140824
68134JS00018B/937